Shakespeare, Ecology and Adaptation

Online resources to accompany this book are available at bloomsbury.pub/shakespeare-ecology-adaptation. If you experience any problems, please contact Bloomsbury at: onlineresources@bloomsbury.com

SHAKESPEARE AND ADAPTATION

Shakespeare and Adaptation provides in-depth discussions of a dynamic field and showcases the ways in which, with each act of adaptation, a new Shakespeare is generated. The series addresses the phenomenon of Shakespeare and adaptation in all its guises and explores how Shakespeare continues as a reference-point in a generically diverse body of representations and forms, including fiction, film, drama, theatre, performance and mass media. Including sole authored books as well as edited collections, the series embraces a mix of methodologies and espouses a global perspective that brings into conversation adaptations from different nations, languages and cultures.

Series Editor:

Mark Thornton Burnett (Queen's University Belfast, UK)

Advisory Board:

Professor Ariane M. Balizet (Texas Christian University, USA)

Professor Sarah Hatchuel (Université Paul-Valéry Montpellier, 3, France)

Professor Peter Kirwan (Mary Baldwin University, USA)

Professor Douglas Lanier ((University of New Hampshire, USA)

Professor Adele Lee (Emerson College, USA)

Professor Joyce Green MacDonald (University of Kentucky, USA)

Dr Stephen O'Neill (Maynooth University, Ireland)

Professor Shormishtha Panja (University of Delhi, India)

Professor Lisa Starks (University of South Florida)

Professor Nathalie Vienne-Guerrin (Université Paul-Valéry Montpellier 3, France)

Professor Sandra Young (University of Cape Town, South Africa)

Published Titles:

Lockdown Shakespeare: New Evolutions in Performance and Adaptation
Edited by Gemma Allred, Benjamin Broadribb and Erin Sullivan

Women and Indian Shakespeares
Edited by Thea Buckley, Mark Thornton Burnett, Sangeeta Datta and Rosa García-Periago

Adapting Macbeth: A Cultural History
William C. Carroll

Shakespeare, Ecology and Adaptation

A Practical Guide

Alys Daroy and Paul Prescott

BLOOMSBURY VISUAL ARTS

LONDON • NEW YORK • OXFORD • NEW DELHI • SYDNEY

THE ARDEN SHAKESPEARE
Bloomsbury Publishing Plc
50 Bedford Square, London, WC1B 3DP, UK
1385 Broadway, New York, NY 10018, USA
29 Earlsfort Terrace, Dublin 2, Ireland

BLOOMSBURY, THE ARDEN SHAKESPEARE and the Arden Shakespeare logo are
trademarks of Bloomsbury Publishing Plc

First published in Great Britain 2025

ISBN: HB: 978-1-3502-8290-2
       PB: 978-1-3502-8291-9
       ePDF: 978-1-3502-8293-3
       eBook: 978-1-3502-8292-6

Series: Shakespeare and Adaptation

Typeset by RefineCatch Limited, Bungay, Suffolk
Printed and bound in Great Britain

To find out more about our authors and books, visit www.bloomsbury.com
and sign up for our newsletters.

CONTENTS

FIGURES

EXTRACTS

ACKNOWLEDGEMENTS

Sections of this book were written on unceded Kaurna, Cammeraygal, and Noongar lands. We pay our respects to Elders past, present and emerging, and recognize their enduring care for Country. We acknowledge the sovereignty of all First Nations peoples, diverse histories and continuation of storytelling and performance, and the importance of Indigenous-led ecological knowledge practices.

We are very grateful to everyone who has given of their time and talent to contribute directly to this book: thank you Patti-Anne Ali, Nicolette Bethel, Katie Brokaw, Rob Conkie, Elizabeth Freestone, Lynne Parker, Craig Pindar, and Roz Symon. We are also grateful to the Odin Theatret for permission to reproduce their poster for *Ur-Hamlet* and to Tomas Ovalle for permission to print his photo of Shakespeare in Yosemite. We thank Michelle Terry and Will Tosh at Shakespeare's Globe and Randall Martin and Gretchen Minton for their expertise, encouragement and generosity. We are grateful for Helena Grehan's feedback and support, and to Dr John Welch for his advice on evolutionary biology. We also thank Murdoch University and Alys' colleagues there. Joshua Zeunert has been instrumental in offering his ecological and sustainability knowledge. Mark Thornton Burnett, Mark Dudgeon and our editors at Bloomsbury, Lara Bateman and Ella Wilson, have been models of support, wisdom and patience. Finally, love and thanks to our friends and families and, especially, to our (long-suffering) partners, Josh and Jenny.

A NOTE ON THE TEXT

All Shakespeare quotes are taken from the Arden Shakespeare Third Series *Complete Works*, edited by Richard Proudfoot, Ann Thompson, David Scott Kasten, and H.R. Woudhuysen, 2021.

1

Shakespeare, Ecology, Adaptation: An Introduction

O mighty poet! Thy works are not as those of other men, simply and merely great works of art; but are also like the phenomena of nature, like the sun and the sea, the stars and the flowers; like frost and snow, rain and dew, hail-storm and thunder, which are to be studied with entire submission of our own faculties, and in the perfect faith that in them there can be not too much or too little, nothing useless or inert but that, the farther we press in our discoveries, the more shall we see proofs of design and self-supporting arrangement where the careless eye had seen nothing but accident!

(THOMAS DE QUINCEY, 'ON THE KNOCKING AT THE GATE IN *MACBETH*',

THE LONDON MAGAZINE, OCT 1823 [DE QUINCEY 1889–90: 395])

This book is both a guide and an invitation. It is a guide to the ecological dimensions of three Shakespeare plays and an invitation to you to transform them to fit the times in which we live.

Shakespeare is the most widely performed playwright on our planet. The vast majority of his plays can be viewed as adaptations of pre-existing materials which he refashioned to speak to the joys and challenges of his own time. These plays have since offered an inexhaustible and open-access resource of artworks that continue to survive through adaptation. It is a commonplace that each generation retells and remakes the plays in their own image. If this is so, our own era of climate crisis, biodiversity loss and species extinction is surely the time for ecological readings and re-imaginings of these canonical texts.

Every adaptation of Shakespeare strives to give the action 'a local habitation and a name' (*Dream* 5.1.17), to place the characters in an environment that helps tell their story and explain their behaviour. We argue that ecologically conscious interpretations can foreground environmental localism and this inevitably intersects with wider issues of power and inequality. Shakespearean eco-adaptations can also draw from the plays' rich inclusions of more-than-human life and human-nature relationships to foster greater recognition of kinship and interconnectedness.

Theatre, as both a sensory and emotion-based medium, is particularly effective in creating an affective experience and encouraging empathy. Our emphasis, therefore, is on the theatre and live performance as the natural habitats of Shakespeare's plays. Here, we think, they have the greatest capacity to generate emotion, but there is no reason why an ecological focus shouldn't be applied to adaptations into other media.

We focus on Shakespeare as the most widely performed playwright on our endangered planet. This is not a question of ancestor worship but of descendent survival. Given the frequency and ubiquity with which Shakespeare is performed across the globe, we can be sure of two things: 1) There are hearts and minds to be won by telling old stories in new ways; 2) There are practical efficiencies to be made in the *ways* we tell these stories. This guide hopes to show you how to do both. The ideal outcome of the reader's interaction with this book would be the creation of a new adaptation of one of the key texts, or indeed any in Shakespeare's canon.

Prologue: Shakespeare's bones

On Shakespeare's tombstone in Holy Trinity Church, Stratford-upon-Avon, you can still read the following words:

> Good friend for Jesus' sake forbeare,
> To dig the dust enclosèd here.
> Blessed be the man that spares these stones,
> And cursed be he that moves my bones.

We don't know whether Shakespeare himself was responsible for these lines, but it is noticeable that they say nothing about his plays or poems. They are rather a stern warning against extraction, a prohibition against the removal of earth and bones. They say, in effect, 'Let what is in the ground stay in the ground'. But there is no prohibition on disturbing or extracting from the *works* which have outlived the hand that wrote them. Four hundred years later, and in the midst of a climate crisis, we know that we need to move from an extractive economy to a regenerative one. We need to stop digging. The beauty of Shakespeare's works is that we can extract freely from them knowing that we're doing no lasting damage. Each time we remake Shakespeare, we stir those old bones and the skeleton begins to dance.

To be Shakespearean is to take a pre-existing story and transform it. As you can see from the extracts in Chapter 2, Shakespeare drew on a range of texts to forge the new materials of his plays. As Emma Smith has written: 'While his works have prompted centuries of adaptations, they are themselves as much adaptation as original' (Smith 2022: 62). When we adapt Shakespeare, we enter into a process that he knew intimately: one of sifting, editing, streamlining, rearranging and reimagining. If anything, we have a key advantage in that we are collaborating with a writer who has more fame and cultural capital than any other in history, even including the great writers such as Ovid who inspired him. It is therefore more likely that our adaptation will be noticed, and may even thrive, in a crowded ecosystem of competing stories.

In 2018, the scientist Jem Bendell published the paper 'Deep Adaptation: A Map for Navigating Climate Tragedy', in which he persuasively argued that irreversible anthropogenic climate change will lead to 'a near-term collapse in society with serious ramifications for the lives of readers'. Bendell also analysed some of the reasons for 'collapse-denial' (2018: 2). One clear reason lies in the stories we tell ourselves as a culture. A 2019 study by Deloitte on the priorities of mainstream media found that UK television news in 2017–18 referred more often to Shakespeare (5,444 mentions) than it did to climate change (3,126) (Townsend 2019). If Shakespeare is getting more airtime than the most existential threat to human life on this planet, perhaps it is time to use one to make people think about the other. As environmental activist Bill McGibben has asked:

> If the scientists are right, we're living through the biggest thing that's happened since human civilization emerged [. . .] But oddly, though we know about it, we don't *know* about it. It hasn't registered in our gut; it isn't part of our culture. Where are the books? The poems? The plays? The goddamn operas?
>
> (McKibben 2005)

McGibben's call has been heeded by many writers and artists since 2005, but has been taken up only recently by makers of Shakespearean theatre (many of whom you will read about in this book). Given the cultural capital of this playwright in not just the UK but around the world, it seems clear that Shakespearean theatre can, and should, be adapted to address the climatic, social and ecological emergencies facing the planet.

Shakespeare and the Anthropocene

The devastating extent of global biophysical change since the nineteenth century Industrial Revolution, and its hyper-acceleration since the mid twentieth century, has been labelled the 'Anthropocene' – a new geological epoch in which, for the first time in the earth's history, human activity has been the dominant influence on the planet's health. The 'daunting, indeed, horrifying, coincidences of human history and terrestrial geology' (Morton 2013: 9) have ushered in an era of crisis and 'environmental violence' (Clark 2015: 2), in which global capitalism reaches a threshold of self-destruction. Timothy Clark posits that within the humanities (and specifically, ecocriticism), the 'Anthropocene' has come to be used as a shorthand for 'all the new contexts and demands—cultural, ethical, aesthetic, philosophical and political—of environmental issues that are truly planetary in scale, notably climate change, ocean acidification, effects of overpopulation, soil-erosion, overfishing and the general and accelerating degradation of ecosystems' (Clark 2015: 2).

What has all this got to do with Shakespeare? There is a range of opinion among scientists, geographers and historians as to when the Anthropocene began. Some think it very recent, a product of the 'Great Acceleration' of the last seventy or so years in which the world's population has exploded and global economic systems and trends have made deep and devastating impacts on the Earth's own systems of self-regulation. Others point to the Industrial Revolution of the eighteenth and nineteenth centuries as a combined tipping point. But others have gone back further still. In their 2015 article 'Defining the Anthropocene', geographers Simon L. Lewis and Mark A. Maslin suggested that the Anthropocene began during Shakespeare's lifetime at a moment that they name the Orbis spike and date to 1610. At this point, there was a pronounced dip in the amount of CO_2 in the earth's atmosphere, a dip they attribute to the arrival of Europeans in the Americas in the century before and the subsequent deaths of tens of millions of Indigenous people from the imported disease of smallpox. These deaths vastly reduced farming activity across the Americas and led to the effectual reforestation of large parts of South America, leading to a global reduction in CO_2 levels in the early 1600s. The collision of the Old and New Worlds led to the global exchange not only of diseases, but also of species, crops, drugs and animals. This, they argue, qualifies the early 1600s as the first moment in which human activity became the key determinant of planetary health. As they wrote: 'The choice of 1610 [. . .] as the beginning of the Anthropocene would probably affect the perception of human actions on the environment. The Orbis spike implies that colonialism, global trade and coal brought about the Anthropocene' (177).

Citing this article, theatre historian Patrick Lonergan has pointed to the near coincidence of the composition of *The Tempest* and the Orbis Spike. He asks what it might mean to think of Shakespeare's plays as being 'written and staged at the beginning of the Anthropocene', and adds: 'Shakespeare is one of the stories that people can construct about the ongoing development of our societies. To say that the Anthropocene started during the time of Shakespeare is to understand that human activity can have an impact that lasts far longer than the span of a single human life' (Lonergan 2021). It is also to say that, in long geological terms, Shakespeare is still our contemporary: we are all Anthropoceans, even if we (unlike Shakespeare) are living at a time when we have overwhelming scientific evidence of planetary decline and when the damage feels irreversible. That said, Lewis and Maslin concluded their article by reminding us of the agency we have as a species:

> To a large extent the future of the only place where life is known to exist is being determined by the actions of humans. Yet, the power that humans wield is unlike any other force of nature, because it is reflexive and therefore can be used, withdrawn or modified.
>
> (Lewis and Maslin 2015: 178)

As Maslin elsewhere summarized: 'The first stage of solving our damaging relationship with our environment is recognising it' (Maslin 2015: np). With this in mind, consider the image below.

It is an adaptation – almost a desecration – of the painting 'Ophelia' (1851–2) by Sir John Everett Millais. (If you can't picture the original, type 'Millais Ophelia' into a search engine.) The cartoon by Morten Morland was published in *The Times* newspaper in 2023 and shows Shakespeare/ Millais' delicate heroine in her watery grave, but now with the addition of a pipe dumping raw sewage directly onto her head. In the early 2020s, news stories proliferated of water companies releasing unprecedented amounts of sewage into British waterways and coastal areas. But Morland was probably thinking of the specific revelation that, in May 2022, the Thames Water company pumped raw sewage into the Hogsmill River, Malden, where 170

FIGURE 1.1 *Ophelia. Cartoon by Morten Morland,* The Times, *13.02.2023* © *The Times / News Licensing, 2023.*

years earlier Millais had made a detailed study of the river and riverbank's flora for his painting 'Ophelia'.

The cartoon's message is clear: look, it says, at how far we have fallen, at how far we have allowed greed and profit to pollute this once green and pleasant land. But – as many critics have shown – there was pollution in Shakespeare's time, as indeed there was when Millais painted the picture. They, too, were living in the Long Anthropocene. Millais was part of an artistic collective, the Pre-Raphaelites, who recoiled in disgust from the smoky horrors of the British Industrial Revolution and sought refuge in idealised visions of a pre-industrial, pre-lapsarian past (the clue is in the Pre-fix). But even as he painted 'Ophelia', some perceptive Victorian geologists were suggesting that the earth had already entered a new, perhaps final, geological era. One of them, Thomas Jenkyn, defined this as 'the human epoch', or what we would now call the Anthropocene (qtd. Lewis and Maslin 2015: 172).

If '[t]he first stage of solving our damaging relationship with our environment is recognising it' (Maslin 2015), then Morland's cartoon helps us to do that. The artist has adapted something Shakespeare(an) to raise awareness, cause outrage, and shift opinion.

Inspired by this example, and thinking more broadly across the body of Shakespeare's work, we might next ask: What processes of 'deep adaptation' do the works require to make them fit for raising environmental awareness in the Anthropocene? And what do we mean by adaptation?

Environmental adaptation

There has been much critical discussion over the last few decades about the nature and theory of adaptation as it relates to the afterlives of Shakespeare's plays. What counts as an adaptation? How much should an adaptation be measured against the 'original' or 'source' text? What happens when we transfer a story that was written for one medium (e.g. the theatre) and put it in another (e.g. film, dance, novel, etc)? How much should 'fidelity' to the 'original' be valued or derided? Who has the responsibility to decide on what is an adaptation? What ethical work might adaptations engender? These are complicated questions that have generated a wide range of answers. For our purposes, it is helpful to think of some basic definitions of adaptation as offered by evolutionary biology, specifically those formulated by the great Ukrainian biologist Theodosius Dobzhansky. These might be summarized as follows:

1   *Adaptation* is the evolutionary process by which an organism becomes better able to live and survive in its habitat or habitats.

2   An *adaptive trait* is an aspect of the developmental pattern of the organism which enables or enhances the probability of that organism surviving and reproducing.

(See Dobzhansky 1970)

The process of adaptation happens unconsciously in plant and animal life. The adaptation of artworks, on the other hand, involves agency and intention (although it will also be driven by some impulses of which the adaptor is unaware). But what unites both evolutionary and cultural adaptation is the goal of *survival within a particular habitat*. From this perspective, we can see Shakespeare's 'original' plays as adaptations, not only because they fitted old stories into new contexts, but also because we know he and others revised and adapted them in his lifetime to better serve a 'given set of habitats'. We may never know exactly why there are two versions of *King Lear* but one of those versions must, in effect, be an adaptation of the other (or a missing third text, perhaps handwritten by Shakespeare). Something in the story needed fixing.

George Orwell observed that 'the first test of a work of art is survival' (Orwell 2022: 45). This endows the artwork with a kind of agency, as if it survives or fails by its own efforts. On one level, this is misleading: the success of an artwork clearly depends on a range of human agents – producers, actors, directors, publishers, designers, publicists – and their efforts to attract and then please an audience. But on a deeper level we can see that some works of art might have stronger *adaptive traits* than others, qualities that enable or enhance the probability of that (cultural) organism surviving and reproducing. This quality has been named 'adaptogenecity' by the critic Thierry Groensteen (1998: 270). Here we can consider two such possible traits: simplicity and complexity.

The non-specific simplicity and often allegorical quality of Shakespeare's stories makes them highly 'adaptogenic' across times, spaces and cultures. Think of the simplicity of our texts' opening plot outlines: 1) a young woman wants to marry a young man, but her father won't allow it; 2) a powerful old man wants to know which of his daughters loves him the most; 3) a man and his daughter are stranded on an island; the man dreams of revenge. If we take the opening scenario of *King Lear*, we can see how its fairy-tale simplicity provides a springboard for adaptation: the creators of recent TV shows like *Empire* (2015–20) and *Succession* (2018–23) took this as their starting point before more or less abandoning the source text and proceeding to tell the stories they wanted to tell. Seeking to distinguish between 'adaptation' and 'appropriation', Julie Sanders has written that 'an adaptation signals a relationship with an informing sourcetext or original [. . .] on the other hand, appropriation frequently affects a more decisive journey away from the informing source into a wholly new cultural product and domain' (2006: 26). In the cases of *Empire* and *Succession*, both series 'signalled' their relationship with *King Lear* before then breaking away on 'a more decisive journey'. What the writers needed to get going on that journey was the simplicity of the opening scenario (and, perhaps, the cultural capital that comes from riffing off Shakespeare).

If Shakespeare's plots and characterization can be adaptogenically simple, this simplicity coexists with an extraordinary level of complexity in the language he used and the thoughts he explores. Gary Taylor has argued that the possible interpretations of great works of art are 'for all practical purposes, incalculable. And the more interpretations, the more likely that some will seem particularly relevant and important to the unpredictable

FIGURE 1.2 *The poster for* Ur-Hamlet *by Eugenio Barba, Odin Teatret, Norway, 2006. (Poster designed by Luca Ruzza, by kind permission of the Odin Teatret.)*

changing cultures of the future. The more variously interpretable a work is, the more adaptable it is – and the more likely to survive' (1996: 87). Taylor's book is called *Cultural Selection* and he is one of many thinkers to draw the analogy between Darwin's theory of natural selection and the ways in which stories are adapted and modified to fit in new cultural environments that would otherwise be inhospitable to the story in its original form.

Many theorists of adaptation reach for analogies with the natural world to describe this cultural process. Douglas Lanier (2014) has adapted Gilles Deleuze and Félix Guattari's concept of the 'rhizome' – a nonlinear network of roots – to make the case for 'Shakespearean Rhizomatics', in effect inviting an 'ecosystemic' way of thinking about Shakespeare's texts and adaptations. As Diane Henderson and Stephen O'Neill note, 'Adaptation resembles a plant in its capacity to replicate, to change, and even to blur origin and offshoots'; they then cite Poonam Trivedi's metaphor of Shakespearean adaptation as resembling a banyan tree, which develops 'a dense, weblike canopy of branches, roots and trunks, intermeshing and supporting each other' (Henderson and O'Neill 2022: 20). When the Norwegian theatre company Odin Teatret produced *Ur-Hamlet* by Eugenio Barba in 2006, their research on the play led them to produce a poster that anticipated Trivedi's imagery.

Beneath the trunk of a multi-stemmed tree sits the words 'Saxo Grammaticus', the medieval author of the earliest known account of the Hamlet story (and the one on which Barba based his new play). 'Shakespeare' is superimposed on the base of the trunk, and from this base we see branches and limbs stretching upwards and multiplying, each bearing the names of significant adapters and interpreters of the play.

There is a long history of associating Shakespeare himself with Nature and of conceiving of him as an ecological phenomenon. In 1916, for example, the novelist John Galsworthy claimed that:

> When the human spirit, joyful or disconsolate seeks perch for its happy feet, or stay for flagging winds, it comes back again and again to the tree of Shakespeare's genius whose evergreen no heat withers, no cold blights, whose security no wind can loosen.
>
> (Galsworthy 1916: 37)

But the Hamlet poster above represents more than 'the tree of Shakespeare's genius'. It recognizes the ground from which that genius grew and the seeds that were planted there by the works of others. It also shows the evolution and growth of that tree to be *collaborative*. In Galsworthy's image, the tree is monolithic, unchanging and impervious to weather and climate: a ready-made mature oak that is Pure Shakespeare. The Oden Teatret image suggests something quite different: that a work of art *grows* through adaptation, that 'Shakespeare' is the sum of the collaborators who have come after him. To such an extent that it becomes more meaningful to think of *Hamlet* not as one text, but as an organism containing all the *Hamlets* there have ever been and ever will be. If the image ended one centimetre above the word 'Shakespeare', we would be left with a sapling. Adaptation is, therefore, the medium of Shakespeare's survival, and we agree with Henderson and O'Neill when they write: 'Adaptation is no longer simply a facet of Shakespeare or the field of study based in his works and their afterlives but is, rather, a key driver of Shakespeare's ongoing vitality in the contemporary world' (Henderson and O'Neill 2022: 24).

To return to definitions of adaptation found in evolutionary biology, here is how Richard Dawkins summarized the term in 1982:

> Adaptation: A technical term which has evolved somewhat away from its common usage as a near synonym for 'modification'. From sentences like 'cricket wings are adapted (modified from their primary function of flying) for singing' (and by implication are well designed for singing). 'An adaptation' has come to mean approximately an attribute of an organism that is 'good' for something. Good in what sense?, and good for what or for whom?, are difficult questions [. . .]
>
> (Dawkins 1982: 283)

Fortunately, these questions are easier to answer in the field of cultural reproduction than they are in biology. As adaptors of Shakespeare, we know what our adaptations are (or should be) 'good' for: for ourselves, for our audiences, for our communities, for the planet.

Florilegium, or: What's in this book

This is a heterogeneous book that pulls together a range of materials. We offer it as a florilegium – originally and etymologically, the word means a gathering of flowers but it has since become used for a gathering of texts, of fine extracts from the bodies of larger works. In botanical terms, this book presents a range of samples, specimens, and cuttings. In ecological terms, it offers 'eco-assemblages', or communities of like beings within habitats that exist within a larger ecosystem. It consists of five sections:

1 **Sources:** What resources did Shakespeare draw upon to write his plays? This section consists of a range of short extracts from early modern and classical texts. These extracts will give the reader examples of the 'raw materials' which Shakespeare recycled and adapted into his plays. Some extracts will be direct sources for the play (i.e. we know that Shakespeare read them and absorbed them into his new works), others will have a more contextual relationship and will provide insights into early modern environmental attitudes and other concerns. You might find images and ideas to inspire your own adaptations.

2   **Eco-tables:** Having considered some of the literary and social contexts in which the plays were produced, we next move to the three focus plays themselves. This section largely consists of Shakespeare's words, but not as you have ever seen them before. Each text has been carefully gleaned for its references to the environment and to ecology. These references have then been placed in categories and subcategories. In the epigraph to this Introduction, we quote Thomas De Quincey's comparison of the works of Shakespeare with the phenomena of the natural world, and his conclusion that the more we study each, 'the more shall we see proofs of design and self-supporting arrangement where the careless eye had seen nothing but accident!' (De Quincey 1889–90: 395). The Eco-tables amply demonstrate that the suffusion of natural imagery in the texts were *designed in* by Shakespeare and indeed mark one of the key adaptations he has made to his sources.

3   **Ecocriticism:** This section continues our chronological journey by considering the contribution of ecocriticism to our understanding of the ecological dimensions of the plays. We introduce some key terms, offer a brief history of ecocriticism, and then summarize some of the most important books, articles and chapters that have appeared in the last three or so decades. Many of the sub-sections begin with a series of questions that aim to focus your thinking on a set of issues and dynamics in each text.

4   **Eco-adaptations:** We now move from criticism to performance. In this section we briefly introduce you to some adaptive strategies before offering ten examples of how playwrights and directors have adapted our key texts to foreground the environment. These examples are drawn from a range of contexts (professional, college and semi-amateur stage productions, a web series) and countries (including the Bahamas, New Zealand, Ireland and Martinique). In some cases we offer an extract from the adapted script, in others we speak to the creatives who made these productions. We hope that each of the examples will inspire you to create your own adaptation.

5   **Eco-Theatre:** The last section of this book is subtitled 'how to make Shakespearean eco-theatre'. It explores some key concepts, including theatre ecology, ecodramaturgy and ecoscenography. The aim of these practices is both to foreground the environment in the stories we tell and also, crucially, to minimize the material impacts and resource consumption involved in theatre-making. In *The Tempest*, Prospero stages a piece of theatre – the masque – that magically dissolves at its conclusion, leaving 'not a rack [a wispy cloud] behind' (4.1.156). In our world, and lacking as we do Prospero's

magic, theatre-making has a tendency to leave a lot of stuff behind: set pieces, costumes, props, food waste, fuel bills, and so on. How might we leave the smallest possible trace? And can we imagine a form of eco-Shakespeare production that is not only sustainable, but also regenerative?

Epilogue: Building back better

This book aims to infuse you with optimism and with a sense of agency and purpose. Multinational companies and national governments are mostly happy to outsource the responsibility for climate change to individuals, individual responsibility being the default ideology of contemporary capitalism. It is all too easy to internalize this responsibility, becoming first guilty, then paralysed, then 'sicklied o'er with the pale caste of thought.' It is too easy, as Hamlet knew, to 'lose the name of action' (3.1.84, 3.1.87). But we want to encourage a resilient and active optimism. Two of our three plays are generically comedies, the point of which genre is that Life Goes On. The third, *King Lear*, is, on the face of it, a monument to despair. But we believe even the bleakest of plays can be mobilized as a parable and a premonitionary caution: watching it, we might feel, with Lear, that we 'have ta'en / Too little care of this' (3.4.323).

In January 2019, sixteen-year-old Greta Thunberg addressed the delegates of the World Economic Forum in Davos, Switzerland.

> I don't want you to be hopeful. I want you to panic. I want you to feel the fear I feel every day. And then I want you to act. I want you to act as you would in a crisis. I want you to act as if the house was on fire – because it is.
>
> (Thunberg 2019: np)

Thunberg was addressing an audience of business people and political leaders – these were the people she needed to panic and then act. Four hundred years earlier, in the summer of 1613, a very different audience gathered at the Globe Theatre on Bankside to watch *All is True* (now known as *Henry VIII*), a new play by William Shakespeare and John Fletcher. That audience did not need to act as if the house was on fire. It *was* on fire. A piece of flaming material from a stage cannon ignited the Globe's thatched roof and, very quickly, the fire consumed the wooden structure. There was no loss of life, and the most colourful anecdote of the event is that of the man who, finding that his breeches were ablaze, put out that fire with a bottle of ale.

The Globe was burning then. Our globe is burning now. The first time as farce, the second time as tragedy. The reaction back in 1613 was to rebuild the theatre with more resilient materials, primarily replacing the thatched roof with less flammable tiling. First, we panic. Next, we act. For this we have a range of approaches and materials to hand, not least the plays of William Shakespeare. While many of the Earth's resources will never come back after being extracted and exhausted, Shakespeare's plays are not diminished when plundered to energize a new work of art. Quite the opposite: free and creative adaptation of these plays has generally ensured their survival better than conservative preservation. Shakespeare will not save life on this planet. He is quietly decomposing in that grave in Stratford. But with your help, he can play his part.

2

Sources

What resources did Shakespeare draw upon to write his plays? This section consists of a range of short extracts from early modern and classical texts. These extracts will give the reader examples of the 'raw materials' which Shakespeare recycled and adapted. Some extracts will be direct sources for the play (i.e. we know that Shakespeare read them and absorbed them into his new works), others will have a more contextual relationship and will provide insights into early modern environmental attitudes and other concerns. You might find images and ideas to inspire your own adaptations.

What you will notice in the case of many of these extracts is that one of Shakespeare's key adaptive strategies was to introduce to the source text an environmental awareness and richness that is untapped in the original. This is amply demonstrated in the following chapter (Eco-tables) and substantiates Tom MacFaul's contention that: 'there was an extraordinary range of thinkable ideas about nature in his time, and [Shakespeare] was able, with the unique eclecticism of the dramatist, to make suggestive imaginative patterns out of mixtures of those ideas' (2015: 9).

A Midsummer Night's Dream

Overview: Unlike most of Shakespeare's plays, there is no single defined source text for *A Midsummer Night's Dream*. (The same, as we will see, is true of *The Tempest*.) This does not mean that the play is purely a product of Shakespeare's imagination, but rather that he mashed up a variety of pre-existing stories, legends and beliefs into an extraordinary new artwork. From classical literature, we have the characters of Theseus and Hippolyta, the legend of Pyramus and Thisbe, and a fable of a man turned into an ass; from medieval literature, we have the mythical figure of Oberon and rival male lovers who recall those in Chaucer's *The Knight's Tale*; from English folklore, Robin Goodfellow or Puck. Finally, despite the Athenian setting, we have an amateur dramatic group of distinctly English-sounding workers. As in an actual dream, worlds collide and impossible things happen. Before we consider some written sources, we begin by thinking of climate as a stimulant and inspiration.

1) Weird weather

We don't know exactly when Shakespeare wrote *A Midsummer Night's Dream* but it was certainly sometime in the mid-1590s in a time marked by social disorder and famine. England had unseasonably cold summers from 1594–6 and these led to very poor harvests. In Simon Forman's diary of 1594, he recorded: 'The months of June and July were very wet and wonderful cold like winter, that the 10th day of July many did sit by the fire, it was so cold; and so was it in May and June; and scarce two fair days together all that time, but it rained every day more or less. If it did not rain, then it was cold and cloudy' (qtd Chiari 2019: 41). And as Ludwig Lavater and William Barlow observed in relation to the dearth of 1596, 'Many times the years prove unseasonable: in our time we may remember that on Midsummer Day we have been fain to use baths and stoves against the extremity of cold, and on New Year's Day again, we have dined abroad in our terraces and open galleries for the great heat. This is not man's but God's doing' (qtd Borlik 2019: 511). In short: *Dream* was written when the weather felt uncanny, unsettling, and out of joint. This is the most immediate environmental source for Titania's litany of extreme weather:

> 1a)
> Therefore the winds, piping to us in vain,
> As in revenge, have suck'd up from the sea
> Contagious fogs; which falling in the land
> Have every pelting river made so proud
> That they have overborne their continents:
> The ox hath therefore stretch'd his yoke in vain,
> The ploughman lost his sweat, and the green corn
> Hath rotted ere his youth attain'd a beard;
> The fold stands empty in the drowned field,
> And crows are fatted with the murrion flock;
> The nine men's morris is fill'd up with mud,
> And the quaint mazes in the wanton green
> For lack of tread are undistinguishable:
> The human mortals want their winter here;
> No night is now with hymn or carol blest:
> Therefore the moon, the governess of floods,
> Pale in her anger, washes all the air,
> That rheumatic diseases do abound:
> And thorough this distemperature we see
> The seasons alter: hoary-headed frosts

Far in the fresh lap of the crimson rose,
And on old Hiems' thin and icy crown
An odorous chaplet of sweet summer buds
Is, as in mockery, set: the spring, the summer,
The childing autumn, angry winter, change
Their wonted liveries, and the mazed world,
By their increase, now knows not which is which:
And this same progeny of evils comes
From our debate, from our dissension;
We are their parents and original.

(*A Midsummer Night's Dream*, 2.1.81-117)

1a) *Thomas Nashe*, Summer's Last Will and Testament *(1592)*

Thomas Nashe wrote this dramatic interlude personifying the changing of the seasons in 1592 but may well have revised it before its publication in 1600 to capture the extreme weather of the mid-1590s. He invents a malicious new semi-season, 'Backwinter', to personify the frosty and unwelcome eruption of wintry weather in springtime. We can compare the following speech to Titania's catalogue of unseasonal weather, but also to Prospero's account of the unnatural upheavals prompted by his own magic (see below). Backwinter is described by Autumn as 'the veriest dog in Christendom', to which he snarls:

Would I could bark the sun out of the sky,
Turn Moon and stars to frozen Meteors,
And make the Ocean a dry land of Ice!
With tempest of my breath turn up high trees,
On mountains heap up second mounts of snow,
Which melted into water might fall down
As fell the deluge on the former world!
I hate the air, the fire, the Spring, the year,
And whatso'er brings mankind any good.
O that my looks were lightnings to blast fruits!
Would I with thunder presently die,
So I might speak in thunder and slay men.
Earth, if I cannot injure thee enough,
I'll bite thee with my teeth; I'll scratch thee thus!
I'll beat down the partition with my heels,
Which as a mud-vault severs hell and thee!

> Spirits, come up! 'Tis I that knock for you:
> One that envies [scorns] the world far more than you.
> Come up in millions! Millions are too few
> To execute the malice I intend. [. . .]
> I will peep forth, thy [Summer's] kingdom to supplant.
> My father [Winter] will I quickly freeze to death
> And then sole Monarch will I sit and think
> How I may banish thee as thou dost me. . .
>
> (Nashe 1972: 201–02)

Nashe's interlude ends with the prayer: 'From winter, plague, and pestilence, good Lord, deliver us!'

2) Extreme weather and the fairy world

How to explain these extreme weather events? According to conventional wisdom, and in the words of Lavatar and Barlow, 'This is not man's but God's doing'. But this is something of a false binary, as conventional wisdom also held that the reason for God's intervention might be to punish the moral degradation of human beings. Other explanations for climate disruption were found in other less-than-God but more-than-human sources, including planetary influence, witches or fairies, as in *A Midsummer Night's Dream*.

2a) *Oberon in* Huon of Bordeaux *(c. 1540)*

The figure of the fairy king Oberon makes a memorable cameo in a French story first published in English in the 1530s and adapted for the theatre in a now-lost play staged in 1593, shortly before Shakespeare wrote *Dream*. He dwells in a wood 'full of Fairies and strange things' and 'is of height but of three foot, and crooked shouldered, but yet he hath an angel-like visage' (Muir 1977: 67). The hero Huon has 'great desire [. . .] to see that Dwarf King of the Fairies' (Bullough 1957: 391). When Huon and his companions first encounter Oberon, he is benign and munificent, blowing a magic horn that cures their hunger and thirst, and which fills their hearts with such joy that they sing and dance. But when the humans refuse to speak to Oberon, things turn environmentally nasty:

> When that Huon and his company heard the Dwarf speak, they mounted on their Horses, and rode away as fast as they might, without speaking of any word; and the Dwarf seeing how that they rode away and would not speak, he was sorrowful and angry. Then he set one of his fingers on his

> Horn, out of the which issued such a wind and a tempest so horrible to hear, that it bore down Trees, and therewith came such a rain and hail, that it seemed heaven and the earth had fought together, and the world should have ended; the beasts in the woods brayed and cried, and the fowls of the air fell down dead for fear [. . .]; there was no creature but he would have been afraid of that tempest. Then suddenly appeared before them a great River that ran swifter than the birds did fly, and the water was so black and so perilous, and made such a noise that it might be heard ten leagues off. 'Alas!' (quoth Huon) 'I see well now we be all lost; we shall here be oppressed without God have pity of us. I repent me that I ever entered into this wood.'
>
> (qtd in Bullough 1957: 393)

3) The wood

Most of the action of *A Midsummer Night's Dream* takes place in a wood outside Athens. Lysander describes the distance between city and wood as a 'league' (i.e. three miles; 1.1.164), although Peter Quince will later describe the wood as a 'mile without [outside] the town' (1.2.94). Whatever the actual distance, the symbolic distance between city and wood is vast. The city stands for stability, civilization, order, patriarchy and law. The wood, by comparison, is an anarchic space fraught with danger, madness and sudden metamorphoses. The wood in *Dream* is Theseus' hunting ground and therefore technically what early modern people would have called a forest, a privatized space for royalty and aristocracy to hunt animals. But in Theseus' absence, the forest acquires the mysterious, unsettling and dangerous qualities of a wood. Unlike the Forest of Arden in *As You Like It*, this green space has no human occupants. It is the preserve of fairies, flora and fauna. Some early moderns saw such spaces as increasingly rare. Shakespeare lived through an era of extensive deforestation as trees were felled for timber, fuel, and to create space for agriculture. Tristram Risdon, writing about the Devonshire countryside in the 1630s, observed that: 'For trees, it hath the like variety as are found in other places of this kingdom, with which in former times it hath more abounded. For now, what with good husbandry and cleansing of the ground, and what by ill husbandry in felling and selling, the trees and timber are well shortened; which we in part feel and future times will find wanting' (qtd in Borlik 2019: 289).

There was a strong association between woods and wild beasts. In *As You Like It*, we hear reports of a snake and a lion in the Forest of Arden. In *Dream*, Hermia dreams of a snake attack and in 'Pyramus and Thisbe' we see a burlesque of a lion attempting to prey on the heroine. This link between woods and bestiality can be clearly seen in John Manwood's *Treatise of Forest Laws* of 1598:

> As I do take it, a great part of our ancient forests in England had their first beginning in this manner: when this realm, at the first being a wilderness full of huge great woods because it was not inhabited with people, the same was also full of wild beasts [. . .] and after [it] began to be inhabited with people, they did daily more and more destroy the woods and great thickets that were near unto the places where they did inhabit, so that still as the land increased and flourished with people, whose nature could not endure the abundance of savage beasts so cruelly to annoy them as they then did, they sought by all means possible how to destroy such great woods and coverts [. . .] and so by that means the wild beasts were all driven to resort to those places where the woods were left remaining . . .
>
> (qtd in Borlik 2019: 272)

4) Seasonal festivity

The title of the play locates the action in the summer solstice, the longest day of the year, and for millennia, across all northern hemisphere cultures, a moment of celebration of the life-giving power of the sun. In Elizabethan England, Midsummer Eve (23 June) was recognized by communal celebrations that included the lighting of bonfires and torches, and the gathering of plants believed to have therapeutic or even magical properties. It was a moment in which people gave thanks for the fertility of the natural world and of the human animal: it was thought to be a time when young women's dreams would reveal the identity of their future husbands and, by extension, the father of their offspring-to-be. Fairies and spirits were thought to be abundant, playing their part in the 'midsummer madness'.

While the title of Shakespeare's play more than hints at a Midsummer setting, the most specific reference is to 'the rite of May' that Theseus assumes explains the lovers' presence in the wood (4.1.132). The celebrations of May Day (which lasted throughout that month) were, in spirit, so similar to those of Midsummer that we might think of the play as happening *both* on May Day *and* on Midsummer's Eve. Both consisted of a conscious super-charging of the relationship between human animals and the natural world. As John Stow recorded in 1603:

> In the month of May, namely on May day in the morning, every man [. . .] would walk into the sweet meadows and green woods, there to rejoice their spirits with the beauty and the savour of sweet flowers, and with the harmony of birds, praising God in their kind.
>
> (qtd in Nostbakken 2003: 81)

The pre-Christian, pagan origins of May Day and Midsummer celebrations were obvious to Elizabethans, however much the Church sought to rebrand these as religious holidays devoted to the feast of St Philip and St James (May Day) and to the feast of St John (Midsummer's Eve). For a Puritan such as Phillip Stubbes, the celebrations stank of idolatry:

> Against May[day], Whitsunday, or other time, all the young men and maids, old men and wives run gadding over night to the woods, groves, hills, and mountains, where they spend all night in pleasant pastimes, and in the morning they return, bringing with them birch and branches of trees, to deck their assemblies withal, and no marvel, for three is a great Lord present among them, as superintendent and Lord over their pastimes and sports, namely Satan, prince of hell: But the chiefest jewel they bring from thence is their Maypole, which they bring home with veneration, as thus. They have twenty or forty yoke of oxen, every ox having a sweet nosegay of flowers placed on the tip of his horns, and these oxen draw home this Maypole (this stinking idol, rather) which is covered all over with flowers, and herbs bound round about with two or three hundred men, women and children following it with great devotion. And thus being reared up with handkerchiefs and flags hovering on the top, they straw the ground round about, bind green boughs about it, set up summer halls, bowers, and arbours hard by it. And then they fall to dance about it like as the heathen people did at the dedication of the idols [. . .] I have heard it credibly reported [. . .] by men of great gravity and reputation, that of forty, threescore [60], or a hundred maids going to the wood over night, there have scarcely the third part of them returned home again undefiled. These be the fruits which these cursed pastimes bring forth.
>
> (qtd in Nostbakken 2003: 84)

5) Metamorphoses

When Bottom is transformed into a donkey, an astonished Peter Quince exclaims 'Bless thee, Bottom, bless thee! Thou art translated!' (3.1.114–15). *Dream* is indeed full of translations and metamorphoses, from the male lovers' and Titania's drug-induced affections, to the translational power of theatre (Flute becomes Thisbe, a lantern becomes the moon, etc). Writing the play also involved the translation and up-cycling of classical stories in which humans are metamorphosed into other animals.

5a) The Golden Ass *by Lucius Apuleius, translated by William Adlington (1566)*

Lucius Apuleius was a descendant of Plutarch and studied, appropriately enough, in Athens. In the preface to his translation of 1566, William Adlington wrote of *The Golden Ass* that 'there be many who would rather entitle it "Metamorphosis", that is to say, a transfiguration or transformation, by reason of the argument and matter within.' In this passage, Apuleius wishes to be transformed into an Owl, so that he might 'nest' perpetually with his lover, Fotis. (Romeo says to Juliet 'I would I were thy bird'.) To which end, he rubs himself in an ointment prepared by Fotis's 'mistress', a witch, but Fotis has accidentally given him the wrong ointment.

After that I had well rubbed every part and member of my body, I hovered with mine arms, and moved my self, looking still when I should be changed into a Bird, and behold neither feathers nor appearance of feathers did burgeon out, but verily my hair did turn in ruggedness, and my tender skin waxed tough and hard, my fingers and toes losing the number of five, changed into hooves, and out of mine arse grew a great tail, now my face became monstrous, my nostrils wide, my lips hanging down, and mine ears rugged with hair: neither could I see any comfort of my transformation, for my members increased likewise, and so without all help (viewing every part of my poor body) I perceived that I was no bird, but a plain Ass.

Then I thought to blame Fotis, but being deprived as well of language as of human shape, I looked upon her with my hanging lips and watery eyes. Who as soon as she espied me in such sort, cried out, 'Alas poor wretch that I am, I am utterly cast away. The fear I was in, and my haste hath beguiled me, but especially the mistaking of the [ointment] box, hath deceived me. But it forceth [matters] not much, in regard a sooner medicine may be gotten for this than for any other thing. For if thou couldst get a rose and eat it, thou should be delivered from the shape of an Ass, and become my Lucius again. And would to God I had gathered some garlands this evening past, according to my custom, then thou should not continue an Ass one night's space, but in the morning I shall seek some remedy.' Thus Fotis lamented in pitiful sort, but I that was now a perfect ass, and for Lucius a brute beast, did yet retain the sense and understanding of a man. And did devise a good space with my self, whether it were best for me to tear this mischievous and wicked harlot with my mouth, or to kick and kill her with my heels. But a better thought reduced me from so rash a purpose: for I feared lest by the death of Fotis I should be deprived of all remedy and help.

Then shaking mine head, and dissembling [hiding] mine ire, and taking my adversity in good part, I went into the stable to my own horse, where I found another ass of Milos, sometime my host, and I did verily think that mine own horse (if there were any natural conscience or knowledge in brute beasts) would take pity on me, and proffer me lodging for that night: but it chanced far otherwise. For see, my horse and the ass as it were consented together to work my harm, and fearing lest I should eat up their provender, would in no wise suffer me to come nigh the manger, but kicked me with their heels from their meat, which I my self gave them the night before. Then I being thus handled by them, and driven away, got me into a corner of the stable, where while I remembered their uncourtesy, and how on the morrow I should return to Lucius by the help of a Rose, when as I thought to revenge my self of mine own horse, I fortuned to espy in the middle of a pillar sustaining the rafters of the stable the image of the goddess Hippone, which was garnished and decked round about with fair and fresh roses: then in hope of present remedy, I leaped up with my fore feet as high as I could, stretching out my neck, and with my lips coveting to snatch some roses.

But in an evil hour I did go about that enterprise, for behold the boy to whom I gave charge of my horse, came presently in, and finding me climbing upon the pillar, ran fretting towards me and said, 'How long shall wee suffer this wild Ass, that doth not only eat up his fellows' meat, but also would spoil the images of the gods? Why doe I not kill this lame and weak wretch?' And therewithal looking about for some cudgel, he espied where lay a fagot of wood, and choosing out a crabbed truncheon of the biggest he could find, did never cease beating of me, poor wretch, until such time as by great noise and rumbling, he heard the doors of the house burst open, and the neighbours crying in most lamentable sort, which enforced him being stricken in fear, to fly his way.

(Apuleius 1566: n.p.)

5b) *Reginald Scot,* The Discovery of Witchcraft *(1584)*

Scot's book was a bracingly sceptical attempt to debunk popular beliefs and superstitions about witchcraft. Shakespeare almost certainly read it (see *King Lear* sources). As with Lucius' account above, Scot presents the experience as an entirely unpleasant sequence of human cruelty towards the animal, an experience that Shakespeare transforms utterly in his depiction of Bottom. Scot understandably doubted the veracity of such stories and sternly concluded: 'Whosoever believeth, that any creature can be made or changed into better or worse, or transformed into any other shape, or into any other similitude, by any other than by God himself the creator of all things, without all doubt is an infidel, and worse than a pagan' (qtd in Nostbakken 2003: 117). Shakespeare was more than happy to flirt with such paganism for the rich dramatic payoff of a lusty romance between a donkey and a fairy.

[An Englishman in Cyprus buys some eggs from a woman who will later transpire to be a witch].

The young fellow returned towards his ship: but before he went aboard, he would needs eat an egg or twain to satisfy his hunger, and within a short space he became dumb and out of his wits (as he afterwards said.)

When he would have entered into the ship, the mariners beat him back with a cudgel, saying: 'What a murren lacks the ass? Whither the devil will this ass?' The ass or young man (I cannot tell by which name I should term him) being many times repelled, and understanding their words that called him ass, considering that he could speak never a word, and yet could understand every body; he thought that he was bewitched by the woman, at whose house he was. And therefore, when by no means he could get into the boat, but was driven to tarry and see her departure; being also beaten from place to place, as an ass. He remembered the witch's words, and the words of his own fellows that called him ass, and returned to the witch's house, in whose service he remained by the space of three years, doing nothing with his hands all that while, but carried such burdens as she laid on his back; having only this comfort, that although he were reputed an ass among strangers and beasts, yet that both this witch, and all other witches knew him to be a man.

After three years were passed over, in a morning betimes he went to town before his dame; who upon some occasion (of like to make water) stayed a little behind. In the mean time being near to a church, he heard a little sacring bell ring to the elevation of a morrow mass, and not daring to go into the church, least he should have been beaten and driven out with cudgels, in great devotion he fell down in the churchyard, upon the knees of his hinder legs, and did lift his forefeet over his head, as the priest doth hold the sacrament at the elevation. Which prodigious sight when certain merchants of Genoa espied, and with wonder beheld; anon commeth the witch with a cudgel in her hand, beating forth the ass. And because (as it hath been said) such kinds of witchcrafts are very usual in those parts, the merchants aforesaid made such means, as both the ass and the witch were attached by the judge. And she being examined and set upon the rack, confessed the whole matter, and promised, that if she might have liberty to go home, she would restore him to his old shape: and being dismissed, she did accordingly [. . .] notwithstanding they apprehended her again, and burned her. And the young man returned into his country with a joyful and merry heart.

(Scot 1584: 95–6)

King Lear

Overview: In adapting the story of a legendary Celtic king, Shakespeare followed his default pattern of lifting the outline of a plot from extant narratives then filling in and refashioning that outline in bold, even shocking ways. The bones/roots of the story are ancient: cultures around the world have long told themselves parables about ungrateful children, unwise fathers, the perils of old age and the controversies of inheritance. More directly, Shakespeare was inspired by the accounts of King Lear found in Geoffrey of Monmouth's *History of the Kings of Britain* (*c.* 1135) and Raphael Holinshed's *Chronicles of England, Scotland, and Ireland*, the latter of which he consulted for nearly all of his British history plays. Not content with these, he added a subplot of Gloucester and his sons that was suggested by an episode in Sir Philip Sidney's *Arcadia* (1590) in which the heroes meet a blind, old king being led through a storm by his loyal son after being betrayed by his other, wicked son. There is no mention of a storm in Monmouth or Holinshed, so this powerful image – of an old man contending against the elements – had a crucial bearing on Shakespeare's decision to make the storm so central to the action and climate of his play. Perhaps the most influential source for *King Lear* was theatrical rather than literary. The anonymously written play *The True Chronicle History of King Leir and His Three Daughters, Gonorill, Ragan, and Cordella* had been performed in London at least as early as 1594, but was published in 1605, which is probably when Shakespeare was writing his play. As Kenneth Muir has written: 'Shakespeare [. . .] created *King Lear* from the most heterogeneous materials. As was his custom, he amplified and complicated his original fable by using incidents, ideas, phrases, and even words from a variety of books. He found material for his purposes in the most unlikely places' (Muir 1977: 206). Here we focus on two of the most obvious places from which he drew his plot.

1) Geoffrey of Monmouth

Geoffrey of Monmouth wrote his *Historia regium Britanniae* (*History of the Kings of Britain*) some time around 1135, almost five centuries before *King Lear*. If, as seems likely, Shakespeare read this, he did so in a Latin manuscript, as no English translation had been published. The outline and much of the detail Geoffrey offers would be lifted by subsequent historians. This, in effect, became the standard account of the 'historical' King Lear (even though such a person never existed). As you read through the following modern translation, think of it as a 'treatment' – i.e. the plot pitch sent to film producers to persuade them to finance a film – and ask yourself which bits must have leapt out at Shakespeare, and which failed to spark his interest. Note too that in Geoffrey's account (as in all subsequent spin offs before Shakespeare), Leir and Cordelia are successful in battle, and Leir is restored to his throne for three years before his death. Cordelia then inherits the kingdom for a further five years before a tragic ending.

Leir ruled the country for sixty years. It was he who built the city on the River Soar which is called Kaerleir after him in the British tongue, its Saxon name being Leicester. He had no male issue, but three daughters were born to him. Their names were Goneril, Regan and Cordelia. Their father was very fond indeed of them and above all he loved Cordelia, his youngest daughter. When he felt himself becoming a really old man, he made up his mind to divide his kingdom between these three daughters of his and to marry them to husbands whom he considered to be suited to them and capable of ruling the kingdom along with them. In an attempt to discover which of the three was most worthy of inheriting the larger part of his realm, he went to them each in turn to ask which of them loved him most. When he questioned Goneril, she immediately called the gods of heaven to witness that he was dearer to her than the very soul which dwelt within her body. 'My dearest daughter,' answered Leir, 'since you have preferred me, even in my old age, to your own life, I will marry you to any young man you choose and I will give you a third part of the kingdom of Britain.' Regan, the second daughter, was determined to wheedle her own way into Leir's favour, just as her sister had done. It was her turn next to be questioned. She swore that her only possible answer could be that she loved Leir more than any other living person. Her credulous father thereupon decided to marry Regan with the same pomp that he had promised to his eldest child and to give her at the same time another third of his kingdom.

When she heard how Leir had been deceived by the blandishments of her two older sisters, Cordelia, the King's youngest daughter, made up her mind to test him by giving quite a different answer. 'My father,' she said, 'can there really exist a daughter who maintains that the love she bears her own father is more than what is due to him as a father? I cannot believe that there can be a daughter who would dare to confess to such a thing, unless, indeed, she were trying to conceal the truth by joking about it. Assuredly, for my part, I have always loved you as my father, and at this moment I feel no lessening of my affection for you. If you are determined to wring more than this out of me, then I will tell you how much I love you and so put an end to your inquiry. You are worth just as much as you possess, and that is the measure of my own love for you.'

Cordelia's father, who was angry because she had spoken in this way and apparently really meant what she had said, immediately lost his temper with her. 'Since you have so much scorn for me your old father that you refuse to love me as much as your sisters do, then I in my turn will scorn you. You shall never share my kingdom with your sisters. All the same, you are still my daughter. I do not say that I shall be unwilling to marry you off to some foreigner, if fate should offer you such a husband; but this I do make clear to you, that I shall never attempt to marry you with the same honour as your sisters. Until this moment I have loved you more than the others. Now, indeed, you say that you love me less than they do.'

With the advice of the nobles of his realm he proceeded there and then to give the older girls in marriage to two of his Dukes, Cornwall and Albany, and to share between them one half of the island for as long as he, Leir, should live. He agreed that after his own death they should inherit the entire kingdom of Britain. Soon afterwards it happened that Aganippus, King of the Franks, heard Cordelia's beauty being greatly praised. He immediately sent messengers to Leir to ask if the King would let Cordelia go back with them so that he could marry her. Cordelia's father was still as angry as ever. He said that he would willingly give her to Aganippus, but that there would be no land or dowry to go with her; for he had shared his kingdom, with all his gold and silver, between her two sisters Goneril and Regan. Aganippus' love for the girl was not damped when he received this answer. He sent a second time to King Leir to say that he had plenty of gold and silver himself, and other possessions, too, for he ruled over a third of Gaul. He wanted the girl for one reason only, so that he might have children by her. The bargain was struck. Cordelia was dispatched to Gaul and there she was married to Aganippus.

Some long time after, when King Leir began to grow weak with old age, the Dukes whom I have mentioned, with whom, as the husbands of his daughters, he had shared Britain, rebelled against him. They took the remainder of his kingdom from him and with it the royal power which up to then he had wielded manfully and in all glory.

By the time that Leir had stayed two years with his son-in-law, his daughter Goneril made up her mind that he had too many attendants, especially as they kept wrangling with her own servants. . . Then she ordered her father to content himself with the service of thirty soldiers and to dismiss the others whom he had with him. Leir was infuriated by this. He left Maglaurus [Albany] and went off to Henwinus, the Duke of Cornwall, to whom he had married Regan, his second daughter. Leir was received honourably by the Duke, but a year had not passed before a quarrel arose between the two households. Regan was annoyed by this and she ordered her father to dismiss all his retainers except five who should remain to do him service. . . Leir, who was greatly aggrieved by what had happened, went back again to his eldest daughter, thinking that she might take pity on him and let him stay with his full retinue. . .[Goneril] upbraided her father for wanting to go about with such a huge retinue now that he was an old man with no possessions at all. She refused steadfastly to give way to his wish. For his part he had to obey her, and so the other attendants were dismissed and he was left with a single soldier.

[. . .] Leir developed such a loathing for the misery to which he had been reduced that he began to wonder whether he would not be better off with his youngest daughter across the sea. . . For all that, he could not bear his poverty-stricken existence any longer and he set off across the sea to the lands of Gaul.

As he made the crossing, he observed that he was held third in honour among the princes who were on the boat [. . .] 'Oh, spiteful Fortune! Will the moment never come when I can take vengeance upon those who have deserted me in my final poverty? Oh, Cordelia, my daughter! How true were the words you spoke to me when I asked you how much you loved me!. . . How shall I dare to ask favours of you, the dearest of my daughters – I who, in my anger at those very words of yours which I have just quoted, decided to marry you off less honourably than I did your sisters?'

At last Leir landed [. . .] He waited outside the city and sent a messenger to Cordelia to tell her into what poverty he had fallen. It was simply because he had nothing to eat and nothing with which to clothe himself that he had come to seek her compassion. Cordelia was greatly moved by what she heard and she wept bitterly. She asked how many armed attendants Leir had with him. The messenger replied that he had no one, except a certain knight who was waiting with him outside the city. Cordelia then took as much gold and silver as was necessary and gave it to the messenger, telling him to accompany her father to some other city and to bathe him, dress him and nurse him there, giving it out that he was ill. Cordelia also commanded that Leir should take into his retinue forty properly-equipped and fully-armed knights and that only when this was done should he announce his arrival to King Aganippus and his own daughter [. . .] As soon as Leir was dressed in royal robes, equipped with royal insignia and accompanied by a household, he announced to Aganippus and his own daughter that he had been expelled from the realm of Britain by his own sons-in-law and that he had come to them so that he might recover his kingdom. . .[Aganippus and Cordelia] received him honourably and they granted him the rank which he held in his own country until such time as they should have restored him to his former dignity.

Meanwhile Aganippus sent messengers throughout the whole of Gaul to summon all the men there who could bear arms, so that with their help he might endeavour to restore the kingship of Britain to his father-in-law Leir. When this was done, Leir marched at the head of the assembled army, taking his daughter with him. He fought with his sons-in-law and beat them, thus bringing them all under his dominion again.

Three years later Leir died; and Aganippus, King of the Franks, died too. As a result Leir's daughter Cordelia inherited the government of the kingdom of Britain. She buried her father in a certain underground chamber which she had ordered to be dug beneath the River Soar, some way downstream from Leicester.

[. . .]

After a peaceful possession of the government for five years, Cordeilla began to meet with disturbances from the two sons of her sisters, being both young men of great spirit, whereof one, named Margan, was born to Maglaunus [Albany], and the other, named Cunedagius, to Henuinus [Cornwall]. These, after the death of their fathers, succeeding them in their dukedoms, were incensed to see Britain subject to a woman, and raised forces in order to raise a rebellion against the queen; nor would they desist from hostilities, till, after a general waste of her countries, and several battles fought, they at last took her and put her in prison, where for grief at the loss of her kingdom she killed herself.

(Monmouth 1904: 29–35)

2) *The True Chronicle History of King Leir and His Three Daughters, Gonorill, Ragan, and Cordella,* Anonymous (published 1605)

Although published in 1605 (and around the time that Shakespeare was writing *King Lear*), this play had been performed as early as 1594 and may have enjoyed some popularity in the decade after. As can be seen in the first extract below, the anonymous playwright offers a transparent motivation for Leir's abdication and the ensuing love-test.

Leir's wife has very recently died, leaving Leir at a loss how to relate to or 'govern' his daughters. He regrets not having a son to whom to leave the kingdom. The playwright gives him two advisors, one bad (Skalliger) and one good (Perillus, a model for Kent in Shakespeare's play). The main point of the love-test is to corner Cordelia into accepting the King of Brittany as her husband. What follows has been summarised by R.A. Foakes:

> The business of the love-test, the marriages of the daughters and the division of the kingdom take up the first third of the text. The middle part of the action is expanded with much comic or romantic invention involving messengers, murderers, mariners [...] The ending also includes two scenes of English watchmen who get drunk and fail to light a beacon.
>
> (Foakes 1997: 96–7)

Which is to say, both the plot and the atmosphere of *King Leir* were overwhelmingly transformed by Shakespeare into his dark masterpiece. As Kenneth Muir observed: 'There is no underplot, no storm, no Fool, no madness and no deaths' (201). Most notably perhaps – and as can be seen in the second extract – *King Leir* ends with the King, Cordilla and the King of Brittany triumphant in battle and the happy restoration of Leir to his throne. In effect, the genre of this story depends on the point at which you terminate it: tragedy is comedy plus time.

2a) Scene 1

[Enter King Leir, Skalliger, Perillus and Nobles.]

LEIR: Thus to our grief, the obsequies performed
Of our too late deceased and dearest queen,
Whose soul, I hope, possessed of heavenly joys,
Doth ride in triumph 'mongst the cherubims.
Let us request your grave advice, my lords,
For the disposing of our princely daughters,

For whom our care is specially employed,
As nature bindeth, to advance their states,
In royal marriage with some princely mates;
For wanting now their mother's good advice,
Under whose government they have received
A perfect pattern of a virtuous life –
Left, as it were, a ship without a stern,
Or silly sheep without a pastor's care –
Although ourselves do dearly tender them,
Yet are we ignorant of their affairs,
For fathers best do know to govern sons,
But daughters' steps the mother's counsel turns.
A son we want for to succeed our crown,
And course of time hath canceled the date
Of further issue from our withered loins;
One foot already hangeth in the grave,
And age hath made deep furrows in my face.
The world of me, I of the world am weary,
And I would fain resign these earthly cares
And think upon the welfare of my soul,
Which by no better means may be effected
Than by resigning up the Crown from me
In equal dowry to my daughters three.
SKALLIGER: A worthy care, my liege, which well declares,
The zeal you bare unto our quondam [former] queen.
And since your grace hath licensed me to speak,
I censure thus: your majesty, knowing well
What several suitors your princely daughters have,
To make them each a jointure – more or less,
As is their worth – to them that love profess.
LEIR: No more, nor less, but even all alike.
My zeal is fixed: all fashioned in one mold,
Wherefore unpartial shall my censure be;
Both old and young shall have alike for me.
NOBLE: My gracious lord, I heartily do wish
That God had lent you an heir indubitate,
Which might have set upon your royal throne
When fates should loose the prison of your life,
By whose succession all this doubt might cease
And as by you, by him we might have peace.
But after-wishes ever come too late
And nothing can revoke the course of fate;
Wherefore, my liege, my censure deems it best,
To match them with some of your neighbor kings,
Bord'ring within the bounds of Albion,

By whose united friendship, this our state,
May be protected 'gainst all foreign hate.
LEIR: Herein, my Lords, your wishes sort with mine,
And mine, I hope, do sort with heavenly powers:
For at this instant two near-neighboring kings
Of Cornwall and of Cambria, motion love
To my two daughters, Gonorill and Ragan.
My youngest daughter, fair Cordella, vows
No liking to a monarch, unless love allows.
She is solicited by divers peers,
But none of them her partial fancy hears.
Yet, if my policy may her beguile,
I'll match her to some king within this isle,
And so establish such a perfect peace
As fortune's force shall ne're prevail to cease.
PERILLUS: Of us and ours, your gracious care, my lord,
Deserves an everlasting memory
To be enrolled in chronicles of fame
By never-dying perpetuity;
Yet, to become so provident a prince,
Lose not the title of a loving father.
Do not force love where fancy cannot dwell,
Lest streams, being stopped, above the banks do swell.
LEIR: I am resolved, and even now my mind
Doth meditate a sudden stratagem
To try which of my daughters loves me best,
Which, till I know, I cannot be in rest.
This granted, when they jointly shall contend,
Each to exceed the other in their love,
Then at the vantage will I take Cordella,
Even as she doth protest she loves me best;
I'll say, 'Then, daughter, grant me one request:
To show thou lovest me as thy sisters do,
Accept a husband, whom myself will woo.'
This said, she cannot well deny my suit,
Although, poor soul, her senses will be mute.
Then will I triumph in my policy,
And match her with a king of Brittany.
SKALLIGER [*Aside*]: I'll to them before, and bewray your secrecy.
PERILLUS [*Aside*]: Thus fathers think their children to beguile,
And oftentimes themselves do first repent,
When heavenly powers do frustrate their intent. [*Exeunt.*]

(Lee 1909: 1–4)

2b) Scene 32 [The final scene]

[Alarums and excursions, then sound victory.

Enter Leir, Perillus, King, Cordella, and Mumford.]

KING [OF BRITTANY]: Thanks be to God, your foes are overcome,
And you again possessed of your right.
KING LEIR: First to the heavens; next, thanks to you, my son,
By whose good means I repossess the same,
Which if it please you to accept yourself,
With all my heart I will resign to you,
For it is yours by right, and none of mine.
First, have you raised, at your own charge, a power
Of valiant soldiers – this comes all from you –
Next have you ventured your own person's scathe,
And lastly, worthy Gallia never stained,
My kingly title I by thee have gained.
KING: Thank heavens, not me; my zeal to you is such,
Command my utmost, I will never grutch [complain].
CORDELLA: He that with all kind love entreats his queen
Will not be to her father unkind seen.
LEIR: Ah, my Cordella, now I call to mind
The modest answer which I took unkind;
But now I see, I am no whit beguiled,
Thou loved'st me dearly, and as ought a child.
And thou, Perillus, partner once in woe,
Thee to requite, the best I can, I'll do;
Yet all I can, ay, were it ne'er so much,
Were not sufficient, thy true love is such.
Thanks, worthy Mumford, to thee last of all,
Not greeted last 'cause thy desert was small,
No, thou hast lion-like laid on today,
Chasing the Cornwall king and Cambria,
Who with my daughters – 'daughters,' did I say? –
To save their lives, the fugitives did play.
Come son and daughter, who did me advance,
Repose with me awhile, and then for France.

Sound drums and trumpets. Exeunt.

(Lee 1909: 106–07).

The Tempest

Overview: *The Tempest*, like *A Midsummer Night's Dream*, has no obvious single-source text and the plotline and characters all seem to be of Shakespeare's own invention. The short time scheme of the play is also very unusual in Shakespeare's work. For inspiration, he clearly drew on contemporary accounts of travel to exotic and sometimes dangerous places previously largely unseen by Europeans. While the play is ostensibly set in the Mediterranean Sea somewhere between Italy and North Africa, it is suffused with a sense of the 'New World' of the Americas, and the reports of encounters with indigenous peoples that fascinated readers such as the French essayist Michel de Montaigne. Shakespeare would also have heard (or heard of) sermons and pamphlets justifying or opposing the settlement of these lands by European plantationers and colonialists. Finally, given that this is Shakespeare's last solo-authored play, he drew on his own vast body of work as source material: shipwrecks, wicked brothers, usurpation, love at first sight, supernatural beings, plays-within-plays, magic – many of the themes and motifs of his life's work have all been mashed-up into something that is at once familiar and 'rich and strange' (1.2.402).

1) William Strachey, extracts from *A true repertory of the wreck and redemption of Sir Thomas Gates, Knight, upon and from the islands of the Bermudas* (1610)

William Strachey appears to have tried a number of careers – including holding shares in a theatrical company – before purchasing two shares in the Virginia Company (see below) and tying his financial prospects to the enterprise of transatlantic plantation. He travelled aboard the flagship *Sea Venture*, which was blown off course by a hurricane and ran aground off the coast of Bermuda (the notorious danger of the area is registered in Ariel's line about the 'still-vexed Bermudas' [1.2.229]). The would-be plantationers were stranded for almost a year on the island before they could complete their voyage to Virginia, where Strachey would become Secretary of the Colony. Note the emphasis in Strachey's account of the solidarity between everyone on board: even 'the better sort' pitch in to the collective effort. How does this compare with the class dynamics of the opening scene of *The Tempest*? And what is the difference between a *written* account of a hazardous sea voyage and the *theatrical* representation of one?

A most dreadful tempest, the manifold deaths whereof are here to the life described, their wrack on Bermuda, and the description of those islands.

We had followed this course so long as now we were within seven or eight days at the most, by Captain Newport's reckoning, of making Cape Henry upon the coast of Virginia, when on Saint James his day, July 24, being Monday, preparing for no less all the black night before – the clouds gathering thick upon us, and the winds singing and whistling most unusually, which made us to cast off our pinnace, towing the same until then astern – a dreadful storm and hideous began to blow from out the northeast, which swelling and roaring, as it were, by fits, some hours with more violence than others, at length did beat all light from heaven, which like an hell of darkness turned black upon us, so much the more fuller of horror, as in such cases horror and fear use to overrun the troubled and overmastered senses of all, which, taken up with amazement, the ears lay so sensible to the terrible cries and murmurs of the winds and distraction of our company, as who was most armed and best prepared was not a little shaken.

For four and twenty hours the storm in a restless tumult had blown so exceedingly as we could not apprehend in our imaginations any possibility of greater violence. Yet did we still find it not only more terrible but more constant, fury added to fury, and one storm urging a second more outrageous than the former, whether it so wrought upon our fears or indeed met with new forces. Prayers might well be in the heart and lips, but drowned in the outcries of the officers, nothing heard that could give comfort, nothing seen that might encourage hope.

It could not be said to rain. The waters like whole rivers did flood in the air. And this I did still observe that whereas upon the land when a storm hath poured itself forth once in drifts of rain, the wind, as beaten down and vanquished therewith, not long after endureth. Here the glut of water, as if throttling the wind erewhile, was no sooner a little emptied and qualified but instantly the winds, as having gotten their mouths now free and at liberty, spake more loud, and grew more tumultuous and malignant. There was not a moment in which the sudden splitting or instant oversetting of the ship was not expected. Howbeit this was not all. It pleased God to bring a greater affliction yet upon us, for in the beginning of the storm we had received likewise a mighty leak.

There might be seen master, master's mate, boatswain, quartermaster, coopers, carpenters, and who not with candles in their hands, creeping along the ribs viewing the sides, searching every corner, and listening in every place, if they could hear the water run. Many a weeping leak was this way found and hastily stop'd, and at length one in the gunner room made up with I know not how many pieces of beef. Then men might be seen to labor (I may well say) for life, and the better sort, even our governor and admiral themselves, not refusing their turn, and to help each the other to give example to other.

Once, so huge a sea brake upon the poop and quarter upon us as it covered our ship from stern to stem. Like a garment or a vast cloud, it filled her brim full for a while within from the hatches up to the spar deck. This source or confluence of water was so violent as it rush'd and carried the helmman from the helm, and wrested the whipstaff out of his hand, which so flew from side to side that when he would have seized the same again, it so tossed him from starboard to larboard as it was God's mercy it had not split him.

One thing, it is not without his wonder whether it were the fear of death in so great a storm or that it pleased God to be gracious unto us: There was not a passenger, gentleman or other, after he began to stir and labor but was able to relieve his fellow and make good his course. And it is most true such as in all their lifetimes had never done hours' work before (their minds now helping their bodies) were able twice fortyeight hours together to toil with the best.

During all this time, the heavens look'd so black upon us that it was not possible the elevation of the Pole might be observed, nor a star by night, not sunbeam by day was to be seen. Only upon the Thursday night, Sir George Summers, being upon the watch, had an apparition of a little round light like a faint star, trembling and streaming along with a sparkling blaze half the height upon the mainmast, and shooting sometimes from shroud to shroud, attempting to settle as it were upon any of the four shrouds. And for three or four hours together, or rather more, half the night it kept with us, running sometimes along the main yard to the very end, and then returning; at which Sir George Summers called divers about him and showed them the same, who observed it with much wonder and carefulness. But upon a sudden, towards the morning watch, they lost the sight of it and knew not what way it made.

The superstitious seamen make many constructions of this sea fire, which nevertheless is usual in storms. The Spaniards call it Saint Elmo, and have an authentic and miraculous legend for it. Be it what it will, we laid other foundations of safety or ruin than in the rising or falling of it. Could it have served us now miraculously to have taken our height by, it might have strucken amazement and a reverence in our devotions, according to the due of a miracle. But it did not light us any whit the more to our known way, who ran now as do hoodwinked men at all adventures, sometimes north and northeast, then north and by west, and in an instant again varying two or three points, and sometimes half the compass.

East and by south we steered away, as much as we could to bear upright, which was no small carefulness nor pain to do, albeit we much unrigged our ship, threw overboard much luggage, many a trunk and chest (in which I suffered no mean loss), and staved many a butt of beer, hogsheads of oil, cider, wine, and vinegar, and heaved away all our ordnance on the starboard side, and had now purposed to have cut down the mainmast the more to lighten her, for we were much spent, and our men so weary as their strengths together failed them with their hearts, having travailed now from Tuesday till Friday morning, day and night, without either sleep or food.

But see the goodness and sweet introduction of better hope by our merciful God given unto us: Sir George Summers, when no man dreamed of such happiness, had discovered and cried LAND!

We found it to be the dangerous and dreaded island, or rather islands, of the Bermuda, whereof let me give Your Ladyship a brief description before I proceed to my narration; and that the rather, because they be so terrible to all that ever touched on them, and such tempests, thunders, and other fearful objects are seen and heard about them that they be called commonly 'the Devil's Islands,' and are feared and avoided of all sea travelers alive above any other place in the world. Yet it pleased our merciful God to make even this hideous and hated place both the place of our safety and means of our deliverance.

And hereby also I hope to deliver the world from a foul and general error: it being counted of most that they can be no habitation for men, but rather given over to devils and wicked spirits; whereas indeed we find them now by experience to be as habitable and commodious as most countries of the same climate and situation, insomuch as if the entrance into them were as easy as the place itself is contenting, it had long ere this been inhabited as well as other islands. Thus shall we make it appear that truth is the daughter of time, and that men ought not to deny everything which is not subject to their own sense.

(Strachey 1906: 5–14)

2) William Symonds, 'Virginia: a sermon preached at Whitechapel' (1609)

William Symonds regularly preached at St Saviour's church (now known as Southwark Cathedral) on the south bank of the Thames and only a few hundred yards from the Globe theatre. (Indeed, Shakespeare's brother Edmund was buried there in 1607.) This sermon was delivered over the river in Whitechapel and subsequently published as a pamphlet. In it, Symonds sought to defend the ethics and operations of the Virginia Company, which had been founded by King James in 1606 with the aim of colonizing a large part of the eastern seaboard of America. The hope was that gold and silver would be discovered and that valuable commodities such as tobacco could be cultivated for profit. In common with other preachers, Symonds focuses on the question of land ownership, a question that haunts *The Tempest* ('this island's mine', says Caliban) and informs postcolonial readings of the play (see Césaire below). The colonial project was clearly controversial in the years in which Shakespeare wrote the play. As Joshua Eckhardt has noted: 'each of the 1609 company preachers first answered the principal objection that people were making to the Virginia Company in 1609: that it was unconscionable, unjust, and even unlawful to take land that others have rightly inherited and were peaceably governing. For those of us who have presumed that such a criticism, so obvious to virtually everyone now, was unthinkable in Jacobean England, its prominence and persistence in Virginia Company sermons can come as a shock' (Eckhardt 2013: 10). Surprising, too, is Symonds' argument that England was once 'as wild as a forest' with barbaric inhabitants but was made a 'paradise' by 'conquerors and planters'.

And here might we have proceeded to the next point, were it not for one scruple, which some, that think themselves to be very wise, do cast in our way; which is this in effect. The country, they say, is possessed by owners, that rule, and govern it in their own right: then with what conscience, and equity can we offer to thrust them, by violence, out of their inheritances? For answer to this objection: first it is plain, that the objector supposeth it not lawful to invade the territories of other princes, by force of sword. [Symonds then lists examples from the Bible of invasions that were justified because they spread the Word of God.]

I am not ignorant, that many are not willing to go abroad and spread the Gospel, in this most honorable and Christian voyage of the Plantation of Virginia. Their reasons are diverse according to their wits. One says, 'England is a sweet country'. True indeed, and the God of glory be blessed, that whereas the country was as wild a forest, but nothing so fruitful as Virginia, and the people in their nakedness did arm themselves in a coat armor of Woad [. . .]: by the civil care of conquerors and planters it is now become a very paradise in comparison of that it was.

The land [in Virginia], by the constant report of all that have seen it, is a good land, with the fruitfulness whereof, and pleasure of the Climate, the plenty of Fish and Fowl, England, our mistress, cannot compare, no not when she is in her greatest pride. [. . .] As for the opportunity of the place, I leave it to the grave Politician: and for the commodities, let the industrious Merchant speak: but for food and raiment, here is enough to be had, for the labour of mastering and subduing the soil.

Again, this text doth teach us thus much, that in a strange Country, we must look for enemies; even cursing enemies, under whose tongues is the poison of Asps, and whose right hand is a right hand of iniquity. [. . .] If the children of Israel had known as they ought, they would never have refused to enter the land which God commanded them to possess: because there were cursing and killing enemies, no better than Cannibals. Be not then discouraged, though you light on enemies: for that did God foretell unto Abram, that he and his seed must find. Rather be strong, and of good courage : because the Lord is with you; and with them, but an arm of flesh.

(Symonds 1609: 10–18)

3) Michel de Montaigne, 'On Cannibals', translated by John Florio (1603)

The essays of Michel de Montaigne were published in an English translation by John Florio in 1603. The extent to which Shakespeare knew them and how often he consciously drew on them is 'ultimately undecideable' (Mack 2010: 1), but there is one instance – Gonzago's speech in the second act of *The Tempest* – that is clearly inspired by Montaigne's essay 'On Cannibals'. Here Shakespeare would have found a sympathetic account of New World inhabitants that contrasts their simplicity and adherence to the 'laws of nature' with the artificiality, cruelty and corruption of European culture. Montaigne finds cannibalism itself barbaric, but, in a characteristic move, finds 'more barbarity' in European practices of torture that inflict suffering on 'a body still fully able to feel things' (Montaigne 1991: 236). The last few lines of this extract are closely recycled in Gonzago's fantasy of a new commonwealth, but its sceptical questioning of the merits of 'nature' versus 'civilization' reverberate throughout *The Tempest*.

Now (to return to my purpose) I find (as far as I have been informed) there is nothing in that nation, that is either barbarous or savage, unless men call that barbarism which is not common to them. As indeed, we have no other aim of truth and reason, then the example and *Idea* of the opinions and customs of the country we live in. Where is ever perfect religion, perfect policy, perfect and complete use of all things. They are even savage, as we call those fruits wild, which nature of herself, and of her ordinary progress hath produced: whereas indeed, they are those which our selves have altered by our artificial devices, and diverted from their common order, we should rather term savage. In those are the true and most profitable virtues, and natural properties most lively and vigorous, which in these we have bastardized, applying them to the pleasure of our corrupted taste. And if notwithstanding, in divers fruits of those countries that were never tilled, we shall find, that in respect of ours they are most excellent, and as delicate unto our taste; there is no reason, art should gain the point of honour of our great and puissant mother Nature. We have so much by our inventions, surcharged the beauties and riches of her works, that we have altogether over-choked her. [. . .]

All our endeavours or wit, cannot so much as reach to represent the nest of the least birdlet, it's contexture, beauty, profit and use, no nor the web of a silly spider. *All things* (says *Plato*) *are produced, either by nature, by fortune, or by arte. The greatest and fairest by one or other of the two first, the least and imperfect by the last.* Those nations seem therefore so barbarous unto me, because they have received very little fashion from human wit, and are yet near their originall naturalitie. The laws of nature do yet command them, which are but little bastardized by ours. And that with such purity, as I am sometimes grieved the knowledge of it came no sooner to light, at what time there were men, that better than we could have judged of it. I am sorry *Licurgus* and *Plato* had it not: for me seemeth that what in those nations we see by experience, doth not only exceed all the pictures wherewith licentious Poetry hath proudly embellished the golden age, and all her quaint inventions to fein a happy condition of man, but also the conception and desire of Philosophy. They could not imagine a genuitie so pure and simple, as we see it by experience; nor ever believe our society might be maintained with so little art and human combination. It is a nation, would I to answer *Plato,* that hath no kind of traffic, no knowledge of Letters, no intelligence of numbers, no name of magistrate, nor of politic superiority; no use of service, of riches, or of poverty; no contracts, no successions, no dividences, no occupation but idle; no respect of kindred, but common, no apparell but naturall, no manuring of lands, no use of wine, corn, or metal. The very words that import lying, falshood, treason, dissimulation, covetousnes, envy, detraction, and pardon, were never heard of amongst them.

(Montaigne 1603: 101–02)

4) Medea's incantation from Ovid's *Metamorphoses* translated by Arthur Golding (1567)

Shakespeare would have studied the Roman poet Ovid at school and the influence of Ovidian mythology is clear throughout his plays and poems. We find Medea, the sorceress, in Book 7 of the *Metamorphoses*. Stephen Orgel has argued that the figure of Sycorax in *The Tempest* is 'largely based' on Ovid's Medea, so it is fascinating that, at the moment in which he renounces his magic, Prospero, too, seems to be channelling the character (Orgel 1987: 19–20). Medea has used magic and witchcraft to help her would-be lover Jason through a series of challenges. Here she offers an autobiographical catalogue of ecocidal destruction, extraction and inversion that directly inspired Prospero's soliloquy beginning 'Ye elves of hills, brooks, standing lakes, and groves. . .' (5.1.33).

Before the Moon should circlewise close both her horns in one
Three nights were yet as then to come. As soon as that she shone
Most full of light, and did behold the earth with fulsome face,
Medea with her hair not trussed so much as in a lace,
But flaring on her shoulders twain, and barefoot with her gown
Ungirded, got her out of doors and wandered up and down
Alone the dead time of the night. Both Man, and Beast, and Bird

Were fast asleep: the Serpents sly in trailing forward stirred
So softly as ye would have thought they still asleep had been.
The moisting Air was whist. No leaf ye could have moving seen.
The starrs alonely faire and bright did in the welkin shine
To which she lifting up her hands did thrice herself incline:
And thrice with water of the brook her hair besprinkled she:
And gasping thrice she opened her mouth: and bowing down her knee
Upon the bare hard ground, she said: 'O trusty time of night
Most faithful unto privities [secret matters], O golden stars whose light
Doth jointly with the Moon succeed the beams that blaze by day
And thou three headed Hecate who knowest best the way
To compass this our great attempt and art our chiefest stay:
Ye Charms and Witchcrafts, and thou Earth which both with herb and
    weed
Of mighty working furnishest the Wizards at their need:
Ye Ayres and winds: ye Elves of Hills, of Brookes, of Woods alone,
Of standing Lakes, and of the Night approach ye every one,
Through help of whom (the crooked banks much wondering at the
    thing)
I have compelled streams to run clean backward to their spring.
By charms I make the calm Seas rough, and make the rough Seas plain,
And cover all the Sky with Clouds and chase them thence again.
By charms I raise and lay the winds, and burst the Vipers jaw.
And from the bowels of the Earth both stones and trees doe draw.
Whole woods and Forests I remove. I make the Mountains shake,
And even the Earth it self to groan and fearfully to quake.
I call up dead men from their graves: and thee O lightsome Moon
I darken oft, though beaten brass abate thy peril soon.
Our Sorcery dims the Morning faire, and darks the Sun at Noon.
The flaming breath of fiery Bulls ye quenched for my sake
And caused their unwieldy necks the bended yoke to take.
By means whereof deceiving him that had the Golden fleece
In charge to keep, you sent it thence by Jason into Greece.
Now have I need of herbs that can by virtue of their juice,
To flowering prime of lusty youth old withered age reduce'.

(Golding 1567: 83–4)

3

Eco-tables

I prithee, let me bring thee where crabs grow,
And I with my long nails will dig thee pignuts,
Show thee a jay's nest and instruct thee how
To snare the nimble marmoset. I'll bring thee
To clust'ring filberts, and sometimes I'll get thee
Young scamels from the rock. Wilt thou go with me?
(*TEMPEST* 3.1.165–70)

The eco-tables capture a selection of Shakespeare's numerous environmental references within our focus plays of *A Midsummer Night's Dream, King Lear* and *The Tempest*. These are grouped into various assemblages, such as animals, plants and elements, to help you locate them. We hope that they invite consideration of how they converge and interact within Shakespeare's textual ecosystem. Like our own planet, each play is populated with differing topographies, geologies, systems and species. The eco-tables therefore prompt creative inspiration from the plays' more-than-human presences. The concept is somewhat akin to literary 'ecological restoration', or George Monbiot's concept of 'rewilding' biologically denuded landscapes, to increase species diversity and support ecosystems in light of the extinction crisis (2014). Shakespeare's biodiversity, or rather, *eco*diversity, offers a presentist resource to spur more ecologically diverse adaptations.

There are many valuable texts that can be read as companion works for historical context – see, for example, Nikki Faircloth and Vivian Thomas' *Shakespeare's Plants and Gardens* (2014), Karen Raber and Karen Edwards' *Shakespeare and Animals* (2022), and Sophie Chiari and Sandra Clark's edited volume *Shakespeare and the Environment* (2022). In some cases, Shakespeare's environment has kept its secrets. Are *The Tempest's* 'crabs' crabapples or crustations? What about the mysterious 'scamels', which have been interpreted as everything from sea-birds to walruses (Fitzpatrick 2016)? These historical questions illuminate and inform how we interpret texts. Here, though, we are chiefly concerned with how we can reimagine the plays anew in response to Anthropocene's shifting ecological predicaments. The following section frames some questions to help guide your exploration of the eco-tables.

* * *

How might the characters' thoughts and emotions help us to contemplate our species' intra- and interdependencies with the more-than-human world? Along with the plays' settings, environmental events and material elements, Shakespeare's natural references frequently harness simile and metaphor. This enables us to view the way Shakespeare's landscapes exist *within* as well as *without*. Thus, we may note Helena's description of Hermia's eyes as 'lode-stars' (*Dream* 1.1.183), or humankind's 'goatish disposition' (*Lear* 1.2.128). This is a circulating material exchange. More-than-human forces are personified, as in Sebastian's description of the island's air as breathing upon them 'As if it had lungs, and rotten ones' (*Tempest* 2.1.50). Rather than nature as a static backdrop, observe how Shakespeare's characters are enmeshed within a lively and active ecosystem.

How does Shakespeare's text draw attention to human attitudes towards different species? Viewing Shakespeare's text as an ecosystem does not imply a utopic vision of harmony. The plays reveal distinct preferences towards certain species and environments. Alongside 'lovely berries' (*Dream* 3.2.208–11) we find 'beauty's canker' (*Tempest* 1.2.416). Note how characters feel about other species. Which are described favourably, such as the gentle dove (*Dream* 1.2.79), and which invoke fear, like the 'sharp-toothed' vulture (*Lear* 2.4.326–7)? It is useful to become more attuned to human attitudes towards other species and reflect on any privileges or prejudices. Thinking ecologically involves considering all species' roles within an ecosystem, not merely those that we find beautiful or useful. Noticing Shakespeare's spectrum of responses to the more-than-human prompts us to consider the cultural or ideological influences that underpin conceptions of species' worth or utility.

How might the plays help us to think about the way we manage landscapes? Traditionally, studies of Shakespeare and the natural world focussed on pastoral or wilderness conceptions of untouched green (or blue) spaces. An ecological look at the text reminds us that Shakespeare's natural landscapes are a mosaic of agricultural, industrial and urban zones through which materials are grown, produced, extracted, machined and constructed into new forms. Consider how the plays' horticultural and agricultural metaphors reveal the way in which humans manage landscapes or how they are valued based on their productivity. Also note the use of animal products, visible in lines such as 'owe the worm no silk, the beast no hide, the sheep no wool, the cat no perfume' (*Lear* 3.4.102–04). Shakespeare's text can therefore help us understand the interconnectedness of productive and consumptive systems and our land management processes and impacts.

How do the plays assist ecological systems thinking? Note the plays' diversity of species, elements, habitats and ecotones. These sit within a wider holistic conception of Earth and space that moves from terrestrial earth, rocks and metals to celestial stars and planets. Weather is a dominant presence, as are the seasons, from winter (*Lear* 2.4.239–40) to spring's hawthorn buds (*Dream* 1.1.184) and summers eventual fade into autumn (*Tempest* 4.1.134). Diurnal shifts pervade the text, from 'Fair daylight' (*Lear* 4.7.52) to 'threading dark-eyed night' (*Lear* 2.1.121), and back again, 'as the morning steals upon the night, / Melting the darkness' (*Tempest* 5.1.65–6). The plays are imbued with ecological cycles from growth to decay as a reminder that we will all eventually return to 'wormy beds' (*Dream* 3.2.384). Rather than focussing on singular ecocritical foci, such as green spaces, blue worlds, or grey atmospheres, the eco-tables remind us that Shakespeare's plays traverse a holistic ecosystem.

How you can create your own eco-assemblages from Shakespeare's plays? See what surprising elements, connections, or patterns emerge when you assemble Shakespeare's textual references divorced from their dominant settings and contexts. These may be *re*assembled through the adaptation process in unique ecodramaturgical and ecoscenographic ways. Reading the plays for their material content also nudges us to consider how we can create ecologically sensitive adaptations. Gather what resonates for you, adapt to your own contexts and disperse it into the world.

Adaptation prompts

Like interconnected ecosystem components, the eco-tables' categories overlap. Some references are repeated when relevant to more than one category. *Dream*'s eco-table has fewer references than *Lear*'s and *The Tempest*'s, as it is a shorter play. The number of references should also be balanced against their significance to the play's action and presence within the text. We have included the characters who speak these lines to help readers (especially actors) chart additional patterns. The following adaptation prompts may be used following a table-read in the rehearsal room, in the classroom or for your own contemplation.

OUR MORE-THAN-HUMAN KIN

1　Which animals are present within the text?

2　What type of insects are mentioned?

3　Are there any animal products (such as leather, silk or honey)?

4　Which species of plants do you note and what is their diversity?

5　What type of plant forms, growths or communities are present?

6   Which specific features are mentioned (for example, thorns or wings)?

7   Are there any plant products, materials, distillations or extractions?

8   Where is biodiversity (variety of life) visible in single passages?

9   Are microbes or microbial presences visible at all?

10 Which mythical or supernatural beings or presences do you observe? What may these suggest about heightened, hyperbolic extensions of attitudes towards other species or phenomena?

HUMAN–NATURE RELATIONSHIPS

1   When, where and how do the characters 'other' (distance or separate themselves from) nature?

2   What are the characters' attitudes towards more-than-human species?

3   When and how do the characters think or feel through metaphors of plants, animals, weather or other elements?

WEATHER AND NATURAL CYCLES

1   What type of weather phenomena or events are present?

2   Which meteorological conditions or effects do you notice (e.g. rain, snow or ice)?

3   Which seasons are present?

4   What are the play's diurnal (day–night) changes?

5   How are life cycles represented within the play?

ELEMENTS, METALS, MINERALS AND GEOLOGICAL FRAGMENTS

1   Which elements (fire, water, earth, air) do you notice within the text?

2   Do any elements dominate others?

3 Is earth (as soil, rather than planet Earth) mentioned and if so, in what forms does it appear (for instance, dirt or dust)?

4 Which metals are present?

5 Are any minerals observable?

6 Are there any other extracted materials, for example, coal or saltpetre?

7 How do geological fragments appear, for example, as rocks, stones or pebbles?

8 Are there other weathered geological fragments, such as sand or chalk?

9 Are there gemstones within the text and how do their descriptions differ from rocks?

10 What other forms and materials do you notice, such as coral, mud, shells or pearls?

11 Where are organic materialities present in their natural state and where have they been modified by humans, for instance, as jewellery or other products/materials?

TOPOGRAPHIES AND LANDSCAPES

1 What are the play's topographical (physical landscape) features?

2 Are there any hills or mountains?

3 Are there valleys?

4 Are meadows or plains present?

5 Which agricultural (farmed) spaces do you note (such as fields or orchards)?

6 What, if any, horticultural (gardens) sites or references are present?

7 When, where and how is the sea mentioned?

8 How does the sea appear in different forms (e.g. ocean, salt brine or flood)?

9 Are there any references to rivers, streams or other freshwater sources?

10 What are the plays' urban environments?

11 Are there any hybrid or mixed urban-rural landscapes?

SKIES AND PLANETS

1 Is Earth mentioned within the play?
2 Where does the sun appear in the play?
3 Is the moon present?
4 Are stars present within the play?
5 Are any other planets mentioned?
6 Is there any additional astrological activity?
7 How do the planets and/or stars affect characters or the more-than-human world?

DESIGN PROMPTS

1 What colours and tones come to mind when reading the text?
2 What textures are present in different materials?
3 Which shapes and forms do you observe?
4 What motion, movement and dynamics are present?
5 What organic and/or built structures and materials can you observe?
6 How do these colours, textures, motions, forms and materials impress upon or affect the mind and body? How do they make you feel?
7 Do they invite, intrigue, repel or alienate? How may they make the audience feel?
8 Which senses are evoked within the text?
9 What physiological states and temperatures are described?
10 What melodies and sounds are implied or directly referred to?
11 How could any of these singular or multiple forms or behaviours inform design?

ADDITIONAL QUESTIONS

1 What is present in, and absent from, the play?
2 How do the eco-tables' categories function together as assemblages, life-webs, interconnections or linkages?

A Midsummer Night's Dream

Animals

Animality, monstrosity

Beast, monstrous	Tom Snout, character name, etc. 'For beasts that meet me run away for fear' (Helena 2.2.94) 'Like horse, hound, hog, bear, fire' (Puck 3.1.105) '. . .grisly beast' (Prologue 5.1.138) 'Two noble beasts in, a man and a lion' (Theseus 5.1.215) '. . .monstrous little voice' (Bot 1.2.49) *See further references to monstrosity and the unnatural, e.g. Bottom's transformation

Hunting & cruelty

Bait, hunt	'Demetrius being bated' (Helena 1.1.190) '. . .fond chase' (Helena 2.2.87) *See Geese, Jackdaw 'Our purpos'd hunting shall be set aside' (Theseus 4.1.182)

Birds

Birds, general	'Begin these wood-birds but to couple now' (Theseus 4.1.139) 'Hop as light as bird from briar' (Oberon 5.1.388)
Blackbird	'The ousel cock, so black of hue, / With orange-tawny bill' (Bottom 3.1.119)
Crow	'. . .crows are fatted with the murrion flock' (Titania 2.1.97) '. . .turns to a crow' (Demetrius 3.2.142)
Cuckoo	'. . .plain-song cuckoo grey' (Bottom 3.1.125) 'so foolish a bird? [. . .]though he cry "cuckoo"' (Bottom 3.1.128–9)
Dove	'By the simplicity of Venus' doves' (Hermia 1.1.171) '. . .I will roar you as gently as any sucking dove' (Bottom 1.2.78–9) 'The dove pursues the griffin' (Helena 2.1.232)

	'Who will not change a raven for a dove' (Lysander 2.2.113)
Finch	'The finch' (Bottom 3.1.124)
Fowl	'. . .there is not a more fearful wild-fowl than your lion living' (Bottom 3.1.29–30)
Geese, jackdaw	'As wild geese that the creeping fowler eye, / Or russet-pated choughs, many in sort, / Rising and cawing at the gun's report, / Sever themselves, and madly sweep the sky' (Puck 3.2.20–3) '. . .a goose for his discretion' (Theseus 5.1.228) '. . .the goose carries not the fox' (Theseus 5.1.232)
Lark	'More tuneable than lark to shepherd's ear' (Helena 1.1.184) '. . .the lark' (Bottom 3.1.124) 'I do hear the morning lark' (Puck 4.1.93)
Owl	'The clamorous owl, that nightly hoots' (Titania 2.2.6) '. . .the screech-owl, screeching loud' (Puck 5.1.370)
Raven	'Who will not change a raven for a dove' (Lysander 2.2.113)
Robin	Robin Goodfellow, character name, etc.
Rooster	'. . .first cock crow' (Oberon 2.1.267)
Thrush	'The throstle, with his note so true' (Bottom 3.1.121)
Sparrow	'. . .the sparrow' (Bottom 3.1.124)
Wren	'The wren with little quill' (Bottom 3.1.122)

Insects

Bee	'The honey-bags steal from the humble-bees, / And for night-tapers crop their waxen thighs, / And light them at the fiery glow-worms' eyes' (Titania 3.1.160–2) '. . .kill me a red-hipped humble-bee on the top of a thistle; and good mounsieur, bring me the honey-bag [. . .] have a care the honey-bag break not; I would be loathe to have you overflowen with a honey-bag' (Bottom 4.1.11–17)
Beetle	'Beetles black, approach not near' (1 Fairy 2.2.21)
Butterfly	'And pluck the wings from painted butterflies' (Titania 3.1.164)
Moth	Character name, etc.
Spider	'Weaving spiders, come not here; / Hence, you long legg'd spinners, hence!' (1 Fairy 2.2.19–20) Cobweb, character name, etc.

Amphibians, reptiles & invertebrates

Canker	'Some to kill cankers in the musk-rose buds' (Titania 2.2.3)
	'You canker-blossom' (Hermia 3.2.282)
Glow-worm	'. . .fiery glow-worms' eyes' (Titania 3.1.162)
Newt	'Newts and blind-worms, do no wrong' (1 Fairy 2.2.11)
Snail	'Worm nor snail, do no offence' (1 Fairy 2.2.22)
Snake	'And there the snake throws her enamell'd skin, / Weed wide enough to wrap a fairy in' (Oberon 2.1.255–6)
	'You spotted snakes with double tongue' (1 Fairy 2.2.9)
	'To pluck this crawling serpent from my breast!' (Hermia 2.2.145)
	'Methought a serpent ate my heart away' (Hermia 2.2.148)
	'Could not a worm, an adder, do so much? / An adder did it; for with doubler tongue / Than thine, thou serpent, never adder stung' (Hermia 3.2.71–4)
	'Or I will shake thee from me like a serpent' (Lysander 3.2.261)
	'Now to 'scape the serpent's tongue' (Puck 3.1.427)
Worm	'. . .blind worms' (1 Fairy 2.2.12)
	Note that worm may sometimes refer to a snake
	'Worm nor snail, do no offence' (1 Fairy 2.2.22)
	'. . .to their wormy beds' (Puck 3.2.384)

Mammals

Ass	'ass' (3.1.110, 114; 3.2.17, 34, 4.1.76, etc.)
Ape, monkey	'On medling monkey, or on busy ape' (Oberon 2.1.181)
Bear	'bear' (Oberon 2.1.180)
	'. . .or bear' (Oberon 2.2.29)
	'. . .as ugly as a bear' (Helena 2.2.93)
	'. . .a headless bear' (Puck 3.1.103)
Bat	'Some war with reremice for their leathern wings' (Titania 2.2.4)
	'. . .batty wings doth creep' (Oberon 3.2.365)
Boar	'. . .or boar with bristled hair' (Oberon 2.2.30)
Bull	'bull' (Oberon 2.1.180)
	'Crook-knee'd and dewlapp'd like Thessalian bulls' (Theseus 4.1.121)

Cat	'. . .to tear a cat in' (Bottom 1.2.26–7) 'cat' (Oberon 2.2.29) 'Hang off, thou cat, thou burr! Vile thing, let loose' (Lysander 3.2.260)
Deer, tiger	'. . .the mild hind / Makes speed to catch the tiger' (Helena 2.1.232)
Dog	'I am your spaniel; and, Demetrius / The more you beat me, I will fawn on you. / Use me but as your spaniel' (Helena 2.1.203–05) '. . .as you use your dog' (Helena 2.1.210) '. . .sometime a hound' (Puck 3.1.102) 'I had rather give his carcase to my hounds' (Demetrius 3.2.64) 'Out, dog! Out, cur!' (Hermia 3.2.65) 'My hounds are bread out of the Spartan kind, / So flew'd, so sanded; and their heads are hung / With ears that sweep away the morning dew; Crook-knee'd and dewlapp'd like Thessalian bulls; / Slow in pursuit, but match'd in mouth like bells / Each under each: a cry more tuneable / Was never holla'd to' (The 4.1.118–24) '. . .with lantern, dog, and bush of thorn' (Prologue 5.1.134)
Dolphin	'. . .heard a mermaid on a dolphin's back' (Oberon 2.1.150)
Fox	'She was a vixen when she went to school' (Helena 3.2.234) 'This lion is a very fox for his valour' (Lysander 5.1.226) '. . .for the goose carries not the fox' (Theseus 5.1.232)
Hedgehog	'Thorny hedgehogs, be not seen' (1 Fairy 2.2.10)
Horse	'a fat and bean-fed horse beguile, / Neighing in likeness of a filly foal' (Puck 2.1.45–6) 'As true as truest horse that yet would never tire' (Flute 3.1.96) 'Sometime a horse I'll be' (Puck 3.1.102) 'The man shall have his mare again' (Puck 3.2.463) 'He hath rid his prologue like a rough colt' (Lysander 5.1.199)
Leopard	'Pard, or boar with bristled hair' (Oberon 2.2.30)
Lion	Lion (1.2.61, 63; 2.1.180; 3.1.25, 28, 30, 35), etc. Roar (1.2.66, 67,68) 'This lion is a very fox for his valour' (Lysander 5.1.227)

	'Now the hungry lion roars' (Puck 5.1.365)
Lynx	'Be it ounce, or cat, or bear' (Oberon 2.2.29)
Mouse	'The smallest monstrous mouse that creeps on floor' (Lion 5.1.217) '. . .not a mouse / Shall disturb' (Puck 5.1.381–82)
Ox	'The ox hath therefore stretch'd his yoke in vain' (Titania 2.1.93) '. . .giant-like ox-beef' (Bottom 3.1.184)
Pig	'A hog, a headless bear, sometime a fire' (Puck 3.1.103) 'Like horse, hound, hog' (Puck 3.1.105)
Sheep	'. . .murrion flock' (Titania 2.1.97)
Squirrel	'The squirrel's hoard' (Titania 4.1.35)
Wolf	'wolf' (Oberon 2.1.180) '. . .the wolf behowls the moon' (Puck 5.1.366)

Microbes

Germs, bacteria & decay

| *Disease, rot* | 'Contagious fogs' (Titania 2.1.90)
'Hath rotted' (Titania 2.1.95)
'. . .rheumatic diseases' (Titania 2.1.105) |

Ecosystems and ecotones

Ecosystems and landscape features

Bog, bush, brake, briar	'Through bog, through bush, through brake, through briar' (Puck 3.1.101)
Forest	'. . .to trace the forests wild' (Puck 2.1.25) '. . .forest' (Titania 2.1.83) 'Through the forest have I gone' (Puck 2.2.65)
Grass	'To dew her orbs upon the green' (Fairy 2.1.9) '. . .in grove or green' (Puck 2.1.28) 'wanton green' (Titania 2.1.99) 'This green plot shall be our stage' (Quince 3.1.3–4)
Hill, dale, park, pale, mead, bank	'Over hill, over dale' (Fairy 2.1.2) 'Over park, over pale' (Fairy 2.1.4) 'Met we on hill, in dale, forest or mead' (Titania 2.1.83) 'I know a bank where the wild thyme blows' (Oberon 2.1.249) 'I upon this bank will rest my head' (Hermia 2.2.39)

	'One turf shall serve as pillow for us both' (Lysander 2.2.40)
Mountain	'Like far-off mountains turned into clouds' (Demetrius 4.1.187)
Promontory, prospect mountain	'Since I sat upon a promontory' (Oberon 2.1.149) 'Like far-off mountains turned into clouds' (Demetrius 4.1.187)
Wood	'And in the wood' (Lysander 1.1.165) 'And in the wood' (Hermia 1.1.214) '. . .to the wood' (Helena 1.1.247) '. . .palace wood' (Quince 1.2.95) 'How long within this wood' (Oberon 2.1.138) '. . .wood within this wood' (Demetrius 2.1.192) 'Nor doth this wood lack worlds of company' (Helena 2.1.222) '. . .wand'ring in the wood' (Lysander 2.2.34) '. . .get out of this wood' (Bottom 3.1.142–3) 'Out of this wood do not desire to go' (Titania 3.1.144) 'About the wood go swifter than the wind' (Oberon 3.2.94) '. . .unto this wood' (Helena 3.2.310) '. . .behind the wood' (Oberon 4.1.47) '. . .hither to this wood' (Demetrius 4.1.160)

Rivers and freshwater

Brook	'. . .rushy brook' (Titania 2.1.84)
River	'. . .every pelting river made so proud / That they have overborne their continents' (Titania 2.1.91–2)

Sea

Beach	'Or in the beached margent of the sea' (Titania 2.1.85) 'Neptune's yellow sands' (Titania 2.1.126)
Flood	'Thorough flood' (Fairy 2.1.5) 'Therefore the moon, the governess of floods' (Titania 2.1.103) 'Marking th'embarked traders on the flood' (Titania 2.1.127) 'That in cross-ways and floods have burial' (Puck 3.2.383)

Sail	'. . .under sail' (Hermia 1.1.174)
	'When we have laugh'd to see the sails conceive / And grow big-bellied with the wanton wind' (Titania 2.1.128–9)
	'. . .sail upon the land' (Titania 2.1.132)
Sea	'. . .suck'd up from the sea' (Titania 2.1.89)
	'. . .rude sea grew civil' (Oberon 2.1.152)
	'. . .fetch thee jewels from the deep' (Titania 3.1.150)
	'salt green' (Oberon 3.2.393)
Sunrise over the sea	'Even till the eastern gate, all fiery red, / Opening on Neptune with fair blessed beams, / Turns into yellow gold his salt green streams' (Oberon 3.2.391–3)

Elements

Air

Air	'. . .washes all the air' (Titania 2.1.104)
	'. . .spiced Indian air' (Titania 2.1.124)
	'. . .like an airy spirit' (Titania 3.1.153)

Earth

Dust	'. . .sweep the dust behind the door' (Puck 5.1.384)
Ground	'. . .dank and dirty ground' (Puck 2.2.74)
	'On the ground' (Puck 3.2.448)
	'. . .rock the ground' (Oberon 4.1.85)
	'With these mortals on the ground' (Titania 4.1.101)
Mud	'The nine-men's-morris is fill'd up with mud' (Titania 2.1.98)
	'Crystal is muddy' (Demetrius 3.2.139)

Fire

Fire	'. . .fire which burn'd' (Hermia 1.1.173)
	'. . .thorough fire' (Fairy 2.1.5)
	'. . .run through fire' (Lysander 2.2.102)
	'. . .sometime a fire [. . .] and burn' (Puck 3.1.103–04)
	'. . .fiery glow-worms' eyes' (Titania 3.1.162)
	'By the dead and drowsy fire' (Oberon 5.1.386)

Water

Dew	'Decking with liquid pearl the bladed grass' (Lysander 1.1.211)
	'To dew her orbs upon the green' (Fairy 2.1.9)
	'I must go seek some dew-drops here, / And hang a pearl in every cowslips' ear' (Fairy 2.1.14–15)
	'Bedabbled with the dew' (Hermia 3.2.443)
	'And that same dew, which sometime on the buds / Was wont to swell like round and orient pearls' (Oberon 4.1.52–3)
	'. . .morning dew' (Theseus 4.1.120)
	'dewlapp'd' (Theseus 4.1.121)
	'With this field-dew consecrate' (Oberon 5.1.409)
Water	'wat'ry glass' (Lysander 1.1.210)
	'The moon, methinks, looks with a watery eye' (Titania 3.1.190)

Extractive processes and products

Chemicals and compounds

Medicine	'Out, loathed medicine! O hated potion, hence!' (Lysander 3.2.264)
Potion	*See Love-in-idleness
	'All the power this charm doth owe' (Puck 2.2.78)
	'. . .has thou yet latch'd the Athenian's eyes / With the love-juice, as I did bid thee do?' (Oberon 3.2.36–7)
	'laid the love-juice' (Oberon 3.2.89)
	'Then crush this herb' (Oberon 3.2.366)

Materials

Materials	'. . .let him have some plaster, or some loam, or some roughcast about him' (Bottom 3.1.63–5)
	'. . .with lime and rough-cast' (Prologue 5.1.130)
	'Would you desire lime and hair to speak better?' (Theseus 5.1.164)

Metals

Gold	'. . .best arrow with the golden head' (Hermia 1.1.170)
	'In their gold coats' (Fairy 2.1.11)

	'. . .for shining now so bright; / For by thy gracious, golden, glittering gleams' (Pyramus 5.1.267–8)
Iron	'But yet you draw not iron' (Helena 2.1.196)
	'The iron tongue of midnight' (Theseus 5.1.357)
Silver	'. . .silver visage' (Lysander 1.1.210)
Steel	'. . .true as steel' (Helena 2.1.197)

Managed and built environments

Agriculture

Corn	'. . .pipes of corn' (Titania 2.1.67)
	'. . .green corn' (Titania 2.1.94)
Field	'The fold stands empty in the drowned field' (Titania 2.1.96)
	'. . .the field' (Helena 2.1.238)
	'. . .in field and town' (Puck 3.2.398)
	'. . .field-dew' (Oberon 5.1.409)
Oats, hay	'. . .peck of provender' (Bottom 4.1.31)
	'. . .good dry oats' (Bottom 4.1.32)
	'. . .bottle of hay: good hay, sweet hay' (Bottom 4.1.33)
Pastoral	'More tuneable than lark to shepherd's ear, / When wheat is green, when hawthorn buds appear' (Helena 1.1.184–5)
	'Upon faint primrose beds were wont to lie' (Hermia 1.1.215)
	'And in the shape of Corin, sat all day / Playing on pipes of corn, and versing love / To amorous Phillida' (Titania 2.1.66–8)
Wheat	'. . .wheat is green' (Helena 1.1.185)

Horticulture

Growth, wither	'. . .withering on the virgin thorn, / Grows, lives, and dies' (Theseus 1.1.76–7)
	'. . .wither'd dewlap' (Puck 2.1.50)
	'Things growing are not ripe until their season' (Lysander 2.2.116)
	'O how ripe in show / Thy lips, those kissing cherries, tempting grow' (Demetrius 3.2.139–40)
	'So we grew together, / Like to a double cherry' (Helena 3.2.209–10)

Nature

Natural & unnatural

Art	'Nature shows art' (Lysander 2.2.103)
Unnatural	'. . .thorough this distemperature we see / The seasons alter' (Titania 2.1.106–7)
	'And the blots of Nature's hand [. . .] mole, hare-lip, scar' (Oberon 5.1.403–5)

Supernatural

Dragon	'For night's swift dragons cut the clouds full fast' (Puck 3.2.379)
Elves	'. . .her elves' (Fairy 2.1.17)
	'Nod to him, elves' (Titania 3.1.166), etc.
Fairies	See all references to, and interactions with, fairies, the fairy kingdom, spirits, sprites, elves, goblins, etc.
Ghost	'. . .ghosts wandering here and there / Troop home to churchyards. / Damned spirits all, / That in cross-ways and floods have burial, / Already to their wormy beds are gone' (Puck 3.2.381–4)
Griffin	'The dove pursues the griffin' (Helena 2.1.232)
Hobgoblin	'Those that Hobgoblin call you, and sweet Puck' (Fairy 2.1.40)
Mermaid	'. . .heard a mermaid on a dolphin's back' (Oberon 2.1.150)
Nymph	'Fare thee well, nymph' (Oberon 2.1.245)
Spirit	'How now, spirit!' (Puck 2.1.1)
	'That thou shalt like an airy spirit go' (Titania 3.1.153)
	'But we are spirits of another sort' (Oberon 3.2.388)

Wilderness/wild

Wild	'to trace the forests wild' (Puck 2.1.25)
	'And the ill counsel of a desert place' (Demetrius 2.1.218)
	'And leave thee to the mercy of wild beasts' (Demetrius 2.1.228)
	'The wildest hath not such a heart as you' (Helena 2.1.229)
	'. . .wild thyme' (Oberon 2.1.249)
	'When lion rough in wildest rage doth roar' (Lion 5.1.219)

Plants

Flowers, fruits, nuts, grasses, etc.

Apricot	'apricocks' (Titania 3.1.158)
Apple	'Sink in apple of his eye' (Oberon 3.2.104)
Cherry	'. . .kissing cherries' (Demetrius 3.2.140)
	'So we grew together, / Like to a double cherry, seeming parted, / But yet an union in partition, / Two lovely berries moulded on one stem' (Helena 3.2.208–11)
	'This cherry nose' (Thisbe 5.1.326)
Cowslip	'The cowslips tall [. . .] In their gold coats' (Fairy 2.1.10–11)
	'. . .hang a pear in every cowslip's ear' (Fairy 2.1.15)
	'. . .yellow cowslip cheeks' (Thisbe 5.1.327)
Crab-apple	'roasted crab' (Puck 2.1.48)
Dewberries	'dewberries' (Titania 3.1.158)
Eglantine	'eglantine' (Oberon 2.1.252)
Flowers (general)	'Crowns him with flowers' (Puck 2.1.27)
	'. . .odorous chaplet of sweet summer buds' (Titania 2.1.110)
	'Fetch me that flower; the herb I show'd thee once' (Oberon 2.1.169)
	'Lull'd in these flowers' (Oberon 2.1.254)
	'. . .flower's force' (Puck 2.2.68)
	'. . .flowery bed' (Titania 3.1.123)
	'. . .pressed flowers dost sleep' (Titania 3.1.151)
	'. . .weeps every little flower' (Titania 3.1.191)
	'Flower of this purple dye' (Oberon 3.2.102)
	'. . .both one flower' (Helena 3.2.204)
	'. . .this flowery bed' (Titania 4.1.1)
	'. . .coronet of fresh and fragrant flowers' (Oberon 4.1.51)
	'And that same dew, which sometime on the buds' (Oberon 4.1.52)
	'. . .pretty flowerets' eyes' (Oberon 4.1.54)
	'Dian's bud o'er Cupid's flower' (Oberon 4.1.72)
Fig	'green figs' (Titania 3.1.159)
Garlic	'. . .nor garlic' (Bottom 4.2.40)
Grape	'grapes' (Titania 3.1.159)
Grass	'Decking with liquid pearl the bladed grass' (Lysander 1.1.211)
	'To dew her orbs upon the green' (Fairy 2.1.9)
	'. . .hindering knot-grass' (Lysander 3.2.329)

Herb	'Fetch me this herb' (Oberon 2.1.173)
	'(As I can take it with another herb)' (Oberon 2.1.184)
	'Then crush this herb' (Oberon 3.2.366)
Honeysuckle	'So doth the woodbine the sweet honeysuckle / Gently entwist' (Titania 4.1.41–2)
Ivy	'. . .the female ivy so / Enrings the barky fingers of the elm' (Titania 4.1.42–3)
Lily	'These lily lips' (Thisbe 5.1.325)
Love-in-idleness	'Before milk-white, now purple with love's wound: / And maidens call it 'love-in-idleness'' (Oberon 2.1.167–8)
	'Hast thou the flower there' (Oberon 2.1.247)
Mustardseed	Mustardseed, character name, etc.
Nuts	'The squirrel's hoard, and fetch thee new nuts' (Titania 4.1.35)
Oat	'good dry oats' (Bottom 4.1.32)
Onion	'no onions' (Bottom 4.2.40)
Oxlips	'Where oxlips and the nodding violet grows' (Oberon 2.1.250)
Pea	Peaseblossom, character name, etc.
	'Master Peascod' (Bottom 3.1.179)
	'. . .handful or two of dried peas' (Bottom 4.1.36)
Primrose	'. . .primrose beds' (Hermia 1.1.215)
Quince	Peter Quince, character name, etc.
Rose	'But earthlier happy is the rose distill'd' (Theseus 1.1.76)
	'How chance the roses there do fade so fast?' (Lysander 1.1.128)
	'crimson rose' (Titania 2.1.108)
	'With sweet musk-roses' (Oberon 2.1.252)
	'. . .musk-rose buds' (Titania 2.2.3)
	'. . .stick musk-roses in thy sleek smooth head' (Titania 4.1.3)
Thistle	'. . .on the top of a thistle' (Bottom 4.1.12)
Thyme	'I know a bank where the wild thyme blows' (Oberon 2.1.249)

Trees, bushes, shrubs, etc.

Bush, briar, brake, thorn	'Thorough bush, thorough briar' (Fairy 2.1.3)
	'. . .bush of thorns' (Quince 3.1.55–6)
	'Through bog, through bush, through brake, through briar' (Puck 3.1.101)
	'. . .enter'd in a brake' (Puck 3.2.15)

	'For briars and thorns at their apparel snatch' (Puck 3.2.28)
	'In some bush?' (Demetrius 3.2.406)
	'Telling the bushes that thou look'st for wars' (Puck 3.2.408)
	'...torn with briars' (Hermia 3.2.443)
	'...with lantern, dog, and bush of thorn' (Prologue 5.1.134)
	'...this thorn-bush, my thorn-bush' (Moonshine 5.1.252–3), etc.
Elm	'Enrings the barky fingers of the elm' (Titania 4.1.43)
Grove	'...in grove or green' (Puck 2.1.28)
	'...not from this grove' (Oberon 2.1.146)
	'...do leave this grove' (Oberon 2.1.245)
	'...this grove' (Oberon 2.1.259)
	'...haunted grove' (Oberon 3.2.5)
	'...besides the groves' (Hippolyta 4.1.114)
Hawthorn	'...hawthorn buds' (Helena 1.1.185)
	'...this hawthorn-brake our tiring-house' (Quince 3.1.4)
Mulberry	'...tarrying in mulberry shade' (Prologue 5.1.147)
Oak	'...at the Duke's oak' (Quince 1.2.104)

Skies

Day, night & diurnal cycles

Day	'...four happy days' (Theseus 1.1.2)
	'...comfort of the day' (Lysander 2.2.37)
	'...the sun was not so true unto the day' (Hermia 3.2.50)
	'...shines Aurora's harbinger' (Puck 3.2.380)
	'...by daylight' (Demeter 3.2.427)
	'...daylight' (Helena 3.2.433)
	'...fresh days of love' (Theseus 5.1.29)
	'...break of day' (Oberon 5.1.395, 416)
Day to night	'Four days will quickly steep themselves in night; / Four nights will quickly dream away the time' (Hippolyta 1.1.7–8)
Night	'...collied night' (Lysander 1.1.145)
	'...tomorrow night' (Helena 1.1.247)
	'night-wanderers' (Fairy 2.1.39)
	'...merry wanderer of the night' (Puck 2.1.43)
	'...glimmering night' (Oberon 2.1.77)

	'. . .spiced Indian air, by night' (Titania 2.1.124)
	'. . .I am not in the night' (Helena 2.1.221)
	'Night and silence' (Puck 2.2.69)
	'night-rule' (Oberon 3.2.5)
	'Dark night' (Hermia 3.2.177)
	'. . .more engilds the night / Than all yon fiery oes and eyes of light' (Lysander 3.2.187–88)
	'. . .black-brow'd night' (Puck 3.2.387)
	'. . .the story of the night' (Hippolyta 5.1.23)
	'. . .heavy gait of night' (Theseus 5.1.362)
Light, dark	'The jaws of darkness do devour it up' (Lysander 1.1.148)
	'So quick bright things come to confusion' (Lysander 1.1.149)
	'From the presence of the sun, / Following darkness like a dream' (Puck 5.1.379–80)
Moonlight	'Thou hast by moonlight at her window sung' (Egeus 1.1.20)
	'. . .by moonlight' (Quince 1.2.96)
	'Ill met by moonlight' (Oberon 2.1.60)
	'. . .moonlight revels' (Titania 2.1.141)
	'Quench'd in the chaste beams of the watery moon' (Oberon 2.1.162)
	'moonlight' (Quince 3.1.45, 46P)
	'Doth the moon shine that night' (Snout 3.1.49)
	'moonshine' (3.1.50,50)
	'. . .moon may shine in at the casement' (Bot 3.1.54)
	'. . .the person of Moonshine' (Quince 2.2.57)
	'To fan the moonbeams' (Titania 3.1.165)
Shine, shadow	'Shall shine from far' (Bottom 1.2.32)
	'spangled starlight sheen' (Puck 2.1.29)
	'glimmering night' (Oberon 2.1.77)
	'give glimmering light' (Oberon 5.1.385)
	'. . .look as bright, as clear, / As yonder Venus in her glimmering sphere' (Demetrius 3.2.60–1)
	'Let her shine as gloriously / As the Venus of the sky' (Oberon 3.2.106–07)
	'Crystal is muddy' (Demetrius 3.2.139)
	'. . .more engilds the night / Than all yon fiery orbs and eyes of light' (Lysander 3.2.187–8)
	'Trip we after night's shade' (Oberon 4.1.95)
	'. . .for shining now so bright; / For by thy gracious, golden, glittering gleams' (Pyramus 5.1.267–8)
Time of day	'. . .a morn of May' (Lysander 1.1.167)
	'. . .deep midnight' (Lysander 1.1.223)

'. . .with the Morning's love' (Oberon 3.2.389)
'break of day' (Hermia 4.1.446; Oberon 5.1.395;
Oberon 5.1.416)
'. . .I do hear the morning lark' (Puck 4.1.93)
'The iron tongue of midnight hath told twelve'
(Theseus 5.1.357)
'. . .outsleep the coming morn' (Theseus 5.1.359)

Planets & stars

Earth

'I'll believe as soon / This whole earth may be bor'd,
and that the moon / May through the centre creep,
and so displease / Her brother's noon-tide with
th'Antipodes' (Hermia 3.2.52–5)
'We the globe can compass soon / Swifter than the
wandering moon' (Oberon 4.1.96–7)

Stars

'Your eyes are lode-stars' (Helena 1.1.183)
'. . .spangled starlight sheen' (Puck 2.1.29)
'. . .more engilds the night / Than all yon fiery oes
and eyes of light' (Lysander 3.2.187–8)
'. . .overcast the night; / The starry welkin cover
thou anon / With drooping fog' (Oberon 3
.2.355–7)
'. . .bragging to the stars' (Puck 3.2.407)
'She will find him by starlight' (Theseus 5.1.309)

Stars: Constellation
Stars: Shooting star

'. . .high Taurus' snow' (Demetrius 3.2.141)
'. . .four happy days bring in / Another moon: but O,
methinks, how slow / This old moon wanes'
(Theseus 1.1.2–4)
'. . .the moon, like to a silver bow / New bent in
heaven' (Hippolyta 1.1.9–10)
'. . .cold fruitless moon' (Theseus 1.1.73)
'Phoebe doth behold / Her silver visage in the wat'ry
glass' (Lysander 1.1.209–10)
'. . .moon's sphere' (Fairy 2.1.7)
'Flying between the cold moon and the earth'
(Oberon 2.1.156)
'The moon, methinks, looks with a watery eye'
(Titania 3.1.190)
'. . .let us listen to the moon' (Theseus 5.1.233)
'. . .the horned moon' (Moonshine 5.1.234)
'I am aweary of this moon' (Hippolyta 5.1.245)
*etc. for Moonshine and Mechanicals' references.

Venus

'. . .look as bright, as clear, / As yonder Venus in her
glimmering sphere' (Demeter 3.2.60–1)

'Let her shine as gloriously / As the Venus of the sky'
(Oberon 3.2.106–7)

Stone

Gems

Jewels	'. . .fetch thee jewels from the deep' (Titania 3.1.150)
Pearl	'Decking with liquid pearl the bladed grass' (Lysander 1.1.211) '. . .hang a pearl in every cowslip's ear' ([dew] Fairy 2.1.15) '. . .like round and orient pearls' (Oberon 4.1.53)
Ruby	'Those be rubies' ([Cowslips] Fairy 2.1.12)

Rocks & minerals

Rock, stone	'The raging rocks' (Bottom 1.2.28) '. . .kissed thy stones, / Thy stones with lime and hair knit up in thee' (Thisbe 5.1.188–9)

Weather

Climate, weather elements & events

Cloud	'For night's swift dragons cut the clouds full fast' (Puck 3.2.379) 'Like far-off mountains turned into clouds' (Demetrius 4.1.187)
Fog	'Contagious fogs' (Titania 2.1.90) '. . .overcast the night; / The starry welkin cover thou anon / With drooping fog, as black as Acheron' (Oberon 3.2.355–7)
Hail, Hail shower	'He hail'd down oaths that he was only mine; / So he dissolv'd and show'rs of oaths did melt' (Helena 1.1.244–5)
Rain	'Belike for want of rain' (Hermia 1.1.130)
Snow	'. . .high Taurus' snow' (Demetrius 3.2.141) 'Melted as the snow' (Dem 4.1.165) '. . .wondrous strange snow' (Theseus 5.1.59)
Storm	'. . .tempest of my eyes' (Hermia 1.1.131)

Storm: Lightening	'Brief as the lightening in the collied night' (Lysander 1.1.145)
Storm: Thunder	'So musical a discord, such sweet thunder' (Hippolyta 4.1.117)
Wind	'…whistling wind' (Titania 2.1.86)
	'Therefore the winds, piping to us in vain, / As in revenge have suck'd up from the sea / Contagious fogs' (Titania 2.1.89–90)
	'When we have laugh'd to see the sails conceive / And grow big-bellied with the wanton wind' (Titania 2.1.128–29)
	'Fann'd with the eastern wind' (Demetrius 3.2.142)

Seasons

Seasons	'…we see / The seasons alter' (Titania 2.1.106–07)
	'…the spring, the summer, / The childing autumn, angry winter, change / Their wonted liveries; and the mazed world, / By their increase, now knows not which is which' (Titania 2.1.111–14)
	'Things growing are not ripe until their season' (Lysander 2.2.116)
Spring	'….a morn of May' (Lysander 1.1.167)
	'When wheat is green, when hawthorn buds appear' (Helena 1.1.185)
	'the right of May' (Theseus 4.1.132)
Summer	'…middle summer's spring' (Titania 2.1.82)
	'The summer still doth tend upon my state' (Titania 3.1.147)
Winter	'…winter cheer' (Titania 2.1.101)
	'…old Hiem's thin and icy crown' (Titania 2.1.109)

King Lear

Animals

Animality, monstrosity

Animals: General	'Things that love night / Love not such nights as these' (Kent 3.2.43–3, natural/supernatural) '. . .these things sting / His mind so venomously that burning shame / Detains him from Cordelia' (Kent 4.3.46–8)
Beast	'You beastly knave' (Cornwall 2.2.69) 'That ever penury in contempt of man / Brought near to beast' (Edgar 2.3.182–3) 'Allow not nature more than nature needs / Man's life is cheap as beast's.' (Lear 2.4.458–9) '. . .the beast no hide' (Lear 3.4.103)
Monstrosity	'Commit a thing so monstrous' (France 1.1.218) '. . .her offence / Must be of such unnatural degree / That monsters it' (France 1.1.219–21) 'He cannot be such a monster' (Gloucester 1.2.94) 'More hideous [. . .] / Than the sea-monster' (Lear 1.4.252–3) '. . .monster ingratitude' (Lear 1.5.37) '. . .what a monstrous fellow art thou' (Oswald 2.2.24) 'Women will all turn monsters' (3 Servant 3.7.101) 'Humanity must perforce prey on itself, / Like monsters of the deep' (Albany 4.2.50–1) 'Be-monster not thy feature' (Albany 4.2.64) 'Most monstrous!' (Albany 5.3.157)

Hunting & cruelty

Cruelty	'Horses are tied by the heads, dogs and bears by the neck, monkeys by the loins and men by the legs' (Fool 2.4.201–03) 'Cry to it, nuncle, as the cockney did to the eels when she put 'em i'the paste alive: she knapped 'em o'the coxcombs with a stick, and cried 'Down, wantons, down!' 'Twas her brother that in pure kindness to his horse buttered his hay' (Fool 2.4.314–18) 'As flies to wanton boys are we to the gods, / They kill us for their sport.' (Gloucester 4.1.39)

Animals: Hunt, trap	'When he returns from hunting' (Gonzalo 1.3.8) '. . .by the happy hollow of a tree / Escaped the hunt' (Edgar 2.3.176–7) 'Look, look, a mouse: peace, peace, this piece of toasted cheese will do't' (Lear 4.6.88–90) '. . .to kill vermin' (Edgar 3.4.155) 'That fellow handles his bow like a crow-keeper' (Lear 4.6.86–7) '. . .fire us hence like foxes' (Lear 5.3.23)

Birds

Birds, general	Coxcomb [fool's cap](1.4.96, 100, 103, 104, 106, etc.) 'Till you have drenched our steeples, drowned the cocks' (Lear 3.2.3) 'With plumed helm' (Gonzalo 4.2.58) 'Hadst thou been aught but gossamer, feathers, air' (Edgar 4.6.49) 'This feather stirs' (Lear 5.3.263) 'Bring up the brown bills. O well flown, bird, i'the clout, i'the clout' (Lear 4.6.91–2) 'We two alone will sing like birds i'the cage' (Lear 5.3.9)
Crow	'The crows and choughs that wing the midway air' (Edgar 4.6.13) 'This fellow handles his bow like a crow-keeper' (Lear 4.6.87–8)
Cock	'. . .till the first cock' (Edgar 3.4.114)
Crow, chough	'The crows and choughs that wing the midway air' (Edgar 4.6.13)
Goose	'Goose, if I had you upon Sarum plain, / I'd drive ye cackling home to Camelot' (Kent 2.2.84–5) 'Winter's not gone yet, if the wild geese fly that way' (Fool 2.4.239–40)
Kite	'Detested kite' (Lear 1.4.254)
Lark	'. . .the shrill-gorged lark' (Edgar 4.6.58)
Nightingale	'. . .in the voice of a nightingale' (Edgar 3.6.29–30)
Owl	'. . .wage against the enmity o'th' air — / To be a comrade with the wolf and owl' (Lear 2.4.401–02)
Pelican	'. . .'twas this flesh begot / Those pelican daughters' (Lear 3.4.73–4)
Sparrow, Cuckoo	'The hedge-sparrow fed the cuckoo so long / That it's had it head bit off by it young' (Fool 1.4.206–07)

Vulture	'. . .she hath tied / Sharp-toothed unkindness, like a vulture, here' (Lear 2.4.326–7)
Wren	'The wren goes to't and the small gilded fly / Does lecher in my sight. Let copulation thrive' (Lear 4.6.111–12)

Fish

Eel	'Cry to it, nuncle, as the cockney did to the eels when she put 'em i'the paste alive: she knapped 'em o'the coxcombs with a stick, and cried 'Down, wantons, down' (Fool 2.4.314–17)
Fish	'. . .with champaigns riched' (Lear 1.1.64) '. . .to eat no fish' (Kent 1.4.17) '. . .angler in the lake of darkness' (Edgar 3.6.7) 'fishermen' (Edgar 4.6.17)

Insects

Ant	'We'll set thee to school an ant, to teach thee there's no labouring i'the winter' (Fool 2.4.260–1)
Beetle	'Show scarce so gross as beetles' (Edgar 4.6.14)
Butterfly	'. . .and laugh / At gilded butterflies' (Lear 5.3.12–13)
Fly	'As flies to wanton boys are we to the gods, / They kill us for their sport.' (Gloucester 4.1.38–9) 'The wren goes to't and the small gilded fly / Does lecher in my sight. Let copulation thrive' (Lear 4.6.111–12)
Louse	'The head and he shall louse' (Fool 3.2.29)
Spiderweb	'. . .gives the web and the pin' (Edgar 3.4.114–15) 'Hadst thou been aught but gossamer, feathers, air' (Edgar 4.6.49)

Amphibians, reptiles & invertebrates

Worm: Canker	'. . .canker-bit' (Edgar 5.3.120)
frog, tadpole	'. . .eats the swimming frog, the frog, the tadpole' (Edgar 3.4.126–7)
Newt	'. . .the wall-newt' (Edgar 3.4.127)
Oyster	'Canst tell how an oyster makes his shell' (Fool 1.5.25)
Snail	'I can tell why a snail has a house' (Fool 1.5.27)

	'Why, to put's head in, not to give it away to his daughters and leave his horns without a case' (Fool 1.5.29–30)
Snake	's. . .harper than a serpent's tooth' (Lear 1.4.280)
	'. . .struck me with her tongue / Most serpent-like, upon the very heart' (Lear 2.4.352–3)
	'Each jealous of the other as the stung / Are of the adder' (Edmund 5.1.57–8)
	'This gilded serpent' (Albany 5.3.85)
Toad	'. . .the toad' (Edgar 3.4.126–7)
	'. . .toad-spotted traitor' (Edgar 5.3.136)
Worm	'. . .made me think a man a worm' (Gloucester 4.1.35)

Mammals

Ape	'Their manners are so apish' (Fool, song, 1.4.161)
Ass	'. . .thou bor'st thine ass on thy back o'er the dirt' (Fool 1.4.154)
	'May not an ass know when the cart draws the horse?' (Fool 1.4.215–16)
	'Thy asses are gone about 'em' (Fool 1.5.33)
Bear	'. . .dogs and bears by the neck' (Fool 2.4.202)
	'This night wherein the cub-drawn bear would couch' (Knight 3.1.12)
	'Thou'dst shun a bear, / But if thy flight lay toward the roaring sea, / Thoud'st meet the bear i'the mouth' (Lear 3.4.9–11)
	'Whose reverence even the head-lugged bear would lick' (Albany 4.2.43)
Boar	'. . .stick boarish fangs' (Gloucester 3.7.57)
Cat	'. . .the cat no perfume' (Lear 3.4.104)
	'Purr, the cat is grey' (Edgar 3.6.45)
Cow	'. . .cow-dung for salads' (Edgar 3.4.129)
	'. . .the cowish terror of his spirit' (Gonzalo 4.2.12)[5]
Deer	'But mice and rats and such small deer / Have been Tom's food' (Edgar 3.4.135–6)
Dog	'. . .where's that mongrel' (Lear, re fool, 1.4.48)
	'. . .you whoreson dog, you slave, you cur! (Lear 1.4.78–9)
	'Truth's a dog that must to kennel; he must be whipped out' (Fool 1.4.109–10)
	'. . .son and heir of a mongrel bitch' (Kent 2.2.21)

'With every gale and vary of their masters, /
Knowing naught, like dogs, but following' (Kent
2.2.80–1)
'. . .if I were your father's dog / You should not use
me so' (Kent 2.2.136–7)
'. . .dogs and bears by the neck' (Fool 2.4.202)
'. . .dog in madness' (Edgar 3.4.92–93)
'. . .ditch-dog' (Edgar 3.4.130)
'The little dogs and all, Trey, Blanch and Sweetheart,
see, they bark at me' (Lear 3.6.60–61)
'. . .avaunt, you curs' (Edgar 3.6.62–3)
'Be thy mouth or black or white, / Tooth that
poisons if it bite; / Mastiff, greyhound, mongrel
grim, / Hound or spaniel, brach or him, / Or bobtail
tyke or trundle-tail, / Tom will make him weep and
wail; / For with throwing thus my head, / Dogs leap
the hatch and all are fled' (Edgar 3.6.64–71)
'How now, you dog' (Regan 3.7.74)
'. . .dog-hearted daughters' (Kent 4.3.46)
'Thou hast seen a farmer's dog bark at a beggar'
(Lear 4.6.150–1)
'And the creature run from the cur — there thou
mightst behold the great image of authority: a dog's
obeyed in office' (Lear 4.6.153–5)
'Mine enemy's dog / Though he had bit me should have
stood that night / Against my fire' (Cordelia 4.7.36–8)
'Why should a dog, a horse, a rat have life / And
thou no breath at all' (Lear 5.3.305–06)

Fox   'A fox when one has caught her' (Fool 1.4.310)
'. . .fox in stealth' (Edgar 3.4.92)
'Ingrateful fox' (Regan 3.7.28)
'. . .fire us hence like foxes' (Lear 5.3.23)

Goat   '. . .goatish disposition' (Edmund 1.2.128)
Horse   'Ride more' (Fool 1.4.119)
'. . .cart draws the horse' (Fool 1.4.215–16)
'Saddle my horses' (Lear 1.4.244)
'Prepare my horses' (Lear 1.4.250)
'away to horse' (Gonzalo 1.4.332)
'Be my horses ready' (Lear 1.5.31–2)
'are the horses ready' (Lear 1.5.46)
'Where may we set our horses' (Oswald 2.2.4) 'I'the
mire' (Kent 2.2.5)
'took horse' (Kent 2.4.228)
'horses are tied by the heads' (Fool 2.4.201–02)

'Twas her brother that in pure kindness to his horse buttered his hay' (Fool 2.4.317–18)
'. . .to ride on a bay trotting horse over four-inched bridges' (Edgar 3.4.55–6)
'He met the nightmare and her nine foal' (Edgar 3.4.119)
'Horse to ride' (Edgar 3.4.134)
'. . .a horse's health' (Fool 3.6.18–19)
'Get horses for your mistress' (Cornwall 3.7.20)
'The fitchew, nor the soiled horse, goes to't with a more riotous appetite.' (Lear 4.6.120–1)
'. . .a troop of horse' (Lear 4.6.181)
'Why should a dog, a horse, a rat have life / And thou no breath at all?' (Lear 5.3.305–06)

Lion   'The lion and the belly-pinched wolf / Keep their fur dry' (Knight 3.1.13–14)
'. . .lion in prey' (Edgar 3.4.93)

Mouse   'But mice and rats and such small deer / Have been Tom's food' (Edgar 3.4.135–6)
'Appear like mice' (Edgar 4.6.18)
'Look, look, a mouse: peace, peace, this piece of toasted cheese will do't' (Lear 4.6.88–90)

Monkey   '. . .monkeys by the loins' (Fool 2.4.202–03)

Pig   '. . .hog in sloth' (Edgar 3.4.92)
'To hovel thee with swine and rogues forlorn / In short and musty straw' (Cordelia 4.7.39–40)
*See also 'boar'.

Polecat: Fitchew   'The fitchew, nor the soiled horse, goes to't with a more riotous appetite.' (Lear 4.6.120–1)

Rat   'Like rats oft bite the holy cords atwain' (Kent 2.2.75)
'. . .set ratsbane by this porridge' (Edgar 3.4.54)
'. . .swallows the old rat' (Edgar 3.4.129)
'But mice and rats and such small deer / Have been Tom's food' (Edgar 3.4.135–6)
'. . .to kill vermin' (Edgar 3.4.155)
'Why should a dog, a horse, a rat have life / And thou no breath at all' (Lear 5.3.305–06)

Sheep   '. . .the sheep no wool' (Lear 3.4.103–04)
'. . .jolly shepherd? / Thy sheep be in the corn; / And for one blast of thy minikin mouth / Thy sheep shall take no harm' (Edgar 3.6.41–4)

Tiger   'Tigers, not daughters' (Albany 4.2.41)

Wolf   '. . .thy wolvish visage' (Lear 1.4.300)

'To be a comrade with the wolf and owl' (Lear
2.4.402)
'The lion and the belly-pinched wolf / Keep their fur
dry' (Knight 3.1.13–14)
'. . .wolf in greediness' (Edgar 3.4.92)
'He's mad that trusts in the tameness of a wolf'
(Fool 3.6.18)
'If wolves had at thy gate howled that stern time, /
Thou shouldst have said, 'Good porter, turn the key,
/ All cruels else subscribed' (Gloucester 3.7.62–4)

Microbes

Germs, bacteria & decay

Decay   '. . .this great decay' (Albany 5.3.296)
Disease   '. . .the foul disease' (Kent 1.1.165)
       '. . .plague of custom' (Edmund 1.2.3)
       'A pestilent gall' (Lear 1.4.112)
       'A plague upon your epileptic visage' (Kent 2.2.82)
       '. . .plague, death, confusion' (Lear 2.4.287)
       '. . .a disease that's in my flesh [. . .] a boil, / A plague
       sore, or embossed carbuncle / In my corrupted
       blood' (Lear 2.4.414–17)
       '. . .all the plagues that in the pendulous air / Hang'
       (Lear 3.4.66–7)
       '. . .time's plague' (Gloucester 4.1.49)
       '. . .whom the heaven's plagues' (Gloucester 4.1.67)
       '. . .to plague us' (Edgar 5.3.169)
       'A plague' (Lear 5.3.267)

Fungi and protists

Algae   '. . .drinks the green mantle of the standing pool'
       (Edgar 3.4.130–1)
Mildew   '. . .mildews the white wheat' (Edgar 3.4.116)

Ecosystems & ecotones

Ecosystem connections and features

Eco-relationships   Thou ow'st the worm no silk, the beast no hide, the
       sheep no wool, the cat no perfume' (Edgar 3.4.102–04)
       '. . .hurts the poor creature of earth' (Edgar 3.4.116–17)

Landscape features

Bog, quagmire	'. . .o'er bog and quagmire' (Edgar 3.4.52)
cave	'The wrathful skies / Gallow the very wanderers of the dark, / And make them keep their caves' (Kent 3.2.43–5)
Cliff, verge	'Nature in you stands on the very verge / Of her confine' (Regan 2.4.339–40) 'There is a cliff whose high and bending head / Looks fearfully in the confined deep: / Bring me but to the very brim of it' (Gloucester 4.1.76–8) 'From the dread summit of this chalky bourn. / Look up a-height: the shrill-gorged lark so far / Cannot be seen or heard' (Edgar 4.6.57–9) 'Upon the crown o'the cliff' (Edgar 4.6.67)
Hill	'. . .a great wheel runs down a hill' (Fool 2.4.264–5) 'Pillicock sat on Pillicock hill' (Edgar 3.4.75) 'When shall I come to the top of that same hill' (Gloucester 4.6.1) 'You do climb up it now' (Edgar 4.6.2) 'Methinks the ground is even' (Gloucester 4.6.3) 'Horrible steep' (Edgar 4.6.3)
Hovel	'. . .hard by here is a hovel: / Some friendship will it lend you 'gainst this tempest' (Kent 3.2.61–2) 'Come; your hovel' (Lear 3.2.71) 'Come, bring us to this hovel' (Lear 3.2.77) 4.1 *Enter Fool, as from the hovel* '. . .into the hovel; keep thee warm' (Gloucester 3.4.170)
Landscape variability	'With shadowy forests and with champaigns riched, / With plenteous rivers and wide-skirted meads' (Lear 1.1.64–5) '. . .led through fire and through flame, through ford and whirlpool, o'er bog and quagmire' (Edgar 3.4.51–2)
Meadow	'wide-skirted meads' (Lear 1.1.65)
Mire	'I'the mire' (Kent 2.2.5)
Sands	'Here in the sands / Thee I'll rake up' (Edgar 4.6.267–8)

Rivers and freshwater

Lake	'. . .angler in the lake of darkness' (Edgar 3.6.7)
Pond	'. . .drinks the green mantle of the standing pool' (Edgar 3.4.130–1)

River	'. . .with plenteous rivers' (Lear 1.1.65)
Spring	'That good effects may spring from words of love' (Kent 1.1.186)
Ford, whirlpool	'. . .through ford and whirlpool' (Edgar 3.4.52)

Sea

Beach	'The fishermen that walk upon the beach' (Edgar 4.6.17) 'The murmuring surge / That on th'unnumbered idle pebble chafes, / Cannot be heard so high' (Edgar 4.6.20–2)
Sea	'Bids the wind blow the earth into the sea, / Or swell the curled waters 'bove the main' (Knight 3.1.5–6) 'Thou'dst shun a bear, / But if thy flight lay toward the roaring sea, / Thoud'st meet the bear i'the mouth' (Lear 3.4.9–11) 'The sea, with such a storm as his bare head / In hell-black night endured, would have buoyed up / And quenched the stelled fires' (Gloucester 3.7.58–60) 'As mad as the vexed sea' (Cordelia 4.4.2) '. . .do you hear the sea?' (Edgar 4.6.4) 'Horns whelked and waved like the enraged sea' (Edgar 4.6.71)

Elements

General

General	'. . .down, thou climbing sorrow, / Thy element's below' (Lear 2.4.250–1) 'Contending with the fretful elements' (Knight 3.1.4) 'Nor rain, wind, thunder, fire are my daughters; / I tax not you, you elements, with unkindness. / I never gave you kingdom, called you children; / You owe me no subscription. Why then, let fall your horrible pleasure' (Lear 3.2.15–19)

Air

Air	'. . .taking airs' (Lear 2.4.356) '. . .wage against the enmity o'th' air' (Lear 2.4.401)

'. . .all the plagues that in the pendulous air / Hang' (Lear 3.4.66)

'Here is better than the open air' (Gloucester 3.6.1)

'Welcome then, / Thou unsubstantial air that I embrace; / The wretch that thou hast blown unto the worst / Owes nothing to thy blasts' (Edgar 4.1.6–9)

'. . .stretch thy spirits up into the air' (Gonzalo 4.2.23)

'The crows and choughs that wing the midway air' (Edgar 4.6.13)

'Hadst thou been aught but gossamer, feathers, air' (Edgar 4.6.49)

'. . .the first time that we smell the air' (Lear 4.6.175)

Earth

Earth	'Bids the wind blow the earth into the sea' (Knight 3.1.5) 'She's dead as earth' (Lear 5.3.259)
Earth: Clay	'. . .temper clay' (Lear 1.4.296)
Earth: Dirt	'. . .thou bor'st thine ass on thy back o'er the dirt' (Fool 1.4.154)
Earth: Dunghill	'Throw this slave / Upon the dunghill' (Cornwall 3.7.94–5) 'Out, dunghill' (Oswald 4.6.239)
Earth: Dust	'You are not worth the dust which the rude wind / Blows in your face.' (Albany 4.2.31–2) '. . .dust below thy foot' (Edgar 5.3.135)
Earth: Grime	'My face I'll grime with filth' (Edgar 2.3.183)

Fire

Fire	'My love should kindle to inflamed respect' (France 1.1.257) '. . .may stand by the fire and stink' (Fool 1.4.110–11) 'Bring oil to fire' (Kent 2.2.78) '. . .radiant fire' (Kent 2.2.108) '"Fiery"? The fiery Duke, tell the hot Duke' (Lear 2.4.296) '. . .the fiery quality of the Duke' (Gloucester 2.4.284) '. . .blinding flames' (Lear 2.4.357) '. . .comfort and not burn' (Lear 2.4.365)

'. . .thought-executing fires' (Lear 3.2.4)
'Spit fire, spout rain!' (Lear 3.2.14)
'Nor rain, wind, thunder, fire are my daughters'
(Lear 3.2.15)
'No heretics burned' (Fool 3.2.83)
'. . .through fire and through flame' (Edgar 3.4.51)
'Now a little fire in a wild field were like an old
lecher's heart, a small spark, all the rest on's body
cold: look, here comes a walking fire' (Fool 3.4.110–
12)
'. . .bring you where both fire and food is ready'
(Gloucester 3.4.149)
'. . .red burning spits / Come hizzing in upon 'em!'
(Lear 3.6.15–16)
'My snuff and loathed part of nature should / Burn
itself out' (Gloucester 4.6.39)
'. . .wheel of fire' (Lear 4.7.47)
'Tis hot, it smokes' (Gentleman 5.3.222)

Water

Water

'. . .waterish Burgundy' (France 1.1.260)
'. . .cast you with the waters that you loose / To
temper clay' (Lear 1.4.295–6)
'. . .water-drops' (Lear 2.4.469)
'. . .court holy-water in a dry house is better than
this rain-water out o'door' (Fool 3.2.10–11)
'When brewers mar their malt with water' (Fool
3.2.81)
'. . .the wall-newt and the water' (Edgar 3.4.127)
'The holy water from her heavenly eyes' (Gentleman
4.3.31)
'To use his eyes for garden water-pots' (Lear
4.6.192)
'Be your tears wet' (Lear 4.7.71)

Extractive processes & products

Chemicals & compounds

Balm   '. . .balm of your age' (France 1.1.216)
Civet   'Give me an ounce of civet, good apothecary, to
sweeten my imagination' (Lear 4.6.126–7)

Medicine	'Thy medicine on my lips' (Cordelia 4.7.27)
	'I'll ne'er trust medicine' (Gonzalo 5.3.97)
Poison	'I perceived had poisoned mine' (Kent 2.4.232)
	'. . .set ratsbane by his porridge' (Edgar 3.4.54)
	'Tooth that poisons if it bite' (Edgar 3.6.65)
	'. . .these things sting / His mind so venomously that burning shame / Detains him from Cordelia' (Kent 4.3.46–8)
	'If you have poison for me, I will drink it' (Lear 4.7.72)
	'. . .the other poisoned for my sake' (Edmund 5.3.239)
Salt	'. . .this would make a man a man of salt' (Lear 4.6.191)
Sulpher	'. . .there is the sulphurous pit, burning, scalding, stench, consumption! Fie, fie, fie! Pah, pah' (Lear 4.6.124–5)

Materials

Materials	'. . .glass-glazing' (Kent 2.2.17)
	'. . .glass eyes' (Lear 4.6.166)
	'Lend me a looking-glass; / If that her breath will mist or stain the stone, / Why then she lives' (Lear 5.3.259–60)
	'. . .in a glass' (Fool 3.2.36)
	'. . .blanket my loins' (Edgar 2.3.184)
	'. . .wear rags' (Fool 2.4.241)
	'. . .a madman's rags' (Egdar 5.3.186)
	'. . .rags, a pigmy's straw' (Lear 4.6.163)
	'Thou ow'st the worm no silk, the beast no hide, the sheep no wool, the cat no perfume' (Lear 3.4.102–04)
	'I'll fetch some flax and whites of eggs' (3 Servant 3.7.105)
	'With plumed helm' (Goneril 4.2.58)
	'Hadst thou been aught but gossamer, feathers, air' (Edgar 4.6.49)
	'This feather stirs' (Lear 5.3.263)
	'Robes and furred gowns' (Lear 4.6.161)
	'. . .to shoe / A troop of horse with felt' (Lear 4.6.180–1)
	'. . .gentle wax' (Edgar 4.6.254)

Metals

Metal	'. . .fire-new' (Edgar 5.3.130)
Gold	'. . .gav'st thy golden one away' (Fool 1.4.156) 'When usurers tell their gold i'the field' (Fool 3.2.88) 'Plate sin with gold' (Lear 4.6.161)
Lead	'. . .mine own tears / Do scald like molten lead' (Lear 4.7.47–8)

Managed & built environments

Agriculture

Cornfield	'. . .all the idle weeds that grow / In our sustaining corn (Cordelia 4.4.5–6)
Farm	'Poor pelting villages, sheepcotes and mills' (Edgar 2.3.192)
Field, battlefield	'When usurers tell their gold i'the field' (Fool 3.2.88) 'Search every acre in the high-grown field' (Cordelia 4.4.7)
Pastoral	'Sleepest or wakest thou, jolly shepherd? / Thy sheep be in the corn; / And for one blast of thy manikin mouth / Thy sheep shall take no harm' (Edgar 3.6.41–4)
Straw	'Where is this straw' (Lear 3.2.69) 'What art thou that dost grumble there i'the straw?' (Kent 3.4.43–4) 'To hovel thee with swine and rogues forlorn / In short and musty straw' (Cordelia 4.7.39–40)
Wheat	'. . .mildews the white wheat' (Edgar 3.4.116)

Horticulture

Gnawn plants	'By treason's tooth bare-gnawn and canker-bit' (Edgar 5.3.120)
Fruitful	'. . .time and place will be fruitfully offered' (Edgar, letter, 4.6.259–60)
Garden	'To use his eyes for garden water-pots' (Lear 4.6.192)
Graft	'. . .long-engrafted condition' (Gonzalo 1.1.298)
Grow	'And my invention thrive, Edmund the base / Shall top the legitimate. I grow, I prosper' (Edmund 1.2.20–1)
Plant	'Should never plant in me' (France 1.1.224)
Ripen	'Ripeness is all' (Edgar 5.2.11)

Nature

Natural & unnatural

Human nature	'Which nor our nature, nor our place can bear' (Lear 1.1.172) 'Whose nature is so far from doing harms' (Edmund 1.2.178) 'I will forget my nature' (Lear 1.5.31) 'Natures of such deep trust' (Cornwall 2.1.116) '. . .the natures of their lords rebel' (Kent 2.2.77) '. . .from his nature' (Cornwall 2.2.99) 'When nature, being oppressed, commands the mind / To suffer with the body' (Lear 2.4.300–01) 'Thy tender-hafted nature' (Lear 2.4.363) 'Man's nature cannot carry / Th'affliction, nor the fear' (Kent 3.2.48–9) 'The tyranny of the open night's too rough / For nature to endure. *Storm still*' (Kent 3.4.2–3) '. . .nature thus gives way to loyalty' (Edmund 3.5.2–3) 'Oppressed nature sleeps' (Kent 3.6.95) 'That nature which contemns its origin / Cannot be bordered certain in itself. / She that herself will sliver and disbranch / From her material sap perforce must wither, / And come to deadly use' (Albany 4.2.33–7) 'My snuff and loathed part of nature should / Burn itself out' (Gloucester 4.6.39–40) 'Cure this great breach in his abused nature' (Cordelia 4.7.15) 'Despite of mine own nature' (Edmund 5.3.242)
Nature	'Where nature doth with merit challenge' (Lear 1.1.53) 'Than on a wretch whom nature is ashamed / Almost t'acknowledge hers' (Lear 1.1.213–14) '. . .tardiness in nature' (France 1.1.237) 'Thou, Nature, art my goddess; to thy law / My services are bound.' (Edmund 1.2.1–2) '. . .lusty stealth of nature' (Edmund 1.2.11) '. . .wrenched my frame of nature / From the fixed place' (Lear 1.4.260–1) 'Hear, Nature, hear, dear goddess, hear: / Suspend thy purpose if thou didst intend / To make this creature fruitful. / Into her womb convey sterility, / Dry up in her organs of increase, / And from her

derogate body never spring / A babe to honour her'
(Lear 1.4.267–73)
'. . .nature disclaims in thee' (Kent 2.2.53)
'Nature in you stands on the very verge / Of her
confine' (Regan 2.4.339–40)
'The offices of nature, bond of childhood' (Lear
2.4.370)
'Allow not nature more than nature needs /
Man's life is cheap as beast's. Thou art a lady; /
If only to go warm were gorgeous, / Why nature
needs not what thou gorgeous wear'st' (Lear
2.4.458–61)
'Crack nature's moulds, all germens spill at once /
That make ingrateful man' (Lear 3.2.8–9)
'Nor rain, wind, thunder, fire are my daughters; / I
tax not you, you elements, with unkindness. / I never
gave you kingdom, called you children; / You owe
me no subscription. Why then, let fall / Your
horrible pleasure' (Lear 3.2.15–19)
'Nothing could have subdued nature / To such
lowness' (Lear 3.4.69–70)
'Is there any cause in nature that make these hard
hearts' (Lear 3.6.75–6)
'Our foster nurse of nature is repose' (Gentleman
4.4.12)
'Nature's above art in that respect' (Lear 4.6.86)
'O ruined piece of nature' (Gloucester 4.6.130)
'Thou hast one daughter / Who redeems nature from
the general curse' (Gentleman 4.6.201–02)

Nature: Breed, grow   'What grows of it no matter . . . / I would breed
from hence occasions' (Gonzalo 1.3.24–5)
Crack nature's moulds, all germens spill at once /
That make ingrateful man' (Lear 3.2.8–9)

Nature: Power   'Strives in his little world of man to outscorn / The
to and fro conflicting wind and rain' (Knight
3.1.10–11)
'When the rain came to wet me once and the wind
to make me chatter; when the thunder would not
peace at my bidding' (Lear 4.6.100–03)

Natural   'Loyal and natural boy' (Gloucester 2.1.84)
'The wren goes to't and the small gilded fly / Does
lecher in my sight. Let copulation thrive' (Lear
4.6.111–12)
'The fitchew, nor the soiled horse, goes to't with a
more riotous appetite' (Lear 4.6.120–1)

	'I am even / The natural fool of fortune' (Lear 4.6.186–7)
Unnatural	'Sure her offence / Must be of such unnatural degree / That monsters is' (France 1.1.219–21)
	'Unnatural, detested, brutish / villain' (Gloucester 1.2.77–8)
	'Though the wisdom of Nature can reason it thus and thus, yet nature finds itself scourged by the sequent effects' (See full speech: Gloucester 1.2.103–114)
	'. . .as of unnaturalness between the child and the parent, death, dearth, dissolutions of ancient amities, divisions in state, menaces and maledictions against King and nobles, needless diffidences, banishment of friends, dissipation of cohorts, nuptial breaches and I know not what' (Edmund 1.2.144–9)
	'. . .thwart disnatured torment to her' (Lear 1.4.275)
	'To his unnatural purpose' (Edmund 2.1.50)
	'. . .unnatural hags' (Lear 2.4.470)
	'. . .unnatural and bemadding sorrow' (Kent 3.1.34)
	'I like not this unnatural dealing' (Gloucester 3.3.1–2)
	'Most savage and unnatural' (Edmund 3.3.7)

Supernatural

Dragon	'Come not between the dragon and his wrath!' (Lear 1.1.123)
	'. . .under the dragon's tail' (Edmund 1.2.129)
Fairies	'Fairies and gods' (Gloucester 4.6.29)
Fiend	'. . .methought his eyes / Were two full moons. / He had a thousand noses, / Horns whelked and waved like the enraged sea. / It was some fiend' (Edgar 4.6.69–72)
Nightmare	'He met the nightmare and her nine foal' (Edgar 3.4.119)
Sea-monster	'More hideous [. . .] / Than the sea-monster' (Lear 1.4.252–3)
	'Humanity must perforce prey on itself, / Like monsters of the deep' (Albany 4.2.50–1)
Spirit	'. . .here's a spirit' (Fool 3.4.39)
	'A spirit, a spirit' (Fool 3.4.42)

Wilderness/wild

Wild	'Shut up your doors, my lord; 'tis a wild night. / My Regan counsels well; come out o'the storm' (Cornwall 2.4.501–02)
	4.6. Enter Lear mad, crowned with wild flowers
Wild: Human in wilderness	Unaccommodated man is no more but such a poor, bare, forked animal as thou art' (Lear 3.4.106–07)
Wild: Savage	'Most savage and unnatural' (Edmund 3.3.7)

Plants

Flowers, fruits, nuts, grasses, etc.

Burdock	'With burdocks' (Cordelia 4.4.4)
Crabapple	'. . .though she's as like this as a crab's like an apple' (Fool 1.5.15)
	'She will taste as like this as a crab does to a crab' (Fool 1.5.18)
Corn	'. . .grow / In our sustaining corn' (Cordelia 4.4.5–6)
Cuckoo-flowers	'. . .cuckoo-flowers' (Cordelia 4.4.4)
Darnel	'Darnel' (Cordelia 4.4.5)
Flowers	*4.6. Enter Lear mad, crowned with wild flowers*
Fumiter	'Crowned with rank fumiter' (Cordelia 4.4.3)
Furrow	'. . .furrow-weeds' (Cordelia 4.4.3)
Hawthorn	'Through the sharp hawthorn blows the cold wind' (Edgar 3.4.45–6)
	'Still through the hawthorn blows the cold wind' (Edgar 3.4.97–8)
Hemlock	'hemlock' (Cordelia 4.4.4)
Lily	'. . .lily-livered' (Kent 2.2.16)
Marjoram	'Sweet marjoram' (Edgar 4.6.93)
Nettle	'nettles' (Cordelia 4.4.4)
Oats	'. . .eat dried oats' (Captain 5.3.39)
Peascod	'That's a shelled peascod' (Fool 1.4.190)
Rosemary	'. . .sprigs of rosemary' (Edgar 2.3.190)

Trees, bushes, shrubs, etc.

Body, trunk	'Thy banished trunk' (Lear 1.1.178)
bush	'. . .for many miles about / There's scarce a bush' (Gloucester 2.4.493–4)
Cork	'. . .bind fast his corky arms' (Cordelia 3.7.29)
Forest	'With shadowy forests' (Lear 1.1.64)
Hedge	'hedge-sparrow' (Fool 1.4.206)

Oak	'. . .oak-cleaving thunderbolts' (Lear 3.2.5)
Tree	'. . .by the happy hollow of a tree / Escaped the hunt' (Edgar 2.3.176–7)
	'She that herself will sliver and disbranch / From her material sap perforce must wither, / And come to deadly use' (Albany 4.2.35–7)
	'Here, father, take the shadow of this tree / For your good host' (Edgar 5.2.1–2)

Skies

Day, night & diurnal cycles

Day	'Fair daylight?' (Lear 4.7.52)
	'. . .this day's battle's fought' (Kent 4.7.97)
	'. . .this day's strife' (Albany 5.3.43)
Day and night	'By day and night he wrongs me' (Gonzalo 1.3.4)
	'Till noon? Till night, my lord, and all night too' (Regan 2.2.135)
Night	'The mysteries of Hecate and the night' (Lear 1.1.111)
	'. . .the night gone by' (Edgar 1.2.152)
	'. . .good advantage of the night' (Edmund 2.1.23)
	'. . .threading dark-eyed night?' (Regan 2.1.121)
	'. . .it be night, yet the moon shines' (Kent 2.2.30)
	'The night before' (Knight 2.4.198)
	'. . .travelled all the night?' (Lear 2.4.281)
	'Alack, the night comes on, and the high winds / Do sorely ruffle' (Gloucester 2.4.493–4)
	'This night wherein the cub-drawn bear would crouch, / The lion and the belly-pinched wolf / Keep their fur dry, unbonneted he runs' (Knight 3.1.12–14)
	'Things that love night / Love not such nights as these. The wrathful skies / Gallow the very wanderers of the dark, / And make them keep their caves' (Kent 3.2.42–5)
	'This is a brave night to cool a courtesan' (Fool 3.2.78)
	'The tyranny of the open night's too rough / For nature to endure. *Storm still*' (Kent 3.4.2–3)
	'In such a night / To shut me out? Pour on, I will endure. / In such a night as this' (Lear 3.4.17–19)
	'. . .'tis a naughty night to swim in' (Fool 3.4.109)
	'. . .this tyrannous night' (Gloucester 3.4.147)
	'What a night's this?' (Gloucester 3.4.166)
	'What, i'the storm, i'the night?' (Gentleman 4.3.29)
	'His nighted life' (Regan 4.5.15)

Passage of time	'. . .some twelve or fourteen moonshines / Lag of a brother' (Edmund 1.2.5–6)
	'. . .he begins at curfew and walks till the first cock' (Edgar 3.4.113–14)
Shine, shadow; dark light	'With shadowy forests' (Lear 1.1.64)
	'. . .our darker purpose' (Lear 1.1.35)
	'. . .the maidenliest star in the firmament twinkled' (Edmund 1.2.132–3)
	'Lear's shadow' (Fool 1.4.222)
	'Darkness and devils!' (Lear 1.4.243)
	'Here stood he in the dark' (Edmund 2.1.37)
	'like the wreath of radiant fire / On flickering Phoebus' front' (Kent 2.2.108–09)
	'Gallow the very wanderers of the dark, / And make them keep their caves' (Kent 3.2.44–5)
	'. . .course his own shadow' (Edgar 3.4.56)
	'. . .the act of darkness' (Edgar 3.4.86)
	'The prince of darkness' (Edgar 3.4.139)
	'. . .to the dark tower' (Edgar 3.4.178)
	'. . .angler in the lake of darkness' (Edgar 3.6.7)
	'. . .small gilded fly' (Lear 4.6.111)
	'. . .and laugh / At gilded butterflies' (Lear 5.3.12–13)
	'This gilded serpent' (Albany 5.3.85)
	'. . .there's hell, there's darkness' (Lear 4.6.123–4)
	'Here, father, take the shadow of this tree / For your good host' (Edgar 5.2.1–2)
	'All's cheerless, dark and deadly' (Kent 5.3.288)
	*see also sunshine and moonshine
Shine: Candle, torch	'So out went the candle and were left darkling' (Fool 1.4.208)
	'Light, ho, here' (Edmund 2.1.32)
	'Torches, torches' (Edmund 2.1.33–4)
	Enter Gloucester and servants, with torches 2.1
	3.3 *Enter Gloucester and Edmund, with lights*
	3.4 *Enter Gloucester with a torch*

Planets & stars

Earth	'. . .they shall be / The terrors of the earth!' (Lear 2.4.473–4)
	'. . .hurts the poor creature of earth' (Edgar 3.4.116–17)
	'Strike flat the thick rotundity o'the world' (Lear 3.2.7)

	'All you unpublished virtues of the earth, / Spring with my tears' (Cordelia 4.4.15–16)
Eclipse	'These late eclipses in the sun and moon portend no good to us' (Gloucester 1.2.103–04)
	'O, these eclipses do portend these divisions. Fa, sol, la, mi' (Edmund 1.2.136–7)
	'. . .a prediction I read this other day, what should follow these eclipses' (Edmund 1.2.140–1)
Fixed course	'How unremovable and fixed he is / In his own course' (Gloucester 2.4.285–6)
Moon	'. . .some twelve or fourteen moonshines / Lag of a brother?' (Edmund 1.2.5–6)
	'Mumbling of wicked charms, conjuring the moon / To stand's auspicious mistress' (Edmund 2.1.38–9)
	'. . .it be night, yet the moon shines. I'll make a sop o'the moonshine of you' (Kent 2.2.30–1)
	'For all beneath the moon / Would I not leap upright' (Edgar 4.6.26–7)
	'. . .his eyes / Were two full moons' (Edgar 4.6.9–10)
	'That ebb and flow by the moon' (Lear 5.3.19)
Sun, orb, globe	'For by the sacred radiance of the sun, / The mysteries of Hecate and the night, / By all the operation of the orbs / From whom we do exist and cease to be' (Lear 1.1.110–13)
	'. . .like the wreath of radiant fire / On flickering Phoebus' front' (Kent 2.2.108–09)
	'Thou out of heaven's benediction com'st / To the warm sun. / Approach, thou beacon to this under-globe, / That by thy comfortable beams I may / Peruse this letter.' (Kent 2.2.162–6)
	'You fen-sucked fogs, drawn by the powerful sun' (Lear 2.4.59)
	'Were all thy letters suns, I could not see one' (Gloucester 4.6.136)
Stars	'The reason why the seven stars are no more than seven is a pretty reason' (Fool 1.5.33–4)
	'. . .their great stars / Throned and set high' (Kent 3.1.22–3)
	'. . .bless thee from whirlwinds, star-blasting and taking' (Edgar 3.4.58)
	'The sea, with such a storm as his bare head / In hell-black night endured, would have buoyed up / And quenched the stelled fires' (Gloucester 3.7.58–60)

Stone

Gems

Diamond	'As pearls from diamonds dropped' (Gentleman 4.3.22)
Jewel	'The jewels of our father' (Cordelia 1.1.270)
	'. . .in it a jewel / Well worth a poor man's taking' (Gloucester 4.6.28–9)
	'precious stones' (Edgar 5.3.189)
Pearl	'As pearls from diamonds dropped' (Gentleman 4.3.22)

Rocks & minerals

Chalk	'. . .this chalky bourn' (Edgar 4.6.57)
Marble	'. . .thou marble-hearted fiend' (Lear 1.4.251)
Stone	'. . .a stone-cutter' (Kent 2.2.57)
	'. . .while I to this hard house —/ More harder than the stones whereof 'tis raised' (Kent 3.2.63–4)
	'. . .th'unnumbered idle pebble chafes' (Edgar 4.6.21)
	'. . .precious stones' (eyes, Edgar 5.3.189)
	'O, you are men of stones!' (Lear 5.3.255)

Weather

Climate, weather elements & events

Cataract, hurricane	'You cataracts and hurricanoes, spout / Till you have drenched our steeples, drowned the cocks!' (Lear 3.2.2–3)
Fog	'Blasts and fogs upon thee!' (Lear 1.4.291)
	'Infect her beauty, / You fen-sucked fogs, drawn by the powerful sun / To fall and blister!' (Lear 2.4.357–9)
Rain	'Will pack when it begins to rain' (Fool 2.4.272)
	'Strives in his little world of man to outscorn / The to and fro conflicting wind and rain' (Knight 3.1.10–11)
	'. . .court holy-water in a dry house is better than this rain-water out o'door' (Fool 3.2.10–11)
	'Nor rain, wind, thunder, fire are my daughters' (Lear 3.2.15)

'Such groans of roaring wind and rain' (Kent
3.2.47)
'With heigh-ho, the wind and the rain' (Fool 3.2.74)
'Though the rain it raineth every day' (Fool 3.2.76)
'. . .bide the pelting of this pitiless storm' (Lear
3.4.29)
'. . .he holp the heavens to rain' (Gloucester 3.7.61)
'Sunshine and rain at once' (Gentleman 4.3.18)
'When the rain came to wet me once and the wind
to make me chatter; when the thunder would not
peace at my bidding' (Lear 4.6.100–03)

Sky   'The wrathful skies / Gallow the very wanderers of
the dark, / And make them keep their caves' (Kent
3.2.43–5)
'. . .thou wert better in a grave than to answer with
thy uncovered body this extremity of the skies' (Lear
3.4.100–01)

Snow   'Snow to their colder moods' (Kent 2.2.78)
'. . .presages snow' (Lear 4.6.117)

Storm   'Will pack when it begins to rain, / And leave thee in
the storm' (Fool 2.4.272–3)
'Let us withdraw; 'twill be a storm' (Cornwall
2.4.479)
'Shut up your doors, my lord; 'tis a wild night. / My
Regan counsels well; come out o'the storm'd
(Cornwall 2.4.501–02)
3.1 *Storm still*
'Fie on this storm' (Kent 3.1.45)
3.2 *Storm still.*
'Blow winds and crack your cheeks! Rage, blow! /
You cataracts and hurricanoes, spout / Till you have
drenched our steeples, drowned the cocks! / You
sulphurous and thought-executing fires, / Vaunt-
couriers of oak-cleaving thunderbolts, / Singe my
white head! And thou, all-shaking thunder, / Strike
flat the thick rotundity o'the world, / Crack nature's
moulds, all germens spill at once / That make
ingrateful man' (Lear 3.2.1–9)
'. . .bide the pelting of this pitiless storm' (Lear
3.4.29)
'This tempest will not give me leave to ponder / On
things would hurt me more' (Lear 3.4.24–5)
3.4 *Storm still.*
'Thou think'st 'tis much that this contentious storm /
Invades us to the skin' (Lear 3.4.6–7)

'The sea, with such a storm as his bare head / In hell-black night endured, would have buoyed up / And quenched the stelled fires. (Gloucester 3.7.58–60)

'. . .last night's storm' (Gloucester 4.1.34)

'What, i'the storm, i'the night?' (Gentleman 4.3.29)

'Was this a face / To be opposed against the warring winds? / To stand against the deep dread-bolted thunder, / In the most terrible and nimble stroke / Of quick-cross lightning? / To watch, poor perdu, / With this thin helm? Mine enemy's dog / Though he had bit me should have stood that night / Against my fire' (Cordelia 4.7.31–8)

'That heaven's vault should crack' (Lear 5.3.257)

Storm: Lightning

'You nimble lightnings, dart your blinding flames / Into her scornful eyes! Infect her beauty, / You fen-sucked fogs, drawn by the powerful sun / To fall and blister' (Lear 2.4.356–9)

'You sulphurous and thought-executing fires, / Vaunt-couriers of oak-cleaving thunderbolts, / Singe my white head' (Lear 3.2.4–6)

'Such sheets of fire' (Kent 3.2.46)

'In the most terrible and nimble stroke / Of quick cross-lightning' (Cordelia 4.7.34–5)

Storm: Psychological

'One minded like the weather, most unquietly' (Knight 3.1.2)

'Contending with the fretful elements' (Knight 3.1.4)

'When the mind's free, / The body's delicate: this tempest in my mind / Doth from my senses take all feeling else, / Save what beats there, filial ingratitude' (Lear 3.4.11–14)

Storm: Thunder

''Gainst parricides did all their thunders bend' (Edmund 2.1.46)

'I did not bid the thunder-bearer shoot, / Nor tell tales of thee to high-judging Jove' (Lear 2.4.419–20)

'. . .oak-cleaving thunderbolts' (Lear 3.2.5)

'And thou, all-shaking thunder, / Strike flat the thick rotundity o'the world, / Crack nature's moulds, all germens spill at once / That make ingrateful man' (Lear 3.2.6–9)

'Nor rain, wind, thunder, fire are my daughters' (Lear 3.2.15)

'. . .such bursts of horrid thunder' (Kent 3.2.46)

	'What is the cause of thunder?' (Lear 3.4.151) 'When the rain came to wet me once and the wind to make me chatter; when the thunder would not peace at my bidding' (Lear 4.6.100–03) 'To stand against the deep dread-bolted thunder' (Cordelia 4.7.33)
Sunshower	'Sunshine and rain at once' (Gentleman 4.3.18)
Weather	'Who's there, besides foul weather' (Kent 3.1.1) 'One minded like the weather, most unquietly' (Knight 3.1.2)
Wind	'. . .thou canst not smile as the wind sits, thou'lt catch cold shortly' (Fool 1.4.99–100) 'Blasts and fogs upon thee!' (Lear 1.4.291) 'With every gale' (Kent 2.2.80) 'And with presented nakedness outface / The winds and persecutions of the sky' (Edgar 2.3.185–6) '. . .the high winds / Do sorely ruffle' (Gloucester 2.4.493–4) 'Bids the wind blow the earth into the sea, / Or swell the curled waters 'bove the main' (Knight 3.1.5–6) '. . .the impetuous blasts with eyeless rage / Catch in their fury and make nothing of, / Strives in his little world of man to outscorn / The to and fro conflicting wind and rain' (Knight 3.1.8–11) 'Blow winds and crack your cheeks! Rage, blow' (Lear 3.2.1) 'Nor rain, wind, thunder, fire are my daughters' (Lear 3.2.15) 'Such groans of roaring wind and rain' (Kent 3.2.47) 'With heigh-ho, the wind and the rain' (Fool 3.2.74) 'Through the sharp hawthorn blows the cold wind.' (Edgar 3.4.45–6) 'Still through the hawthorn blows the cold wind' (Edgar 3.4.97–8) 'You are not worth the dust which the rude wind / Blows in your face' (Albany 4.2.31–2) 'When the rain came to wet me once and the wind to make me chatter; when the thunder would not peace at my bidding' (Lear 4.6.100–02) 'Was this a face / To be opposed against the warring winds?' (Cordelia 4.7.31–2)
Whirlwind	'. . .bless thee from whirlwinds, star-blasting and taking' (Edgar 3.4.58)

Seasons

Season	'Thus out of season' (Regan 2.1.121)
	'How shall your houseless heads and unfed sides, / Your looped and windowed raggedness, defend you / From seasons such as these?' (Lear 3.4.30–2)
Autumn	'To use his eyes for garden water-pots. / Ay, and laying autumn's dust' (Lear 4.6.192–3)
Winter	'Winter's not gone yet, if the wild geese fly that way' (Fool 2.4.239–40)
	'We'll set thee to school an ant, to teach thee there's no labouring i'the winter' (Fool 2.4.260–1)

The Tempest

Animals

Animality, monstrosity

Animals: Beast, monster

'. . .make thee roar, / That beasts shall tremble at thy din' (Prospero 1.2.371–2)
'Heavens keep him from these beasts' (Gonzalo 2.1.326)
'There would this monster make a man; any strange beast there makes a man' (Trinculo 2.2.30–1)
'. . .dead mooncalf's' (Trinculo 2.2.110)
'How now, mooncalf' (Stephano 2.2.133–4)
'I saw such islanders / (For certes, these are people of the island), / Who, though they are of monstrous shape, yet note / Their manners are more gentle, kind, than of / Our human generation you shall find / Many —nay, almost any' (Gonzalo 3.3.29–34)
'. . .the beast Caliban' (Prospero 4.1.140)
'This is some monster of the isle' (Stephano 2.2.65)
'Four legs and two voices — a most delicate monster!' (Stephano 2.2.89–90)
'. . .a very shallow monster [. . .] very weak monster [. . .] poor credulous monster! Well drawn, monster' (Trinculo 2.2.142–3, 143, 144–5)
'perfidious and drunken monster' (Trinculo 2.2.148–9)
'. . .puppy-headed monster. A most scurvy monster' (Trinculo 2.2.152–3)
'. . .poor monster's in drink. An abominable monster!' (Trinculo 2.2.156–7)
'. . .most ridiculous monster' (Trinculo 2.2.163)
'. . .brave monster' (Stephano 2.2.184) See 3.2 ('servant monster' Stephano 3.2.3, Trinculo 3.2.4, Stephano 3.2.8; 'brave monster' (Trinculo 3.2.11); 'man-monster' (Stephano 3.2.12) and so forth).

Hunting & cruelty

Animals: Hunt

'. . .go a bat-fowling' (Sebastian 2.1.186)
'To snare the nimble marmoset' (Caliban 2.2.168)
4.1 *A noise of hunters heard. Enter diverse spirits in shape of dogs and hounds, hunting them about, Prospero and Ariel setting them on.*
'Let them be hunted soundly' (Prospero 4.1.263)

Birds

Birds, general	'One dowl that's in my plume.' (Ariel 3.3.65) '. . .my bird' (Prospero 4.1.184) 'chick' (Prospero 5.1.318)
Chough	'A chough of as deep chat' (Antonio 2.1.268)
Cock	'The strain of strutting chanticleer / Cry cock a diddle dow' (Ariel, song, 1.2.386–7) '. . .first begins to crow' (Antonio 2.1.31) 'The old cock' (Sebastian 2.1.32) 'The cockerel' (Antonio 2.1.32)
Dove	'Dove-drawn with her' (Iris 4.1.94)
Duck	'Swum ashore, man, like a duck. I can swim like a duck' (Trinculo 2.2.126–7) 'Though thou canst swim like a duck' (Stephano 2.2.129)
Goose	'. . .thou art made like a goose' (Stephano 2.2.130)
Jay	'Show thee a jay's nest' (Caliban 2.2.167)
Owl	'There I couch when owls do cry' (Ariel, song, 5.1.90)
Peacock	'Her peacocks fly amain' (Iris 4.1.74)
Phoenix	'There is one tree, the phoenix' throne, one phoenix / At this hour reigning there' (Sebastian 3.3.23–4)
Raven	'As wicked dew as e'er my mother brushed / With raven's feather from unwholesome fen / Drop on you both.' (Caliban 1.2.322–4)
Scamel	[unclear] 'Young scamels from the rock' (Caliban 2.2.170)
Sparrow	'. . .play with sparrows' (Iris 4.1.100)

Fish

Fish	'. . .well fished for' (Antonio 2.1.105) '. . .what strange fish / Hath made his meal on thee?' (Alonso 2.1.113–14) '. . .What have we here, a man or a fish? Dead or alive? A fish: he smells like a fish, a very ancient and fish-like smell, a kind of—not of the newest—poor-John. A strange fish!' (See Trinculo's full speech 2.2.24–9) '. . .this is no fish' (Trinculo 2.2.35) '. . .fins like arms' (Trinculo 2.2.33–4) 'I'll fish for thee' (Caliban 2.2.159) 'No more dams I'll make for fish' (Caliban 2.2.177) '. . .thou deboshed fish [. . .] half a fish and half a monster' (Trinculo 3.2.26,29)

'…make a stockfish of thee' (Stephano 3.2.69–70)
'…a plain fish and no doubt marketable' (Antonio 5.1.267)

Insects

Bees	'…thou shalt be pinched / As thick as honeycomb, each pinch more stinging / Than bees that made 'em' (Prospero 1.2.329–31) 'Diffusest honey-drops' (Ceres 4.1.79) 'Where the bee sucks, there suck I' (Ariel, song 5.1.88)
Beetle	'All the charms / Of Sycorax—toads, beetles, bats' (Caliban 1.2.340–1)
Fly	'The flesh-fly blow in my mouth!' (Ferdinand 3.1.63) '…not fear fly-blowing' (Trinculo 5.1.285)
Wasp	'Her waspish-headed son' (Iris 4.1.99)

Amphibians, reptiles & invertebrates

Canker	'…his mind cankers' (Prospero4.1.192) 'beauty's canker' (Prospero 1.2.416)
Mussel	'The fresh-brook mussels' (Prospero 1.2.464)
Toad	'All the charms / Of Sycorax —toads, beetles, bats' (Caliban 1.2.340–1)
Tortoise	'Come, thou tortoise, when?' (Prospero 1.2.317)
Worm	'Poor worm, thou art infected!' (Prospero3.1.31)
Snake	'Sometime am I / All wound with adders, who with cloven tongues / Do hiss me into madness' (Caliban 2.2.12–14)

Mammals

Dog	'…incharitable dog' (Sebastian 1.1.40) 'Hang, cur!' (Antonio 1.1.42) 'Bow-wow, / The watch dogs bark, bow-wow' (Spirits 1.2.383–4) '…thy dog and thy bush' (Caliban 2.2.139) '…puppy-headed monster' (Trinculo 2.2.152–3) '…lie like dogs' (Trinculo 3.2.19) 4.1 *Enter diverse spirits in shape of dogs and hounds, hunting them about, Prospero and Ariel setting them on.*
Hedgehog	'…like hedgehogs which / Like tumbling in my barefoot way and mount / Their pricks at my footfall' (Caliban 2.2.10–12)

Horse	'Phoebus' steeds' (Ferdinand 4.1.30)
	'. . .like unbacked colts they pricked their ears' (Ariel 4.1.176)
	'I do smell all horse piss' (Trinculo 4.1.199)
Leopard	'. . .more pinch-spotted make them / Than pard or cat o'mountain' (Prospero 4.1.261–2)
Lion	'. . .or rather lions' (Sebastian 2.1.313)
	'Sure it was the roar / Of a whole herd of lions' (Antonio 2.1.317–18)
Marmoset	'. . .snare the nimble marmoset' (Caliban 2.2.168)
Mole	'Pray you tread softly, that the blind mole may / Not hear a footfall' (Caliban 4.1.194–5)
Monkey	'. . .jesting monkey' (Caliban 3.2.44)
Rat	. . .'the very rats / Instinctively have quit it.' (Prospero 1.2.147–8)
Sheep	'Thy turfy mountains where live nibbling sheep' (Iris 4.1.62)
Wolf	'Did make wolves howl' (Prospero 1.2.288)

Microbes

Germs, bacteria & decay

Disease, infect	'A plague upon' (Boatswain 1.1.35)
	'A pox o'your throat' (Sebastian 1.1.39)
	'. . .infect his reason' (Prospero 1.2.208)
	'. . .fever of the mad' (Ariel 1.2.209)
	'The red plague rid you' (Caliban 1.2.365)
	'A pox o'that' (Antonio 2.1.78)
	'All the infections that the sun sucks up / From bogs, fens, flats, on Prosperoper fall, and make him / By inchmeal a disease!' (Caliban 2.2.1–3)
	'A plague upon' (Caliban 2.2.160)
	'. . .a pox [. . .] A murrain' (Trinculo 3.2.78,79)
	'I will plague them all' (Prospero 4.1.192)
	'Would even infect my mouth' (Prospero 5.1.132)
Rot	'As if it had lungs, and rotten ones' (Sebastian 2.1.50)

Fungi

Mushroom	'. . .make midnight-mushrooms' (Prospero 5.1.39)
Toadstool	'By moonshine do the green sour ringlets make, / Whereof the ewe not bites' (Prospero 5.1.37–8)

Ecosystems & ecotones

Ecosystem connections & features

Ecosystem dependencies	'Here is everything advantageous to life' (Gonzalo 2.1.52). 'True, save means to live' (Antonio 2.1.53) 'Of that there's none, or little' (Sebastian 2.1.54)
Connected ecosystems	'. . .all the qualities o'th' isle: The fresh springs, brine pits, barren place and fertile.' (Caliban 1.2.338–9) 'All the infections that the sun sucks up / From bogs, fens, flats' (Caliban 2.2.1–2) 'Ceres, most bounteous lady, thy rich leas / Of wheat, rye, barley, vetches, oats and peas; / Thy turfy mountains where live nibbling sheep, / And flat meads thatched with stover them to keep; / Thy banks with pioned and twilled brims, / Which spongy April at thy hest betrims / To make cold nymphs chaste crowns; and thy broomgroves / Whose shadow the dismissed bachelor love, / Being lass-lorn; thy pole-clipped vineyard, / And thy sea-marge, sterile and rocky-hard, / Where thou thyself dost air — the queen o'th' sky, / Whose watery arch and messenger am I, / Bids thee leave these, and with her sovereign grace, / Here on this grass-plot, in this very place, / To come and sport. Her peacocks fly amain. / Approach, rich Ceres, her to entertain' (Iris 4.1.60–75) 'Ye elves of hills, brooks, standing lakes and groves, / And ye that on the sands with printless foot / Do chase the ebbing Neptune' (Prospero 5.1.33–5)

Landscape features

Bog, swamp	'From bogs' (Caliban 2.2.2) '. . .pitch me i'th' mire' (Caliban 2.2.5)
Broomgrove	'. . .thy broomgroves / Whose shadow the dismissed bachelor loves, / Being lass-lorn' (Iris 4.1.66–8)
Cave	'. . .you sty me / In this hard rock' (Caliban 1.2.343–4) 'Deservedly confined into this rock' (Miranda 1.2.362) 'My cellar is in a rock by th' seaside' (Stephano 2.2.132–33)
Den	'. . .murkiest den' (Ferdinand 4.1.25)
Downs	'. . .unshrubbed down' (Ceres 4.1.81)

Ecotone	'In the line grove which weather-fends your cell' (Ariel 5.1.10)
Fen	'. . .unwholesome fen' (Caliban 1.2.323)
	'. . .as 'twere perfumed by a fen' (Antonio 2.1.51)
	'fens' (Caliban 2.2.2)
Flats	'flats' (Caliban 2.2.2)
	'. . .flat meads' (Iris 4.1.63)
	'My bosky acres' (Ceres 4.1.81)
Grass-plot	'Here on this grass-plot' (Iris 4.1.73)
	'. . .this short-grassed green?' (Ceres 4.1.83)
Heath	'Now would I give a thousand furlongs of sea for an acre of barren ground — long heath, brown furze, anything' (Gonzalo 1.1.65–7)
Hill	'Ye elves of hills' (Prospero 5.1.33)
Island, isle	'Here in this island' (Prospero 1.2.171)
	'. . .dispersed them 'bout the isle' (Ariel 1.2.220)
	'In an odd angle of the isle' (Ariel 1.2.223)
	'This island's mine by Sycorax' (Caliban 1.2.332)
	'. . .all the qualities o'th' isle' (Caliban 1.2.338)
	'Though this island seem to be desert' (Ad 2.1.37)
	'And sowing the kernels of it in the sea, bring forth more islands!' (Antonio 2.1.93–94)
	'. . .fertile inch o'th' island' (Caliban 2.2.146)
	'In this bare island' (Prospero *Epilogue* 8), etc.
Mead	'. . .flat meads thatched with stover' (Iris 4.1.63)
Mountain	'Thou shalt be as free / As mountain winds' (Prospero 1.2.499–500)
	'. . .there were mountaineers / Dewlapped like bulls' (Gonzalo 3.3.44–5)
	'Thy turfy mountains where live nibbling sheep' (Iris 4.1.62)
	'Hey, Mountain, hey!' (Prospero 4.1.256)

Rivers & freshwater

Bank	'Thy banks with pioned and twilled brims, / Which spongy April at thy hest betrims' (Iris 4.1.64–5)
Brook	'. . .windring brooks [. . .] leave your crisp channels' (Iris 4.1.128, 130)
	'Ye elves of hills, brooks' (Prospero 5.1.33)
Spring	'The fresh springs' (Caliban 1.2.339)
	'I'll show thee the best springs' (Caliban 2.2.158)
River, stream	'He shall drink nought but brine, for I'll not show him / Where the quick freshes are' (Caliban 3.2.65–6)

Still Water, lake, pool	'Well, I am standing water.' (Sebastian 2.1.224) 'I'll teach you how to flow.' (Antonio 2.1.225) 'Do so. To ebb' (Sebastian 2.1.225) 'I'th' filthy-mantled pool beyond your cell, / There dancing up to th' chins, that the foul lake / O'erstunk their feet' (Ariel 4.1.182–4) '. . .standing lakes' (Prospero 5.1.33)

Sea

Sea	'Nay, good, be patient.' (Gonzalo 1.1.15) 'When the sea is!' (Boatswain 1.1.16) 'Set her two courses off to sea again!' (Boatswain 1.1.48–9) 'This wide-chopped rascal—would thou mightst lie drowning the washing of ten tides!' (Antonio 1.1.56–7) 'Now would I give a thousand furlongs of sea for an acre of barren ground' (Gonzalo 1.1.65–6) 'Put the wild waters in this roar, allay them' (Miranda 1.2.2) 'The sky, it seems, would pour down stinking pitch / But that the sea, mounting to th' welkin's cheek, / Dashes the fire out.' (Miranda 1.2.3–5) 'sunk the sea within the earth' (Miranda 1.2.11) 'To cry to th' sea that roared to us' (Prospero 1.2.149) 'I have decked the sea with drops full salt' (Prospero 1.2.155) '. . .sea-sorrow' (Prospero 1.2.170) '. . .to tread the ooze / Of the salt deep (Prospero 1.2.252–3) '. . .suffer a sea-change' (Ariel, song, 1.2.401) 'Sea water shalt thou drink' (Prospero 1.2.463) 'our garments being, as they were, drenched in the sea [. . .] being rather new-dyed than stained with salt water' (Gonzalo 2.1.63–6) 'And sowing the kernels of it in the sea, bring forth more islands!' (Antonio 2.1.93–4) 'We all were sea-swallowed' (Antonio 2.1.252) 'I shall no more to sea, to sea' (Stephano, song 2.2.42) '. . .to sea, boys' (Stephano, song 2.2.54) '. . .the sea mocks / Our frustrate search on land' (Alonso 3.3.9–10)

'. . .never-surfeited sea / Hath caused to belch up you' (Ariel 3.3.55–6)

'Exposed unto the sea, which hath requit it' (Ariel 3.3.71)

'Incensed the seas and shores — yea, all the creatures' (Ariel 3.3.74)

'Therefore my son i'th' ooze is bedded, and / I'll seek him deeper than e'er plummet sounded, / And with him there lie mudded' (Alonso 3.3.100–02)

'that on the sands with printless foot / Do chase the ebbing Neptune, and do fly him / When he comes back' (Prospero 5.1.34–6)

'. . .mudded in that oozy bed' (Alonso 5.1.152)

'Though the seas threaten, they are merciful' (Ferdinand 5.1.179)

'. . .calm seas, auspicious gales' (Prospero 5.1.316)

Sea: Ecotone   '. . .thy sea-marge, sterile and rocky-hard' (Iris 4.1.69)

Sea: Ecotone, shore   '. . .came we ashore' (Miranda 1.2.159)

'Brought to this shore' (Prospero 1.2.180)

'. . .not this nigh shore' (Prospero 1.2.216)

'To th' shore' (Francisco 2.1.121)

'Here shall I die ashore' (Stephano 2.2.43)

'. . .cast ashore' (Stephano 2.2.122)

'My cellar is in a rock by th' seaside' (Stephano 2.2.132–3)

'. . .the sea cannot drown me. I swam, ere I could recover the shore, five and thirty leagues off and on.' (Stephano 3.2.13–15)

'Incensed the seas and shores' (Ariel 3.3.74)

'. . .thy sea-marge, sterile and rocky-hard' (Iris 4.1.69)

'. . .the approaching tide / Will shortly fill the reasonable shore / That now lies foul and muddy' (Prospero 5.1.80–2)

'. . .wrecked upon this shore' (Alonso 5.1.138)

'Upon this shore where you were wrecked' (Prospero 5.1.162)

'. . .on shore' (Gonzalo 5.1.220)

Sea: Sand   'Come unto these yellow sands' (Ariel, song 1.2.376)

'. . .that on the sands with printless foot' (Prospero 5.1.34)

Sea: Tide   'Their understanding / Begins to swell, and the approaching tide / Will shortly fill the reasonable shore / That now lies foul and muddy' (Prospero 5.1.79–82)

Sea: Waves	'. . .the most mighty Neptune / Seem to besiege and make his bold waves tremble, / Yea, his dread trident shake.' (Ariel 1.2.204–06) 'Plunged in the foaming brine' (Ariel 1.2.211) 'kissed / The wild waves whist' (Ariel 1.2.378–9) 'I saw him beat the surges under him / And ride upon their backs. He trod the water, / Whose enmity he flung aside, and breasted / The surge most swoll'n that met him. His bold head / 'Bove the contentious waves he kept and oared / Himself with his good arms in lusty stroke / To th' shore, that o'er his wave-worn basis bowed, / As stooping to relieve him' (Francisco 2.1.115–22)

Elements

General

Elements	'. . .if you can command these elements to silence and work the peace of the present, we will not hand a rope more' (Boatswain 1.1.21–3) 'The elements / Of whom your swords are tempered may as well / Wound the loud winds, or with bemocked-at stabs / Kill the still-closing waters, as diminish / One dowl that's in my plume.' (Ariel 3.3.61–5) 'Then to the elements / Be free, and fare thou well!' (Prospero 5.1.319–20)

Air

Air	'Where should this music be? I'th' air, or th'earth?' (Ferdinand 1.2.388) '. . .cooling of the air with sighs' (Ariel 1.2.222) 'The air breathes upon us here most sweetly' (Ad 2.1.49) 'Where thou thyself dost air— the queen o'th' sky, / Whose watery arch' (Iris 4.1.70–1) 'Are melted into air, into thin air; / And — like the baseless fabric of this vision — / The cloud-capped towers, the gorgeous palaces, / The solemn temples, the great globe itself, / Yea, all which it inherit, shall dissolve, / And like this insubstantial pageant faded, / Leave not a rack behind' (Prospero 4.1.150–6)

	'. . .smote the air / For breathing in their faces' (Ariel 4.1.172–3)
	'Shalt have the air at freedom' (Prospero 4.1.266)
	'Hast thou, which art but air' (Prospero 5.1.21)
	'. . .airy charm' (Prospero 5.1.54)
	'I drink the air before me' (Ariel 5.1.102)
Air: Smoke	'. . .so their rising senses / Begin to chase the ignorant fumes that mantle / Their clearer reason' (Prospero 5.1.66–8)

Earth

Earth	'. . .sunk the sea within the earth' (Miranda 1.2.11)
	'. . .in the veins o'th' earth / When it is baked with frost' (Prospero 1.2.255–6)
	'. . .earthy and abhorred commands' (Prospero 1.2.273)
	'Thou earth, thou' (Prospero 1.2.314)
	'Where should this music be? I'th' air, or th'earth?' (Ferdinand 1.2.388)
	'. . .no sound / That the earth owes' (Ferdinand 1.2.407–08)
	'All corners else o'th' earth' (Ferdinand 1.2.492)
	'When he is earthed' (Antonio 2.1.235)
	'No better than the earth he lies upon' (Antonio 2.1.283)
	'. . .the liquor is not earthly' (Caliban 2.2.124)
	'And with each end of thy blue bow dost crown / My bosky acres and my unshrubbed down, / Rich scarf to my proud earth.' (Ceres 4.1.80–2)
	'Earth's increase' (Ceres 4.1.110)
	'. . .the strong-based promontory / Have I made shake' (Prospero 5.1.46–7)
	'Bury it certain fathoms in the earth' (Prospero 5.1.55)
Earthquake	'To make an earthquake!' (Antonio 2.1.317)
	'. . .the strong-based promontory / Have I made shake' (Prospero 5.1.46–7)
Earth: Ground	'. . .an acre of barren ground' (Gonzalo 1.1.66)
	'Lead off this ground' (Alonso 2.1.325)
	'. . .beat the ground / For kissing of their feet' (Ariel 4.1.173–4)
Earth: Ooze, mud	'Therefore my son i'th' ooze is bedded, and / I'll seek him deeper than e'er plummet sounded, / And with him there lie mudded' (Alonso 3.3.100–02)

'. . .now lies foul and muddy' (Prospero 5.1.82)
'. . .mudded in that oozy bed' (Alonso 5.1.152)

Fire

Fire

'. . .sea, mounting to th' welkin's cheek, / Dashes the fire out.' (Miranda 1.2.4–5)
'. . .to dive into the fire' (Ariel 1.2.191)
'I flamed amazement. Sometime I'd divide / And burn in many places — on the topmast, / The yards and bowsprit would I flame distinctly, / Them meet and join.' (Ariel 1.2.198–201)
'. . .the fire and cracks / Of sulphurous roaring' (Ariel 1.2.203–04)
'. . .all afire with me' (Ariel 1.2.212)
'. . .make our fire' (Prospero 1.2.312)
'The strongest oaths are straw / To th' fire i'th' blood' (Prospero 4.1.52–3)
'Have I given fire' (Prospero 5.1.45)

Water

Water: Dew

'. . .to fetch dew / From the still-vexed Bermudas' (Ariel 1.2.228–9)
'As wicked dew as e'er my mother brushed / With raven's feather from unwholesome fen / Drop on you both' (Caliban 1.2.322–4)
'Dewlapped like bulls' (Gonzalo 3.3.45)
'. . .with thy saffron wings, upon my flowers / Diffusest honey-drops' ([unclear, predominantly rain] Ceres 4.1.78–9)

Water

'. . .every drop of water swear against it and gape at widest to glut him' (Gonzalo 1.1.58–9)
'Put the wild waters in this roar, allay them' (Miranda 1.2.2)
'. . .fresh water' (Prospero 1.2.160)
'Water with berries in't' (Caliban 1.2.335)
'This music crept by me upon the waters' (Ferdinand 1.2.393)
'Sea water shalt thy drink' (Prospero 1.2.463)
'He trod the water' (Francisco 2.1.116)
'Well, I am standing water.' (Sebastian 2.1.224) 'I'll teach you how to flow.' (Antonio 2.1.225) 'Do so. To ebb' (Sebastian 2.1.225)
'. . .we will drink more' (Stephano 3.2.1–2)

	'Kill the still-closing waters' (Ariel 3.3.64)
	'. . .watery arch' (Iris 4.1.71)
	Enter Ariel, loaden with glistering apparel etc. Enter Caliban, Stephano and Trinculo, all wet 4.1
	'. . .my wetting' (Trinculo 4.1.211)
Water: Lack	'So dry he was for sway' (Prospero 1.2.112)
	'. . .an acre of barren ground' (Gonzalo 1.1.66)

Extractive processes & products

Chemicals & compounds

Poison	'Thou poisonous slave' (Prospero 1.2.320)
	'Like poison given to work a great time after, / Now 'gins to bite the spirits' (Gonzalo 3.3.106–07)
Salt	'I have decked the sea with drops full salt' (Prospero 1.2.155)
	'. . .to tread the ooze / Of the salt deep' (Prospero 1.2.252–3)
	'. . .stained with salt-water' (Gonzalo 2.1.66)
Sulphur	'. . .the fire and cracks / Of sulphurous roaring' (Ariel 1.2.203–04)
Poison	'Thou poisonous slave' (Prospero 1.2.320)
	'Like poison given to work a great time after, / Now 'gins to bite the spirits' (Gonzalo 3.3.106–07)

Materials

Materials & products	'Rich garments, linens, stuffs' (Prospero 1.2.164)
	'our garments being, as they were, drenched in the sea [. . .] being rather new-dyed than stained with salt water' (Gonzalo 2.1.63–6)
	'. . .creep under his gaberdine' (Trinculo 2.2.37–8)
	'. . .neat's leather' (Stephano 2.2.70)
	'. . .my glass' (Miranda 3.1.50)
	'Rich scarf to my proud earth.' (Ceres 4.1.82)
	4.1. *Enter Ariel, loaden with glistering apparel etc.*
Materials: Wood	'Fetch in our wood' (Prospero 1.2.313)
	2.2 *Enter Caliban, with a burden of wood*
	'. . .bringing wood in slowly' (Caliban 2.2.16)
	'There's wood enough within' (Caliban 1.2.315)
	'. . .bring my wood home' (Caliban 2.2.71–2)
	'. . .get thee wood enough' (Caliban 2.2.159)
	'I'll bear him no more sticks' (Caliban 2.2.161)
	3.1 *Enter Ferdinand, bearing a log*

'. . .wooden slavery' (Ferdinand 3.1.62)
'. . .log-man' (Ferdinand 3.1.67)
'. . .with a log / Batter his skull, or paunch him with
a stake' (Caliban 3.2.90–1), etc.

Metals

Metal: general	'No use of metal' (Gonzalo 2.1.154) 'Sword, pike, knife, gun, or need of any engine' (Gonzalo 2.1.162)
Gold	'T'excel the Golden Age' (Gonzalo 2.1.169) 'With gold on lasting pillars' (Gonzalo 5.1.209)
Silver	'. . .piece of silver' (Trinculo 2.2.29) 'Silver! There it goes, Silver!' (Ariel 4.1.257)
Steel	'. . .this obedient steel—three inches of it' (Antonio 2.1.285)

Industry

Industries and processes	'. . .stinking pitch' (Miranda 1.2.3) '. . .savour of tar nor of pitch' (Stephano, song 2.2.52) 'As fast as millwheels strike' (Prospero 1.2.281) '. . .or need of any engine / Would I not have; but nature should bring forth' (Gonzalo 2.1.162–3)

Managed & built environments

Agriculture

Agriculture	'. . .thy rich leas / Of wheat, rye, barley, vetches, oats and peas' (Iris 4.1.60–1)
Agriculture: Barren, fertile	'. . .barren ground' (Gonzalo 1.1.66) '. . .barren place and fertile' (Caliban 1.2.339) '. . .fertile inch o'th' island' (Caliban 2.2.146) '. . .barren hate' (Prospero 4.1.19) 'Ceres, most bounteous lady, thy rich leas' (Iris 4.1.60) '. . .bounteous sister' (Juno 4.1.103) 'Earth's increase, foison plenty, / Barns and garners never empty. / Vines with clustering bunches growing; / Spring come to you at the farthest, / In the very end of harvest. / Scarcity and want shall shun you, / Ceres' blessing so is on you' (Juno 4.1.110–17)

Agriculture: Corn	'No use of metal, corn, or wine or oil' (Gonzalo 2.1.154)
Agriculture: Field	'My bosky acres' (Ceres 4.1.81)
Agriculture: Furrow,	'You sunburned sicklemen, of August weary, / Come
country	hither from the furrow and be merry; / Make holiday! Your rye-straw hats put on /And these fresh nymphs encounter every one / In country footing' (Iris 4.1.134–8)
Agriculture: Plantation	'Had I plantation of this isle' (Gonzalo 2.1.144)
agriculture: sheep	'Thy turfy mountains where live nibbling sheep' (Iris 4.1.62)
Agriculture: Sow, yield	'And sowing the kernels of it in the sea, bring forth more islands' (Antonio 2.1.93–4)
	'He'd sow't with nettle-seed' (Antonio 2.1.144)
	'. . .much to yield' (Sebastian 2.1.232)
Agriculture: Straw	'The strongest oaths are straw' (Prospero 4.1.52)
	'Your rye-straw hats' (Iris 4.1.136)
Agriculture: Vineyard	'. . .bound of land, tilth, vineyard' (Gonzalo 2.1.153)
	'. . .the pole-clipped vineyard' (Iris 4.1.68)
Aquaculture: (Indigenous)	'No more dams I'll make for fish' (Caliban 2.2.177)

Horticulture

Garden	'In the line grove which weather-fends your cell' (Ariel 5.1.10)
Roots	'. . .withered roots' (Prospero 1.2.464)
	'As rootedly as I' (Caliban 3.2.96)

Nature

Natural & unnatural

Nature: Body	'Of his bones are coral made; / Those are pearls that were his eyes, / Nothing of him that doth fade / But doth suffer a sea-change / Into something rich and strange' (Ariel, song, 1.2.398–02)
Nature, Divine	'I might call him / A thing divine, for nothing natural / I ever saw so noble' (Miranda 1.2.418–20)
Nature: Human nature	'Awaked an evil nature' (Prospero 1.2.93)
	'. . .good natures' (Miranda 1.2.359–60)
	'. . .of a better nature' (Miranda 1.2.497)
	'. . .a born devil, on whose nature / Nurture can never stick' (Prospero 4.1.188–9)
	'Expelled remorse and nature' (Prospero 5.1.76)

Nature: Instinct, genes	'. . .the very rats / Instinctively have quit it' (Prospero 1.2.147–8) 'Hag-seed' (Prospero 1.2.366) 'And sowing the kernels of it in the sea, bring forth more islands' (Antonio 2.1.93–4) 'He'd sow't with nettle-seed' (Antonio 2.1.145) 'Hereditary sloth instructs me' (Sebastian 2.1.224)
Nature: Provision	'All things in common nature should produce / Without sweat or endeavour, treason, felony, / Sword, pike, knife, gun, or need of any engine / Would I not have; but nature should bring forth / Of its own kind of foison, all abundance, / To feed my innocent people' (Gonzalo 2.1.160–5)
Nature: Body	'Of his bones are coral made; / Those are pearls that were his eyes, / Nothing of him that doth fade / But doth suffer a sea-change / Into something rich and strange' (Ariel, song, 1.2.398–02)
Unnatural	'Unnatural though thou art' (Prospero 5.1.79) '. . .more than nature / Was ever conduct of' (Alonso 5.1.244–5)

Supernatural

Devils	"Hell is empty, / And all the devils are here" (Ariel 1.2.214–15) '. . .these are devils' (Trinculo 2.2.88) 'This is a devil and no monster' (Stephano 2.2.97) 'If thou be'st a devil' (Stephano 3.2.130) 'A devil, a born devil' (Prospero 4.1.188)
Elf	'Ye elves of hills, brooks, standing lakes and groves' (Prospero 5.1.33)
Fairy	'. . .your fairy, which you say is a harmless fairy' (Stephano 4.1.196–7) '. . .harmless fairy' (Trinculo 4.1.212)
Goblin	'. . .charge my goblins' (Prospero 4.1.259)
Harpy	'. . .the figure of this harpy' (Prospero 3.3.83)
Nymph	'Go make thyself like a nymph o'th' sea' (Prospero 1.2.304) 'Sea nymphs hourly ring his knell' (Ariel 1.2.403) 'You nymphs, called naiads, of the windring brooks, / With your sedged crowns and ever-harmless looks [. . .] Come, temperate nymphs' (Iris 4.1.128–9, 132)
Phoenix	'There is one tree, the phoenix' throne, one phoenix / At this hour reigning there' (Sebastian 3.3.23–4)
Spirit, sprite	'Hast thou, spirit' (Prospero 1.2.193)

'Why, that's my spirit!' (Prospero 1.2.215)
'. . .for thou wast a spirit too delicate / To act her earthy and abhorred commands' (Prospero 1.2.272–3)
'. . .do my spriting' (Ariel 1.2.298)
'. . .sweet sprites' (Ariel, song, 1.2.381)
'What is't, a spirit? [. . .] But 'tis a spirit.' (Miranda 1.2.410, 412)
'His spirits hear me' (Caliban 2.2.3)
'The spirit torments me!' (Caliban 2.2.64)
'These be fine things, an if they be not sprites' (Caliban 2.2.115)
'May I be bold / To think these spirits?' (Ferdinand 4.1.119–20) 'Spirits, which by mine art / I have from their confines called to enact / My present fancies' (Prospero 4.1.119–22)
4.1. *Enter diverse spirits in shape of dogs and hounds.*

Supernatural

'If by your art, my dearest father, you have / Put the wild waters in this roar' (Miranda 1.2.1–2)
'pluck my magic garment from me' (Prospero 1.2.24)
'The foul witch Sycorax' (Prospero 1.2.258)
'. . .mischiefs manifold and sorceries terrible' (Prospero 1.2.264)
'. . .by sorcery he got this isle' (Caliban 3.2.51)
'My high charms work' (Prospero 3.3.88)
'Some wanton charm' (Iris 4.1.95)
'Or else our spell is marred' (Prospero 4.1.127)
'My charms crack not; my spirits obey' (Prospero 5.1.2)
'. . .you are spell-stopped' (Prospero 5.1.61)
'The charm dissolves' (Prospero 5.1.64)
'. . .some enchanted trifle' (Alonso 5.1.112)
'Untie the spell' (Prospero 5.1.254)
'His mother was a witch, and one so strong / That could control the moon, make flows and ebbs, / And deal in her command without her power' (Prospero 5.1.270–72)
'Now my charms are all o'erthrown' (Prospero, Epi 1)
'Spirits to enforce, art to enchant' (Prospero, Epilogue 14)

Unicorn

'Now I will believe / That there are unicorns' (Sebastian 3.3.21–2)

Urchin	'. . .urchins / Shall forth at vast of night' (Prospero 1.2.327–8) 'Fright me with urchin-shows' (Caliban 2.2.5)

Wilderness/wild

Uninhabitable	'Uninhabitable and almost inaccessible' (Ad 2.1.40)
Wild	'Put the wild waters in this roar, allay them' (Miranda 1.2.2) '. . .kissed / The wild waves whist' (Ariel 1.2.378–9) '. . .too wildly' (Miranda 3.1.58)

Plants

Flowers, fruits, nuts, grasses, etc.

Apple	'. . .give it his son for an apple' (Sebastian 2.1.92)
Berries	'Water with berries in't' (Caliban 1.2.335) 'I'll pluck thee berries' (Caliban 2.2.158)
Cowslip	'In a cowslip's bell I lie; / There I couch when owls do cry' (Ariel 5.1.89–90)
Crabapple	'. . .let me bring thee where crabs grow' (Caliban 2.2.165)
Dock	'Or docks' (Sebastian 2.1.145)
Flower, blossom	'. . .upon my flowers / Diffusest honey-drops' (Ceres 4.1.78–9) 'Under the blossom that hangs on the bough' (Ariel, song, 5.1.94)
Furze	'. . .brown furze' (Gonzalo 1.1.66–7) '. . .sharp furzes' (Ariel 4.1.180)
Gorse	'. . .pricking gorse' (Ariel 4.1.180)
Grape	'Vines with clustering bunches growing' (Ceres 4.1.112)
Grass	'How lush and lusty the grass looks! How green!' (Gonzalo 2.1.55) 'Here on this grass-plot' (Iris 4.1.73) '. . .this short-grassed green?' (Ceres 4.1.83)
Hazelnuts	'. . .clust'ring filberts' (Caliban 2.2.169)
Heather	'. . .long heath' (Gonzalo 1.1.66)
Ivy	'The ivy which had hid my princely trunk / And sucked my verdure out on't' (Prospero 1.2.86–7)
Mallow	'. . .or mallows' (Sebastian 2.1.145)
Nettle	'He'd sow't with nettle-seed' (Antonio 2.1.144)
Nut	'. . .though the ship were no stronger than a nutshell' (Gonzalo 1.1.45–6)

Pignut	'And I with my long nails will dig thee pignuts' (Caliban 2.2.166)
Pioned	[Unclear]
Plants	'Plants with goodly burden bowing' (Ceres 4.1.113)
Reed	'. . .like reeds, not hair' (Ariel 1.2.213) '. . .like winter's drops / From eaves of reeds' (Ariel 5.1.16–17)
Roots	'. . .withered roots' (Prospero 1.2.464) 'As rootedly as I' (Caliban 3.2.96)
Rye	'Your rye-straw hats' (Iris 4.1.136)
Saffron crocus	'. . .thy saffron wings' (Ceres 4.1.78)
Sedge	'With your sedged crowns' (Iris 4.1.129)
Weeds	'. . .with weeds so loathly' (Prospero 4.1.21)

Trees, bushes, shrubs, etc.

Bush, shrub	'Here's neither bush nor shrub to bear off any weather' (Trinculo 2.2.18–19) '. . .thy dog and thy bush' (Caliban 2.2.139) 'Toothed briars, sharp furzes, pricking gorse and thorns, / Which entered their frail shins' (Ariel 4.1.180–1)
Cedar	'. . .by the spurs plucked up / The pine and cedar' (Prospero 5.1.47–8)
Hedgerow	'My bosky acres' (Ceres 4.1.81)
Linden	'In the line grove which weather-fends your cell' (Ariel 5.1.10)
Oak	'I will rend an oak / And peg thee in his knotty entrails' (Prospero 1.2.294–5) '. . .husks / Wherein the acorn cradled' (Prospero 1.2.464–5)
Pine	'Into a cloven pine, within which rift / Imprisoned thou didst painfully remain' (Ariel 1.2.277–8) '. . .made gape / The pine' (Prospero 1.2.292–3) '. . .by the spurs plucked up / The pine and cedar' (Prospero 5.1.47–8)
Tree	'The ivy which had hid my princely trunk / And sucked my verdure out on't' (Prospero1.2.86–7) 'I made of the bark of a tree' (Stephano 2.2.121–2) 3.1 *Enter Ferdinand, bearing a log* 'Some thousands of these logs' (Ferdinand 3.1.10) '. . .the next tree' (Stephano 3.2.35) 'There is one tree, the phoenix' throne, one phoenix / At this hour reigning there' (Sebastian 3.3.23–4) 'Under the blossom that hangs on the bough' (Ariel, song, 5.1.94)

Skies

Day, night & diurnal cycles

Day	'. . .woe the day' (Miranda 1.2.15)
	'. . .once a day' (Ferdinand 1.2.491)
	'. . .high-day; high-day freedom; freedom high-day' (Caliban 2.2.182–3)
	'. . .day's celebration' (Ferdinand 4.1.29)
	'. . .till this day' (Miranda 4.1.144)
	'. . .day by day' (Prospero 5.1.164)
	'. . .in the morn' (Prospero 5.1.308)
Night	'. . .one midnight' (Prospero 1.2.128)
	'. . .vast of night' (Prospero 1.2.328)
	'. . .night kept chained below' (Ferdinand 4.1.31)
	'. . .good night your vow!' (Prospero 4.1.54)
	'All's hushed as midnight' (Caliban 4.1.207)
	'. . .this thing of darkness' (Prospero 5.1.276)
	'. . .this one night' (Prospero 5.1.304)
Night, day	'. . .tis fresh morning with me / When you are by at night' (Ferdinand 3.1.33–4)
	'. . .as the morning steals upon the night, / Melting the darkness' (Prospero 5.1.65–6)
Passage of Time	'What is the time o'th' day?' (Prospero 1.2.239)
	'Past the mid-season' (Ariel 1.2.239) 'At least two glasses. The time 'twixt six and now / Must by us both be spent most preciously' (Prospero 1.2.240–1)
	'time / Goes upright with his carriage' (Prospero 5.1.2–3)
Shine, shadow, light, dark	'. . .the dark backward and abysm of time' (Prospero 1.2.50)
	'. . .dead of darkness' (Prospero 1.2.130)
	'. . .like a firebrand in the dark' (Caliban 2.2.6)
	'By this good light' (Trinculo 2.2.142)
	'By this light' (Stephano 3.2.15)
	'Whose shadow the dismissed bachelor loves' (Iris 4.1.67)
	'dusky' (Ceres 4.1.89)
	'. . .melting the darkness' (Prospero 5.1.66)
	'. . .hath gilded 'em' (Alonso 5.1.281)
Shine: Lights	'To name the bigger light and how the less / That burn by day and night' (Caliban 1.2.336–7)
	'Hymen's lamps shall light you' (Prospero 4.1.23)
	'Till Hymen's torch be lighted' (Iris 4.1.97)
Sunset	'The sun will set' (Ferdinand 3.1.22)

Planets & stars

Earth	'O heaven, O earth, bear witness' (Ferdinand 3.1.68) '. . .the great globe itself' (Prospero 4.1.153)
Moon	'You would lift the moon out of her sphere, if she would continue in it five weeks without changing' (Gonzalo 2.1.183–5) 'Out o'th' moon, I do assure thee. I was the man i'th' moon when time was' (Stephano 2.2.136–7) '. . .thy dog and thy bush' (Caliban 2.2.139) '. . .man i'th' moon' (Trinculo 2.2.144) 'By moonshine do the green sour ringlets make' (Prospero 5.1.37) '. . .control the moon, make flows and ebbs' (Prospero 5.1.271)
Sky	'The sky, it seems, would pour down stinking pitch / But that the sea, mounting to th' welkin's cheek, / Dashes the fire out.' (Miranda 1.2.3–5) 'Where thou thyself dost air— the queen o'th' sky, / Whose watery arch' (Iris 4.1.70–1) '. . .'twixt the green sea and the azured vault' (Prospero 5.1.43)
Stars	'I find my zenith doth depend upon / A most auspicious star, whose influence / If now I court not, but omit, my fortunes / Will ever after droop' (Prospero 1.2.181–4)
Sun, moon	'To name the bigger light and how the less / That burn by day and night' (Caliban 1.2.336–7) 'Can have no note unless the sun were post — / The man i'th' moon's too slow' (Antonio 2.1.249–50)
Sun	'All the infections that the sun sucks up / From bogs, fens, flats' (Caliban 2.2.1–2) 'Phoebus' steeds' (Ferdinand 4.1.30) '. . .bedimmed / The noontide sun' (Prospero 5.1.41–2)

Stone

Gems

Coral	'Of his bones are coral made' (Ariel 1.2.398)
Jewel	'The jewel in my dower' (Miranda 3.1.54)
Pearl	'Those are pearls that were his eyes' (Ariel 1.2.399)

Rocks & minerals

Chalk	'. . .chalked forth the way' (Gonzalo 5.1.204)
Rock	'. . .you sty me / In this hard rock' (Caliban 1.2.343–4)
	'Deservedly confined into this rock' (Miranda 1.2.362)
	'My cellar is in a rock by th' seaside' (Stephano 2.2.132–3)
	'Young scamels from the rock' (Caliban 2.2.170)
	'rocky-hard' (Iris 4.1.69)

Weather

Climate, weather elements & events

Climate	'It must needs be of subtle, tender and delicate temperance' (Ad 2.1.44–5)
	'It is the quality o'th' climate' (Antonio 2.1.201)
Clouds	'. . .to ride / On the curled clouds' (Ariel 1.2.191–2)
	'It is foul weather in us all, good sir, / When you are cloudy' (Gonzalo 2.1.142–3)
	'Yond same black cloud, yond huge one looks like a foul bombard that would shed his liquor. If it should thunder as it did before, I know not where to hide my head. Yond same cloud cannot choose but fall by pailfuls.' (Trinculo 2.2.20–4)
	'The clouds, methought, would open and show riches / Ready to drop upon me, that when I waked / I cried to dream again' (Caliban 3.2.142–4)
	'Cutting the clouds towards Paphos' (Iris 4.1.93)
	'The cloud-capped towers' (Prospero 4.1.152)
	'. . .bedimmed / The noontide sun' (Prospero 5.1.41–2)
Frost	'. . .in the veins o'th' earth / When it is baked with frost' (Prospero 1.2.255–6)
Rain	'The sky, it seems, would pour down stinking pitch' (Miranda 1.2.3)
	'Yond same black cloud, yond huge one looks like a foul bombard that would shed his liquor. If it should thunder as it did before, I know not where to hide my head. Yond same cloud cannot choose but fall by pailfuls' (Trinculo 2.2.20–4)
	'Heavens rain grace' (Prospero 3.1.75)
	'. . .upon my flowers / Diffusest honey-drops, refreshing showers' (Ceres 4.1.78–9)

Rainbow	'. . .many-coloured messenger [. . .] Rich scarf to my proud earth' (Ceres 4.1.76, 82) '. . .heavenly bow' (Ceres 4.1.86)
Sky	'The sky, it seems, would pour down stinking pitch / But that the sea, mounting to th' welkin's cheek, / Dashes the fire out.' (Miranda 1.2.3–5) 'Where thou thyself dost air— the queen o'th' sky, / Whose watery arch' (Iris 4.1.70–1) 'And with each end of thy blue bow dost crown / My bosky acres and my unshrubbed down, / Rich scarf to my proud earth.' (Ceres 4.1.80–2)
Snow	'. . .white cold virgin snow' (Ferdinand 4.1.55)
Storm	1.1 *A tempestuous noise of thunder and lightning heard* '. . . [*to the storm*] Blow till thou burst thy wind, if room enough.' (Boatswain 1.1.7–8) 'You do assist the storm' (Boatswain 1.1.14) '. . .this sea-storm' (Miranda 1.2.177) 'Performed to point the tempest' (Prospero 1.2.194) 'Here's neither bush nor shrub to bear off any weather at all, and another storm brewing; I hear it sing i'th' wind. Yond same black cloud, yond huge one looks like a foul bombard that would shed his liquor. If it should thunder as it did before, I know not where to hide my head. Yond same cloud cannot choose but fall by pailfuls' (Trinculo 2.2.18–24) 'Alas, the storm is come again. My best way is to creep under his gaberdine; there is no other shelter hereabout. Misery acquaints a man with strange bedfellows! I will here shroud till the dregs of the storm be past' (Trinculo 2.2.37–41) 'Is the storm overblown?' (Trinculo 2.2.109) 'I hid me under the dead mooncalf's gaberdine for fear of the storm' (Trinculo 2.2.109–11) 'I raised the tempest' (Prospero 5.1.6) 'In this last tempest' (Prospero 5.1.154)
Storm: Thunder, lightning	'Jove's lightning, the precursors / O'th' dreadful thunderclaps, more momentary / And sight-outrunning were not; the fire and cracks / Of sulphurous roaring' (Ariel 1.2.201–04) 'Hell is empty, / And all the devils are here' (Ariel 1.2.214–15) 'They dropped, as by a thunderstroke' (Antonio 2.1.205)

2.2 *Enter Caliban, with a burden of wood; a noise of thunder heard.*
'. . .an islander that hath lately suffered by a thunderbolt' (Trinculo 2.2.35–6)
'. . .killed with a thunderstroke' (Trinculo 2.2.107)
'I would the lightning had / Burnt up those logs that you are enjoined to pile' (Miranda 3.1.16–17)
3.3 *Thunder and lightning. Enter Ariel, like a harpy, claps his wings upon the table, and with a quaint device the banquet vanishes*
3.3 *He vanishes in thunder*
'. . .to the dread-rattling thunder / Have I given fire and rifted Jove's stout oak / with his own bolt' (Prospero 5.1.44–6)

Sunshine   'You sunburned sicklemen' (Iris 4.1.134)
Weather: General 'A plague upon this howling. They are louder than the weather or our office' (Boatswain 1.1.35–6)
'It is foul weather in us all, good sir, / When you are cloudy' (Gonzalo 2.1.142–3)
'Foul weather?' (Sebastian 2.1.143)
'Very foul' (Antonio 2.1.143)
'In the line grove which weather-fends your cell' (Ariel 5.1.10)

Wind   '. . . [*to the storm*] Blow till thou burst thy wind, if room enough.' (Boatswain 1.1.7–8)
'. . .to sigh / to th' winds, whose pity, sighing back again, / Did us but loving wrong' (Prospero 1.2.149–51)
'. . .sharp wind of the north' (Prospero 1.2.254)
'A southwest blow on ye / And blister you all o'er' (Caliban 1.2.324–35)
'Thou shalt be as free / As mountain winds' (Prospero 1.2.499–500)
'. . .another storm brewing; I hear it sing i'th' wind' (Trinculo 2.2.19–20)
'The elements / Of whom your swords are tempered may as well / Wound the loud winds' (Ariel 3.3.61–3)
'Methought the billows spoke and told me of it; / The winds did sing it to me, and the thunder—/ That deep and dreadful organpipe — pronounced / The name of Prospero' (Alonso 3.3.96–9)
'. . .called forth the mutinous winds' (Prospero 5.1.42)
'Gentle breath of yours my sails / Must fill' (Prospero Epi 11–12)

Seasons

Spring   'Thy banks with pioned and twilled brims, / Which
                    spongy April at thy hest betrims' (Iris 4.1.64–5)
                    'Spring come to you at the farthest, / In the very end
                    of harvest' (Ceres 4.1.114–15)
Summer   'You sunburned sicklemen, of August weary, / Come
                    hither from the furrow and be merry; / Make
                    holiday! Your rye-straw hats put on' (Iris 4.1.134–6)
                    'After summer merrily' (Ariel, song, 5.1.92)
Winter   '. . .howled away twelve winters' (Prospero 1.2.296)
                    '. . .like winter's drops / From eaves of reeds' (Ariel
                    5.1.16–17)

4

Ecocriticism

This chapter offers a survey of critical terms and works relating to the study of ecology in Shakespeare's plays. Academic books can be expensive and articles often very hard to access, so we hope this gives you an overview and a flavour of the insights offered by Shakespearean ecocriticism. Many of the sections begin with a series of questions that aim to focus your thinking on a set of issues and dynamics in each text.

* * *

We begin with some baseline definitions. Ecology is the 'science dealing with the structure, dynamics and functions of nature' (Urban et al. 2021: 1). Literary criticism is the 'consideration or analysis of a text' (OED 2023). 'Ecocriticism' is therefore a portmanteau word melding the two. Joseph W. Meeker introduced the concept of literary ecology in his proto-ecocritical work, *The Comedy of Survival* (1974). Meeker applied ecology to literary analysis, interestingly choosing *Hamlet* to support his argument. Shakespeare is therefore a part of ecocriticism's inception. The term 'ecocriticism' itself was coined by William Reuckert, whose essay 'Literature and Ecology: An Experiment in Ecocriticism' applies a 'considerable number of concepts from pure, biological ecology' (1978: 73). Reuckert's aim was to 'understand the processes through which *interactions* among species over long periods of time produce the various biological communities and environments found in the natural world' [our emphasis] (Reuckert 1978: 13–14).

This notion of interactions is key to both ecology and ecocriticism. One of the major charges against Western Enlightenment scientific thought is the artificial separation of humans from 'nature'. Perceived human exceptionalism and anthropocentric (human-centred) ethics drives the exploitation of other species and environments. Ecology recognizes interactions, interconnections, and interdependencies. It applies 'ecological systems thinking', a holistic way of thinking that considers interactions between elements comprising the total Earth system. Similarly, ecocriticism is *inter-* and *intra*disciplinary. It looks for linkages and connections and applies multidimensional theories to analyze texts' relationships to what David Abram calls, instead of 'non-human', the 'more-than-human' world (1996).

This chapter therefore offers a selection of ecocritical 'eco-assemblages' (related groups existing in particular habitats) to highlight convergences, reciprocities and exchanges. A complete survey of the vast field is impossible here but we offer a selection of key ecocritical readings to inspire further analysis. For context, we begin with a 'flyover' of ecocriticism's origins and evolution. We then move to ecocritical texts that discuss more than one of our focus plays, before looking at singular studies in greater depth. Each assemblage is followed by adaptation prompts, comprising questions and key words to spark your own ecodramaturgical interpretations of the play and ecoscenographic designs. The focus plays of *A Midsummer Night's Dream*, *King Lear* and *The Tempest* are themselves an 'eco-assemblage' of sorts from Shakespeare's wider dramatic ecosystem. Rather than restrict adaptations to these three plays, this chapter aims to highlight patterns of ecocritical thinking applicable to all of Shakespeare's plays.

Origins and evolution

The classical pastoral literary tradition, British Romanticism, and American transcendentalism brought the human–environment relationship to the attention of the Western literary canon. Early ecocriticism was heavily informed by the (largely) Anglo-American environmental movement that advocated for immersion in nature and 'wilderness' conservation. The 'early beginnings of a distinctly contemporary, consciously environmentalist criticism', however, first 'stirred in the 1960s' (ibid.). The environmental movement infused fledgling ecocriticism with key philosophical and ethical principles and an activist intent. This included a holistic view of Earth systems, as derived from James Lovelock's view of Earth as a self-regulating organism (1979). Other foundational concepts are ecocentric (Earth-centred) ethics, as present in Bill Devall and George Sessions' *Deep Ecology* (1985), and interrogations of human exceptionalism and speciesism from the animal rights movement.

As the field developed, it drew on ecofeminism's attention to gendered ideas of nature, postcolonialism's interrogation of racial oppression and exploitation, and Marxism's critique of capitalist power structures. More recently, ecocriticism has incorporated additional fields. These include new materialism, recognizing matter as active, vital and agential, and posthumanism, which decentres humans and acknowledges enmeshment with other species and forms. Shakespearean ecocriticism further includes traditional Shakespearean historically inflected scholarship. Tensions were once present between historicist critics who argued that historical context is critical and presentist scholars who focussed on Shakespeare's application to present day environmental crises. Lynne Bruckner and Dan Brayton, for instance, note the significance of the divide, arguing that the 'presentist/ historicist dialectic is central to the field and resonates in different ways' (2011: 4). Shakespearean ecocriticism is now supported by a raft of historical and presentist perspectives, at times distinct but more often intermingled.

As the (upstart) crow flies: The terrain

The following section offers an aerial view of Shakespearean ecocriticism's key ecological communities and theoretical 'habitats'. They reflect broader ecocriticism's trajectory, as evident in early proto-ecocritical works in which we can see the environmental movement's influence. Glen A. Love's 'Ecocriticism and Science' (1999) applied biologist E.O. Wilson's notion of consilience to advocate for interdisciplinary literary analysis bridging the historic science/arts divide, with his later *Practical Ecocriticism: Literature, Biology and the Environemnt* (2003) further advocating for greater systems-thinking in the humanities. Bruce Boeher's *Shakespeare Among the Animals: Nature and Society in Early Modern England* (2002) countered traditionally anthropocentric readings through drawing on animal studies. Frank O. Waage's 'Shakespeare Unearth'd' drew attention to Shakespeare's correlations between life, death and organicism, arguing that he 'implicitly takes what we would call today an ecocentric view of the human condition' (2005: 154). Simon Estok's 'Shakespeare and Ecocriticism: An Analysis of 'Home' and 'Power' in *King Lear*' advocated for a 'vocabulary for environmental ethics' as a counter to traditional thematicism and symbolic readings (2005: 13). Early works also reflected a preoccupation with pastoral and post-pastoral notions of wilderness and the green, as evident in the titles of Gabriel Egan's *Green Shakespeare: From Ecopolitics to Ecocriticism* (2006) and Robert N. Watson's *Back to Nature: The Green and the Real in the Late Renaissance* (2006), both of which consolidated the field.

As Shakespearean ecocriticism evolved, it more comprehensively critiqued idealized notions of the green and pastoral nested within Romantic conceptions of nature and wilderness. Works such as Sharon O'Dair's 'The State of the Green' (2008a) and 'Slow Shakespeare' (2008b) called for greater activism and ecological impact. We can also see a wider focus in Glen Love's evolutionary reading of 'Shakespeare's Origin of Species and Darwin's Tempest' (2010). Estok's *Ecocriticism and Shakespeare: Reading Ecophobia* inverted nature-love with his introduction of the 'ecophobia' construct, defined as the 'pathological aversion toward nature, an aggravated form of anthropocentricism expressed variously as fear of, hatred of, or hostility toward nature at least in part motivated by a sense of nature's imagined unpredictability' (2011: 128). The field continued to expand into a multitude of intersectional approaches visible in Bruckner and Brayton's edited collection *Ecocritical Shakespeare* (2011) and Julian Yates and Garrett Sullivan's '"Forum" on Shakespeare and Ecology' (2011).

This is not to say that a green focus disintegrated but rather that Shakespeare's pastoral, arboreal and botanical contexts continued to be interrogated, including through a historicist lens. Jeffrey Theis' *Writing the Forest in Early Modern England* (2009), for instance, examined Shakespeare's sylvan pastoral in relation to early modern forests, while Boehrer's *Environmental Degradation in Jacobean Drama* reconfigured Shakespeare's pastoral spaces as places of civil butchery against a background of Jacobean land use and politics (2013). Nardizzi's *Wooden Os: Shakespeare's Theatres and England's Trees* (2013) examined early modern woodland ecology, connecting forests with their representations on stage and other uses of wooden materials. Ann Barton's posthumously published *The Shakespearean Forest* (2017) also traced the decline of England's forests.

Recent criticism continues to take an interest in Shakespeare's green. Andoni Cossio and Martin Simonson's 'Arboreal Tradition and Subversion' (2020), for example, analyze the role of trees on stage together with Shakespeare's symbolism of forests and woodlands. Keir Elam's 'Romancing the Oak' (2022) is interested in Shakespeare's arboreal lexicon but with particular reference to the oak tree, which he puts in the context of Warwickshire's oak forest. Jennifer Munroe and Rebecca Laroche's *Shakespeare and Ecofeminist Theory* takes an ecomaterialist and ecofeminist look at the 'dynamism in plants' in Shakespeare's works, and the trope of '(boys as) women as plants' (2017), inviting consideration of shared cross-species materialities.

Shakespearean ecocriticism, however, also continues to multiply in tones and textures. Downing Cless' *Ecology in European Drama* (2010) embraces environmental philosophy. Randall Martin's *Shakespeare and Ecology* (2015) and 'Shakespeare, Ecology, and Ecocriticism' (2017) examines early modern natural history and issues such as deforestation, localism, as well as environmental activism. Todd Borlik's *Ecocriticism and Early Modern Literature* (2011), *Literature and Nature of the English Renaissance* (2019) and *Shakespeare Beyond the Green World* (2022) extend to social and environmental contexts and contemporary texts. Borlik, in particular, departs from singular ecocritical foci to embrace an ecosystemic perspective. Tom McFaul's *Shakespeare and the Natural World* (2015) also draws attention to environmental exploitation while highlighting Shakespeare's plays' 'natural *sympathy*' between their 'human characters and multiple other species' [original emphasis] (16). Elizabeth Gruber's *Renaissance Ecopolitics from Shakespeare to Bacon: Rethinking Cosmopolis* (2017) takes up the age's 'interlinked and fraught conceptions of "self" and "world"' (6, 133). Diverse ecocritical approaches are further reflected in Jennifer Munroe, Lynne Bruckner and Edward Geisweidt's *Ecological Approaches to Early Modern Texts* (2015).

Beyond green into blue worlds, Steve Mentz' *At the Bottom of Shakespeare's Ocean* (2009) highlights the shift from 'the supposed stability of land, with its pastoral and georgic master narratives, to a broader vision of the maritime world' (98). Dan Brayton's *Shakespeare's Ocean: An Ecocritical Exploration* (2012) further applies a blue ecocritical lens to

Shakespeare's oceans. Mentz' 'Shakespeare and the Blue Humanities' (2019) is another instrumental work canvassing Shakespeare's seas, oceans, floods, bays, brooks and tides, amongst other watery spaces. Richard Kerridge's 'All is Deep: All is Shallow—Literary Springs, Wells and Depths, from Shakespeare to Ecocriticism' (2021) is noteworthy for including freshwater within blue Shakespeare.

Moving now from sea to sky, Ken Hiltner's *What Else is Pastoral? Renaissance Literature and the Environment* (2011) examines air pollution and environmental destruction within early modern England. Gwilym Jones' *Shakespeare's Storms* (2015) discusses the Jacobean theatre's use of the storm trope in an ecocritical context. Jennifer Mae Hamilton's *This Contentious Storm* (2017) similarly applies a meteorological reading of Shakespeare's use of the storm but specifically in relation to a performance history *King Lear*. Sophie Chiari's *Shakespeare's Representations of Weather, Climate and Environment: The Early Modern 'Fated Sky'* (2018) examines environmental conditions ranging from climate change in *A Midsummer Night's Dream*, to thunder and lightning in *King Lear*, and 'clime and slime' in *Antony and Cleopatra*. Her edited volume, *The Experience of Disaster in Early Modern English Literature* (2022), further reassesses early modern texts from an ecocritical perspective and discusses plays such as *A Midsummer Night's Dream*.

It is also worth noting that Shakespearean ecocriticism intersects with animal studies through shared interests in challenging speciesism, namely, the privileging of certain species above others. For a review of early ecocriticism's inclusion and exclusion of animal studies, see Sharon O'Dair's 'The State of the Green' (2008b). Shakespearean animal studies is a field in its own right with a vast array of texts. For further reading, see Boehrer's *Shakespeare Among the Animals* (2002) as well as Erica Fudge's *Perceiving Animals: Humans and Beasts in Early Modern English Culture* (2002) and *Brutal Reasoning: Animals, Rationality and Humanity in Early Modern England* (2006). Benjamin Bertram's *Bestial Oblivion: War, Humanism, and Ecology in Early Modern England* (2018) is noteworthy for unsettling the illusion of human autonomy in warfare through a multispecies lens. Tiffany Jo Werth, Kristen Poole and Lauren Shohet offer a useful study of the early modern fascination with more-than-human entanglements in *The More-than-Human in English Renaissance Literature* (2023). Other key works include Andreas Höfele's *Stage, Stake and Scaffold: Humans and Animals in Shakespeare's Theatre* (2008), Laurie Shannon's *The Accommodated Animal: Cosmopoly in Shakespeare's Locales* (2013), Rebecca Ann Bach's *Birds and Other Creatures in Renaissance Literature: Shakespeare, Descartes, and Animal Studies* (2017), and Karen Raber's *Animal Bodies, Renaissance Culture* (2013) (see also Raber and Mattfield 2017 and Raber and Dugan 2021).

Shakespearean ecocriticism offers innumerable artistic possibilities for informing dramaturgical analysis and scenographic design. These exist at different scales, from vast ecosystem concerns such as climate change to the minute of small organisms and materialities. What might Shakespeare's venomous snakes, spiders and toads, for example, teach us about racial otherness (Borlik 2023)? Can *Coriolanus'* 'ecology of combustion', or *Antony and Cleopatra's* fire and air be harnessed scenographically for the stage to create a 'disorderly, threatening world' (Mentz 2015: 589) of ecological catastrophe? How might ecocritical readings of Shakespeare's mud, slime, ooze, bog or decay (Yates 2015: 217) shine light on the importance of ecosystem components and processes, ecotones (transition zones between ecological communities) and lifewebs (interaction networks)? As you read through the following ecocritical analyses of our focus plays, consider how they might inspire creative ecological adaptations.

Focus plays: Multi-play studies

Can fairies be staged as microbes? What might *King Lear* have to say about ecological catastrophe? Does Prospero really control the weather or does the weather control him? The four extracts below are examples of how ecocritics apply different ecological lenses while finding convergences across the plays.

Frederick O. Waage's 'Shakespeare Unearth'd' (2005) considers *Dream* to offer the 'most detailed circumstance of environmental distress' of all the plays, as captured in Titania's description of climate disorder (2.1.81–117) (149). He finds *King Lear* to be 'almost topographically determined, in that the movements of [. . .] plot and action are closely tied to changes in place as defined by vegetation and topographical features' (149). Similarly, he notes that landscape is key to *The Tempest,* which juxtaposes the 'island's less than hospitable topography' with Ceres and Iris' descriptions of an 'idealized and generic rural landscape, cultivated fields, sheep-covered uplands, meadows, stream banks, vineyards and seacoast' (ibid.). All three plays, he suggests, are examples of how Shakespeare's works evoke Earth 'holistically in [a] complex and sometimes contradictory relationship with humanity' (147). Waage finds that Shakespare's characters display a 'terrocentric identity' in which '[b]ody and earth are interchangeable', thus Shakespeare takes an 'ecocentric view of the human condition' (154).

Gabriel Egan's *Green Shakespeare: From Ecopolitics to Ecocriticism* (2006), focuses on the supernatural and the weather in the plays. He links *A Midsummer Night's Dream's* disrupted weather patterns and *Lear's* storm with the late sixteenth century's climactic instability. Egan reframes *Lear's* biological terminology of 'all germens spill at once' (3.2.8) in the storm scene as evidence that 'Lear's speech is about *Mother* Earth, rising up to chastise her children' [original emphasis] (142). He suggests that in the

'Globe playhouse in 1605, as across the globe today, the cause of unseasonal weather is not divine and not mysterious, it is human action' (145). Moving to *The Tempest*, he ties the play's preoccupation with wood to the colonization of both Ireland and Virginia. He notes the 'self-referential circuit' of the playhouse's timber structure with *The Tempest's* wood, while the rushes-strewn stage evokes *Dream's* 'green plot' (3.1.1) (159). Egan also comments that it is noteworthy that William Strachey's description of the *Sea Venture's* shipwreck in Bermuda claimed that meteorological equipment was being used to control the weather (153). Prospero's magical powers are thus allied to technological advancement, while the extreme weather of both *The Tempest* and *Lear* nevertheless remind us that 'Gaia's responses can easily eliminate the cause of global harm by eliminating us' (170).

Downing Cless' *Ecology and Environment in European Drama* (2010) considers *Dream* and *The Tempest* to be 'Shakespeare's most nature-laden plays' (91). He argues that each play's lack of a principal source, together with extensive natural imagery, suggests that Shakespeare's inspiration was drawn from nature rather than literature. Like older thematic studies of Shakespeare and nature drawing on Shakespeare's rural upbringing, likely annual return and retirement in his 'beloved countryside', Cless paints Shakespeare as a 'naturalist who refers in detail to exact flora and fauna' (115–17). Cless holds that: '[a]cutely aware of nature's minutiae and balance, Shakespeare lived and worked with an ecological sensibility' (118). He asks whether 'Shakespeare's wildness leads to containment or subversion' (102), noting that nature is 'not a happy place of escape in either play, yet through the agency of nature in regard to culture, a benevolent life with nature is the outcome' (112).

Robert N. Watson's 'The Ecology of Self in *Midsummer Night's Dream*' (2011) compares Renaissance philosophy's invisible microcosmic world to current scientific analysis of the body's microbial diversity. He proposes viewing *Dream* as a 'prescient allegory of these facts, with fairies in the role of microbes' (24). Other influences include the juice of the flower love-in-idleness and the brain's chemical cocktail giving rise to the feeling of being in love and the play's links to endocrine rhythms and the lunar cycle. He further notes that in *Lear*, even before Cordelia's army fails to 'cleanse the agents of evil from the body-politic, Lear's pride has been punctured by a virus' (48). When Lear refers to Goneril as the 'disease that's in my flesh' (2.4.222) he thus also acknowledges the multitudes contained within him, 'even at the viral scale' (48). Watson further links Ariel's song 'Of his bones are coral made' (1.2.398) to recent orthopaedic discoveries that coral is a suitable substitute for bone-mass. Watson concludes that Shakespeare's intuitive recognition of shared connection between lifeforms and matter points towards the 'key to developing the individual and collective selflessness needed to avoid an ecological catastrophe' through the 'recognition that we are already largely selfless' (51).

ADAPTATION PROMPTS

- **Dramaturgical concepts:** Shakespeare's ecocentric view of the human condition, the Earth's power to eliminate us as the cause of global harm the shared connection between lifeforms and matter.

- **Scenographic possibilities:** Ecological complexity, local flora and fauna, the self-referential circuit of plants and stage materials.

- **Questions:** How do we know what it is to be human without our relationship to other species? What does the play's natural world suggest about human attitudes to the more-than-human world?

Focus Plays: Single studies

A Midsummer Night's Dream

How have ecocritics interpreted *A Midsummer Night's Dream*? What might it mean to stage a love affair between a fairy queen and a man transformed into a donkey? Why is 'Nature' so often conceived as female and what are the consequences? Is Shakespeare's weather alive? Here are some examples of how posthumanism unsettles what it means to be human, ecofeminism rethinks gendered ideas of Earth and how we can think about Shakespeare's climate in new ways that are relevant to our own.

Eco-assemblage: A posthuman Dream

Bruce Boehrer's 'Economies of Desire in *A Midsummer Night's Dream'* (2004) explores the play's cross-species eroticism in a manner that may be seen to anticipate later posthumanism. Boehrer argues that the comedy 'develops a zoophiliac subdiscourse correlative to its more obvious concern with heteroerotic courtship and marriage' (2004: 100). He considers the play to present male/female and human/animal identity as 'competing impulses to embrace and to repudiate alterity [otherness]' (2004: 114). He finds *Dream* to 'embody the anxieties—of encounter with the other, of confinement to the self', and concludes that the play 'seems more nervous than reassuring, less convinced of its own happy fantasies than aware of their evanescence' (2004: 115). Boerher's reading asks us to question fixed notions of self and species, inviting further posthuman readings.

Timothy Ryan Day's 'With parted eye: A Midsummer Night's Dream, Richard Powers' Orfeo, and Biosemiotics' (2018) investigates the 'strange evolutionary encoding that traverses life and all the networks of meaning that emanate from it' (2018: 249). He considers that what appears to be Oberon's magic (2.1.249–58) is in fact the effect of a psychotropic plant. Nonhuman forces thus pervade the text as agents generating events within complex ecosystems. When Hermia awakens at the edge of the forest, she looks back on the night's events with 'parted eye, / When everything seems double' (4.1.186–87) revealing that she is in a liminal space. He compares this to a cultural-bacterial nexus that unsettles the fantasy of selfhood (2018: 252). Day states that while it would be 'absurd to claim that Shakespeare was aware of the inner workings of cells and DNA', the play 'demonstrates the dynamic relationship between Narrative and Nature' (2018: 252–53).

Vin Nardizzi's "Shakespeare's Trans*plant* Poetics: Vegetable Blazons and the Seasons of Pyramus's Face" (2019) also sees the play as unsettling species categorization. Nardizzi focuses on Thisbe's lament as a vegetable blazon (a poetic form of praise in which the loved ones' parts are praised separately):

> These lily lips,
> This cherry nose,
> These yellow cowslip cheeks,
> Are gone, are gone!
> Lovers, make moan.
> His eyes were green as leeks.

(5.1.318–23)

Putting aside the passage's comic elements, the article examines the 'poetic crossing of taxonomic kingdoms' (Nardizzi 2019: 168–9). Leeks, for instance, may be viewed a 'limn fissures and faultiness in the concatenated discourses of gender, beauty, and humanness that operate only in binary terms (female/male, beautiful/not beautiful, and human/nonhuman animal)' (Nardizzi 2019: 169). Nardizzi also observes that the passage's seasonal cyclic order is jumbled. In the early modern calendar, cherries and cowslips were understood to bloom in April, May and even winter, lilies from May to June and leeks in autumn (Nardizzi 2019: 169). The play's trans*plant* poetics opens up non-anthropocentric perspectives that also unsettle racist, classist and gendered assumptions of contemporary beauty.

ADAPTATION PROMPTS

- **Dramaturgical concepts:** Anxieties of otherness, nature's dynamic narrative, non-human forces, jumbled seasonal cycles.

- **Scenographic possibilities:** Non-binary and non-anthropocentric beauty, psychotropic plants, vegetable and fruit forms and colours.

- **Questions:** How may *Dream*'s liminal and in-between identities and spaces unsettle human exceptionalism? What may this reveal about our interrelated identities with and dependencies on the more-than-human world?

Eco-assemblage: An ecofeminist Dream

Angela Schumann's 'But as a Form in Wax' (2015) is one of the first ecofeminist studies of *Dream*. Schumann applies key concepts from Carolyn Merchant's seminal *The Death of Nature: Women, Ecology and the Scientific Revolution* (1980) and Val Plumwood's influential *Feminism and the Mastery of Nature* (2002). Both critique androcentric (male-centred) and anthropocentric paradigms that consider woman and nature to be inferior to men and civilization. Schumann also locates Western culture's dual oppression of women and nature in the early modern period's scientific and economic revolutions that accelerated older classical patriarchal notions. She argues that *Dream* undermines, rather than reinforces, this view and consideres the play's 'natural', 'feminine' elements of imagination, instinct and emotion' to surpass those of order and convention (Schumann 2015: 46). Schumann holds that Shakespeare subverts contemporary expectations of not only feminine 'nature' but that of the physical environment, revealing the power of both.

Lynne Bruckner's 'Reprocentric Ecologies: Pedagogy, Husbandry and *A Midsummer Night's Dream*' (2016) reads *Dream*'s 'patriarchal desire to control social reproduction [that] is underscored by Titania and Oberon's fight for the Indian boy' (159). Bruckner highlights early modernity's equation of the female body with the natural world expressed in works such as Raynalde's *Byrth of Mankynde* (1545). She notes that early modern husbandry manuals frequently consider the concept of earth-as-womb, describing, for example, 'unfertill places' and 'unnaturall and bastardly issues' (Markham 1625: 8 in Bruckner 2016: 156). She further holds that the notion of feminized Nature-as-goddess may be seen to view it as an exploitable resource (2016: 157). *Fitzharberts Booke of Husbandrie* (1598), for instance, describes the plough as the 'first good instrument, by which the husband rips from the Earths wombe a well pleasing living' (B2 in Bruckner 2016: 157). The essay offers a selection of student readings of *Dream*, including considering Titania as a gardener with a sometime violent stewardship approach, as well as the play's sexualization of natural spaces, as in Hermia's reference to 'primrose beds' (1.1.215) and Titania's 'flowery bed' (3.1.114).

Susan Rowland's 'Jung and Literary Studies for the Anthropocene, Climate Change and Ecocriticism' (2018) views the play as representing unbalanced gendered energies between sky-father and Earth-mother. Utilizing Jungian psychological concepts such archetypes from a collective unconscious, Rowland reads the play's court and forest as sites of erotic dalliance. She considers *Dream* to 'show complex adaptive systems of social organisation around sexuality, individuality desires, and human-nature connections and distinctions' that 'fall into chaos before they can find creativity and creative patterning' (174). This grounds the play's supernatural characters and events within mythic consciousness. She therefore considers that humans and fairies are not distinct species but subject to a process of 'dismembering and re-mending' in the natural world (174). Rowland holds that the play's comedy is nested within symbols that create multiple realities for the audience and serve to 're-knit' the psyche with nature. The play thus 're-makes us as part of nature' through its mythic content (157).

ADAPTATION PROMPTS

- **Dramaturgical concepts**: Dual oppression of women and nature, subversion of feminine expectations, Earth-as-womb, nature-as-goddess, a reunion with nature through mythic archetypes.

- **Scenographic possibilities**: Feminine versus masculine spaces and border crossings, unfertile and fertile places, sexualized nature and botanical fecundity, chaos versus ordered patterns.

- **Questions**: How may *Dream* reinforce or subvert patriarchal views of women and the exploitation of nature? In what ways does the play prompt us to rethink gendered nature?

Eco-assemblage: Weathering the Dream

Sophie Chiari's *Shakespeare's Representation of Weather, Climate and Environment: The Early Modern 'Fated Sky'* (2017) observes that despite being set in Mediterranean Athens, the play's environment is closer to a damp and chilly English forest. This reminds us that 'Shakespeare fashioned his personal geography and imagined his exotic settings with his immediate surroundings in mind' (Chiari 2017: 2). Chiari posits that the drop in temperatures during the late sixteenth century and subsequent unsettled weather events were interpreted theologically as a post-Lapsarian corruption of nature due to human sin. She argues that while Titania's monologue (2.1.81–117) evokes the Biblical flood, Shakespeare positions the characters as responsible for the environmental destruction rather than as passive victims of divine retribution. This contrasts with contemporary works such as Samuel Daniel's *The Queenes Arcadia* (c.1606), in which two shepherds see themselves as victims of England's harsh weather. Shakespeare's play therefore stands apart from those of his contemporaries in that the 'weather is not the source but the consequence of discord', aligning it with current anthropogenic climate change (Chiari 2017: 5).

Steve Mentz' 'Green Comedy: Shakespeare and Ecology' (2018) offers a post-pastoral reconsideration of Northrop Frye's model of comic form in *The Anatomy of Criticism* (1957) and Meeker's 'The Comedy of Survival' (1974). Mentz disrupts Frye and Meeker's concepts of ecological harmony in his reading of *Dream*. Ecological stability, he suggests, promulgates an idealised literary pastoral that does not account for dynamism and catastrophe. Instead, he moves towards Jeffrey Jerome Cohen's concept of prismatic ecology (2013) that diffracts Frye's green world into a multi-hued rainbow and includes hybrid ecologies. He views *A Midsummer Night's Dream's* forest, like Shakespeare's ocean, as a destabilizing force rather than utopian space. Mentz suggests that the 'catastrophic weather-visions of *A Midsummer Night's Dream* articulate the darker qualities of the comic forest' (2018: 256). He finds *Dream* to express the human view of nature as a vast and unpredictable force. The play's environments reveal chaos, illegibility and rupture, rendering it a fitting play for discussion of the Anthropocene.

ADAPTATION PROMPTS

- **Dramaturgical concepts:** Environmental destruction, anthropogenic climate instability, ecological dynamism and catastrophe, chaos and rupture.

- **Scenographic possibilities:** Harsh weather, a destabilized and dark forest, hybrid ecologies.

- **Questions:** Is the play's unstable weather an active force or a consequence of human action? How is the forest presented as either beneficent or hostile and how might this reflect human attitudes to more-than-human phenomena?

Further reading

Recent texts continue to draw attention to *Dream's* green and grey worlds. Grace Tiffany's 'Shakespeare's Savage Trees' (2020) argues that the forest 'owe[s] more to the threatening woods of European folk tales and medieval romance than to the pastoral "Green Worlds" of classical and romantic poetry' (197). Lisa Hopkin's '"Thou art translated": Plants of Passage in *A Midsummer Night's Dream*' (2023) investigates human-vegetable affinities and transformations. Mary Thomas Crane's 'Meteorology, Embodiment, and Environment in Shakespeare's *A Midsummer Night's Dream*' (2020) examines *Dream's* fairies as unruly meteorological agents in a transgressive and changeable world. She argues that although the play's ending may seem to reinstate institutional control over the natural elements, it leaves a question mark over how lasting that control may be.

King Lear

Does *King Lear* predict our ecological future? How can we stage a storm that is powerfully present but never localized? These ecocritical readings consider how *Lear*'s violent and unpredictable world relates to ecological catastrophe.

Eco-assemblage: Ecophobic Lear

Simon Estok's 'Shakespeare and Ecocriticism: An Analysis of 'Home' and 'Power' in *King Lear*' (2005) and *Ecocriticism and Shakespeare: Reading Ecophobia* (2011) focus on *Lear*'s ecophobic fear or hatred of the natural world. Estok argues that all of *Lear*'s main characters 'share a utilitarian view of Nature' which 'represents an object space that must be controlled, uncontrolled, it is a dangerous space of chaotic nothingness' (2005: 20). As Lear's authority, control, power and identity unravel, he is displaced by his daughters into a hostile natural space. Estok suggests that *Lear* positions women and nature as 'a profound threat to masculine control when things go awry' (2005: 22–3), as 'women and the environment are each viciously unpredictable and dangerous, and women who communicate freely are monsters' (2011: 27). Lear's 'dispossessing himself of his lands, his giving away of space' therefore reflects a 'dispossession of masculine identity' and a fear of uncontained wildness (2005: 24). Estok's 2011 study further considers Cordelia as nature itself, positioned in between Lear, Gloucester, Albany and Kent as the old Medieval orthodoxy and Edmund, Cornwall, Goneril and Regan as a rapacious new early modern world. *Lear*, Estok concludes, is not merely about power, property and inheritance but an unpredictable and uncontrollable 'natural world, with bad weather, horrifying indifference, and countless dangers and paradoxes' (2011: 32).

Elizabeth Gruber's 'Nature on the Verge: Confronting "Bare Life" in *Arden of Faversham* and *King Lear*' (2015) argues that the play 'draws attention to shifting apprehensions of nature, and their consequence for the meanings of humanness' (Gruber 2015: 98). Like the play *Arden of Faversham* (which was falsely attributed to Shakespeare), *Lear* is concerned with the division of resources in an 'acknowledgment of how identity is intimately bound up with land' (104). Lear's confrontation with mortality raises further questions of how 'identity and mortality both shape and reflect conceptions of nature' (104). Lear's journey takes him from 'fantasies of separation' in which he calls upon luxuries to be exposed within the storm (115). This leads to 'profound empathy with 'Poor naked wretches' burdened by 'houseless heads and unfed sides' (105). She employs an ecofeminist lens, reading the storm as a 'savage, feminized force' that finds its stark expression of ecocide in Lear's final address to Cordelia, in which she is pronounced as 'dead as earth' (5.3.262). Gruber finds that *Lear* anticipates scientific modernity, 'which will rely upon "anatomization" and also vivisection in the interests of "discovering" all of nature's secrets', founding an 'epistemology grounded in violent domination' (108).

<hr>

ADAPTATION PROMPTS

- **Dramaturgical concepts**: Nature as an uncontrollable feminine threat, identity as bound up with land, new technologies and the violent domination of nature.

- **Scenographic possibilities**: Hostile chaotic environments, dangerous weather, ecocide.

- **Questions**: What does *King Lear*'s bleak and violent landscape reveal about human fears of nature's power? How may this contribute to human attempts to destroy, control or tame the more-than-human world?

<hr>

Eco-assemblage: Stormy Lear

Steve Mentz' 'Strange Weather in *King Lear*' (2010) and 'Tongues in the Storm: Shakespeare, Ecological Crisis, and the Resources of Genre' (2011), critique earlier green Romantic ecocritical thinking. Instead of pastoral homeostasis, Mentz likens *Lear*'s natural chaos to a post equilibrium shift in which constant change and instability are considered fundamental to natural systems. He argues that *Lear*'s turbulent natural world is one of complexity and variability. This parallels early modern understanding of human–nature relationships derived from Aristotle's *Meterologica*, the Royal Society's Baconians, an 'Ovidian legacy of mutability and flux', and incorporates 'micro-macrocosmic reciprocity between the body's humours and the world's weather' (2010: 140–1). *Lear*'s storm is also grounded in the material world, offering 'Shakespeare's most direct interrogation of how a Providential storm feels against your skin' (2010: 141). The play's thirty-two references to 'nature' (a third more than any other Shakespearean play) draw attention to sensory experience and an 'opaque world of catastrophe and crisis' evoking our own age's ecological destruction (2010: 146). Mentz argues that *Lear*'s many invocations of nature – human nature, sexual nature, the father–daughter natural relationship, and natural weather events – all 'underscore the dilemmas of living in an unstable environment' (2011: 166). The play can therefore 'help write new responses to the old stories about the humanity-nature relationship' (171).

Gwilym Jones' '*King Lear*: Storm and the Event' (2015) argues that the play is 'subtly but consistently misunderstood by the tendency to imagine the storm happening in a particular place' (59). Jones considers the storm to be characterized by an absence of location – rather, the storm itself sustains the play both aesthetically and structurally. He traces the play's critical history in which the storm is considered to take place on the heath rather than the 'fluidity or placelessness of the original context' (66). Asking why the heath continues to appeal to the popular imagination, Jones posits that this particular form of wilderness links Lear's isolation to Christian narratives of suffering and redemption. He further holds that wilderness 'has an almost sacramental value' for ecocriticism and acts as a metaphorical, albeit problematic, conceit (69). By instead considering nature as an 'event', we may participate in climate change debates relevant to the now (ibid.). Considering the storm as an unlocalized weather event thus frees us to imaginatively reconceive the play from its historical context in relation to current and future ecological disasters.

Jennifer Mae Hamilton's *This Contentious Storm: An Ecocritical and Performance History of* King Lear (2017) is also devoted to *Lear*'s storm trope. Like Jones, she 'practices an ecocriticism that is suspended between humanist and posthumanist thought, exploring how [the play's] canonical representation of the human condition is troubled and transformed by the storm' (3–4). Hamilton is concerned with 'looking at the dialogue between Lear and the storm, and the quality of the storm's eruption or interruption in the story' (4). More than merely highlighting human dynamics, Hamilton reads *Lear* as a 'meditation on the way the sky and the body delimit power' (6). Her historically situated meteorological interpretation examines how 'human-weather relations are complicated by moral, political and social ecologies' (28). Hamilton's conclusion highlights the play's potential for eco-adaptation through the storm's 'metonymy, metaphor, synecdoche or symbol, and an irreducibly elemental otherness that call[s] out the ridiculousness of some creatures that call themselves human' (193).

ADAPTATION PROMPTS

- **Dramaturgical concepts**: Ecological systems' change and instability, weather catastrophe and crisis as emblems of environmental destruction, elemental otherness and agency.

- **Scenographic possibilities**: The weather as a material force, the storm is tangibly present and felt by the characters (and possibly, depending on staging, the audience!).

- **Questions**: How does the play invoke or contest human-weather relations? How might the play's storm relate to climate change instability and extreme weather events?

Eco-assemblage: More-than-human Lear

Laurie Shannon's 'Poor, Bare, Forked: Animal Sovereignty, Human Negative Exceptionalism and the Natural History of *King Lear*' (2009) unearths the 'animal underpinnings of Lear's exclamation' in the article's title (2008: 175). Drawing on Renaissance natural history, Shannon animates 'a broad concept of "zoography": those discourse and modes of writing that are undergirded by animal or broadly taxonomic structures of reference across species' (175). Citing sources depicting and describing animals' coats, skins, bristles or other exteriors, Shannon argues that *Lear's* conception of nakedness as portrayed by Edgar speaks to 'all humankind as a kind' (195). *Lear* 'thus not only anatomizes man, philosophically, and finds him wanting, it taxonomizes man, literally, and finds him naked' (196). In contrast to an early modern human exceptionalism as evident in the anatomist Andreas Vesalius' reference to humans as 'the most perfect of all creatures' and Sir Walter Raleigh's description of a 'brief story of the universal' (174), Shakespeare 'does something quite different' (175). *Lear* 'positions man not as the paragon of creation' but 'creation's *negative* exception' [original emphasis] (175). The play's 'negative-exceptionalist man is a *creature without properties,* a natural-historical oxymoron', or in other words, 'man is that unready animal who lacks a coat' (196).

Jayne Elisabeth Archer, Richard Marggraf Turley and Howard Thomas' 'The Autumn King: Remembering the Land in *King Lear*' (2012) offers a 'botanical-political discourse' to 'open up new ways of reading *King Lear*' (542). They argue that Shakespeare deploys subversive images of crop contamination and weeds to register anxieties about land ownership and natural resource management (519). In contrast to Roz Symon's adaptation prompt that aligns plants to late summer (see Chapter 5), they consider *Lear* to be set in late spring, including the allusion to 'Spring with my tears' (4.4.16). The spring's promise of hope can be seen to counter the play's tragedy, coupling resurrection with death and signals a 'temporal confusion that is encoded in the land and its plants' (524). Given the play's unharvested and overgrown fields, Lear's crown of flowers expose a 'disastrous and seemingly irrevocable breakdown in the production, distribution, and consumption of food' (524). Furthermore, they note that the play's inclusion of the darnel (a weedy ryegrass) signals the end of the Golden Age, as it does in Virgil's *Georgics* (525). The play invites parallels with a 'blighted landscape' and the 'consequent effects upon the natural order, including, of course, the cycles of nature' (534).

Craig Dionne's *Posthuman Lear: Reading Shakespeare in the Anthropocene* (2016) reflects on the play's 'catastrophe and enmeshed co-existence' (22) through a new materialist and posthuman lens. This frames *Lear* within 'our current ecological present', helping us to rethink causality and ecological agency in a 'doubtful posthuman future' (29). *Lear* is thus relevant to surviving the Anthropocene's terrors such as radioactive waste, assisting us to imagine 'physical dissolution' (30). The play's nihilism reproduces the image of a fallen world and functions as a 'parable of the posthuman' (112). It's depiction of a 'trek through the sheepfolds and the green mantle runoff can be seen to provide one of the most vivid artistic representations of a land denuded by disastrous legal ineptitude and economic abuse' (157). Instead of a pastoral claim to blissful or innocent nature, *Lear* gives us 'an agricultural war zone' (158). 'Imagining a post-apocalyptic future is one of the things Shakespeare's *King Lear* is about' (29) and *Lear* can therefore help us fully to realize the bleakness of environmental destruction.

ADAPTATION PROMPTS

- **Dramaturgical concepts:** Human exceptionalism, climate change impacts, catastrophe and enmeshed co-existence within a fallen world.

- **Scenographic possibilities:** Post-apocalyptic landscape, agricultural war zone, weeds, unharvested fields, denuded land.

- **Questions:** How might *Lear* warn us about anthropocentricism and the abuse of land? What does the play suggest about our possible environmental futures?

Further reading

For an interesting account of the influence of medieval traditions, early modern forest laws and monastic spirituality on the play's setting, see Michale Steffes' 'Medieval Wilderness and *King Lear*: Heath, Forest, Desert' (2016). Hamilton's 'Constructing Dying and Death as an Eco-Political Concern in Performances of Shakespeare's *King Lear* and Sarah Kane's *Blasted*' (2018) offers an discussion of the play's dark, violent 'perverse imaginaries' that are underwritten by human exceptionalism, positioning the play's representations of death as an eco-political problem (485). Lowell Duckert's 'Climate of Shakespeare: Four (or More) Forecasts' (2019) poses the interesting question of whether 'we are "of" a mind made up of meteors', namely, materially minded like the play's weather (99). Finally, Borlik's *Shakespeare Beyond the Green World: Drama and Ecopolitics in Jacobean Britain* (2023) examines Lear as 'not simply humanized but bestialized, forced to partake of the agony' inflicted on 'non-human nature' (9), prompting a 'radical questioning of human dominion over the earth and other creatures' (93).

The Tempest

Can the *Tempest*'s many musical and more-than-human voices be staged as a soundscape of the Earth? In what ways do the play's colonial exploitative practices continue to relate to the here-and-now? How might the sea's vitality be artistically configured as a site of loss and hope? Ecocritical readings of *The Tempest* invite us to question the history and legacy of colonization and continuing environmental injustices alongside the play's transformative potential.

Eco-assemblage: Human origins and *The Tempest*

Jonathan Bate's chapter 'A voice for Ariel' (2000) 'represents the first apparent, sustained ecological study of *The Tempest*' (Gray 2020: 2). Bate begins with defining ecocide as 'the systematic destruction of dwelling places in the name of progress, of the globalization of capital' (2000: 78). He advocates for 'ecopoetics' to return to a 'place of dwelling' like a 'recurring cycle, a heartbeat' (83). Bate builds upon a postcolonial conception of Caliban's island as a 'starting-point for an imagining of the voice not of a nation or a race, but of the ravaged earth itself' (88). He interrogates the problematic notion of idealized nature that elicits ideas of the pastoral, primitivism, and as the Romantic tradition of feminized Nature. Though chiefly concerned with analyzing other works inspired by the play, Bate's essay offers an important foundational piece that views the play through an ecological lens.

Glen A. Love's 'Shakespeare's Origin of Species and Darwin's Tempest' (2010) considers the play to be Shakespeare's 'evolutionary fable' set on a 'geographically ambiguous island' (129). Like the Judeo-Christian creation story in Genesis and in Persian, Greek and Roman paradisiacal folklore, Love holds that *The Tempest* evokes an Arcadian conception of the island as the home of original life. He aligns Caliban's ambiguous animality with both Pan and the European Wild Man tradition. He draws particular attention to the play's island setting and the influence of the sea as the 'watery birthplace' of vertebrates as fish and 'fish-like forms' (134). Thus, Shakespeare may be seen to anticipate Darwinian evolution in his depiction of Caliban as part fish. Though Caliban is revealed to be an islander 'that hath lately suffered by a thunderbolt' (2.2.36), Love argues that his continued physical ambiguity and indeterminate future evokes 'a long storm still swirling over the meaning of being human' (140).

ADAPTATION PROMPTS

- **Dramaturgical concepts:** Earth-as-home, evolutionary origins, the destruction of life-sustaining environments for financial gain.

- **Scenographic possibilities:** Earth's 'heartbeat' sustaining life, paradise and pre-human landscapes, Caliban-as-fish.

- **Questions:** Is *The Tempest*'s island an Edenic paradise and return to the original place of human dwelling or a grim warning of an apocalyptic future? How can Ariel and/or Caliban be reinterpreted as embodiments of Earth while continuing to interrogate colonial conceptions of race?

Eco-assemblage: Early modern *Tempests*

Todd Borlik's 'Caliban and the Fen Demons of Lincolnshire: The Englishness of Shakespeare's *Tempest*' (2013) proposes that Shakespeare drew on a lost play based on the life of Anglo-Saxon hermit St Guthlac as well as folktales of Lincolnshire fen spirits. Borlik considers the play's colonial commentary to be closer to home than Virginia, locating a colonial dynamic within England's displacement of locals due to land reclamation projects in which the 'urban elite seizes the communal wilds of the rural poor' (21). He aligns the play's topography with 1,300 square miles of low-lying wetlands or 'fens' around the Wash estuary in a far-reaching network of mudflats, tidal creeks, shallow lakes and oozing brackish morass that also contained an archipelago of 'islands' (23). Borlik argues that the ecologically complex area was held to be a wild site of supernatural magic within the cultural imagination. He offers a useful summary of Caliban's potential sources of inspiration, ranging from First Nation Americans and the Irish to the medieval *wodewose* [wild man], mooncalf [prodigious birth] and 'exotic marine fauna' (25). The ancient 'fen bogey known as Tiddy Mun' offers another prototype, also associated with fens, stagnant water, moon worship, the control of floods and noxious mists from the bogs (24). Furthermore, Caliban's chief tasks – collecting wood and trapping fish – were 'mainstays of the fenland economy' (27). Borlik concludes that Caliban 'shares distinctive characteristics with the Lincolnshire peasantry who believed in such spirits and whose communal land was being taken from them by an educated elite whose scientific knowledge gave them a quasi-magical power to control the elements of earth and water' (29).

Vin Nardizzi's *Wooden Os: Shakespeare's Theatres and England's Trees* (2013) examines the play's relationship to sixteenth- and early-seventeenth-century resource shortages. He considers early modern environmental pressures such as deforestation and natural events amidst the British colonial endeavour in Virginia, citing Francis Bacon's observation that the '[p]lanting of countries is like the planting of woods' (119). The play 'presents hardly any trees on the island' yet implies that a forest must have once been present given its persistent references to lumbered wood (112). This relates to England's timber shortages, as evident in the 'recycling' of timber from the

Theatre in Shoreditch to construct the original Globe on Southbank in 1599. Caliban's bundles of logs are hence emblematic of the 'vital matter of *The Tempest*'s eco-fantasies of colonialist extraction and theatrical production' (112). The early modern timber crisis and colonial plundering of old growth forests therefore highlight 'our age of inconvenient truth, in which fossil fuels supply our energy needs and in which environmental activists warn against the diminishment of the planet's forests' (138).

Rose McKenna's 'Surviving *The Tempest*: Ecologies of Salvage on the Early Modern Stage' (2017) argues that the 'play produces and reproduces itself through salvage' through recollecting and recycling actors, costumes, properties and language within its larger ecology (271). She notes that Shakespeare's company likely obtained stage properties (or 'props') through households and pawn stores, while donated aristocratic clothes allowed the actors to evade the period's sumptuary laws governing clothing of class and rank. Once worn out, clothing scraps would be recycled into paper, resulting in *The Tempest*'s first publication in the First Folio occurring on paper partly made from recycled linen rags (276). She further follows Egan's discussion of Michael Baird Saenger's claim that the 'costumes of Caliban and Arial-as-sea-nymph were first used in a sea-pageant on the Thames celebrating the investiture of Prince Henry as Prince of Wales' (Egan 1997: 62 in McKenna 2017: 276). Like Prospero's cloak and Ariel's lute that were likely shuffled between *The Alchemist* and *The Tempest* in repertory between 1608 and 1610, Caliban's reused water-nymph costume can therefore be seen to recall and rewrite contexts in an 'ecology of salvage' (277). The play thus 'posits a theory of survival as a counter point to Prospero's apocalyptic vision' of the 'great globe itself' (4.1.153) disappearing (278, see also the interview with Elizabeth Freestone).

ADAPTATION PROMPTS

- **Dramaturgical concepts:** Unequal access to land, environmental injustice, deforestation, colonization's plundering of resources, survival versus apocalypse.

- **Scenographic possibilities:** Mudflats, tidal creeks, shallow lakes and brackish ooze, denuded forests, recycled materials, Caliban and Arial as sea-nymphs.

- **Questions:** How might a historical adaptation harness the play's early modern context as a commentary on our current environmental degradation? In what ways can Renaissance practices of salvage be incorporated into ecoscenographic design?

Eco-assemblage: Blue *Tempest*

Steve Mentz's *At The Bottom of Shakespeare's Ocean* (2009) argues for paying closer attention to the materiality of Shakespeare's oceans and thus our own. Like *Lear's* description of Dover Beach (4.6.17–24) and the 'oceanic turn' in the second half of the play that expresses the 'kingdom's disorder in maritime terms', *The Tempest* directs our gaze to the 'water itself' (2009: 15, 18). Frequently interpreted as a 'metaphor for the artistic process or theatricality or mutability itself', Mentz states that the 'real taste of the ocean' and the 'sharp tang of nonhuman immensity' is 'lost in the flux' (1). He draws attention to Ariel's song ('Full fathom five. . .', 1.2.397–403, 405), noting the 'three- and four-beat rhythm recalling the ocean's audible presence', its 'breathless alliterative opening', and its symbolic representation of 'the transforming powers of oceanic magic' (7). Mentz reminds us that the play never delivers Ariel's treasure. Instead, Shakespeare's lyricism is underpinned by tragic intensity issuing a sea-change that 'captures the force, physical and metaphoric, of salt water transfiguring flesh' (8).

Dan Brayton's 'Shakespeare and the Global Ocean' (2011) discusses the sea as a site of geographic otherness that is amorphous, mysterious, and lethal (190). Not only does Prospero's most spectacular magic involve the sea but Ariel has both pyrotechnic and aquatic magic. Ariel hence suggests that nature 'itself is enlisted for political purposes' and evokes 'historical questions about the European ventures at sea in early modernity' (ibid.). Like Love, Brayton notes Trinculo's first encounter with Caliban but adds that his fishlike comparisons extend beyond appearance to odour: 'A fish, he smells like a fish, a very ancient and fish-like smell, a kind of not-of-the-newest-poor-John' (2.2.25–6). He, too, critiques the 'constant animalisation' and monstering of Caliban by other characters, finding him to be instead a 'semi-human creature', a 'stranded merman', 'piece of existential flotsam' and 'marginal creature on the beach without a stable origin or home' (184–5). Caliban is thus a 'conceptually foreign being belonging not to his own social order but to the alien maritime landscape' (183). The play amplifies the 'strangeness of the sea' in the early modern imagination, in which the 'nautical setting seems indistinguishable from the thematics of learning and magic as the mastery of elements' (ibid.).

Claire Hansen's 'Shakespeare, Climate Change and the Blue Humanities: Imagining an Oceanic Education' (2023a) considers how prioritizing Shakespeare's oceanic deepens critical awareness of and engagement with climate change effects in blue spaces. She discusses 'watery ways of thinking' through multiplicity and shipwreck, wherein *The Tempest*'s sea-storm represents anthropogenic climate change and Prospero 'humanity's climatic agency' (195). The play can help us process ecological grief and guilt through 'shared sea-sorrow of humanity, ocean and climate' alongside the 'porous early modern body-environment relationship' (196). Hansen considers the play to provide an 'oppositional mode of thinking where the ocean is anathema to humanity's social hierarchies', complicating human-climate relations, and reconceptualizing disaster as opportunity (195). Hansen concludes that while a blue ecocritical lens 'values uncertainty and complexity, rather than seeking to reduce or contain it', blue pedagogy 'encourages students to linger in a mode of questioning and consideration instead of rushing to answers and conclusions' (195).

ADAPTATION PROMPTS

- **Dramaturgical concepts:** Humanity's shared origins and stories, oceanic, climatic and elemental interplay and influence, harnessing shared sea-stories to process ecological grief and guilt.

- **Scenographic possibilities:** Maritime disorder and flux, oceanic rhythm through music, magical and liminal beach zones, the ocean as a site of transformation.

- **Questions:** In what ways does the play highlight the importance of our planet's ecologically threatened blue spaces? How can the play be adapted to amplify the sea's vibrancy and agency as a more-than-human presence on stage?

Eco-assemblage: An environmentally just *Tempest*

Tarik Monowar's 'Indigeneity and Climate Change in Shakespeare's *The Tempest*: A Postcolonial Study' (2020) examines how *The Tempest* can help to decipher how Indigenous people respond to and resist climate change. This is distinct from the longer history of postcolonial readings of the play in that it takes a specifically ecological focus. Monowar aligns Prospero's 'ecophobic attitude' and 'strong abhorrence for both natural environment and Indigenous people' with the violent control and manipulation enacted on Indigenous populations and ecosystems aggravating climate change. He notes that assessments of climate change impacts have 'mostly been homogenic and ignorant of its diverse consequences' for vulnerable communities at the forefront of direct environmental effects (np). Indigenous communities' dependence on renewable natural resources place them most at risk to climate variability, while being excluded from decision-making processes. Rather than rejecting *The Tempest*, Monowar finds it useful in revealing 'how Indigenous culture, language, and history across the world are alienated and marginalized to the point of extinction' (np). The play thus may be read as a 'rigorous revisiting' of Indigenous values', which can offer a sustainable 'alternative modernity' (np).

Natalie Suzelis' *'Climate Leviathan* and Ecological Accumulation in *The Tempest'* (2021) conisders that viewing humanity as a whole as responsible for the climate crisis obscures the race, class, gender and spatial relations of power causing environmental injustice (181). Drawing on Shakespeare's possible awareness of the Virginia Company's wreck off the coast of the present-day Bahamas, Suzelis observes the play's connection to 'climate apocalypse', given that Hurricane Dorian (2019) was inflicted upon today's Bahamians who are 'largely the descendents of emancipated enslaved laborers' (184, also see, for the Virginia Company, above, and for a Bahamian *Tempest*, below). She calls for acknowledgment of the 'sweat and endeavor that is necessary to nurture and protect life' that, since *The Tempest* was written, has largely been undertaken by 'enslaved, colonized, and exploited peoples' (185). 'While we cannot return to a world before Prospero, we can resist his impulse of accumulation' and 'stand in solidarity' with First Nations and Indigenous peoples (185). To do so, we must move beyond the 'willful naivety of Gonzalo's 'golden age' and beyond Prospero's desire to 'produce, direct, and control nature' (185).

ADAPTATION PROMPTS

- **Dramaturgical concepts**: Indigenous values as an alternative to exploitative Western environmental practices, environmental justice and vulnerable communities, oppression of people and destruction of environments.
- **Scenographic possibilities**: First Nations and Indigenous art and design, Bahamian culture and artistic practice, destructive Western landscape practices.
- **Questions**: What does the play have to say about colonization's exploitation of people and nature? How can the play be reconfigured to reclaim environmental justice and ecological agency?

Eco-assemblage: Designing *The Tempest*

Julia Reinhard Lupton and C.J. Gordon's 'Shakespeare by Design: A Flight of Concepts' (2013) offers a model integrating ecocritical sources within eco-adaptations. Some of the authors' considerations include creating a sonic profile of *The Tempest*'s island. Drawing on acoustic ecology they consider the play's landscapes through the panoramic and material components of 'non-human wilderness and the built environment' (270). Soundscapes, they point out, are the 'product of mutual incursions by multiple species staking out, belligerently defending, and constantly renegotiating their own niches' (271). They find *The Tempest* to be 'Shakespeare's most fully realized soundtrack', exploring 'both the transformative and empowering dimensions of the soundscape while probing its darker, exploitative, abusive potentials' (272). The 'pulsing, wave-like, periodic rhythms of Ariel's melody' therefore 'amplify and intensify the surge of the sea' (ibid.). In a theatrical space, the play's layered interiors and exterior hardscapes hence draw listeners together 'networking human and non-human bodies together in a makeshift assembly' (272–3).

Gwilym Jones' 'The Tempest and Theatrical Reality' in *Shakespeare's Storms* (2015) argues that the 'play presents nature as only accessible through a distorted theatrical lens, one which reflects both subject and object through its self-awareness' (150). He highlights that Ariel is both slave and personification of the weather, positioned in a wider context of 'new world domination' that is 'necessarily also a fantasy of domination over nature' (146). Jones additionally explores early modern staging with particular attention given to stage directions. He holds that *The Tempest*'s storm scene amplifies the play's metatheatricality through its juxtaposition of naturalistic description and simultaneous concealment. This, he suggests, feeds into the play's concern with its 'own process of producing meaning' (144).

Evelyn O'Malley's 'You Do (Not) Assist the Storm' (2016) examines Moving Stories' 2014 production of *The Tempest* directed by Emma Gersch at the outdoor Minack Theatre in Cornwall, England. The production combined recorded soundscape with the real sounds of waves, gulls and wind, suggesting a merging of play and place and linking the text to material landscape. Audience interviews suggested that the seaside setting created a 'disjuncture between performed and real weather' that 'undid as much of the thematic complementarity between performance and location as it generated' (83). In this way, the ocean refused to be wholly appropriated into performance and in fact drew attention to its independence. O'Malley notes that Helen Mirren and *A Midsummer Night's Dream* director Julie Taymor have commented that the 'more realistic the setting, the less realistic the performance seems because the place of performance undermines the credibility of the illusion' (83). She concludes it is anthropocentric hubris to conceive that the ocean may be put to work in work in service of *The Tempest* erasing 'local specificity in response to generic Shakespearean "nature"'. This encourages humility through recognizing that 'the sea always performs in ways that exceed human performance' (84).

ADAPTATION PROMPTS

- **Dramaturgical concepts:** The transformative and empowering dimensions of soundscape and its darker potential, characters as personification of the weather, nature exceeding human performance.

- **Scenographic possibilities:** Shakespeare's soundtrack of the natural world, metatheatricality, non-literal designs.

- **Questions:** How does the play's venue or setting enhance or detract from the play's environmental narrative? How might the play be expressed sonically to amplify the play's many more-than-human voices?

Further reading

Other recent ecocriticism includes Crystal Bartolovich's 'Marxist Ecology and Shakespeare' (2022) and Daniel Vitkus' 'Red-Green Intersectionality Beyond the New Materialism: An Eco-Socialist Approach to Shakespeare's *The Tempest*' (2023). Bartolovich analyzes *The Tempest's* 'unusual physical presence of wood' as both a marker of Caliban's subjugation and reduction of the 'nonhuman world to mere "raw material" (72). Vitkus applies a socio-ecological perspective to *The Tempest*'s 'intensive exploration of nature/ culture boundaries and hierarchies' to target the real, human causes of ecocide' (129). Julia Hoydis' *Posthumanism and Drama: From Shakespeare to Climate Change Plays* (2022) highlights the play's challenge to anthropocentric dominion of nature through its 'man-made storms and entanglements with the more-than-human world, including supernatural elements, spirit beings, and characters kept imprisoned in less-than-human states' (708). Jason C. Hogue's 'Ariels Anguish' also employs posthumanism to examine Ariel's arboreal confinement as an opportunity to think and feel across species and kingdoms (2021). Finally, Jennifer Flaherty's '"This Island's Mine": Ecocritical Caribbean *Tempests*' (2021) examines two Caribbean adaptations: Aimé Césaire's *Une tempête* ([1969] 2000) (see Chapter 5, 'Eco-adaptation' below) and Raquel Carrió and Flora Lauten's *Otra tempestad* (1999). Flaherty argues that '[e]cocritical ideas resonate in each text's approach to colonization' (135). *Une tempête,* for example, 'condemns the colonizers as 'enemies of nature', while *Otra tempestad* suggests that the 'environment can be threatened or protected' by humans alike (ibid.).

5

Eco-adaptation

In the following examples of eco-Shakespearean adaptation, you can read how a range of practitioners have wrestled with the challenge of making the plays speak to the climate emergency. Some have retained Shakespeare's words – or most of them – but experimented with framing devices or design to foreground the environment. Others have freely translated the texts into non-English languages or into contemporary English. Most of the productions and texts described were designed for live performance, whether in an indoor or outdoor setting or a site-specific combination of the two. The case studies take various formats: some are interviews, others written accounts, others are our own descriptions of published works. All support Julie Sander's contention that 'Shakespearean adaptation (and appropriation) [. . .] increasingly orient us towards forward-looking agendas, situating Shakespeare as a potent vehicle for engaging with presentist global issues and challenges from migration to climate to identity politics' (Sanders 2022: 92–3). Below we briefly describe some adaptive prompts and strategies that you will see in many of the extracts, and which you can also use in crafting your own adaptations.

Localization and given circumstances: It may help you to think of a 'local habitation and a name' (*Dream* 5.1.17) through which you can filter these stories. What's happening in your neighbourhood? Your state? Your country? How does the play illuminate or complicate that? What affordances are offered by the lines or plot points for topical issues? If we take ecology in its widest sense, then we are thinking about how to situate these stories in our respective 'dwelling places'. That means thinking across a variety of issues: race, gender, power, land, etc, and not 'just' about ecology in the narrower sense of the natural world. Furthermore, the overwhelmingly outdoor nature of these texts, the fact that most of the action takes place in fictive outside spaces, means that adaptations cannot ignore fundamental environmental questions which we can ask both of ourselves and of the worlds of the plays: Where are we? What does this environment feel like? What is the weather doing? Who owns this land? Is it fit for human habitation? What characterises the animals and other non-human inhabitants of this place?

Casting: Adaptation is not merely a textual operation but a performance *event*. The meaning of that event is determined by a number of factors, but one key component is the identity of the performers. The stage must be peopled and what those people look and sound like, where they come from, and what they represent has implications for the audience experience, and for the reputation of Shakespeare in the wider culture. Can we speak of ecological casting? Yes, if by ecological we refer to the *oikos* – the home or dwelling place – of the production's creation. Ecological casting is therefore a strategy that respects and represents the (bio)diversity of a community. For example: Shakespeare's plays are notoriously gender imbalanced for the very practical reason that his company employed far more adult male actors than boy actors (who played his female characters). How can your adaptation address this? (For examples of representative casting, see extracts 1, 3, 9 and 10.)

Democratizing the text: Shakespeare's plays are often preoccupied with the affairs of 'great ones': kings, queens, dukes, earls, and so on. Some American thinkers of the nineteenth century thought this made the plays, in poet Walt Whitman's words, 'altogether non-acceptable to America and to democracy' (1888: 56). Many adaptors therefore choose to take the characters down a peg or two (or four). In the extracts below, you will see that Lear has been downgraded from a king to a fisherman in Ben Benison's *Jack Lear*, and, in Shakespeare in Paradise's production of *The Tempest*, Prospero became a former CEO.

Mash-ups and collages: The word 'mash-up' was first used to describe a piece of music created by merging elements of two or more existing songs or tracks. The word 'collage' derives from the visual arts where it describes the arrangement of various objects in a limited space. Both techniques are now commonly employed in textual adaptation. None of the extracts below are strictly either, but there are a number of precedents for this in recent performance history. Catalan director Calixto Bieito's *Forests* (2012) mashed up passages relating to woods and forests from a range of Shakespeare plays to create an often dark meditation on the behaviours of humans in 'uncivilized' spaces. Parrabola's project *This Distemperature* (2020), described as 'a conversation between William Shakespeare and the environment', juxtaposed extracts from the plays and poems with a wide variety of other texts (Greenpeace articles, news footage of bushfires, speeches by Greta Thunberg, etc.) to create a moving five-act audio experience (Parrabola 2020). Finally, *Shakespeare's Maritime Dream* (2021) was a collaboration between the University of Buffalo and the Buffalo Maritime Center that explored how Shakespeare's imaginative representation of water and waterways could improve place-based ecological understanding.

Extraction and post-scripting: Can you create a new piece of theatre by extracting characters or scenes from these plays? Or by imagining what happens after Shakespeare's play ends? Actor and writer Tim Crouch has created a series of monologues exploring overlooked or poorly treated Shakespearean characters (these include *I, Peaseblossom* and *I, Caliban*).

Frank Bramwell's *King Lear (Alone)* (2018) is, as the name suggests, a monologue for Lear that takes place in a kind of suspended void after Cordelia's death and before his own. What opportunities can you see in rewriting or adding a sequel to the scripted or 'promised end[s]' (*Lear* 5.3.261) of Shakespeare's plays?

1) Shakespeare in Yosemite's
A Midsummer Night's Dream (2018)
by Brokaw and Prescott

Shakespeare in Yosemite was co-founded by Katie Brokaw and Paul Prescott in 2017. It offers free, outdoor, site-specific adaptations of Shakespeare's plays every April for visitors to Yosemite National Park, California. Yosemite is one of the most-visited and best-loved outdoor spaces in North America. Even those of have not visited the seven-mile Yosemite Valley at its heart will recognize images of Yosemite's staggering granite peaks such as Half Dome and El Capitan, of Yosemite Falls (the largest set of waterfalls in the US), and of the giant sequoia trees found in Mariposa Grove and the adjoining Sequoia and Kings Canyon National Parks. In this piece, Brokaw and Prescott reflect on the adaptive processes behind their 2018 production of A Midsummer Night's Dream.

Our adaptive strategy for the 2018 *Dream* can be summarized in four words: **Reduce, Rewrite/Rewright, Recycle.**

Reducing

In most easily accessible online texts, *A Midsummer Night's Dream* is about 17,000 words long. Uncut productions with an interval tend to run for about two and a half to three hours. Our production needed to last no longer than ninety minutes without an interval. We knew that we wanted to add a few musical numbers not found in Shakespeare's text, so our cut text needed to be about seventy minutes or about 9,500 words long, a substantial reduction of approximately 40 per cent of the original text. This calculation is based on the formula devised by dramaturg Scott Kaiser at the Oregon Shakespeare Festival, who cross-referenced the word count in prompt books with the running times and found that, in an average production, it takes one minute to speak 135 words (Kaiser 2004: 47).

The play is so beautifully plotted that there was no question of removing one of the narrative strands or indeed any of the characters (with the one semi-exception of the Indian Boy, who was replaced with a bear cub puppet), so in this adaptation we stuck broadly with the sequence of scenes found in the original. Reducing the text was, then, a question of sometimes light, sometimes severe internal pruning. Cuts were made for any of the following reasons: obscurity; redundancy; lack of poetic or comedic quality; irrelevance to the production's concept and messages; potential to cause offence. These are highly subjective judgments which led to dozens if not hundreds of textual alterations. They ranged from smallish excisions in the lovers' scenes (no threat of rape from Demetrius to Helena, no racially charged 'tawny Tartar' as an insult from Lysander to Hermia) to the removal of larger blocks of text (no Bergamask, no sweeping and blessing of the house at the end of the play).

Rewrighting/rewriting

The process of devising a world and a concept for the production happened in tandem with the act of cutting the text. The concept for the show was briefly explained to audiences in the program with the following note:

> The play is so weird, so dream-like, that it can be interpreted in all sorts of ways. We want our production to be site-specific and time-sensitive: this play is about being right here in Yosemite National Park, right now in late April 2018. Our lovers leave a fancy wedding party in the valley and flee into the back country; our 'Mechanicals' (i.e. working people) earn their various livings in the Park; the object of Titania and Oberon's quarrel is not an Indian boy (as in Shakespeare's text) but a bear cub; our fairies take the names of Yosemite flora and fauna.

We interpolated a couple of sequences in Act 1 to establish that Theseus and Hippolyta were not regular visitors to the Park but had chosen it as the location for their wedding based on its picturesque, Instagrammable backdrops. Hippolyta casually dropped some litter while taking a selfie; both in their separate pre-nuptial hotel suites called room service for some bottled water (none too subtly, this strand was designed to chime with the World Earth Day 2018 theme to 'End Plastic Pollution'.) At this point, Puck intervened, casting a thunderbolt spell on them with the words 'thou shalt be transformed!' and the pair wheeled offstage to return minutes later as their alter-egos, Oberon and Titania. The Fairies and the Mechanicals were also doubled and their identities made site-specific. The Mechanicals were all Park employees: Bottom the Facilities Operations Specialist, Snout the Wilderness Ranger, Snug the Wildland Firefighter, Flute the Mountaineering Instructor, and Starveling the Majestic Hotel server. Five out of six of the Fairies/Mechanicals were played by and as women, a casting decision designed to highlight the crucial role played by female Park employees (which the National Park Service itself was highlighting on their Instagram feed that spring). The Fairies were renamed and costumed to look like species of Yosemite: Sugar Pine, Orange Poppy, Lacewing, and Mule Deer. In common with Oberon, Titania and Puck, the Fairies occasionally but pointedly used words drawn from Native American languages. We did this under advice and with the blessing of representatives of the South Sierra Miwok and Paiute peoples, two of Yosemite's indigenous tribes. South Sierra Miwuk is a dying language and the man, Tony Cabezut, who taught us these words said one of the best ways to honor his tribe was to speak its endangered language. The Fairies and Puck therefore used the South Sierra Miwuk names for waterfalls and fires, as well as place names like Half Dome (Tessayak), indicating the idea that the fairies had been custodians of the land far before the profit-hunting arrival of white Europeans.

Recycling

The principle of recycling operated on two levels: costumes and props, and music. The latter is always a central component of our Yosemite adaptations and our *Dream* featured snatches of songs by Bob Dylan, Kendrick Lamar, The Beatles, The Proclaimers and Patty Griffin. After Hermia eloped, we had her mother, Egea, wandering through the woods, calling her name, while Oberon – fascinated by human feelings – sang a bit of 'Like A Rolling Stone' ('how does it feel. . .?'); this cross-faded into Hermia and Lysander singing the refrain from 'To Make You Feel My Love', a highly effective musical segue that we gratefully recycled from the superior Bob Dylan jukebox musical *Girl From the North Country*. When Bottom sang to show she was not afraid, she did so to the tune of The Beatles' 'Blackbird' ('Bottom singing in the dead of night! / Take these broken wings and learn to fly. / All your life, you were only waiting / For this moment to arise. . .'). Recycling these bits of folk and pop music in our shows echoes a practice Shakespeare and his contemporaries employed in their plays, whereby popular ballads, drinking songs and psalms were re-performed on the stage by characters from Lear's Fool to Autolycus. As presumably was the case then, these songs and snatches can bring the audience together in a shared cultural referent.

We knew that costume design would be a key element of the show. Constructed sets can be very wasteful (and the ready-made setting in Yosemite is unbeatable anyway), so costume would be the primary visual cue for context and characterisation. We hired local professional costumer Kristine Doiel, who along with two student assistants were in charge of creating our *Dream* world out of recycled clothes and trash. In the programme note, Doiel explained the impact the process had on her work as a designer: 'The exercise of utilizing discarded materials has not only challenged my creative thinking but also increased my awareness that we throw away so many useful materials.' In initial meetings, Doiel came up with several ideas that became important to the show's development – most crucially, the idea that Titania and Oberon would represent two elemental forces in Yosemite: waterfalls and forest fires. The water from Sierra snowmelt and periodic fires are both crucial to the area's ecosystem and potentially destructive when out of joint: the park has been closed for both floods and fire in recent years. The idea to highlight Yosemite's elements was furthered by an early conversation with Lisa Wolpe about her Puck, in which Wolpe had the idea that Puck could synthesize the elements of Earth and Air: she would be a creature who cares deeply for the Earth that she so gracefully circumvents in the air. That idea was enhanced by Doiel's research into the trash problems in Yosemite, when she learned that hiking and climbing gear is often left on trails in the back country. Doiel created Puck wings covered in hiking maps and tangled climbing ropes to convey the idea that when traveling between Earth and sky, Puck gets caught up in a very specific kind of human detritus.

The image of trash in the form of fairy wings, ass heads and discarded water bottles did resonate with many audience members, but first the process of collecting this trash for Doiel's design team affected our cast. James McIntyre, our Demetrius, echoed the sentiment of many when he said that while rehearsing and collecting, 'I found myself becoming overly conscious of the waste I was producing and what efforts I could take to reduce these detriments'. Devon Glover, who as Sonnet Man travels to schools and theatres around the world, said that working on this show 'inspired me to include more natural resources when working on productions with youth groups, and work on practicing and teaching the concept of turning trash to treasure'.

Yosemite is a particularly profound place to observe what Baz Kershaw – adopting an ecological term – calls 'edge effects' (2009: 186); the park's ecosystem rubs up against the theatrical ecosystem of the play, and so Mule Deer the fairy-character beholds a real mule deer in the wings, two squirrels run onto the stage and mimic Helena's chase, Puck calls a wandering toddler a 'woodland sprite' when he gets close. Wolpe describes how the animals, plants, and landscape of Yosemite affected her performance:

> Puck is a goblin of the forest, you couldn't really talk about the forest more effectively than being on this spongy grandmother earth and being so far away from artificial light and being reminded how small we are in connection to this place. There's no tree around me that wasn't here before I was born.

2) Rough Magic's *A Midsummer Night's Dream* (2018)

Lynne Parker has been Artistic Director of Rough Magic Theatre Company since 1984. She is an award-winning director of over fifty productions for Rough Magic and many others for a range of companies both inside her native Ireland and beyond. She directed A Midsummer Night's Dream *at the Kilkenny Arts Festival, Ireland, in the summer of 2018.*

Lynne Parker: The *Dream* was the beginning of our partnership with the Kilkenny Arts Festival and we performed outdoors in the Castle Yard. We really wanted to find a way to do the work that we had become characterized by, which was big ensemble festive shows, and this partnership enabled us to get that muscle back in. It was a steep learning curve as I had never done anything outdoors before. I really felt, 'We can do what we like in the rehearsal room. But it's all gonna have to be reinvented when we get it into the castle yard.' Once there, I realized there was nowhere to hide, so you cannot have a sudden entrance in the open air. I decided to do it in traverse because there's just a more sort of immediate connection when the audience surrounds the action. The castle yard is a sort of semi-circular space and it lends itself to circling, to orbiting. We'll come back to that.

Alys Daroy and Paul Prescott: Visually, were we in the present day, or in some kind of semi-future? Where were we?

LP: Semi-future is closest to it. What I really wanted was the sense that this was a slightly post-apocalyptic world. I wanted to open the show with Theseus and Hippolyta coming on in a car but a car that was drawn by people. There was no engine in it. So we're looking at a world that sort of still wants to believe it's got a Cadillac. In the end, we couldn't get permission to get a car in but that image would have set the tone. We also planned to cover the audience seating banks – these big, ugly aluminium things – with grass and moss, as if they'd been abandoned and left to rust. Again, this proved impracticable. It's the nature of theatre that some of your best ideas sometimes run up against reality.

We began by asking: What is the context of doing something outdoors? And we thought that the climate, which is part of Titania's big speech, had to be key to that. We were very interested in the idea of harnessing natural forces which include electricity. We had all sorts of ambitions to do stuff with electric current and lightning. I'm a huge fan of [science broadcaster] Jim Al-Khalili – he did a radio show called *Shock and Awe* on the story of electricity, and I was just fascinated by the visual effects that you could get from very rudimentary electrical processes. And I wanted to have a system where we could shoot spines of electricity all around the castle yards. I mean, I don't know what budget I thought I was working on! But sometime we'd love to do that because the electricity is most natural thing in the world we have, and we have harnessed it. So I thought the fairies would be very good agents of that power. That sense of a force, a natural force that's really breaking out, out of man's control, would fit very well with the sense of it being a post-apocalyptic world: the whole power supply actually was sort of gaining its own head and its own sense of control.

AD and PP: So you had to abandon that design concept?

LP: Yes, but we instead generated that feeling of energy in perhaps the greenest way possible: through the actors' bodies. I mentioned that there was nowhere to hide in the space and so it was impossible to make sudden entries. It would take what felt like five minutes for everybody to get on stage. It was lugubrious. After the dress rehearsal I went home and thought 'Okay, I've got to reinvent this.' I opened the text and the first thing I saw was '*Enter Demetrius, running*'. And I thought: 'Oh, running: everyone's running. Okay: we're going to *run* this show.' I told the cast the next day: 'You're gonna run into every scene and you're gonna run out of it. In fact, you're gonna keep running as you play the scene.' The actors were young and fit and loved it. They were just hurtling through the play, and it gave it a huge energy. You felt the whole thing was orbiting and with energy, like the electricity which we had failed to get from a conventional power supply.

AD and PP: So by the time Titania gave her speech about the environment, the audience would have sensed that something has gone wrong with this world?

LP: Yes. But it wasn't irreparable. We closed the show with Paul Mescal (who was playing both Demetrius and Peter Quince) singing 'Crazy' by Seal, as the curtain call. We were saying: 'Look, if we're gonna survive, we gotta go crazy, you know, because none of this makes any sense.' It all sounds very daft. And that's exactly what it was: it was daft, and it made sense of a young, sprightly ensemble doing this play in the open air for the sheer, exuberant fun of it. There's such a wonderful ludic energy at the end, and such an innocent celebration of people just having a go, you know, and it doesn't matter whether they can do the parts or not, they have a go. That sense of wonderful human chaos, that's what gives the play a kind of final optimism.

3) *Bright Summer Night* (2016)

Our final case study of an eco-inflected *Dream* adaptation is *Bright Summer Nights* (2016), which can be watched on YouTube. It differs from our previous case studies in two key ways: 1) it is a web series (i.e. a series of short films) rather than a theatrical production; 2) it models a far freer approach to adaptation (only one line from the play is spoken). It was created by The Candle Wasters, a collective of writer-activists who describe themselves as 'four young women and a token dude from New Zealand, who create fierce, funny, feminist web series' (Candle Wasters 2023). Prior to *Bright Summer Night*, they had produced two other Shakespeare-derived vlog series, *Nothing Much to Do* and *Lovely Little Losers* based respectively on *Much Ado about Nothing* and *Love's Labour's Lost*. As with those series, *Bright Summer Night* focuses exclusively on the experiences of young New

Zealanders. It uses *A Midsummer Night's Dream* as a vehicle to ask: what's on young peoples' minds? In Shakespeare's play the answer is simple: love. In *Bright Summer Night*, the answer is far more complex.

The action takes place at an overnight house party in the suburbs of Wellington. There are no adults. The elder partygoers are back from university and in the first episode we see a couple – Bryn and Awhina – arguing about environmental activism in a way that recalls Oberon and Titania's row over the Indian Boy, except here climate change is the subject rather than the result of the argument. Bryn had started an eco-activist group, Kaitiaki, while they were at high school, but no longer believes in making the effort. In a dynamic that recurs throughout the series, one character gives into a fatalistic eco-despair while another argues for activism, however small the difference it makes.

Each subsequent episode tracks one character's experience of the party. The focus is split, as in Shakespeare, between the groupings of the lovers, the fairies and the Mechanicals, and the moments these worlds coincide. Great pain has been taken to make the cast as diverse and representative as possible. Demetrius has been reimagined as Deme, who is non-binary and goes by 'them/they'; Puck is also played by Meesha Rikk, who identifies as bigender. The performers are largely of multiethnic heritage. Eco-anxiety is a generational condition, cutting across a range of racial, sexual and gender identities.

Many of the characters use alcohol and/or drugs to self-medicate their anxieties. The drug of choice is 'Idleness', here not the herbal 'Love in Idleness' of Shakespeare's play, but rather an MDMA-like pill that delivers a euphoric and amnesic rush. As the show's creators relate: 'Millennials arrived at the party too late – our world is on the brink of environmental catastrophe, and we continue to deny it [. . .] Just like the world we live in, we see some of the characters are determined to keep dreaming; putting off tomorrow to indulge in the night' (Whyte 2016). An exception to this yearning for escapism is provided by the very youngest people at the party, a quartet of Gen Z-ers who have formed an experimental performance art group called The Mechanicals. Like Shakespeare's Mechanicals, they are endearingly and entertainingly earnest. At one point, Frankie (i.e. Francis Flute) yells: 'I am a neo-liberal Marxist and I will not be labelled!' Led by pushy, punky Petra (Peter Quince), they brainstorm topics for an activist musical, briefly considering the Holocaust, or the relationship between Israel and Palestine, before plumping for Climate Change. They perform Nicky's (Bottom) new song in the ensemble finale of the series. The song is called 'Relationship Problems and the Environment', which neatly sums up the two major concerns of the series in an analogous way to how the play-within-the-play of Pyramus and Thisbe replays some of the action of *Dream*. In this adaptation, it is the Bottom character that models the least neurotic form of eco-consciousness. 'The earth doesn't care if humans die, but I do,' she says simply to a couple of fairies. Her kindness and concern for others contrasts with the performative cynicism of Puck, and it is telling that the series ends, the morning after the night before, with Nicky gently consoling a distraught Puck.

Web series like *Bright Summer Night* have already redefined what Shakespeare can mean for Millennials and Gen Z-ers. As Luke McKernan writes:

> [. . .] what most distinguishes the series is their focus on youth. Their subjects are young, and usually the filmmakers are too. Just as importantly, the audience is. They have the frankness, idealism, guilelessness and wisdom of a generation that shares its lives online. There is a powerful sense of discovery, of having stumbled across this brave new world of ideas and characters whose situations can be magically transmuted into today. They make Shakespeare young again. The aim of the series is to clarify Shakespeare; to make what the plays say clear to an audience usually thought to have no interest in Shakespeare, by matching them to the world that they do appreciate. They help to make Shakespeare make sense.
>
> (McKernan 2016)

4) Rob Conkie's eco-dramaturgical *King Lear* (2017)

Rob Conkie is Robinson Distinguished Professor of Shakespeare Studies at the University of North Carolina, Charlotte, USA. He has directed, sometimes with professionals, but mainly with students, about a third of Shakespeare's canon for the stage. His production of King Lear *took place around the campus of La Trobe University, Melbourne, Australia, in the winter of 2017. It featured a cast and crew of undergraduate students. The action took place in multiple venues across the campus in a promenade staging (i.e. one in which there is no fixed seating and the audience moves in order to follow the performers).*

Paul Prescott: Why did you chose *King Lear* for this ecodramaturgical approach?

Rob Conkie: Well, there's a surface answer, an obvious answer. And then there are under the surface and more nuanced answers. Some of these only came to me *after* making the show, in a kind of cumulative retrospectivity. To start with the obvious answer: *King Lear* is one of the 'nature' plays. We have a character who goes into nature and is impacted by it. The play has a tripartite structure of beginning in the court, or, let's say an 'accommodated beginning', before it goes into the wild and unaccommodating, before finally returning to some kind of accommodation. At its centre is a sustained weather event, the storm.

Now, a more nuanced way in which *Lear* speaks to the present ecological moment is what I'm going to call the 'Gloucester Precipice Factor'. Our experience of the Anthropocene and environmental catastrophe is of a polarity between grief and hope. I'm on the bleak grief end of the spectrum, but I think Gloucester offers a really interesting case study of the tightrope between grief and hope (see Lesley Head, *Hope and Grief in the Anthropocene: Re-conceptualising Human-nature Relations* [2016] on this). I'm thinking especially of the lines that he says when Edgar has done the work of emotionally resuscitating him, and he says 'Henceforth I'll bear / Affliction till it do cry out itself' (4.6.75-6). He's made a significant emotional journey from wanting to topple over the edge of the cliff at Dover to that moment of being able to bear out affliction. But then a few scenes later, when Edgar reports that Lear and Cordelia have been taken and the war is lost, he refuses to move and says 'No further, sir, a man may rot even here' (5.2.8), and so he pendulums back to despair. Then Edgar reproves him and Gloucester's response is 'that's true too' (5.2.12). And so he swings back. And I think this navigating between grief and hope is an apt metaphor. It reminds me of what Ian Smith, in the context of race relations in the US, has called 'Reparative Hope'.

PP: There's something in there about us needing to be reminded that life is miraculous. As Edgar says to Gloucester after his 'fall': 'Thy life's a miracle'.

RC: Yes. I was thinking about how Edgar stages his own version of 'The Mousetrap' in *Hamlet*. Hamlet's objective is to expose Claudius's culpability. But Edgar uses this weird kind of play-within-the-play – let's call it 'Poor Tom and the Blind Man' – to help his father walk the tightrope, always nudging him towards hope. So, both Gloucester – he who dies ''Twixt two extremes of passion, joy and grief' (5.3.197) – and me as reader/director are caught in this mousetrap, the two of us creatures guilty of potentially paralysing despair. And the Gloucester Precipice Factor is also synedochal of the larger play: *King Lear* also veers between humanity perforce preying on itself and a hoped-for, perhaps after-the-play 'promised end' for 'we that are young'.

PP: What were your ecodramaturgical strategies and tactics?

RC: We really began with two research questions: one, what happens to *King Lear* if you put it in an 'environment'? And two, what happens to that environment if you put *King Lear* in it? Our main strategy was to be open to the elements. It was pretty much: 'Let's put this scene or that scene, or another scene out somewhere, and see what happens.' I spent a lot of time before rehearsals scouting venues for scenes across the campus grounds. Once we were rehearsing in those mostly open spaces, we adopted a tactic from improvised performance which is to take anything random that happens as a gift, as an offer. During one rehearsal, Edgar was crouched in long grass, telling us that 'No port is free, no place / That guard and most unusual vigilance / Does not attend my taking' (2.2.176). Right then, a helicopter flew overheard. 'Use the helicopter!' I shouted, 'they're coming for you!' A few minutes later a group of visiting schoolchildren walked right through our scene. 'Use them: don't let them see you!' From that moment on I encouraged the cast to use everything that the environment presented.

PP: Can you give us an account of the show?

RC: The production began indoors in a large black box theatre with a long table placed diagonally across it. There were twenty-six chairs at the table, twenty of which were for the audience. We used a PowerPoint [presentation] to illustrate the division of the kingdom. I took a screengrab of Tasmania using Google Earth and then turned it sideways. When Lear spoke of dividing 'in three our kingdom', red jagged lines cut the territory into thirds; as he described each daughter's portion, the slides cross-faded into profit projections of the natural resources in each. So, for example, Goneril was due to inherit forests with a net logging value of $4.5m, rivers with a net fishing value of $1.2m, and so on. We wanted to show that here was a ruling class with no concern for the natural world beyond what profit it could yield. By the end of Act One, we were outside, and remained so for the rest of the show. Having looked at a map, an abstract representation of the 'kingdom', we were all now outdoors and navigating a part of that kingdom.

Subsequent locations included a loading dock with a large and beautiful eucalyptus tree to its west for Act Two. Then the audience followed Lear into the storm between two student accommodation wings – here Lear scrambled up a concrete block to rage at the heavens. The hovel in which they all eventually found shelter was another loading dock. Poor Tom popped out of a large paper recycling bin. When Gloucester was arrested, he was frog-marched a few metres away, with the audience hastening to keep up, and bound to a barbed-wire fence, where his eyes were taken from him.

My favourite part of the whole show was when Edgar led his blind father towards 'Dover'. The audience followed the pair as they falteringly walked a significant distance, maybe about 150 metres, between the locations for 4.2 and 4.3. This was the first time the production slowed down, and simply involved silently following the travellers. A space was opened up to attend both to the play and to the surroundings: to listen to the moat, sometimes rushing; to gaze at the stunning branches and trees; to take in the moon and the stars (that Gloucester thinks are so influential to human life below them). I fell in love with the trees, particularly, and looked at them much more closely than I would have normally. I think I experienced an 'enhanced awareness of being-in-the-world' that can often occur during site-specific or site-responsive performance.

PP: How did the production end?

RC: The last scene was staged in the Moat amphitheatre. It's a circle of concrete, really, at the base of tiered seating. It's a big space, and it's a very difficult theatrical space to fill. So there was no attempt to place the spectators in the seating area of the amphitheatre. Instead they stood onstage, circling the final swordfight between Edgar and Edmond and the ensuing deaths. But the image that just keeps coming back to me is of the grand chorus of trees that stand around the amphitheatre. While the onstage audience witnessed the action intimately, these trees seemed to oversee it, even appearing to crane forward to see better. There was a sense of a deeper, ecological time, that would endure beyond the humans who were busily destroying each other on stage (and off it). It wasn't something that I planned, but the spectatorship of the trees was the most powerful thing about the experience for me.

5) *Jack Lear* (2008) by Ben Benison

Jack Lear is a free adaptation of *King Lear* by the playwright and performer Ben Benison (1933–2019). It premiered at the Stephen Joseph Theatre in Scarborough in 2008 and was published in *Five New Plays for the Public Domain* in 2019. As the name of the book implies, Benison chose to waive copyright on his plays in the hope they would reach the widest audience both in performance and, as here, in reproduced extracts. Benison set his version in a coastal town (like Scarborough or Hull) in the north-east of England. Jack Lear is a retired fisherman who has made good money from exhaustive fishing of the tidal waters. He has pushed his workers hard, but, as his middle daughter Freda points out:

> **FREDA** You're right, the men were pushed, but so was he,
> By bosses who sat fat and far away
> In cosy on-shore rooms, white-collared men,
> Who did not care what happened on board ship,
> So long as dad could fill her fit to burst.
>
> (Benison 2019: 30)

Although Benison completely rewrites the text, he does – ambitiously – compose the whole play in iambic pentameter. He cuts the Gloucester subplot but retains the character of Edmund, here a sleazy chancer whose disco moves women find irresistible. *Jack Lear* is a model of several adaptative techniques: how to relocate the action to the present and to a specific community; how to rewrite the backstory in order to create new dynamics; how to change the stakes (in this case, inheritance becomes a question of boats and family houses not land). The play begins with a Prologue performed by Morgana, the eldest daughter:

MORGANA *in male gear: hard-wearing trousers, boots, headscarf knotted gypsy fashion. . .*

MORGANA Morgana is the name I own, prefer,
But Morgan's what I get, Jack wanted men.
It set him back when I was born, the first,
Then Freda, Fred, was breeched: 'I want a son!'
But he soon sorted that, he brought us up
Like men, in oilskin frocks and thigh-high boots,
He made us wear men's gear, he made us men.
So oilskin-frocked and thigh-boot shod, wore too
A pair of fearnoughts, Guernsey; add to these
A gutting knife and stand us all knee-deep
In deck fish, you tell me who's men or not.
To blur the female male distinction more,
Imagine figures swamped by raging seas
And deckies we all were, no more no less.
Men-daughters he has brought us up to be,
A man left wifeless with three budding girls.
Perhaps it all had got too much for mam,
Just after number three was born, our Vic:
'Christ, not another bitch!' then off she'd gone.
I've heard it said that dad then shagged around
To make a son, but he could only make
More daughters, round here's full of bastard kin.
So then he's of a mind his sperm is witched
And liked the thought the more since he found out
That when you meet the sea, you don't meet God.
'The sea, the rocks, the wind, the ice,' he said,
'Are laws unto themselves, they're what they are.
If there's a god it's pagan, witched like me.'
So Jack the godless turned to Nordic lore,
To Thor and Odin, dad has Danish blood,
Became entranced with Scandic gods, with Njord,
Who, throned on high with offspring Frey and Freya,
Presided over clouds and sea and air.
Frey rode the boar Gullbursti, wore a sword
That acted by itself – it thrills me now

As thrill it did, when dad these stories told –
And, God of Spring, wed Gerda, Frozen Earth,
The gleaming daughter of the frost giant Gyme.
This mythic side of Jack enraptured us.

(Benison 2019: 4–5)

As in *King Leir*, the title character is permanently scarred by his lack of a male heir. At the opening of Benison's play he feels himself to be a spent force and sets about distributing his possessions among his three daughter-sons:

JACK My veins are silting up, they throb and ache;
I'm short of breath and gob up too much phlegm;
My eyes are dim from scouring too much sea;
I'm tired, the fight's gone out of Jack the lad.
So witness now my rasping words to you,
My daughters, women-men, I'll say it quick:
The Britta, my first boat, I give to you,
My first-born, Morgan, yes, you know her well.
Oft have you steered her, brought her safe to port,
When forty-footers vied to stave her in;
She's yours to keep, or sell, or what you will.
For you Fred it's the Olbek, small but sleek,
A cleaver of the seas, a Cutty Sark;
A winner, she is yours to love or loathe.
And now, Victoria, to you the Rose –
VICTORIA I cannot promise, dad –
JACK I'm speaking, lass!
A craft most delicate with all mod cons,
A yacht designed for leisure, not for graft.
The other ships divide up as you will. . .

(Benison 2019: 11–12)

Victoria has a boyfriend who's a French lawyer (and whom we never meet). She is disinherited, like Cordelia, and her sisters are left to enjoy a life-changing fortune. Middle sister Freda tells the audience:

FREDA The sea still beckons, yes, I love the sea,
But this time viewed from sun-drenched decks stacked high
Where games are played and pools are swum,
Where lunch is served al fresco, champagne sipped,

> Where luxury is laid on thick, laid on.
> I'll cruise the days away and won't be home
> For Christmas time, the Med stays warm, I hear.
> This place will be as ever is, cold, damp,
> A has-been town, wind-swept, I've done my time.
>
> (Benison 2019: 23)

Benison's equivalent of the storm scenes sees Jack alone on one of his boats in the middle of a gale. His tirade is suicidal but biophilic in the sense that he longs to embraced and engulfed by the waters.

> **JACK LEAR** *stripped to the waist. Behind him a large sail flaps loose and limp in a light breeze. He cups his hands to his mouth, whistles (a taboo action).*
>
> **JACK** I'm married to the sea, I'm one with her;
> Salt-licked, agape, embraced by briny arms,
> I'll rise and fall, go her capricious way,
> Be taken to her bosom when she will.
> The land is set in all its ways, is fixed,
> No joy for dogs like me, who never know
> Which way the sea will turn, she's not so pat.
> I've learned to love her rage. Her tangy wrath
> Holds little fear for one who should by now
> Have sprouted fins, his skin become enscaled,
> So second nature has the sea become. [. . .]
> Give of your best this day of Jack Lear's days,
> I know you can do better, make it good;
> Engulf me, take me, I am ready, lass,
> To be as one with you, gigantic death!
>
> (Benison 2019: 35–6)

He survives and the elder sisters place him in a nursing home. A reconciliation with Victoria takes place there although Jack's mind has deteriorated with the symptoms of either dementia or Alzheimer's, so it is unclear whether he recognizes his daughter or not. In the final scene, he suffers two heart attacks, the second fatal, while Victoria tries to persuade him he's undergoing a death by drowning at sea, the end that he wished for in the 'storm scene'. Meanwhile, Edmund has married Freda but cheated on her with Morgana. Freda wields her revenge by stabbing him with a fisherman's gutting knife. The older sisters then decide to settle everything in Norse fashion, with a swordfight to the death:

> *They fight. They are unskilled swordswomen, the fight no less dramatic*
> *for that. With one final slow motion swing they simultaneously strike*
> *each other in the angle of neck and shoulder, the swords to stay lodged.*
>
> (Benison 2019: 56)

A review of the first production began:

> Why adapt Shakespeare? The simple answer would be that, since
> Shakespeare adapted everyone else, why not? Yet while Shakespeare
> transformed the anonymous *True Chronicle History of King Leir* into
> a work of universal significance, Ben Benison's redrafting focuses on
> the fundamental question: what are you supposed to do with the old
> folk?
>
> (Hickling 2008)

To which we might respond: isn't the question of what 'we that are young'
'do with old folk' of 'universal significance'?

6) Designing *King Lear* – a provocation
by Roz Symon

Roz Symon has devised and led education programmes and Shakespeare
workshops for, among others, RSC Education, the Oxford Stage Company,
Shakespeare Association of America and Shakespeare Birthplace Trust. She
was Director of Education at the California Shakespeare Festival and a
visiting tutor at SOTA in San Francisco (now the Ruth Asawa School of the
Arts). More recently, Roz has been working in French universities and is
currently engaged in a project with asylum seekers and refugees, asking
what King Lear *can mean to us in the twenty-first century?*

For A level, my set texts were *Hamlet* and *King Lear. Hamlet* was more than
great. I knew every word, every beat, and was lucky enough to see four amazing
– four dramatically different – productions, which taught me a great deal about
interpreting texts. But *Lear?* In comparison, *Lear* seemed so *dreary.* The only
live production I saw then failed to fire my imagination: three and a half hours
of an old man (long grey hair, long grey beard, long grey druidy frock) trudging
around what looked like Stonehenge, raving. The text we were using didn't
help. It had photos from a 1950s production that made the play seem remote.
The play doesn't feel at all dreary or remote now. Of all Shakespeare's plays, it

seems the most prescient. Still, *Lear* does pose challenges, not least for designers. Your three **design challenges**, if you chose to accept them, are:

a) **Edgar's animals:** The Earl of Gloucester has two sons: 'legitimate Edgar' and 'the Bastard' Edmund – at whose making, the father says (*in Edmund's hearing!*) there was 'good sport'. Earls are higher up the social scale than Dukes and Gloucester lives in a palace – where later his eyes will be gouged out by visiting members of the royal family. Today you might find Edgar in the pages of *Tatler* or *Vogue* magazine, a rich boy who went to Eton or Harrow, hunts, fishes, rides and plays polo. And yet. When duped by his illegitimate brother and forced to flee, Edgar adopts the disguise of 'Poor Tom' – a Bedlam beggar, naked, filthy, ranting, obsessed by sex. It is perhaps the most difficult role in all of Shakespeare – one directors sometimes cut heavily. But it's an important one – Edgar shows us what's on the other side of a palace door if we're brave enough to look: the homeless, the dispossessed. The world is full of those. My first boss in California was handsome, clever, brilliant and hard-working. He had a wife and a beautiful home in an expensive neighbourhood of San Francisco. And he died, after living on the streets of the Mission for five years, died on the streets, quoting Shakespeare. Let's look at the words and images Edgar gives us:

> **EDGAR:**   The foul fiend haunts poor Tom in the voice of a nightingale. Hopdance cries in Tom's belly for two white herring. Croak not, black angel; I have no food for thee.
>
> (3.6.29–32)

Edgar talks of innocents and devils, traitors and gamblers, foul fiends, brothel-frequenters, shepherds and an array of animals – sheep, cats, hogs, dolphins, foxes, wolves, dogs, lions, mice, deer. He says he eats 'the swimming frog, the toad, the tadpole, the wall-newt', that he eats cow-dung and 'swallows the old rat and the ditch-dog; drinks the green mantle of the standing pool' (3.4.125–9) / When asked what his study is, he replies 'How to prevent the fiend, and to kill vermin.' Poor, cold Tom makes weird noises: 'O, do de, do de, do do [. . .] Pillicock sat on Pillicock-hill: Halloo, halloo, loo, loo! [. . .] sum, mun, ha, no, nonny [. . .] Lurk, lurk'. And so on. Your design challenge is to make something of some – or all – of these elements. Could you, for example, turn them in to a floor projection to use in Act 3 scene 4? Or incorporate them into the costume Edgar wears in Act 1 scene 2? Or into a part of the set?

b) **Lear's 'other' Crown:** I am interested in art-based research – using art and making to understand and solve problems. It's a way of knowing that engages realms inaccessible to linear and logical thought. When Lear enters in 4.6, we know all is not well. He has abdicated – something monarchs are not supposed to do – and lost everything. Including his sanity. It is no longer a golden crown he wears on his head. Here is the stage direction given from three different editions: *Enter LEAR [mad]* – New Cambridge Shakespeare ed. Philip Brockbank (1992); *Enter LEAR mad [crowned with wild flowers]* – Arden ed. R.A. Foakes (1997); *Enter LEAR, fantastically dressed with wild flowers* – New Swan ed. Bernard Lott (1974). This is an important prop that, according to F.G. Butler, has consistently been mis-read by editors and critics. Cordelia has already described what her father looks like:

> Why, he was met even now,
> As mad as the vexed sea: singing aloud,
> Crowned with rank fumiter and furrow-weeds,
> With burdocks, hemlock, nettles, cuckoo-flowers,
> Darnel, and all the idle weeds that grow
> In our sustaining corn.

(4.4.1–6)

The clues are there – yet I had missed them. I think of *Lear* as a dark, wintry play that takes place one stormy November night in a bleak landscape. Not so: 'Search every acre of *the high-grown field*', Cordelia says to the soldiers. I look up the plants Cordelia mentions and find bouquets of blues and yellows, delicate pinks and purples, magenta, white and puce. Lear emerges from the storm into a summery world. Digging deeper, I discover the plants have names like ladies' smocks, ragged robin, corn marigold. The plants in mad Lear's crown are beautiful, but they are also toxic, invasive, make you hallucinate – even kill. Hemlock was used as a powerful narcotic and sedative, and is dangerous at all stages of growth. In a world with an increasingly urban population, few of us can know what the flowers look like. We have forgotten their common names, can't picture the colourful array of insects they attract, know nothing of their medicinal uses or their dangers. Shakespeare clearly had a deep connection to nature. The Warwickshire lad was still very much alive in the successful London playwright. These are not randomly chosen plants; they are in Lear's crown for a reason.

Your challenge for Lear's 'other crown' is to incorporate your findings into a design Lear wears when he enters at 4.6 *fantastically dressed*. First, search online for images of – and information about – ragged robin, ladies' smocks, bedlam cowslips, hardocks also known as hoar or white dock, Beggar's Buttons, Gobo, corn blue-bottle, knapweed, harlocks and burdocks – a common, pesky weed that has powerful medicinal qualities and is full of nutrients rural folk call 'Sticklebacks', 'Sticky Jack' or 'Sticky Bobs'. The leaves of fumiter (or fumitory; Latin name *fumus terrae:* smoke of the earth), for example, have a bitter taste and the juice is poisonous but was used in cases of hypochondria and to treat conjunctivitis (interesting in a play in which eyes, sight and blindness are major themes), skin diseases, black jaundice and to cleanse the kidneys. *Do not try any of these at home!* Do though try to come up with a design for mad Lear's headwear, something that perhaps evokes pity for the tyrannical old man?

c) The storm. *King Lear,* a play about climate change: The play moves from palace to bare heath to hovel, a story of loss whose climax is the storm scene. Too late Lear realises he has taken too little care of his country, his people, his family. The angry old man storms off into a wild, stormy night, his Fool in tow.

Consider the following ideas:

- The storm is an external manifestation of Lear's internal distress and turmoil;
- In order for civilization to function, we need to acknowledge humankind's limitations in the face of nature;
- The role of the storm is to bring about powerful transformation;
- The storm is a way of telling inconvenient truths;
- Lear believes the natural world is in collusion with his daughters;
- The storm should be read as a call to environmental activism.

Consider, too, these lines from the play:

- *Storm still, storm still, storm still*
- Poor naked wretches, [. . .] / That bide the pelting of this pitiless storm (3.4.28–9)
- How shall your houseless head and unfed sides, / Your looped and windowed raggedness, defend you / From seasons such as these? (3.4.30–2)
- O, I have ta'en / Too little care of this (3.4.32–3)
- As mad as the vexed sea (4.4.2)
- Blow, winds, and crack your cheeks! Rage, blow!

  You cataracts and hurricanoes, spout

  Till you have drenched our steeples, drowned the cocks!

  You sulphurous and thought-executing fires,

  Vaunt-couriers of oak-cleaving thunderbolts,

  Singe my white head! And thou, all-shaking thunder,

  Smite flat the thick rotundity o'the world!

  Crack nature's moulds, all germens spill at once

  That make ingrateful man!

(3.2.1–9)

Next, ask yourself **what do you have to lose before you realize what you had?** Make a list. Then make a quick outline sketch of a floor-length coat (or other costume) and fill it with images of things that are precious and worth protecting, things you would hate to loose. Finally a question: what did exploring a piece of text using design add to your understanding of *Lear*?

7) *Une tempête* (1969) by Aimé Césaire

Aimé Césaire (1913–2008) was a poet, playwright and politician from Martinique in the Caribbean. Then, as now, Martinique was an overseas department of the French Republic, and this experience of colonial subjection was crucial to Césaire's political philosophy and career, and to his fictional works. *Une tempête* (1969) is a landmark in the history of *The Tempest*. Subtitled 'an adaptation for a black theatre', it boldly recast the play's power dynamics through the lens of colonialism. The characters' names and much of the plot are the same as in Shakespeare, but Ariel is explicitly described as a 'mulatto' (or mixed-race) slave, and Caliban as 'a black slave'. The conflict that drives the action is between these slaves and their white master, Prospero, a callous and brutal man who is himself enslaved to the ideology of white, western supremacism. Caliban's first word is 'uhuru', the Swahili word for 'freedom'; he ends the play singing 'LIBERTY, OH-AY, LIBERTY!' (62). His response to his colonial master is rebellious, whereas Ariel's is defeatist. Furthermore, as Philip Crispin writes, 'Caliban remains true to his own cultural system, living a symbiotic partnership with nature (personified as his mother Sycorax). Césaire celebrates Caribbean ecology throughout' (Césaire 2000: 11), much as Shakespeare in Paradise's adaptation would forty years later (see below). In *Une tempête*'s final scene, everyone leaves the island except Caliban and Prospero; the latter's decision to stay vindicates Caliban's assessment that Prospero is 'like those men who established the colonies / and can no longer live elsewhere. / An old addict, that's what you are' (60). The play ends with Prospero alone onstage and his closing words unwittingly make clear the links between colonialism, ecophobia and environmental degradation.

> Funny, for some time now, we've been invaded by opossums. They're everywhere... Peccaries, wild boar, all those unclean beasts! But, above all, opossums. Oh, those eyes! And that hideous leer! You'd swear the jungle wanted to invade the cave... But I'll defend myself... I will not let my work perish... (*Roaring.*) I will defend civilisation! (*He fires [his gun] in all directions.*) They've got what was coming to them... Now, this way, I'll have some peace for a blessed while... But it's cold... Funny, the climate's changed... Cold on this island... Have to think about making a fire... Ah well, my old Caliban, we're the only two left on this island, just you and me. You and me! You-me! Me-you! But what the hell's he up to? (*Roaring.*) Caliban!

> *In the distance, above the sound of surf and the mewing of birds, snatches of CALIBAN's song can be heard.*

> LIBERTY, OH-AY! LIBERTY!

> (Césaire 2000: 62)

8) *Shakespeare in Paradise's The Tempest* (2009)

Shakespeare in Paradise was founded in 2009. It was the first, and to date, only international Shakespeare festival in the English-speaking Caribbean. Its inaugural performance was The Tempest. *We discussed that production and its colonial and climatic contexts with Shakespeare in Paradise co-founder* **Nicolette Bethel** *(NB), the show's director* **Patti-Anne Ali** *(PA), and* **Craig Pinder** *(CP), who co-directed and played Prospero.*

Paul Prescott: Why did you chose *The Tempest* for your first ever production?

Nicolette Bethel: *The Tempest* had been used throughout the twentieth century to present the central tropes of anticolonial thinking. Prospero, the magician, the invader of the island, the saviour, the civilizer, the teacher of language, the ruler, is an apt personification of the British in the colonies. And Caliban's very name suggests the Caribbean region. Caliban has been associated with the people of the Caribbean by writers and directors from the 1940s to the present. Shakespeare is, for the Bahamian people, a sort of Prospero. A writer whose language we may be able to speak, but never to understand. Whose art we might learn to appreciate only insofar that it reminds us how far we are from creating it. So *The Tempest* opened up a Bahamian dialogue with our colonisers, with our postcolonial present, and it allowed us to process our changing environment.

Our whole existence is the expression, explicit and subliminal, of living against and amid hurricanes. Historically, the Bahamas were understood to sit outside the Hurricane Belt. Of course, that was before we began to feel the effects of climate change. Recent devastating hurricanes have included Joaquin, which hit Long Island in 2015, Matthew, which hit the capital Nassau in 2016, and most tragically in September 2019, Hurricane Dorian, which destroyed entire communities on the islands of Abaco and Grand Bahama. So in choosing *The Tempest*, we chose a play that speaks both to our colonial past and our environmental present.

PP: Was your production set in the present day?

Patti-Anne Ali: Yes. We tried to create a setting that would be familiar enough to our audiences, most of whom had never read or seen *The Tempest*. So Prospero was a CEO and his brother had taken over his company and banished him. Antonio was now CEO of a big, multi-billion-dollar hotel conglomerate that wanted to develop the island, an island that was sort of like the Bahamas, although we called it Prosperity Cay. And so the hurricane conjured up by Prospero brings all of the people who are negotiating this deal – the company's top executives and the government officials who were negotiating with them – to a point of crisis. So we were setting it in the

Bahamas not only in terms of hurricanes in our region, but also in terms of the socioeconomic reality as well.

PP: How was the audience introduced to that backstory of the warring CEOs and the hotel development and so on?

PA: We put the backstory in a programme note. We wrote, for example: 'Prospero is not the exiled Duke of Milan, but rather the CEO of the Hotel Milan, an exclusive resort in the Bahamas and a family company.' We also tweaked and updated some of the lines of exposition in Act One, Scene Two.

Craig Pindar: The idea was that Prospero had taken a back seat in the running of the company. He was obsessed with studying voodoo and other forms of magic. He was then ousted in a corporate coup and has ended up in this harsh place, with only his books and his daughter for company. And, of course, Caliban and Ariel. Caliban thinks it's his island. It's a bit like the Native American story, I suppose. At first it's all fine, they share the sweetcorn and everything's hunky dory. But then – according to Prospero – there's an attempted assault and Prospero proceeds to treat Caliban with utter contempt.

NB: In our adaptation, we saw Ariel as kind of like the house servant and Caliban as the field servant, the inside and the outside. Ariel is the one who keeps obediently doing her master's bidding, but looking for a freedom that Prospero keeps deferring. And Caliban is more obviously resistant.

PA: Having been born and grown up in a region that came out of 500 years of colonial hegemonic rule, the issues of oppression and liberation are deep, ancestral, resonant themes. I always felt as though the real monster here was Prospero and that the monstrous depiction of Caliban was the product of the lens that Shakespeare had at the time. I always felt as though, in the Caliban that I read, there was a dignity, a humanity, a real tragedy happening in that character. So the dignity and the humanity and the intelligence of Caliban is what I wanted. And without interfering with any of the lines as written. This was all in the process, all in the rehearsal process, all in the characterization, in the embodiment, in the backstory. What if that clash of the monster versus the human was actually flipped? What if the greed and the urge for dominion of characters such as Prospero, Antonio and Sebastian was shown to be the truly monstrous thing in the play?

NB: And we also had Ariel doing the Black Power salute right at the end of the masque.

PA: Yes. Throughout the play, we built Ariel's desire for freedom. There was a consistent motivation for freedom that built and built and built until the end when that moment came. This was her on the cusp of her liberty.

PP: How much of the text did you rewrite?

CP: There were rewrites throughout. We wanted to use Bahamian words and natural images whenever we could. We also wanted to tell this story using the local Bahamian annual festival of Junkanoo, which is the most significant annual cultural event on the Bahamian calendar. The idea was to represent the vibrantly colourful costumes and stirring drumbeat music of Junkanoo and integrate that into the religious ideology of Haitian voodoo – Haitians make up a significant portion of the population of the Bahamas. So Patti made the masque especially full of pan-Caribbean references. Instead of classical European goddesses, we drew on Haitian mythology and the female spirits known as Ezili who communicate between the mortal and divine worlds. I'll read you some lines spoken by Ezili welcoming Yemaya, protector of women, to the celebration:

> **EZILI.** Yemaya, mermaid-queen, your rich shoals
> Of grouper, lobster, snapper, conch, and schools
> Of grunts and jacks and tasty goggle-eye,
> And sharks and 'cudas [barracudas] slinking slyly by;
> Your shores with white and ocean-twillèd sands,
> Whose balmy gulfstream at your hest commands
> The twined seaweed to make your nymphs chaste crowns
> To wear while playing in your own deep sounds,
> And drive the love-starved young fishermen mad
> And your sea-coast, sterile and rocky hard,
> Where you yourself do sun—the Queen o' th' sky,
> Whose love-charged messenger am I,
> Bids you leave these; and with her sovereign grace,
> Here on this grass-plot, in this very place,
> To come and sport. Her peacocks fly amain.
> Approach, Yemaya, her to entertain.

So all those references were changed to make it ecologically more friendly to our local environment and to make it more accessible.

PP: How did the show end?

PA: There was a specific timing that I wanted with the music, with the lights and with Prospero and Caliban. I wanted the very last image to be Prospero and Caliban facing each other as equals. Prospero's last line is 'let your indulgence set me free'. And he said that to Caliban.

PP: Was the idea that on some level that Prospero was seeking forgiveness himself from that?

PA: Yes, absolutely. For me, it wasn't just about the audience or about Prospero. It was about reparations.

9) Elizabeth Freestone's *The Tempest* for the Royal Shakespeare Company (2023)

Elizabeth Freestone directed The Tempest *for the Royal Shakespeare Company, Stratford-upon-Avon, in 2023. It followed the best practices outlined in the Theatre Green Book (REF) and was almost certainly the most sustainable production ever staged at the Royal Shakespeare Theatre. Freestone is also the co-author (with Jeanie O'Hare) of* 100 Plays to Save the World *(2021).*

Paul Prescott: How important was wider community collaboration to this production?

Elizabeth Freestone: Very. We collaborated with a local community group, 'Rubbish Friends', who are a volunteer street-cleaning organization. We worked with a local forestry association who supplied us with all the trees and organic materials. And we partnered with local schools who made various bits and pieces of the show from their own recycling. So community was central to the project and gave it a kind of galvanizing creative momentum. My impression from talking to these partners was that it always had a kind of a proactive, progressive, positive energy about it and became creatively empowering for everybody.

PP: So every prop item, every scene item, very piece of costume had been used before somewhere?

EF: Yes, in some capacity. I think we ended up buying a tiny handful of things but I would guess 98 per cent of everything you saw on stage had had a previous life.

PP: What do you see in *The Tempest* that gives us grounds for ecological optimism?

EF: Well, I have a moral position that I think dystopianism is too easy: presenting only the end game is theatrically lazy and ethically irresponsible. I also feel like we all know what that looks like. We've seen it on films a billion times. But hope is harder. Hope is complex. It's hard won and it's easily lost and it's fragile, but it's deeply powerful. And I think the play is redemptive. It has become very fashionable for theatre-makers to sort of undermine Shakespeare's hopeful endings, and present them as naive or sentimental because we're all so cool these days and we're fabulously über-ironic about everything. I think it's much harder to ask audiences and characters to stare genuine forgiveness in the face. And I don't think that is naive or sentimental. I think it's brave, even radical. It doesn't mean everything has to be resolved entirely. In my production, Antonio kind of crumpled at Prospero's feet. And it was painful. It was agony. It was agony to watch that happen. Prospero wept as Ariel left. Caliban didn't quite know how to face Miranda at the end, brought face to face with the woman he'd tried to rape. But we showed people being brought to the moment where they have to confront those ideas. I feel like there is something in the play that asks us to genuinely look at the possibility of redemption. In this production, interpersonal healing could then lead to the possibility of social transformation.

PP: In your book *100 Plays to Save the World*, you describe Prospero as consisting of a number of identities: the colonizer, the enslaver of the more-than-human, and the refugee. Which of those came into focus in your show?

EF: I would hope that the character has the potential to be all of those things. I think all kind of ecocritical interrogations of these plays should be multifaceted. I'm a little bit suspicious of, you know, *The Tempest* just being about deforestation or colonization or whatever. I think it should be able to be about many of those things. You could easily do a production of this play with Prospero as a sort of geo-engineer, very powerful and hubristic. Or you could do a production where Prospero is attempting to be a very benign power in conversation with the elements in a different way, and that that was the reason for their usurpation and exile. They can be both a refugee and a perpetrator. So it has the potential, I think, to be read in any or all of those ways.

PP: And did you always know you were going to have a female Prospero?

EF: I knew in my head I was picturing a parent because I've never really got on board with the kind of grumpy old man reading of Prospero. I think people have often conflated Shakespeare's end of life retirement as this being a retirement actor part. I wanted to break it away from that. For me it is clearly about a parent making the best of a survival situation. I was thinking about love and humour and heartbreak and great strength and great vulnerability and Alex just kept coming into my head. Casting Alex Kingston opened up this sort of ecofeminist reading of the play. It makes the character pragmatic and loving and protective and it lets us suddenly reframe everything that had happened to her through a different filter. So whether that was the misogyny of the treatment when she was usurped from being the ruler of Milan, or realizing that people might be frightened of a woman with that amount of knowledge, or the parental truth of raising a child. The idea of survival was key: surviving on an island with a man who tried to rape your daughter, wondering about what might happen to you or her if you break your leg when you're out fishing or something. Wondering what kind of future your daughter could have. And it also chimed ecologically. We know from recent UN reports that women are much more liable to be vulnerable to climate events. And I guess having a female Prospero subliminally also suggests a Gaia-like Earth goddess as the understory of the play, which we activated in the masque scene.

PP: Why else do you think *The Tempest* suits an eco reading?

EF: It's a survival situation. Miranda and Prospero have to eke out their own existence in these environmental circumstances. And the island is then a closed space environment, which let's everybody on it be vulnerable. I'm really interested in the wreck as a social leveler – the Boatswain says 'what care these roarers for the name of king?' – and the kind of equitability that comes in the face of a climate event. And then I guess there's the real events that obviously inspired the play, whether the accounts of shipwrecks in the Atlantic or the 1607 floods in Stratford-upon-Avon. It's about being at the mercy of the elements or attempting to be in command of them. And about how people behave in the face of that power. I think it's also both a blue and a green play, with ideas and imagery of both the water and of the land.

PP: Who or what was Ariel in your production?

EF: Ariel and their related spirits are the more-than-human creatures of the place, in some form. Our island has been made toxic and polluted with human rubbish. We tried to make it so that the spirits were cleansing the island of rubbish by turning it into the things that they could then use back against the humans. So washed-up plastic bags became the harpy that then brought the baddies to face the consequences of their actions. Big plastic tubs became the dogs that chased Trinculo and Stephano. As the play went on, the spirits removed pieces of rubbish and we saw them begin to release the island from human pollution.

PP: And Caliban?

EF: Caliban is aware of the life of the island in a different way to everybody else. He's a lost boy. Given the timeline of events that we get told in the beginning, we worked out he's only a few years older than Miranda. He remembers enough about Sycorax because he must have told some of the story to Prospero. So we kind of worked out how old he might have been when Sycorax died, maybe about five or six, and then he's left alone. So we imagined his life as a boy who was left at a old enough age that he didn't just die in the face of the elements, but not so old that he could really manage for himself. So then he's on his own on the island for about four years. And then up rock Prospero and Miranda, who then meet this feral boy and take him in. He becomes a son, and a brother, and that's been the bulk of their backstory together, and, as they all agree, an extremely positive experience. And then of course the children get to sexual maturity and the dynamics begin to shift. And we end up in this situation where he attempts to rape Miranda. And for us, that was the kind of inciting incident of the whole play. That's why Prospero raises the storm, because she realizes they've got to get off the island because she can no longer live on an island with a young man who is now physically very strong and sexually powerful. That's why Prospero did what she did to Caliban. I'm not suggesting that as a justification for it, but that's the complexity of that relationship. It's recent and it's in that context.

PP: We heard languages other than English in this production. What was the thinking behind that?

EF: Many people in the company spoke different languages because it was a diverse company that was globally representative. In rehearsals we talked a lot about freedom, and what freedom really is. It's of course physical liberation. But also Prospero seeks an intellectual freedom. Miranda perhaps finds a social freedom in not being brought up at court. Gonzalo describes a liberal utopia. Stephano seeks a liberation from strict hierarchy. There are so many examples of different types of freedom in the play. I was doing some research into the co-occurrence of biodiversity hotspots and language hotspots. As biodiverse habitats are diminishing, we're also losing languages at the same rate. So maybe two weeks before we went into preview, we began talking in rehearsals about whether there a way that we could express kind of culturally, linguistically, what freedom might mean to some of the characters in the play, especially the ones who are also seeking their physical freedom. So Heledd Gwynn (who is Welsh) as Ariel sang a Welsh translation of 'Where the bee sucks', which became her expression of freedom as she flies away at the end. And then Tommy Sim'aan who played Caliban is of British Iraqi heritage. In consultation with North African and Middle Eastern scholars, we worked out what language Caliban might have learnt from his mother. We know Sycorax is from Algiers, so we researched a range of Algerian languages. In our modern timeline, and with the 1960s revolutionary backstory we created for her, we learnt she might speak Taqbaylit and Darija. We wondered what she would have taught him to say? So he ends up speaking both of those languages, and some Arabic too, when he repeats the key phrase 'This island's mine'. And at the very end, as he exits into the forest, he says, 'Mama, I'm home, Mama, I'm free.'

PP: What did the masque allow you to do within this world?

EF: The masque is a puzzle in the play. I knew straight away that it was not going to be some sort of pseudo-Roman, you know, Ben Jonson in-joke.

That kind of artificiality completely takes me out of the experience and the emotional narrative I'm trying to craft. I *did* know that the masque causes some kind of breakdown in Prospero, but I wasn't sure why. Shakespeare uses it to pull a big emotional lever that then leads into one of the most extraordinary speeches he ever wrote. So it can't just be a theatrical set-piece. The breakthrough came in rehearsal when we took away the Roman names Juno and Ceres and Iris and we started calling them by what those gods represent. So Juno became Sky, Ceres Earth, and Iris became Rain. The moment we did that, we realised how the masque fits into an ecological reading of the whole thing. These are the goddesses of those natural elements and they are hurting and they are in pain and they are burdened with all the terrible things that humankind has done to them. But they can see that a contract between these two young people holds a promise of healing. It became like a deal, with the goddesses saying 'Okay, we'll look after you and we'll bless your love'. We had the lovers plant a seedling – it wasn't just a ritual of marriage, it was a ritual of healing and regeneration. This vision, almost a dream, of a new world was too much for Prospero. She sees that and thinks, 'Oh my God, my generation has messed up. What world are we leaving these young people?'

PP: Boomer's remorse?

EF: Yeah. Basically, 'We've really, really messed up and we can't get to a point of healing unless I complete the task of the day, which is to bring all these people together, to sort Caliban out, and to bring Alonzo here, and. . . oh my God!'. And so she sort of explodes with the weight and the heaviness of it all.

PP: So what, in your mind, happens to the island when the humans have left?

EF: We deliberately left some rubbish tangled up with everything at the end. Our footprint is here. We can't rid the earth of our presence however hard we try. It was more about leaving it in a state that it could be better lived with rather than a complete cleansing. I suppose there's a version of the story where Caliban stays on the island and his awareness of the spirit life of the more-than-human-world helps him to create a better society for himself, or at least achieve some sort of eco balance. Or I guess there's a version where he doesn't learn that and he exploits resources and then the cycle repeats itself.

6

Eco-theatre

'Thou earth, thou! Speak!': Or, how to make Shakespearean eco-theatre

*Please note that this chapter contains the names of
deceased Indigenous people.*

We cannot miss him; he does make our fire,
Fetch in our wood, and serves in offices
That profit us. – What ho, slave! Caliban,
　　Thou earth, thou: Speak!

(Tempest 1.2.311–14)

When Prospero calls forth Caliban in *The Tempest*, he commands: 'Thou earth, thou! Speak!' (1.2.312). 'Earth' is used here as an insult to mean 'dull, dead matter' (Onions 1986: 84). Caliban, assuming Prospero demands fuel, retorts: 'There's wood enough within' (1.2.315), further reminding him: 'This island's mine' (1.2.332). Here, Caliban may be read as an emblem of exploitation yet resistance; enslaved yet agential. He is also allied to resource consumption, inviting interpretations of Western colonial exploitation as well as historical and continuing attitudes towards resource extraction. Digging a little deeper into Shakespeare's 'earth', we may also note that he uses the term in various ways: from 'lifeless materiality', to 'country', 'land,' or the 'human body' (Onions 1986: 84). Early modern 'earth' thus encompassed vital and inert matter; the external environment and the internal self. It perhaps comes closest to the later science of ecology, not introduced until Ernst Haeckel's conception of the 'whole science of the relations of the organism to the environment [. . .] partly organic, partly inorganic' (1866: 286–8). Earth unites all material phenomena. Shakespeare's description of Caliban-as-earth thus easily lends itself to ecological adaptation.

Eco-adaptation demands 'reconceptualization of the nature and purpose of mimesis' (representation) and requires 'finding ways to represent the more-than-human world on stage that do not ineradicably "other" nature' (Arons and May 2012: 2). How can the Earth then 'speak' through Shakespeare's text in performance? One of ecocriticism's foundational scholars, Jonathan Bate, argues that the 'ecocritical project always involves speaking for its subject rather than as its subject, a critic [. . .] cannot speak as a tree' (1991: 72). Lawrence Buell similarly notes: 'One can speak a word for Nature' but 'self-evidently no human can speak *as* the environment, *as* nature, *as* a non-human animal' (original emphasis; 2005: 7). Humans are of course a part of nature – any perceived separation is illusory. Nevertheless, representing Earth on stage requires a degree of speaking *as* other individuals, species and environments. Eco-adaptation therefore requires sensitivity and a light touch, both with respect to textual interpretation and production practices. Our task is to pay close attention to the plays' multihued and diverse presences, uncovering their more-than-human agency while weaving in our creative visions. An eco-Shakespeare adaptation therefore asks, though in a very different sense from Prospero: 'Thou earth, thou! Speak!'

This introduction is subtitled 'how to make Shakespearean eco-theatre' but of course there is no one method and practices continue to evolve. Here we aim to present practical and theoretical guidance for your own eco-adaptation toolbox. We begin by unpacking the underpinning concepts of performance ecology, ecodramaturgy and ecoscenography before moving to place-based adaptation and material impact. We conclude with an 'eco-Shakespeare checklist' for creating your own work. This chapter therefore urges you to draw on your own unique talents and inspired creativity to perform, write, and create with boldness and with passion, for 'The tide is now' (*TGV* 2.2.15).

A Shakespeare performance ecosystem

In her landmark article 'Greening the Theater: Taking Ecocriticism from Page to Stage', Theresa J. May argues that 'ecocritical analyses of dramatic texts do not tap the rich ecological implications of embodied artistic representation' (2005: 85). In contrast, she considers live performance to offer a bridge between metaphoric and material worlds in an 'organic exchange of meaning-making' (May ibid.). May therefore suggests that to discover the 'ecology of theater and its potential to awaken ecological sensibilities in us, ecocritics must come into the theatre and partake' (ibid.). Randall Martin similarly holds 'Shakespeare's greatest possibilities for becoming our eco-contemporary [. . .] lie not in academic discourse but in performance' (2015: 167). Rather than decorative or utilitarian backdrops for human-centred relations, he considers imagined and material environments to have 'independent agency and determining energies of their own' (ibid.). Together with theatre's in-the-moment bodily interactions across players, characters and audiences, Martin determines that

Shakespeare's 'affective and imaginative power' offers a dynamic emotional mix to be harnessed for ecological performance (ibid.).

How, though, do we apply these concepts to creating eco-Shakespeare productions? We first need to understand a little more about how theatre operates as an 'organic exchange of meaning making' if we are to harness Shakespeare's 'affective and imaginative power'. These concepts and practices may help:

1   **Theatre ecology**, for a theoretical basis of how to utilize theatre's circular energy exchange,

2   **Ecodramaturgy**, to analyze and adapt the text through an ecological lens,

3   **Ecoscenography**, to design and create ecological productions.

The following section offers a brief overview of these concepts and breaks down their key ideas and terms.

Why theatre? Theatre ecology and the power of live performance

There are numerous eco-adaptation options open to us beyond theatre, including mediums such as poetry, painting, photography, sculpture and so forth. So why theatre? We focus on theatre due to the plays' original performance context and current eco-theatre's vibrancy. Theatre can also be an impactful medium for ecological messaging, as explained by theatre ecology.

'The terms "theatre ecology" and "performance ecology" reference theatres and performances as ecosystems' (Kershaw 2009: 15). Although often used interchangeably, theatre ecology specifically refers to the theatrical medium, whereas performance ecology encompasses the idea of performativity more generally. Both terms recognize that theatre 'does not float above the material world in some aesthetic ether, but rather plays a part in an immensely complex global system' (Glotfelty 1996: xix). What we create leaves an imprint – mentally, emotionally, and on the Earth.

Theatre ecology builds on the earlier 'environmental theatre' movement of the 1960s. Environmental theatre lifted performance out of the proscenium arch stage arrangement and its implied spectator/performance separation. This led to experimental forms of staging, such as immersive, site-specific, found spaces, and interactive performance. The concept of the *mise-en-scène* (stage design and arrangement) was extended to envelop actors, stage, audience and society (Brook 1968: 44). All performance elements were therefore considered to be vital, or 'alive'. Theatre ecology extends this idea beyond the production to nature itself. Neither production nor nature are static, objectified, devoid of agency, nor viewed from an anthropocentric perspective where 'we are on nature's stage, but we talk and think of it as if it is simply the set-dressing for ours' (Bottoms 2007: 123).

Instead, audience and performance site are connected within an ecosystem that is itself enmeshed within the wider planetary system. The field incorporates environmental philosophies, such as *ecocentricism* (earth-centred ethics) and *holism* (everything is connected within the planetary ecosystem). Important later theoretical concepts include *new materialism* (Bennett 2010) (matter as active and vibrant), *entanglement* (Barad 2007) (a quantum notion of interaction), and *transcorporeality* (Alaimo 2010) (iter- and intraconnected fluidity). This means that matter collides in the performance moment to create a lively and affective event. Theatre ecology therefore considers how live performance can exert pressure on and possibly transform our conception of and attitude toward ecological reality (Arons and May 2012: 8).

Theatre ecology explains performance's impact on audiences through *phenomenological* (consciousness, experienced sensorially), *embodied* (tangible experience), *postcognitivist* (the interconnected mind-body-environment) conceptions, as well as *reflexivity* (affecting and affected by other agents). Put simply, theatre can generate a transformative atmosphere through the *kinaesthetic* (sensory) experience of the performance moment that may generate an empathic response. This can be explained through mirror neurons in the brain and body rhythms, whereby the performer's emotions and body movements stimulate a response in audience minds and bodies. This is an automatic neurocognitive process assisted by a *(syn) aesthetic* (sensation and perception), *ludic* (spontaneous and fun) play within *visceral* (felt) performance (Machon 2009: 13). Because the theatrical ecosystem not only stimulates thought but generates feeling, it offers a powerful cocktail for ecological messaging.

As Bruce McConachie argues, performance may have the potential to create positive ecological impact because it can unite the audience, motivating political engagement and providing a context for political change (2008: 97). Because the audience, actors and stage environment are part of a reciprocal ecosystem creating atmosphere, we must be alert to how we utilize interpret and stage Shakespeare's plays for maximum impact. Techniques can be divided into two practices – *ecodramaturgy* for textual adaptation and *ecoscenography* for design and staging.

Ecodramaturgy

What is ecodramaturgy? First, what is dramaturgy? The word derives from the ancient Greek *dramatourgia* (drama + working/making) and since the eighteenth century has related to the interpretation and creation of a performance. Dramaturgy extends from the analysis of a play's themes, structure, perspectives and historical context to the expression of its language and movement on stage. At its most simplified, dramaturgy is the theory and practice of dramatic composition. By logical extension, *eco*dramaturgy is the ecological theory and ecological practice of dramatic composition.

Ecodramaturgy was coined by Theresa J. May, who defines the practice as 'theatre and performance making that puts ecological reciprocity and community at the center of its theatrical and thematic intent' (Arons and May 2012: 4). May divided ecodramaturgy into three different forms of engagement: 1) lived experiences of historically excluded communities from dominantly white and economically privileged theatre-making and spectatorship; 2) materially sustainably production and 3) adapting plays to present-day and site-specific contexts of the 'community it serves, and the politics into which it speaks' (2018: 1–18 in Martin 2022: np). Martin adds a fourth, vitally important, principle: 'ecodramaturgy also accounts for the interests of non-human bio-communities and earth-systems' (2022: np).

How can you utilize ecodramaturgy for your own adaptations? Consider again the following formula previous discussed in greater depth in relation to Shakespeare and Yosemite's 2018 eco-adaptation of *A Midsummer Night's Dream* (Brokaw and Prescott 2022):

1 **Reduce** the play's length to remove 'obscurity; redundancy; lack of poetic or comedic quality; '(ir)relevance to the production's concept and messages; potential to cause offence' (311),

2 **Rewrite** passages of the play for relevance to context and message, including renaming characters, and integrating local and/or Indigenous languages (311–12),

3 **Recycle** costume, props and music (312).

This offers a practical basis for eco-adaptation. Gretchen Minton further divides the eco-adaptation process into textual changes for relevance to topic and place: setting, characters, naming, language, environmental angles and activism. Approaching Shakespeare's plays in this way can 'encourage audiences to think about language, character, and history, which can open up avenues for change, reconciliation, and regeneration' (Minton in 'Montana InSite Theatre' np).

We highlight that activism is particularly important for eco-adaptation, given that the ultimate aim is to create positive environmental change. Ecodramaturgy is therefore politically artistic by nature. Performance ecology meets activism in a deliberately unstable space of critical reflection of the human 'self', recognizing that such identity is culturally constructed and complicit in the exploitation of oppressed cultures, races, genders and the more-than-human world. This can take multiple creative forms and traverse genres. Rob Conkie's comic book eco-adaptation of *Cymbeline* for Randall Martin's Global Cymbeline Project, for example, integrated political satire, pop culture, art and theatre.

Conkie's ecodramaturgical process interwove direct response to the centre-right Australian Liberal-National Coalition's (ALP) support for coal power, interwoven with traditional Shakespearean language and costume,

FIGURE 6.1 *Image frets for* Cymbeline, 2024. *(Image by Rob Conkie.)*

and critique of the United Arab Emirates' state oil company, Adnoc. It is an example of ecodramaturgical practice in direct response to environmental challenges. Exploring these boundary zones of genre builds on Cathy Turner's concept of dramaturgy as considering 'processual and open-ended structures' that admit the 'aleatory, entropic and chaotic, examining the potential for multiple narratives, frames and forms of textuality' (Turner 2010: 150).

The directors of each of the seven productions in the Global Cymbeline Project, or *Cymbeline in the Anthropocene*, were encouraged to adapt the play to their local environments, political commitments, and community relations. Martin offered directors five ecodramaturgical prompts:

1   Land uses and abuses,
2   Getting physical with the Anthropocene,
3   Ecofeminist adaptation,
4   Decolonization and Indigenous ecologies,
5   Levelling up eco-Shakespeare.

(2022: np)

As Martin highlights, ecodramaturgy 'seeks to awaken awareness of the urgency of freeing the non-human world from oppression by relentless human extraction, commodification, and servitude' (ibid.). To achieve this, we 'need to liberate ourselves from traditional mythologies and cultural narratives of human exceptionalism', including 'entitlements to subdue nature with the utilitarian genius of modern technology' (ibid.). Ecodramaturgy therefore employs concepts such as new materialist *diffraction*, reading texts materially against themes and contexts, and *posthumanism*, decentring humans and viewing us as deeply entangled with other lifeforms.

We can see this process in action in Gretchen E. Minton's eco-adaptation of *Twelfth Night, Salt Waves Fresh*. Minton's adaptation was based in North Queensland and addressed climate-change-driven weather disruptions and the chemical bleaching of the world's largest reef, the Great Barrier Reef.

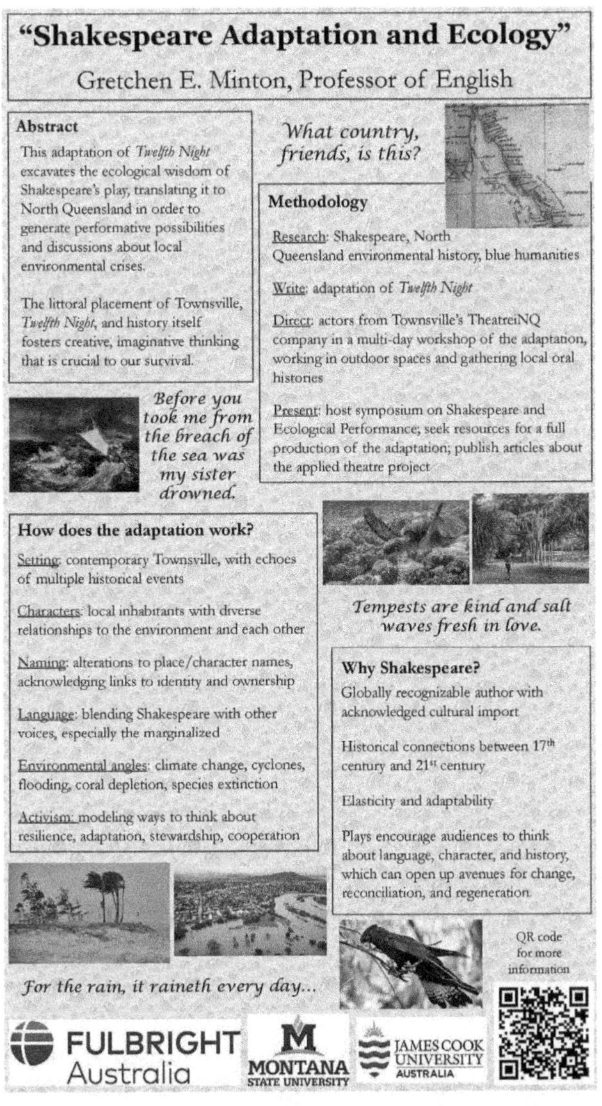

FIGURE 6.2 *Poster image for the Fulbright Australia gala event, February 2023. (By Gretchen E. Minton.)*

Minton adapted Shakespeare's narrative to interweave community stories and Indigenous knowledge. Characters were also transformed for relevance to topic and place – Olivia's fool Feste, for example, was reconceived as an endangered Red-Tailed Black Cockatoo, blurring species boundaries and placing the more-than-human as a central part of the play's action. *Salt Waves Fresh* is therefore a prime example of adapting Shakespeare's plays to place.

Place-based ecodramaturgy

Place-based adaptation includes sensitivity to community. As Katherine Steele Brokaw highlights, in thinking about 'community Shakespeare', we are 'thinking about its embeddedness in anthropological communities – the groupings of people with shared localities and/or concerns' (2017: 445). This includes 'valuing marginalized communities and local knowledge' (ibid.). It recognizes that '[c]limate change, pollution, and biodiversity loss disproportionately affect the people who are least responsible for creating these catastrophes' (Brokaw 2024: 94). Place-based ecodramaturgy therefore requires centring the traditionally marginalized voices in communities, and challenging 'traditionally white, privileged, male, and heteronormative power structures' that exclude BIPOC, female and nonbinary, LGBTQ+, disabled, and neurodivergent people (95). Community also includes the more-than-human community. 'Place' therefore encompasses land, animals, more-than-human living beings and ecological systems. Claire Hansen describes place-based Shakespeare as 'positioning place as a complex, multiperspectival phenomenon with stories and voices' (2023b: iii). Place becomes a 'partner', whether in the learning process or performance (ibid.).

An additional useful concept frequently omitted from eco-theatrical considerations of place is *genius loci,* Latin for 'spirit of place', or the 'intangible quality of a material place, perceived both physically and spiritually' that reveals itself 'through visible, tangible and perceivable non-material features' (Vecco 2020: 225). Why is this important? Thinking about the spirit of place prevents us merely reproducing traditional Shakespeare in an outdoor setting to ensure it ecologically responds to place thematically as well as materially. To consider the land's spirit also brings us closer to performance ecology's notion of circularity and reciprocity and invites more careful listening to the land's multiple voices. This also intersects with Traditional Ecological Knowledge.

Integrating Traditional Ecological Knowledge

Traditional Ecological Knowledge (TEK), often used synonymously with Indigenous Knowledge Systems (IKS), is 'neither static, unchanging, or relegated to the past' but a 'living system of environmental governance rooted in indigenous cosmologies as they relate to environmental change and challenges over many generations' (Latulippe and Klenk 2020: 8). Diverse and vastly different Indigenous people the world over have numerous cosmologies recognizing human-environment interrelationships and responsibilities to what multiple Australian Aboriginal First Nations People express as 'care for Country'. 'Indigenous people are connected to their Country and to each other through totems, law, language, song, story, dance, and through lived experience and knowledge passed across generations over millennia' ('Deadly Story' 2021).

TEK and INS incorporate nuanced understandings of natural patterns and cycles still not recognized within colonized countries. Within northern Australia, for instance, only two seasons are officially recognized – wet and dry. 'Senior knowledge holders of the Ngan'gi set of languages from the Daly River region, Northern Territory', on the other hand, 'recognise 13 overarching seasons within each annual weather cycle' (Woodward and McTaggart 2019 in DCCEEW 2021: np). Changes in seasonal features such as the speargrass Wurr (*Sorghum intrans*) indicate seasonal lifecycle evens and biological indicators of food resources, guiding harvesting (ibid.). Drought, bushfire, disintegration of river systems, biodiversity extinction, erosion of soils and ocean acidification are direct consequences of Western industrial agricultural practices supported by an extractive economy that erases place.

How can Shakespearean eco-adaptation inform better understanding of land-management practices when the early modern Shakespeare is so far removed from Indigenous Knowledge Systems? It would be misplaced and inappropriate to align the English Renaissance playwright to Indigenous ways of knowing. It is also essential to prevent appropriation and seek Indigenous leadership and consultancy. What Shakespeare's plays can do, however, is point us to paying closer attention to the subtleties and minutiae of environments. Like Ngan'gi attention to seasonal cycles and species, we may note how closely the plays reflect ecological elements and processes. In *Dream,* we find diverse topographies 'on hill, in dale, forest or mead' (2.1.83) and seasonal change noted by 'When wheat is green, when hawthorn buds appear' (1.1.184). In *The Tempest,* 'banks with pioned and twilled brims, / Which spongy April at thy hest betrims' (4.1.63–4) introduces the change of season. In *Lear,* 'shadowy forests' meet 'plenteous rivers and wide-skirted meads' (1.1.64–5) and characters are described meteorologically with 'Sunshine and rain at once' (4.3.19).

The plays, through their early modern sense of entanglement with natural processes and a closer relationship to the more-than-human, offer us a more ecologically enmeshed way of viewing our own environments today. We may glimpse this, for example, in Antonio's description of humans as the ocean in the *The Tempest*: 'Ebbing men, indeed' (2.1.227–8). Similarly, Ceres, divine personification of the rainbow, unites nature and selfhood: 'And with each end of thy blue bow dost crown / My bosky acres and my unshrubbed down, / Rich scarf to my proud earth' (4.1.80–2). This added Classical spiritual element, though secular in an early modern sense, nevertheless imbues landscape, human and spirit.

Shakespeare's close alignment of self and environment can be more impactfully informed through Indigenous Knowledges in place-based adaptations. In the Great Lakes region of North America, for example, 'Anishinaabe and Haudenosaunee theoretical frameworks explain *how* one knows is inseparable from *what* one knows, that is, it is inseparable from the world "out there", the land itself, which is alive, intelligent, and willful, and from the values, moral principles, and laws that govern creation and proper conduct' (Latulippe and Klenk 2020: 8). Key concepts include the entwined sense of self-land, physical-social-environmental-spiritual connection, and kinship, or kincentric ecology. The notion of kincentricism was coined by Enrique Salmón as an awareness that 'comes after years of listening to and recalling stories about the land' (2000: 1327). To think kincentrically is to have 'an awareness that life in any environment is viable only when humans view the life surrounding them as kin', and that humans are 'one aspect of the complexity of life' (1332).

Currently, while postcolonial Shakespeare is a vibrant field, TEK and IKS have not yet been substantially integrated within eco-adaptation scholarship and practice. This differs from First Nations and Indigenous Shakespearean performance, such as the Noongar Shakespeare Project, encompassing Yirra Yaakin's *Shakespeare's Sonnets* in Noongar language (Southern Western Australia) at the Globe Theatre's Cultural Olympiad and a current full-length adaptation and translation of *Macbeth*. Similarly, Renelita Arluk's *Pawākan Macbeth*, co-presented by Neptune Theatre and Prismatic Arts Festival told through a combination of Shakespeare's original text, today's English and Plains Cree, is inspired by shared stories from Elders in the Treaty 6 region of Canada. These Indigenous productions are essential to diversifying Shakespearean adaptation but not expressly concerned with ecology.

The process has begun – Minton's *Salt Waves Fresh*, for instance, integrated Indigenous knowledge to 'think about resilience, adaptation, stewardship, cooperation' ('Montana InSite Theatre' 2023). Within expressly ecological adapatation, however, Indigenous-led ecodramaturgy is required for more comprehensively TEK principles and maintaining sovereignty of knowledge systems. Future eco-adaptations of Shakespeare's plays incorporating TEK or IKS must also involve Indigenous-led design and delivery or at the very least, consultancy. In the meantime, we can continue to listen and learn, interrogate privilege and prejudice and de-Westernise nature/culture binaries. This is further discussed below in relation to environmental justice.

Intersectional Shakespeare and environmental justice

Place intersects with multiple converging ideologies and injustices that have together led to the Anthropocene's environmental crises. Eco-Shakespeare adaptation must therefore work to decolonize the text and consider intersectional responses to environmental injustice.

But first, some clarification of terms. *Intersectional* stems from legal scholar Kimberlé Crenshaw's response to the US legal system's 'tendency to treat race and gender as mutually exclusive categories of experience and analysis' (1989: 139). The Center for Intersectional Justice now defines the concept as 'ways in which systems of inequality based on gender, race, ethnicity, sexual orientation, gender identity, disability, class and other forms of discrimination 'intersect' to create unique dynamics and effects' (CIJ 2023). Intersectionality holds that all forms of inequality are mutually reinforcing and therefore require simultaneous consideration.

Environmental justice was coined by Benjamin Chavis, US Director of the United Church of Christ's Commission for Racial Justice (CRJ) in 1982. The concept arose from grassroots activism, where the CRJ, Congressional Black Caucus (CBC) and others protested a toxic waste landfill in Warren County. Subsequent reports and investigations led to wider-scale legislative reform for clean water and air and the protection of resources for minority and low-income groups. Greenpeace UK now defines environmental justice as the 'fair distribution of and access to environmental resources' (2023). The concept nests multiple other constructs, such as equity, exploitation, extractivism, Most Affected People and Areas (MAPA), and neocolonialism (indirect control of an area or group of people by those in power).

Environmental justice and intersectionality are therefore related, with both interrogating power structures and ideologies underpinning environmental sovereignty, climate change and ecocide. Within ecocriticism and ecodramaturgy, environmental justice incorporates intersectional justice's critiques of colonialism, capitalism, patriarchy, racism and their associated oppression and exploitation of the marginalized 'other'. Adaptations may consider how texts respond to, or can be interpreted to consider, climate change, food security, or resource extraction, and their impacts on vulnerable communities.

Shakespeare's plays offer substantive fodder for intersectional ecodramaturgical analysis that can unfold in myriad place-based ways. We see this in eco-adaptations such as Shakespeare and Yosemite's feature film *Imogen in the Wild* (2021) that focusses on environmental justice through highlighting how 'captialism and political greed have long combined with misogyny and racism to destroy lands, plants, animals, and human lives' (Brokaw 2024: 102). Minton's *Timon of Anaconda* (an adaptation of *Timon of Athens*) provides another example of how Shakespeare's 'tragic dimensions' may be interpret ecodramaturgically to serve as 'catharsis for the community' (Minton 2021: 24). Resisting the traditional ending (and staging) of a 'man who literally digs his own grave', the adaptation reflected on the ecological possibilities afforded by a post-industrial legacy reclaiming both ecological and cultural systems. The production emphasized that a 'spirit of collective affective acknowledgment and mourning' is the 'transformative ethos for Anthropocene humans to live more respectfully and responsibly with the non-human world' (Minton 2021: 34).

Finally, *The Shadow King* (2013) is a powerful example of Australian Indigenous-led Shakespearean adaptation incorporating environmental justice. Co-written by Murrungun actor and writer Balang T.E. Lewis and Michael Kantor for Malthouse Theatre and the Melbourne Festival, it was later staged at the Barbican in London. The play reconceived *King Lear* in light of land rights, deaths in custody and environmental destruction. Lewis played Lear as an Elder whose family was made rich from mining contracts. By enabling violence to be enacted on the land, the family unleashes division in itself. The play was performed by a First Nations cast and integrated Kriol and Gupapuyngu languages. The adaptation threaded enduring Indigenous Knowledge with the contemporary complexities of lateral violence and extractive economy. *Shadow King's* melding of past and present, early modern English and Dhuwal, and ecological wisdom with environmental destruction, provides an exemplar of reinvigorated Shakespearean eco-adaptation.

Ecodramaturgical prompts

How might an eco-production adapt Shakespeare's text ecodramaturgically to interrogate environmental injustice? Think about the play's instances of colonialism, racism, sexism, global trade and resource extraction that can be linked to social and ecological impact. As Gary Watt observes, Antonio's trade ships in *The Merchant of Venice* likely carried slaves as well as commodities (2008: 238). *The Tempest's* preoccupation with fuel, or *The Merry Wives of Windsor's* 'sea-coal fire' (2.1.88), point to the period's declining resources but also to issues of resource control and access (See 'Ecocriticism'). It may be useful to observe the manner in which Shakespeare does not merely allude to mining, such as the armour 'locked up in steel' in *Henry IV Part II,* but instils his characters with attitudes towards its extraction. As Hotspur describes in *Henry IV Part 1*: 'And that it was great pity, so it was, / This villainous saltpetre should be digg'd / Out of the bowels of the harmless earth' (1.3.58–60). As an ingredient for gunpowder, saltpetre not only offers an emblem for resource use but also power dynamics. In approaching ecodramaturgical adaptation, you may therefore ask: Who owns the mines? Is Hotspur condemning the practice or mocking those who do and what does this suggest about human attitudes to the Earth? Who has instigated the war and for what purpose? What are the social and more-than-human impacts?

What about our case study plays? Although *The Tempest* is the more obvious choice for an environmental justice lens due to Prospero's control of the isle and enslavement of Caliban and Ariel, while *King Lear*, too, is directly concerned with land ownership, how might colonization's impacts also be visible in *A Midsummer Night's Dream*? The play's premise is based on Theseus conquering Hippolyta's land and people. The male Theseus is aligned with the 'civilized' west and the female Hippolyta with the feminized other, 'woo'd' violently by sword and injury (1.1.16). Think about how the play's human-dominated built landscape may be seen to be constructed from the spoils of other people and lands. You might also like to observe the sense of Orientalism that pervades the play, given that its atmospheric discord hinges on Oberon and Titania's fight over the Indian changeling boy. Oberon's desperation to have the boy as his henchman (or servant/slave) further intersects with androcentric (masculine) desires for control, inviting ecofeminist ecodramaturgical readings of the dual oppression of women and nature.

How you choose to adapt the play is of course up for creative interpretation. Athens may be depicted either as a neoliberal hub for commerce versus the wood as a sacrifice zone with its 'dank and dirty ground' (2.2.74). The play takes place in 'black-brow'd night' (3.2.387), with the urban characters' 'torn with briars' (3.2.443). The forest's sharp 'thornbush' (5.1.251) counters Athens' classical (thus smooth, white) temples, while a sense of nature inching forwards snatches at its edges and 'Enrings the barky fingers of the elm' (4.1.43). Conversely, this interpretation may be flipped to focus on the wood's biodiverse world buzzing with life. Beings 'Creep into acorn cups' (2.1.31), dewberries (3.2.158) grow alongside eglantine (2.1.251), and beetles go about their tasks (2.2.21) watched on by 'fiery glow-worms' eyes' (3.1.162). In this sense, the forest presents a thriving agential world outside of human control. The wood is a place of kinship but also place-based knowledge and pragmatism. Titania, for example, uses shed snakeskin for her bedclothes (2.1.255-6), and is both specific and non-sentimental (even violent) in her use of the 'humble-bee' for 'night-tapers' (3.1.160–2) and fan of butterfly wings (3.1.164). The play therefore provides a sense of human–ecological reciprocity and flow of a close traditional relationship with complex ecosystems while spurring questions of how these practices are carried out and maintained. When viewed against the masculine, Western centre of Athens, adaptations can interrogate these complexities within today's real-world contexts. While your adaptation choices may seek to rekindle attention to and affection for the more-than-human through repudiating class, race and economic inequities, you may prefer to highlight those injustices instead.

Ecoscenography

While ecodramaturgy is well represented within Shakespeare eco-adaptation discourse, ecoscenography is less so. Principles are of course integrated within the productions themselves (see Adaptations) but there is less emphasis on a distinct ecoscenographic eco-Shakespeare field. This is an exciting area for expansion, one we consider to be fundamentally important to harnessing audience attention and affect, and to minimizing negative environmental impact.

The word *scenery* derives from the Greek *skēnē* for the structure at the back of the stage and implies a static backdrop. Rather than static scenery, scenography encompasses the 'total visual-aural sensory creation' (Aronson

2018: 10). Pamela Howard defines scenography as the 'seamless synthesis of space, text, research, art, actors, directors and spectators that contributes to an original creation' (2002: 130). A scenographer unifies all theatrical elements, not only design components (including the theatre architecture, set, costume, lighting and sound) but also place, space and bodies-within-space. Scenography is therefore a reflexive and performative process, wherein '[w]e perform scenographies and they perform us' (Lotker and Gough 2013: 3).

Ecoscenography further adds ecology's concern with the interrelated and interdependent connections between organisms and their environments. Founder Tanja Beer defines ecoscenography as the 'integration of ecological principles into all stages of scenographic thinking and production' (2016a 5–6). Ecoscenography therefore seeks to reveal the 'connections and unsustainable realities of the world, and thus allowing a more considered and valued relationship between materials and humans to occur' (Beer 2016b: 170). Ecoscenographic Shakespeare modes include: 1) incorporating Original Practices, 2) utilizing open-air performance and light-touch design, and 3) experimenting with dynamic staging.

Shakespeare's ecoscenographic synergies

1. Original Practices

Original Practices 'refers to the series of techniques for performance, or preparation for performance, of plays from the early modern period which later-modern practitioners believe may be similar to those of Shakespeare and his theatrical contemporaries' (Weingust 2014: 402). Ecoscenography convergences encompass daylit and open-air performance and direct audience address. Shakespeare's Globe highlights that actors' visibility 'creates an intimate experience where the audience becomes a vital component of the performance' (2020: np.). Additional elements include music to heighten the affective atmosphere, including through additional musicians (other than cast) onstage and sound effects (ibid.). Though we cannot be sure what Shakespeare's original staging looked or sounded like, there are contemporary accounts that highlight how the actors, stage and audience amplified a sense of liveness in the performance ecosystem. Let's think about how one aspect of these synergies might work in a play like *The Tempest*. How might we learn about how to envelop the audience within the play's scenography?

Thomas Middleton and Thomas Dekker's *The Roaring Girl* (1611), staged at the Fortune Theatre by Prince Henry's Men at about the same time Shakespeare's company premiered *The Tempest*, offers a contemporary account of how the groundlings appeared from the stage:

> Within one square a thousand heads are laid,
> So close that of heads the room seems made;
> As many faces there, filled with blithe looks,

Show like the promising titles of new books
Writ merrily, the readers being their own eyes,
Which seem to move and to give plaudites;
The very floor, as t'were, waves to and fro,
And, like a floating island, seems to move,
Upon a sea bound in with shores above.

(12.14–22)

The image of the floor as a 'floating island' upon a moving sea offers an insight into how the original staging of Shakespeare's maritime plays may have harnessed audience bodies as the sea. Ralph Berry argues that there was 'undoubtedly a Stuart taste for exploiting the levels of the playhouse stage in nautical scenes' and he presumes that the 'opening of *The Tempest* has the Master on the upper stage (quarterdeck) and the others on the platform (main deck)' (2016: 5). A thrust stage 'can look like the main deck of a ship, especially if one accepts the theory that the platform was not rectangular but tapered towards the audience' (ibid.).

Berry also observes that there are thirty-five references to *isle, island* and related words in *The Tempest* of the seventy-seven in the entire canon. 'The stage/island, raised above its surroundings, is lapped around by the audience/ sea' (10). Furthermore, the 'decisive linguistic pointer' of *this*, as 'a strong word on the Elizabethan stage, and the more so given the declamatory and emphatic style of Elizabethan acting' (ibid.). He highlights that *The Tempest* couples 'this' frequently with isle/island, which would likely have been accompanied by 'vigorous and expressive gesture' (10–11). The crucial message is that the *size* of *The Tempest's* island is never expressly given: '*This isle* is the territory of the stage' (11). Here we can see how the play's text, the material stage, the actors' physicality and the audiences' bodies combine to create a dynamic seascape and can be incorporated within more experimental staging practices. This is enhanced by the presence of the elements within the playhouse's open structure, including dynamic light and weather conditions.

2. Open-air performance and 'light-touch Shakespeare'

Theatre is notoriously resource intensive. As J.A. Miller observes in relation to adapting *Love's Labour's Lost*:

Theatrical production is inherently wasteful. Scenery is typically made from the cheapest materials possible for temporary use and then thrown away. Perfectly usable items are dismantled so that new ones may be built. Costumes typically require new fabric. The photocopy machine always seems to be running, and the lights left on.

(2012: 192)

Productions require myriad components. Sets, props, costumes, wigs, lighting, programmes, tickets and the building or site itself are the tip of a hefty iceberg. Less visible material practices are extensive. They include everything from cast and audience transport to water use and waste and paints, dyes, glues and solvents. Further material impacts incorporate makeup, catering, rehearsal room components and external supplier practices, amongst others.

Another obvious but powerful eco-adaptation strategy is to perform outdoors. Shakespeare productions need not take place outside but open-air Shakespeare offers an effective, elegant and low-budget eco-strategy to reduce resources, energy consumption and infrastructure. This may be termed 'light touch Shakespeare'. There is a long history of open-air performance on which to draw, from the original semi-open Globe Theatre to the present-day ubiquitous 'Shakespeare in the Park' summer festivals. Open-air Shakespeare's venues and production practices are varied. Some productions utilize built stages and sets, lighting and amplified sound, increasing their 'production footprint', that is, environmental impacts associated with the production. Other daytime or twilight productions create very low negative ecological impact.

Light touch design is a recognized sustainable design mode that reduces environmental intervention and built forms (Zeunert 2017). Original Practices and outdoor, or open-air, productions often fulfill light touch design criteria, sometimes inadvertently. The Cambridge Shakespeare Festival (CSF), for example, is the UK's largest outdoor Shakespeare festival and utilizes around forty professionally trained actors in eight plays across the summer. Audiences for highly popular shows like the annual *Dream* have reached 1,000 per night, with the actors utilizing long, shallow playing spaces to remove the need for amplification and to improve sightlines. Although catering to an appetite for traditional, historically reconstructed Shakespeare, the CSF and the similar numerous Shakespeare festivals and productions worldwide nevertheless abide by:

- No built stage,
- No constructed sets, or use of pre-existing structures,
- Recycled or upcycled costumes (e.g. actors' own/reused within the company),
- No amplification,
- Daylight/twilight productions or minimal, single-state lighting,
- No fixed seating,
- Reduced printed materials (programmes, tickets, banners, posters and flyers),
- No catering (especially meat and dairy products),
- No outside suppliers,
- Predominantly local audiences (reducing transport).

Other open-air Shakespeare productions and venues are consciously ecological, for example the Handlebards' cycling troupe, and the Willow Globe's living globe in Powys, Wales – a scaled-down replica Globe theatre created by living willow trees. These open-air organizations integrate a 'cradle-to-grave' ethos for disassembly and reutilization or 'cradle-to-cradle' conception of materials with a view to their eventual reabsorption into the earth (McDonough and Braungart 2002). Shakespeare in Yosemite offers another example of this practice through using constructed costumes from waste and climbing gear salvaged on site in Yosemite National Park in their outdoor production of *A Midsummer Night's Dream* (2018).

FIGURE 6.3 *Puck (Lisa Wolpe) in upcycled costume in Shakespeare in Yosemite's* A Midsummer Night's Dream, *2018. (Photo: Tomas Ovalle. Credit: UC Merced.)*

Open-air Shakespeare also creates a dynamic ecoscenography resulting in a performance that is co-created by weather and environment. Citing Therese J. May's 'urgent ecological question' of asking *where* rather than *who* are we, Rebecca Salazar notes that 'openair Shakespeare performance literally places the audience in the answer' (2018: 450). In her discussions of 'weathering Shakespeare', Evelyn O'Malley discusses an additional 'green language—of wildlife, light, landscape, and weather—suggesting that atmosphere proceeded from and moved in-between these constellations and things' heightening the production's affective capacity (2020: 155). Meteorological happenstance (sudden showers, storms or bursts of sun) or animal encounters add layers of environmental connection to the text and enable actors to play with the environment as another player on stage. These occurrences may dramatically support or humorously revoke Shakespeare's narrative in what Gwilym Jones calls 'environmental irony' (2017: 7) and Penelope Woods terms 'aleatoric effect' (2012: 246 in Jones 2017: 7) highlighting natural agency as an active performance partner. This, of course, is no guarantee of ecological outcomes – as Carl Lavery states, 'claims for theatre's capacity to bring about behaviour change, more often than not, through some ecstatic or enchanted immersion in "environment" or "nature"' are 'largely hyperbolic' (2016: 229). The most robust eco-Shakespeare production therefore balances ecoscenography with ecodramaturgy.

3. Innovative staging

Without resource and energy intensive lighting, amplification, or built sets, we can still create lively, potent eco-adaptations that absorb the audience into the performance. Strategies include:

- **Promenade staging** in which the audience follows actors around the space or can move about the space,

- **Site-specific theatre** utilizing found spaces, unique sites, scenes on 'loop' and/or simultaneous action taking place across different areas of the site, as in Punchdrunk's adaptation of *Macbeth*, *Sleep No More* (2011–current),

- **Immersive theatre** in which the audience are surrounded by the play's action and surrounded by the actors who may or may not move about the space,

- **Music and soundscape** which can be recorded, but for less environmental impact, created by the actors' voices and physical instruments/objects,

- **Physical theatre** utilizing actors' bodies and voices as part of the play's landscape, for example through choreographed movement, dance, circus or tumbling.

Ecoscenography not only makes theatre practice more sustainable, but also increases the play's dynamic potential. As such, it works together with ecodramaturgy through the design medium, creating opportunities to reveal and support for 'thriv-ability across more-than-human systems' (Beer 2021: 157).

Australian eco-Shakespearean theatrical troupe Come You Spirits, for instance, use novel and experimental staging practices to unify audience and more-than-human world, further incorporating non-traditional healing practices such as sound therapy and meditation. Performance sites have included an outdoor amphitheatre reclaimed by plants, abandoned coal-loading tunnels transformed into a park, a tall ship on Sydney Harbour, and a replica of Stonehenge in Esperance, Western Australia.

FIGURE 6.4 A Midsummer Night's Dream *by Come You Spirits at Stonehenge, Esperance, 2023. (Photographer: Syl Marie. By kind permission of Jo Bloom and Charles Mayer.)*

The troupe further schedule their performances with significant times of the day, including dawn and seasonal equinoxes, connecting audiences to place and planetary rhythm. Other strategies include the integration of ecological aesthetics. Shakespeare South (formerly Shakespeare South Australia), also use biophilic design patterns and principles based on studies of increased psycho-physiological impact in biodiverse environments to heighten audience attention and amplify emotional affect (Browning et al. 2014; Kellert 2018). These include harnessing organic forms, naturally occurring scales, rhythms, colours, sounds, patterns, light, water as well as living environments, air flows and a host of other environmental stimuli (Daroy 2022). These can not only be integrated through aesthetic design components but also through physical ecodramaturgy.

Figure 6.5 shows Viola born aloft the waves in Shakespeare South's *Botanica Lumina: Twelfth Night* (2021). The full cast earlier surrounded the audience (roped off due to Covid-19 requirements) in choreographed ocean

FIGURE 6.5 *Actors-as-ocean in Shakespeare South's* Botanica Lumina: Twelfth Night *open rehearsal at the Adelaide Botanic Garden, 2021. (Photo: Matt Lewis.)*

FIGURE 6.6 *Does the world go round?* Cymbeline *performed by University of Exeter students and directed by Evelyn O'Malley at the Willow Globe (2022). (Photographer Jon Primrose. By kind permission of Evelyn O'Malley.)*

waves with actor-created soundscapes and music. In Figure 6.6, we see Evelyn O'Malley's utilization of physical ecodramaturgy in *Cymbeline* at the Willow Globe for Randall Martin's *Cymbeline in the Anthropocene* project (2022), with students from the University of Exeter as birds and air. In one production, actors and audience 'became' the sea, in another, the air.

Using a foundation of Original Practices that relies on text, voice and bodies, physical ecodramaturgy further incorporates dynamic staging to merge actors, audience and elements within the performance ecosystem.

From sustainable to regenerative Shakespeare?

What is the future of eco-Shakespeare? Adaptation is always a material practice. To produce books, like this one, trees are felled, inks and dyes are absorbed. E-books rely on digital systems sustained by colossal data centres and transmission networks fed by energy sources. As we move towards an increasingly uncertain ecological future, our artistic aims and strategies should be ambitious to the extent that they will make a positive contribution to the audience, the community and the more-than-human world. As a challenge for the future, we can ask: how might we take productions from *sustainable* to *resilient* and even *regenerative*?

First of all, what is 'sustainability'? The most common definition comes from the 'Bruntland Commission Report', or the 'Report of the World Commission on Environment and Development: Our Common Future' (UNWCED 1987). The report defines sustainable development as 'meeting the needs of the present without compromising the ability of future generations to meet their own needs' (1987: 16). Sustainability comprises three pillars: economy, society and the environment. These have generally come to be known ironically as 'profit, people and planet', in descending order of importance. To 'sustain', then, is simply not enough to counter the scale of ecological crises faced within our current age of climate change and mass biodiversity extinction. Additionally, sustainability is conceptually flawed in the same way that neo-pastoral notions of nature and wilderness suggest an ideal state of ecological equilibrium. Fluctuating ecological systems demand revised thinking to account for complexities like hybrid and novel ecosystems impacted by industry and human impact.

Resilience, on the other hand, is a state of 'rebounding or springing back' (OED 2023), implying a greater robustness than merely sustaining life. Ecological resilience refers to the 'capacity of a system to absorb disturbance and reorganize while undergoing change so as to still retain essentially the same function, structure, identity, and feedbacks' (Holling 1973: 2). An eco-Shakespeare production aiming for ecological resilience would hence consider not only the production's carbon impact or aim for 'net zero' but widen the conception of the production's environmental footprint beyond emissions. This would require reducing the production impact beyond stage activities, including rehearsal, cast, crew and supplier materials and activities. Diet is also critical to environmental impact and should be factored into any eco-theatrical production, considering that the 'most effective way to reduce planetary impact' is through a plant-based diet (Poore and Nemecek 2018: 99).

Regeneration goes a step further still. The term 'regenerative' is frequently applied within agriculture, chiefly in relation to food systems that 'rebuild biocapacity and achieve ongoing food system outputs exceeding their environmental footprint' (Zeunert 2018: 242–3). Regenerative Shakespeare would seek to add more positive impact than merely eliminating its negative environmental impact. This is difficult to quantify: how do we, for instance, measure theatre's conceptual of or affective impact in creating change? It is not, however, impossible. Eco-productions already incorporate eco-initiatives to spread awareness and education, whether through social media, aligning with existing charitable organizations to promote campaigns, or through applied community theatre.

As a final eco-theatrical prompt, consider Tanja Beer's *Living Stage* (2013), that included community garden beds woven within ecoscenography to create edible performance art with a community and site-regeneration focus. Imagine a production of *A Midsummer Night's Dream* in which the gardeners below doubled as Mechanicals, simultaneously performing while rehabilitating a degraded section of landscape. This offers a glimpse at a future of Shakespearean eco-theatre that moves from recycle, reuse, and reduce to a more proactive approach in which we rethink, reimagine and regenerate. How else might Shakespearean eco-adaptations continue to increase their outreach and positive impact?

FIGURE 6.7 *Tanja Beer's* The Living Stage, 2013 *with CreateAbility and Born in a Taxi, Castlemaine State Festival, Australia. (Photo: Gisela Beer. With thanks to Tanja Beer and Gisela Beer.)*

ECO-SHAKESPEARE CHECKLIST

Before thinking about ecological messages and production practices (such as site, budget and directorial vision), you might like to consider these aspects.

Strategy. Ask yourself and your cast the following questions. Think back to your favourite Shakespeare production. Why did you enjoy it? Where and how was it staged? Now think of your least favourite Shakespeare production. Why did you dislike it? Was it too long or too short? Was the vision or delivery unclear? This will help to identify how to make the production more affective, hence effective.

Clarity. Strive for absolute clarity across the directorial vision and execution. The audience must understand the play's language and themes but also must follow the additional environmental narrative.

Balance. Consider how to speak *to* rather than *at* the audience. A subtle, nuanced or indeed humorous production will draw the viewer in and have a greater likelihood of convincing them of your message.

Form. Think about how to harness colour, shape, form and environment to create visually enticing and sensorially stimulating designs that invite the audience into the play's world.

Integrity. Strategize how the play can be more diverse, accessible and give back to the community. How will you manage and reduce impact, also ensuring materials and practices are cruelty free?
The impactful eco-Shakespeare adaptation therefore:

1   **Increases conceptual impact** through clear, relevant ecological commentary,
2   **Enhances affective impact** by stimulating emotion and empathy for the more-than-human world,
3   **Reduces/eliminates material impact** through sensitive production practices.

Put more simply:

1   What do you want audience to *think*?
2   How do you want the audience to *feel*?
3   How will the adaptation achieve *ecological sustainability*?

1. Increase conceptual impact

Conceptual impact is achieved when the play leaves an impression on the audience, creating new awareness or motivating change. This is facilitated by ecodramaturgical adaptation of the text for contemporary environmental relevance. Begin by reading and understanding the play in its original context. Consider how characters, settings, themes and/or symbols may be relevant to today's environmental issues. As Shakespeare's work is in the public domain and outside of copyright, you have complete creative freedom. The text may be shortened, modernized, expanded with additional relevant Shakespeare sonnets or passages from other plays, or interwoven with new writing, or diverse voices and languages. Alternatively, you may choose to faithfully preserve the text but translate characters or settings to current contexts.

There are many potential avenues for adapting Shakespeare's work for conceptual impact. You could choose an overarching message; respond to a particular local or global concern; engage in political or social critique; satirize a particular powerful individual, company or sector; promote activism; shed light on a particular species, ecosystem or group of people or inspire hope for the future. There are numerous other possibilities, from warning of apocalyptic future, interrogating anthropocentricism, revealing more-than-human agency, bringing awareness to causes or endangered species or celebrating biodiverse environments. Thus, Lear could face a climate change driven cyclone, Bottom may be transformed into an endangered Australian Quenda, or Prospero satirized as a mining company representative in a biodiversity hotspot on First Nations' land.

GUIDING QUESTIONS:

1   Why this play?
2   Why now?
3   What do I want, or *need*, to say?
4   What might the play have said in its own time?
5   What commentary may the play provide today?

Steps:

1   Choose your Shakespearean play, considering its themes, settings and genre,
2   Read the play for understanding, including the editor's notes, footnotes and glossary,

Research any additional unfamiliar words, concepts or historical contexts,

4 Chart the play's narrative arc, including individual character arcs,

   a. Consider parallels or convergences with today's ecological problems and/or opportunities. How do the themes, characters and/or setting relate to the here-and-now in ways that you, and therefore the audience, may identify with?

   b. Note the play's more-than-human voices, presences and perspectives, as well as human/non-human relationships,

5 Research other productions and ecocritical interpretations. Once you have crystalized your vision, brainstorm how you will convey your message, including tone, theme, message, setting and characterization,

6 Decide whether you will modernize any of the language or references within the play and how you will make the play relevant to local audiences,

7 Decide if and how you will cut the play or interweave current-day voices and/or other languages (if relevant),

8 Draft and seek feedback from trusted individuals. Rewrite as necessary,

9 Undertake further research, ethics approvals and/or community consultation depending on your ecodramaturgical style. Place-based productions on First Nations' land, for example, require consultation, and involvement throughout the pre-production and production process. Verbatim theatre interwoven within Shakespeare's text necessitates ethical treatment of personal stories, including permissions and transparency. You may also need to consult experts with respect to local species or environments depending on your focus,

10 Remain flexible – the best productions are woven from input from the cast and take on their own lifeforce according to the combination of energies and skills of each cast member.

2. Enhance affective impact

Affective impact may be considered to have occurred when the production causes the audience to feel empathy for other species, affected people, environments and/or the Earth. Essentially, designing a play for maximum affective impact involves the stimulation of an emotional response. Part of this process is embedded within the fundamental tenets of performance itself, such as a compelling narrative and truthful performances. It is essential that the audience can, on some level, lose themselves in the production in order to empathize with the characters and be emotionally affected by the play's themes. It is difficult, if not impossible, to capture an audience's hearts and minds when they are bored, confused or physically uncomfortable. Eco-adaptations will therefore arguably be most affective when the audience is captivated, entertained, moved and inspired. Many eco-Shakespeare adaptations are grassroots and may not have the luxury of high-budget, comfortable venues. How, then, can the production keep the audience engaged throughout to ensure that they absorb the play's key takeaways?

GUIDING QUESTIONS:

1   What affects *you* emotionally as you read the play?
2   Which moments and images stand out to you and capture your imagination?
3   What is novel, interesting or different within the text?
4   How can the play's ecological elements be harnessed for greater dynamism?
5   How can the play's more-than-human voices and presences generate pathos and empathy?

Steps:

1   Write a list of your venue's site attributes, depending on whether it is indoor, outdoor, found space, site-specific, or non-specific (e.g. touring or street theatre). Note any unique features, attributes, existing infrastructure or challenges, including those to sightlines and sound,
2   Sketch your performance site, including possible entrances, exits and aisles. Brainstorm how you could utilize the whole performance space, or stage scenes in novel and unexpected ways to hold audience attention,
3   Return to the play's text and note patterns, motifs, symbols, more-than-human voices, elemental presences, and ecological systems for scenographic designs,
4   Unify your design vision. Of this list, are there any particular symbols or themes that evoke the essence of the play? What about colours, animals, plants, or organic forms? How may these relate to play, place and site?
5   Chart the play's settings, season(s), and times of day for lighting and soundscape design. If not using lighting or amplification, think about

how to evoke these changes through human-made soundscapes and choreography to bring the play's living world to life (if this fits your design focus),

6   Note any existing music within the play, including e.g. character songs and trumpet fanfares. Consider how the play's moods and atmospheres may be further underscored musically,

7   Create a costume mood board for your costume designs based on your ecological themes (see Roz Symon's piece in 'Eco-adaptations'),

8   If the play has been cast, consider what performance and design skills you can draw on. These may include singing, musical instruments, dance, physical theatre, circus and tumbling, clowning, stage combat and more. Think about how these can be integrated within performance to increase its liveliness and energy,

9   Plan rehearsal workshops for music and physical dramaturgy, including specialist consultation and guest direction if required.

3. Reduce/eliminate material impact

Material impact relates to the production's effect on the physical environment, including other species, ecological systems and groups of people. Ecological design within the performing arts is 'any form of design that minimizes environmentally destructive impacts by integrating itself with living processes' (van der Ryn and Cowan 2007: 33). Key precepts include ecological accounting, design *with* rather than *on/in* nature, and making nature visible (ibid.). Major principles include eliminating environmental damage, 'bottom up' rather than 'top down' design, recognition and visibility of culture, place, and integration of traditional Indigenous knowledge. Eco-material practice encompasses both eco-processes (such as recycling; upcycling; cradle-to-cradle; closed-loop; carbon positive; regenerative practice) and eco-materials (for instance, local, organic, biodegradable, cruelty-free) (please see Appendix: Glossary).

Resources guiding 'greener' theatrical production continue to grow. Examples include: The Centre for Sustainable Practice in the Arts; Julie's Bicycle; Broadway Green Alliance; Sustainable Theatres Australia; The Green Theatre Programme for London; Mo'olelo Performing Arts Company Green Theatre Choices Toolkit; PGA Green; Theatre Greenbook; Theatres Trust; Ecostage; Artists and Climate Change; and HowlRound Theatre Common. Within eco-theatrical Shakespeare, multiple production initiatives are available online with useful resources and precedents. These include: The EarthShakes Alliance; Shakespeare in Yosemite; the Willow Globe; The Global Cymbeline Project; and Shakespeare's Globe's Globe 4 Globe conference (2021) amongst others (please see Appendix: Resources).

Guiding questions:

1   What are your ecological goals?

2   How can you minimize site and wider environmental footprint?

3   How will you track and measure material impact?

4   How will you integrate local and ethical procurement chains?

5   What kinds of ecological initiatives can you implement beyond reducing/eliminating material impact?

Steps:

1   What is the focus and target for this project? Do you want to work toward carbon neutrality, or zero-waste, or company certification? Start with a 'reduce, reuse, recycle' model and expand outward,

2   What is your budget? How can seek in-kind donations or partnerships to help the production have greater impact and outreach?

3   How visible do you wish the initiatives and process to be? Will they have a public-facing message, for example, but be invisible with respect to aesthetic design?

4   Decide how widely you will draw the production circle when measuring the production effects – will it be duration of the show, or include the rehearsal period? Will you consider the audience, or only the action on stage and backstage processes directly impacting the production?

5   Create a flow chart and timeline with markers and accountability. Depending on the nature and size of your cast and organization, you might like to allocate tasks and responsibilities. This may include electing a sustainability officer to track activities and consumption,

6   Will your ecological initiatives include visible environmental outreach or public-facing communication? In other words, is there an educative or community focus that you will disseminate through social media, workshops, publicity or other means? Will you have full transparency, for example, displaying the outcomes on your website? Consider ways to engage people beyond the theatre audience such as through cast pledges and competitions on social media, partnerships with charities or community initiatives, or special offers with local organizations promoting ethical goods or practices,

7   Consider the material impacts on people, including communities. How will the production be diverse, accessible and financially inclusive?

8   List and assess items, sources, suppliers, lifespan (during and beyond production), embodied energy, packaging, freight, virgin or recycled steel/aluminium fixtures (and percentage), paints, and finishes (Volatile Organic Compounds (VOCs). Set a target from this baseline. Where present, this will also include any set; props; hair items; makeup; costume; printed materials; data usage; cleaning processes and products; cast and crew travel and diet (meat consumption); technology; printed materials (inks, paper, processes); marketing and supporting materials; and waste processes (including: toilets, sanitation; water; waste; cleaning products; e-waste; non-recyclables/landfill),

9   Utilize existing green theatre measurement tools and guides, for example, Julie's Bicycle, the Broadway Green Alliance, Theatre Green Book, carbon calculators, and life-cycle analysis tools (see Appendix),

10 Track impact throughout the rehearsal and production process. If working outside, ensure that you leave the site undamaged,

11 Research any carbon offset companies that you use carefully, paying attention to their regeneration and community programs,

12 Eco-adaptation requires persistence and focussing on ecological disaster can be emotionally taxing. Remember to find the sense of play-within-the-play and joy within the creative process.

The Anthropocene's wicked problems require multifaceted solutions. Shakespeare's plays offer us diverse genres, settings and ecological presences that can be adapted in innumerable ways. What will your story be?

> O wonder!
> How many goodly creatures are there here!
> How beauteous *the more-than-human world* is! O brave new world
> That has such *beings* in't.
>
> (adapted from *The Tempest* 5.1.182–4)

APPENDIX 1: GLOSSARY

Adaptation: 1. Organisms' structural, physiological and/or behavioural change to environmental stimuli; 2. The reinterpretation and reinvention of a source into a new form.

Affect: The embodied experience of intense emotion.

Animal rights: The moral premise that non-human animals have rights to life and to live free from human-inflicted suffering.

Anthropos: Greek for human.

Anthropogenic: Human-generated (usually, pollution, climate change or other environmental destruction).

Anthropocene: A proposed unit on Earth's geologic timescale denoting the shift from natural processes shaping the atmosphere and ecosystems to human activities becoming the dominant planetary agent.

Anthropocentricism: Placing humans at the centre of ethical importance above other species and ecological systems.

Audiencing: The consideration of the audience as co-creators of the performance event.

Biocapacity: An area's biological capacity, or capability of sustaining life based on size and yield.

Biocentricism: Placing all living organisms at the centre of ethical importance.

Biodiversity: The variety of life on Earth, including all organisms, populations and their assemblages within an ecosystem.

Biological: From the Greek *bios*/life and *logos*/study denoting: 1. The study of living organisms and their processes; 2. Related to life and/or living things; 3. A hereditary relationship.

Biophilia/biophilic design: The partially innate affinity for other species and natural phenomena harnessed within design cues to increase human-nature connection.

Bioregion: An ecological measure that classifies similar natural characteristics and environmental processes in an area, such as a desert region or coastal plain.

Blackbox theatre: A typically square or rectangular indoor performance space with black walls that can be used to create a variety of staging configurations.

Carrying capacity: An area's maximum ability to sustain life through available resources.

Carbon dioxide equivalent (CO_2-eq): A metric measurement converting greenhouse gases into carbon dioxide equivalency to calculate their global-warming potential.

Carbon footprint: The total amount of greenhouse gasses generated anthropogenically, including direct emissions (e.g. from fossil-fuel combustion) and indirect (e.g. from goods and services).

Carbon neutral: Balancing a product's or process' generation of greenhouse gases through removing the equivalent amount from the atmosphere.

Carbon offsetting: Purchasing carbon credits from organizations to compensate emissions through investing in environmental projects. One carbon credit typically equates to one tonne of carbon-dioxide-equivalent emissions.

Closed-loop system: 1. A rare or even hypothetical self-regulating system in which there are no inputs to nor outputs from the outside of that system; 2. In ecology, the circle of life from generation to decay and then regeneration; 3. In recycling, the process of making, using and repurposing without requiring additional natural resources.

Cradle-to-cradle: Design for disassembly or reutilization to allow for safe reabsorption into the Earth's nutrient cycles without contamination.

Cradle-to-grave: Ecological assessment of a product's ecological impact at each stage of its life cycle, from creation and use to disposal.

Cruelty-free: Products that are created without harming animals.

Climate change: Anthropogenic alteration of the Earth's atmosphere and climatic patterns, predominantly through the production of greenhouse gas emissions.

Diffraction: The critical practice of reading texts in relation to their contexts, themes, audiences and other texts and considering them as entangled withing matter and discourse.

Dramaturgy: The research and interpretation of a play's text as a dramatic composition for performance.

Dwelling: Mind–body situatedness in environment.

Eco-adaptation: The reinterpretation and environmentally sensitive reinvention of a (usually textual) source into a new literary or artistic form as a mode of ecological activism.

Eco-assemblages: Related groups existing in particular habitats.

Ecocentricism: Placing the wellbeing of the whole Earth system, including its individual organisms and life-sustaining components, at the centre of ethical importance.

Ecocriticism: The application of ecological principles and ethics to the analysis of literary texts.

Ecodramaturgy: The application of ecological principles and ethics to the adaptation of dramatic texts.

Ecofeminism: The examination of the dual oppression of women and nature.

Ecology: The science of the structure, dynamics and functions of planetary life and life-sustaining elements and processes, including organisms, species, habitats, cycles and flows, at various scales from ecosystem niches to the planet's system.

Ecological community: Collections of species within reciprocal food chains and life webs existing together within a habitat.

Ecological footprint: The area of productive land and water required to support life, or the number of Earths required to sustain the current population.

Ecological holism: Consideration of and for the Earth's ecosystems as an interconnected whole.

Ecological systems thinking: A holistic way of thinking that recognizes interactions, interdependencies and interrelationships within a wider system.

Ecomaterialism: A way of thinking about matter as agential, lively, vibrant and dynamic in a system of exchange within and between bodies, and all organic and inorganic ecosystem components.

Ecophobia: An ecocritical theory linking environmental destruction with human fear or hostility toward nature.

Ecoscenography: The design and creation of a production's aesthetic, sensory and material components according to ecological principles, ethics and practices.

Ecosystem processes: The material, biological and chemical processes sustaining and connecting organisms and environments, such as nutrient and water cycles, energy flows and community dynamics.

Eco-theatre: Theatre-making that puts ecological principles and ethics at the centre of all stages of the production process.

Ecotones: Transition zones and boundaries between biological and ecological communities, habitats, regions and ecosystems.

Embodiment: The inextricable connection between the mind, body and environment experienced through perceptual, sensory and motor cues.

Enmeshment: The inseparable interconnections within and between matter, as well as between matter and discourse.

Entanglement: A quantum concept of non-locality applied to discursive and material indivisibility.

Entropy: Energy dispersal and dissipation.

Environment: The total physical, chemical and biological components of an organism's surroundings sustaining and influencing life.

Environmental affordances: The relationships between organisms and their environments.

Environmental ethics: The consideration of humans' moral obligations towards the environment in widening circles of compassion and empathy extending outward from self (ego-), humans (anthropo-) and living beings (bio-) to the whole Earth system (ecocentricism).

Environmental justice: An intersectional understanding of environmental destruction as stemming from multiple interrelated hierarchical power structures and ideologies that are also responsible for social injustice.

Environmental theatre: A predominantly twentieth-century theatre movement encompassing novel forms such as immersive or site-specific theatre and considering elements of the performance to be vital and alive.

Extractivism: The large-scale exploitation of natural resources for economic gain.

Fossil fuel: Finite, combustible organic material containing hydro-carbon such as coal, oil and natural gas formed in the geological past from organisms' remains.

Gaia: 1. Greek goddess of the Earth; 2. The hypothesis that the Earth's ecological components function as a single entity.

Genius loci: Latin for 'spirit of place', expressing the intangible qualities of a place.

Global warming: The rise of the planet's temperature due to greenhouse gas emissions trapping the sun's heat within the atmosphere.

Greenhouse gas emissions: Carbon dioxide, methane and other noxious gases emitted into the atmosphere causing global warming and climate change.

Green theatre: Theatre-making utilizing sustainability tools, guidance and assessments to reduce negative environmental impact irrespective of the play's ecodramaturgical interpretation.

Historicism: Literary criticism that integrates historical analysis.

Immersive theatre: A form of staging in which the audience are surrounded by the play's action, becoming participants within the performance's world.

Intersectional justice: The recognition that social injustices envelop multiple intersecting inequities, identities and systemic barries, including towards race, ethnicity, gender, sexual orientation, class and disability.

Kinaesthetic: Embodied movement and/or sensation.

Kincentric ecology: Indigenous philosophy and practices viewing other lifeforms in/and environments as kin within an intradependent life system.

Landscape: 1. The visual and/or aesthetic features of an environment; 2. A large tract of land.

Life cycle assessment: Assessing the potential environmental impacts across all stages of a product, technology or service's existence, from production to waste.

Light-touch design: Environmentally sensitive design practices based on minimal site intervention.

Ludic theatre: Theatre's potential for re-enchantment through audience participation, play and novel staging.

More-than-human world: A term used to overcome anthropocentric binaries within non-human/human and nature/culture to encompass Earth's multiple lifeforms and the ecological systems.

Nature: A difficult term traditionally used to articulate the living and organic world outside of the self while also being embedded within the idea of 'human nature' as the essence of what it is to be human.

Neocolonialism: The indirect control of an area or group of people by those in power.

Net zero: Achieving a balance between greenhouse gas emissions produced and greenhouse gas emissions removed from the atmosphere.

Oikos: Greek for house/household, from which the root word of 'ecology' is derived, as the 'household of nature'.

Overshoot: Occurs when a population exceeds its environment's carrying capacity, resulting in collapse or 'die-off'.

Organic: 1. Living, derived from or constructed by living matter and capable of decay; 2. A classification system of products produced without chemicals.

Original Practices: The integration of performance principles believed to have taken place in Shakespeare's time, as introduced and championed by Shakespeare's Globe.

Pastoral: A literary mode that emerged in classical antiquity idealizing country life, particularly in relation to shepherds' freedom from urban corruption.

Performance ecology: A mode of scholarship and practice that views performances as ecosystems.

Physical theatre: Theatre that utilizes the body, movement, and/or voice in creative ways to tell stories with minimal or no text.

Plant-based diet: Not consuming animal products, usually in recognition of their environmental impact and the suffering of animals bred and/or killed to create them.

Postcognitive: A movement that considers cognition and affect as linked within an interconnected mind-body-environment nexus.

Posthumanism: In an ecological context, a movement that decentres anthropocentricism through recognizing humans' material interconnections within a web of life.

Presentism: Literary criticism that analyses a text's relation to the present, and in an ecocritical sense, to current day ecological crises.

Proscenium staging: From the Greek division of the stage space, used to relate to the square or arched structure framing the stage and separating the actors and audience.

Promenade staging: Dynamic staging, usually in which the audience follows actors around the space or can move around the space.

Real zero: The elimination of emissions without relying on carbon offsetting.

Recycling: The treatment and/or processing of products for reuse.

Reflexivity: Affecting or being affected by other agents.

Regenerative theatre: The elimination of negative production environmental impact while also generating positive environmental impact during the production itself.

Resilient theatre: Theatrical production that minimizes environmental disturbance to enable the production site to quickly recover.

Scenography: A production's total visual, aural and sensory elements, including text, actors, stage, audience and space.

Site-specific theatre: Performance that takes place within found, unique or outdoor spaces.

Speciesism: The unconscious or conscious belief that certain species have greater inherent worth over others.

Sustainability: 1. The ability to meet present needs without compromising those of future generations; 2. The material practice of ensuring balance and permanence in relation to people, environment, and economic factors.

Sustainable theatre: Production practices that balance social, environmental, and economic impacts for future viability.

(Syn)aesthetic theatre: Theatre that utilizes novel, physical and sensory staging techniques to draw together sensation, perception and space for impact.

Systems thinking: The holistic consideration of the components, linkages and interactions that comprise a system, within the context of larger systems.

Theatre ecology: Performance ecology as relating to theatrical performance, namely, considering the theatrical production as an ecosystem operating within larger ecosystems.

Thrust Stage: From Greek and Elizabethan staging, whereby the stage juts out to allow the audience around three sides, bringing the actors closer to the audience.

Traditional Ecological Knowledge (TEK) or Indigenous Knowledge Systems (IKS): Indigenous knowledge, traditions, cosmologies and practices sustained over millennia through close relationships with and stewardship of the land.

Transcorporeality: The notion that matter is fluid and vital and collides in the performance moment to create affect.

Triple bottom line: The values of traditional sustainability, also referred to as 'people, planet and profit'.

Upcycling: Reusing or transforming discarded products or materials to create a new product of higher value.

Volatile Organic Compounds (VOC): Harmful chemicals emitted from certain materials or liquids.

Weathering: To experience the weather as an active agent within a performance.

Wilderness: 1. A tract of land that is perceived as uncultivated by humans; 2. Barren or inhospitable land.

Zero waste: A whole systems circular approach to waste prevention, incorporating: Refuse (what you don't need); reduce consumption; reuse; recycle and rot or transform.

APPENDIX 2: ONLINE RESOURCES

Links to these resources are also available at bloomsbury.pub/shakespeare-ecology-adaptation. Bear in mind that these may be subject to change over time.

Eco-facts

Climate Clock: https://climateclock.world
Ekō People and Planet over Profits: https://www.eko.org/campaigns/
E.O. Wilson Biodiversity Foundation: https://eowilsonfoundation.org/glossary/species-protection-index/
European Environment Agency: https://www.eea.europa.eu/en
Food and Agriculture Organization of the United Nations (FAO) The State of the World's Biodiversity for Food and Agriculture: https://www.fao.org/state-of-biodiversity-for-food-agriculture/en/
Center for Intersectional Justice: https://www.intersectionaljustice.org/
Environmental Justice Foundation: https://ejfoundation.org/
Environmental Justice Resources (US): https://www.publichealthdegrees.org/resources/environmental-justice-resources/
Food Landscape Impacts: https://www.foodlandscapes.com.au
Global Footprint Network: https://www.footprintnetwork.org
Global Forest Watch: https://www.globalforestwatch.org/dashboards/global/
Greenpeace Publications: https://www.greenpeace.org/international/posts/#publications
Intergovernmental Panel on Climate Change (IPCC): https://www.ipcc.ch
International Panel of Experts on Sustainable Food Systems IPES-Food Resources: https://www.ipes-food.org
International Union for Conservation of Nature (IUCN) Red List of Threatened Species: https://www.iucnredlist.org
Nature Needs Half: https://natureneedshalf.org
Ocean and Climate Platform: https://ocean-climate.org/en/about-us-2/
The World Counts: https://www.theworldcounts.com
World Resources Institute Global Forest Review: https://research.wri.org
World Wildlife Fund (WWF) Living Planet Report: https://livingplanet.panda.org/en-US/

Eco-Shakespeare adaptation resources

Adaptations: blogs and interviews

Flagstaff Shakespeare Festival: https://ucmerced.app.box.
com/s/6kg0302sd1noawcjjt15qgkv6r8i5m5e

'Global Warming and the Globe Theatre': https://www.shakespeareforall.com/blog/
global-warming-and-the-globe-theaterhttps://www.shakespeareforall.com/blog/
global-warming-and-the-globe-theater

Handlebards: https://ucmerced.app.box.com/s/2l8ll8qz6rev2f4vadlq1gxbusl36ce6

LaTrobe University/Rob Conkie: https://www.cymbeline-anthropocene.com/
article/16792-director-interviews-rob-conkie

Montana In-Site Theatre's 'Oguta Island': https://www.cymbeline-anthropocene.
com/article/17149-shakespeare-in-film-oguta-island

Montana Shakespeare in the Park: https://ucmerced.app.box.com/s/
lb5st60tbnu2dt3rh0pnu3xruhl0foxz

New York Classical Theatre: https://ucmerced.app.box.com/s/
hungr3en69o2bc860oouxd1hmlrmzsw2

Parrabbola: https://ucmerced.app.box.com/s/7h2tbwh4bpjk30ch5herd0ekjg0hqi0z

Prague Shakespeare: https://ucmerced.app.box.com/s/
lfwfxt6pm3oxkwg26nn0yaabqc4mrd54

Recycling Magic: *A Midsummer Night's Dream*: https://video.tpt.org/video/
recycling-magic-midsummer-nights-dream-2ko0vo/

Recycled Shakespeare Company: https://ucmerced.app.box.
com/s/147qw9kypjczq5ty3rb73zg470gqwb8t

RSC 'Green Scenery for *The Tempest*': https://www.rsc.org.uk/blogs/whispers-from-
the-wings/green-scenery-for-the-tempest

Shakespeare.Scot: https://ucmerced.app.box.com/s/
bzoeue7qydimx2qt09lqtb70s1ffm4bt

Shakespeare in Yosemite and the EarthShakes Alliance: https://ucmerced.app.box.
com/s/scipmh87stdxxjlzxp5cb3ohojl80jf7

Adaptations: film (full length)

A Nigerian Eco-Tempest: Oguta Island by Montana InSite Theatre (*The Tempest*):
https://ucmerced.app.box.com/s/hungr3en69o2bc860oouxd1hmlrmzsw2

Bound by Laura Elmer (*Macbeth*): https://www.youtube.com/
watch?v=olrm6TwPse8

Queen Mab by Michelle Siu (*Romeo and Juliet*): https://www.youtube.com/
watch?v=67_cW7iPM8s

Imogen in the Wild by Shakespeare in Yosemite (*Cymbeline*): https://earthshakes.
ucmerced.edu/resources/films-and-performances

Mother Nature's Vengeance by Weronika Tomaszewkska (*Julius Caesar*): https://
www.youtube.com/watch?v=ZiAspoL5QQc

Once Upon a Time in the Anthropocene by Cornell University Department of
Drama Students (*Cymbeline*): https://www.youtube.com/watch?v=17s9SgfEOhc

Paddayi by Abhaya Simha (*Macbeth*): https://www.youtube.com/
watch?v=N8afTLW-f0o

The Pulse of Change, by Velina Garabedyan (*A Midsummer Night's Dream*):
https://www.youtube.com/watch?v=eUAjQpw3efw

Tomorrow by Filipache Alexandru, (various Shakespeare sources): https://www.
    youtube.com/watch?v=qnr0puVDH6g

Adaptations: theatre (full length)

Cimbelino en la Patagonia by Setebos Theatre Company: https://www.youtube.
    com/watch?v=h8E3i-VQa3Y
Cymbeline by Montana Shakespeare in the Parks: https://www.youtube.com/
    watch?v=zQEfYgA-SkY
Cymbeline at the Willow Globe: https://www.youtube.com/watch?v=R28H1f_ApU8

Projects and practices

Atmospheric Theatre Project: https://atmospherictheatre.exeter.ac.uk/
Bell Shakespeare: https://www.bellshakespeare.com.au/our-story
Butterfly Theatre: https://www.butterflytheatre.com/theatre/about
Come You Spirits: https://www.comeyouspirits.com/sustainability/
Cymbeline in the Anthropocene: https://www.cymbeline-anthropocene.com/
EarthShakes Alliance: https://earthshakes.ucmerced.edu/
Gift Horse Theatre: https://www.gifthorsetheatre.com/twelfth-night
Handlebards: https://www.handlebards.com
Montana InSite Theatre: https://www.montanainsitetheatre.org
Parrabbola: https://www.parrabbola.co.uk/projects
Recycled Shakespeare Company Archives: https://www.watervillecreates.
    org/?show_organization=recycled-shakespeare-company
Royal Shakespeare Company: https://www.rsc.org.uk/about-us/environmental-
    responsibility
Shakespeare's Globe: https://www.shakespearesglobe.com/discover/blogs-and-
    features/2023/06/05/sustainable-shakespeare-2023/
Shakespeare in Paradise: https://www.shakespeareinparadise.org/our-story
Shakespeare South: http://www.shakespearesouth.com
Shakespeare in Yosemite: https://yosemiteshakes.ucmerced.edu
This Distemperature: http://www.thisdistemperature.co.uk/forest/
Willow Globe: https://www.shakespearelink.org.uk/about-willow-globe

*List of EarthShakes Signatories: https://earthshakes.ucmerced.edu/members-
    organizations-and-individuals

Eco-Shakespeare general resources

Presentations

Globe4Globe: Shakespeare and climate emergency symposium

Keynotes:
Opening: Michelle Terry and Paul Prescott: https://www.youtube.com/watch?v=m3
    B4TOGVrf4&list=PLrjv9JMP90LmQsl9zxQJrjgkID39mND9b&index=2

'Where Does the Story Meet Earth?' by Madeline Sayet: https://www.youtube.com/
    watch?v=kU_yckcSlZs&list=PLrjv9JMP90LmQsl9zxQJrjgkID39mND9b&ind
    ex=3
'Activating Environmental Consciousness through Shakespeare' by Randall Martin:
    https://www.youtube.com/watch?v=HsyGc9J35do&list=PLrjv9JMP90LmQsl9z
    xQJrjgkID39mND9b&index=4&t=1234s
'Using Shakespeare to Change Hearts and Minds' by Solitaire Townsend: https://
    www.youtube.com/watch?v=z-KKT2Pb1JE&list=PLrjv9JMP90LmQsl9zxQJrjg
    kID39mND9b&index=5&t=360s

Producing Eco-Shakespeare: company practices

'Shakespeare in Paradise' by Nicolette Bethal and Philip Smith: https://www.
    youtube.com/watch?v=PlwZJ-jxAwA&list=PLrjv9JMP90LmQsl9zxQJrjgkID39
    mND9b&index=6
'The Handlebards: Shakespeare on Bikes' by Paul Moss and Tom Dixon: https://
    www.youtube.com/watch?v=FbVbIYq_RA0&list=PLrjv9JMP90LmQsl9zxQJrjg
    kID39mND9b&index=8
'Shakespeare in Yosemite' by Katherine S. Brokaw and Collaborators: https://www.
    youtube.com/watch?v=0toKnEfRs48&list=PLrjv9JMP90LmQsl9zxQJrjgkID39
    mND9b&index=8
'The Willow Globe' by Sue Best and Philip Bowen: https://www.youtube.com/
    watch?v=SoIRo5tSUzw
'Butterfly Theatre' by Tracy Irish and Aileen Gonsalves: https://www.youtube.com/
    watch?v=y6fKU3edIlo https://www.youtube.com/watch?v=FNsTyYWJRZk

Eco-Shakespearean projects

'Atmospheric Theatre: Open Air Theatre and the Environment' by Chloe Preedy
    and Evelyn O'Malley: https://www.youtube.com/watch?v=Zwwt44iCXG4
'Cymbeline in the Anthropocene' by Randall Martin: https://www.youtube.com/
    watch?v=PF91_4J1jm4
'Timon of Anaconda' by Gretchen Minton: https://www.youtube.com/
    watch?v=8rnqP5vUB7c

Eco-Shakespearean perspectives

'The Living Globe: Biophilic Shakespeare' by Alys Daroy: https://www.youtube.
    com/watch?v=ACxDGoLdDvY&list=PLrjv9JMP90LmQsl9zxQJrjgkID39mND
    9b&index=18&t=250s
'"Is There not Rain Enough in the Sweet Heavens?": Rain on the Early Modern
    Stage' by Sophie Chiari: https://www.youtube.com/watch?v=U2sQwJLFTu0&lis
    t=PLrjv9JMP90LmQsl9zxQJrjgkID39mND9b&index=19&t=492s
'Shakespeare and the Orbis Spike: Theatre Histories for the Anthropocene Era' by
    Patrick Lonergan: https://www.youtube.com/watch?v=AhBbsvlVCn8&list=PLrj
    v9JMP90LmQsl9zxQJrjgkID39mND9b&index=20

'All the World's a Stag [sic]: *As You Like It*'s Ecologies of Exile' by Bill Kroeger: https://www.youtube.com/watch?v=PbZcJJ8wtc8&list=PLrjv9JMP90LmQsl9zx QJrjgkID39mND9b&index=21

'Shakespeare in Anti-Oil Sponsorship Protests: The Story of BP or not BP' by Claire Frampton: https://www.youtube.com/watch?v=K9ZFhWKjJo8&list=PLrjv9JMP 90LmQsl9zxQJrjgkID39mND9b&index=26&t=403s

'To Trade and Traffic in Affairs of Breath: Shared Air in *Macbeth*' by Theo Black: https://www.youtube.com/watch?v=wPi1DJrMdNM&list=PLrjv9JMP90LmQsl 9zxQJrjgkID39mND9b&index=22

'This Distemperature: A Conversation Between William Shakespeare and the Environment' by Philip Parr and Collaborators: https://www.youtube.com/watch ?v=tyr2moRLUr4&list=PLrjv9JMP90LmQsl9zxQJrjgkID39mND9b&index=25

'The Pathos of Place in *Sam Zimske Noci/A Midwinter Night's Dream*' by Ilana Gilovich: https://www.youtube.com/watch?v=9yG5VdBuXSY&list=PLrjv9JMP 90LmQsl9zxQJrjgkID39mND9b&index=24

'"Where's the Place"?: Shakespeare in the Tropics: Placed-Based Approaches to Teaching *Macbeth* in Regional Australia' by Clare Hansen: https://www. youtube.com/watch?v=UH1OSKmCVL0&list=PLrjv9JMP90LmQsl9zxQJrjgkI D39mND9b&index=29

'The Handlebards and Sustainable Shakespearean Energy' by Ronan Hatfull: https://www.youtube.com/watch?v=Qj6NZnB9Gi4&list=PLrjv9JMP90LmQsl9 zxQJrjgkID39mND9b&index=27&t=23s

'Youth, Age, and Pastoral Guardianship' by Hanh Bui: https://www.youtube.com/ watch?v=AzAJKXyrikU&list=PLrjv9JMP90LmQsl9zxQJrjgkID39mND9b&ind ex=23&t=75s

'"Maiden['s] Blossoms": A Meditation on Climate Grief' by Sujata Iyengar: https:// www.youtube.com/watch?v=U4fE43ggPNg&list=PLrjv9JMP90LmQsl9zxQJrjg kID39mND9b&index=28

Greening the Screen: A Workshop led by Amrita Ramanan (Play On Shakespeare) and Alison Carey (Oregon Shakespeare Festival): https://www.youtube.com/ watch?v=5Lv73y_O8HE&list=PLrjv9JMP90LmQsl9zxQJrjgkID39mND9b&in dex=17

Closing remarks

'Tribute to Emily Fournier, Founder of Recycled Shakespeare Company' by Billy Wolfgang: https://www.youtube.com/watch?v=LJ0_3HuY_XY&list=PLrjv9JMP 90LmQsl9zxQJrjgkID39mND9b&index=30

Launch of EarthShakes Alliance by Katherine S. Brokaw and Paul Prescott: https:// www.youtube.com/watch?v=wwzslwWTQus

Cymbeline in the Anthropocene:
Eco-Shakespeare in performance symposium

Day 1: https://www.youtube.com/watch?v=BNC6XuWUTCE&t=3766s
Day 2: https://www.youtube.com/watch?v=44C4OUP6W9U
Day 3: https://www.youtube.com/watch?v=Y8GBD5Nt8PE&t=1s

Eco-theatre

Ecological assessment tools for the arts

Arts Earth Partnerships (AEP) Green Certification: https://www.artsearthpartnership.org/

Arts and Climate Initiative: https://artsandclimate.org/

Broadway Green Alliance (BGA): https://www.broadwaygreen.com/about-us

Centre for Sustainable Practice in the Arts: https://www.sustainablepractice.org/

Climate Change Theatre Action: https://www.climatechangetheatreaction.com/

Creative Carbon Scotland Green Arts Initiative: https://www.creativecarbonscotland.com/green-arts-initiative/

Creative Carbon Scotland Carbon Management Tools: https://www.creativecarbonscotland.com/carbon-management/tools-and-resources/

Creative Climate Literacy 101: https://juliesbicycle.com/resource/creative-climate-literacy-101/

Creative Green Tools Canada: https://www.cgtoolscanada.org/

Culture for Climate Report Australia: https://apdg.org.au/2023/04/culture-climate-report

Ecovenue (Theatre): https://www.theatrestrust.org.uk/how-we-help/advice

European Theatre Convention (ETC) Green Book: https://www.europeantheatre.eu/page/key-themes/sustainability

Gallery Climate Coalition Carbon Calculator: https://galleryclimatecoalition.org/carbon-calculator/

Greener Live Performance: https://greener.liveperformance.com.au/

Green Production Guide: https://greenproductionguide.com/

Green Theater Choice Toolkit: https://www.sustainablepractice.org/programs/ldi/toolkit/

Green Theatre Programme for London: https://www.sustainablepractice.org/wp-content/uploads/2012/12/Green-Theatre-Report.pdf

Julie's Bicycle Creative Green Tools: https://juliesbicycle.com/our-work/creative-green/creative-climate-tools/

Reel Green–Creative British Columbia: https://creativebc.com/reel-green/tools/

Sustainable Production Toolkit: https://www.sustainableproductiontoolkit.com/

Theatre Green Book: https://theatregreenbook.com/

Tipping Point: https://www.tippingpointaustralia.com/library

Ecodramaturgy

EMOS Ecodrama Playwrights Festival: https://www.earthmattersonstage.com/

Greenturgy at the Oregon Shakespeare Festival: https://www.osfashland.org/en/prologue/fall-2017/prologue-fa17-greenturgy.aspx

Gretchen E. Minton: https://www.gretchenminton.com/dramaturgy

Lisa Woynarski: https://imaginedtheatres.com/lisa-woynarski/

Theresa J. May: https://theresajmay.com/about/ecodramaturgy

'What is Ecodramaturgy?': https://www.kristinidaszak.com/ecodramaturgy

Ecoscenography

EcoStage Ecoscenographers: https://ecostage.online/about/the-team/
'Global Networked Ecoscenography': https://www.critical-stages.org/26/global-
     networked-ecoscenography-creating-sustainable-worlds-for-theatre-through-
     international-collaboration/
Ian Garrett: https://www.ianpgarrett.com/portfolio/#scenography
Tanja Beer: https://ecoscenography.com/blog/
Wallace Heim: https://wallaceheim.com/current/

Stage

Climate Change Theatre Action: https://www.climatechangetheatreaction.com/
Ecostage Global Voices Archive: https://ecostage.online/global-voices/
'Existential Creativity: Making Theatre Sustainable': https://www.
     digitaltheatreplus.com/blog/existential-creativity-making-theatre-sustainable
HowlRound Theatre: https://howlround.com/climate-change-eco-theatre
Superhero Clubhouse: http://www.superheroclubhouse.org/what-is-ecotheater/
See also: Super Hero Clubhouse Publications and Partners: http://www.
     superheroclubhouse.org/publications-partners/
'Storytelling Strategies in Eco-Theatre': https://artistsandclimatechange.
     com/2018/09/06/storytelling-strategies-in-eco-theatre/

Shakespeare and nature

General

Birds of Shakespeare: https://www.birdsofshakespeare.com/
Botanical Shakespeare: https://linktr.ee/botanicalshakespeare
'How Shakespeare's Plays Explore the Same Ecological Issues We Face Today':
     https://insideecology.com/2023/04/22/shakespeares-environmentalism-how-his-
     plays-explore-the-same-ecological-issues-we-face-today/
Shakespeare and Nature Infographic: https://blog.oup.com/2016/08/shakespeare-
     and-nature-graphic/
Shakespeare's Textual Biodiversity: https://www.youtube.com/
     watch?v=Q1aEGrep070
Shakespeare Hour Live—Shakespeare and the Environment: https://www.youtube.
     com/watch?v=7TrHMO-hJXM
Shakespeare's Language of the Sea: https://www.rmg.co.uk/stories/topics/
     shakespeare-quotes-water-sea-maritime-imagery
Shakespeare and Nature: https://www.youtube.com/watch?v=0WthvBKIHcc
Shakespeare's Starling: https://www.bbc.co.uk/programmes/m0006dmc

By collection

Folger Shakespeare Library

'Adapting Shakespeare': https://www.folger.edu/podcasts/shakespeare-unlimited/
adapting-shakespeare/
'Eating Plants in the Early Modern World': https://www.folger.edu/blogs/
shakespeare-and-beyond/eating-plants-in-the-early-modern-world/
'Shakespeare and the Ocean': https://www.folger.edu/podcasts/shakespeare-
unlimited/shakespeare-ocean-mentz/
'Shakespeare, Ecology and the Environment': https://www.folger.edu/blogs/
shakespeare-and-beyond/shakespeare-ecology-environmental-earth-day/
'Quiz: The Animals in Shakespeare's Plays: https://www.folger.edu/blogs/
shakespeare-and-beyond/quiz-the-animals-in-shakespeares-plays/

Royal Shakespeare Company

'At the Forest's Edge': https://www.rsc.org.uk/events/at-the-forests-edge
'RSC Collection' (Archive, artworks, props, costume): https://www.rsc.org.uk/
about-us/history/rsc-collection

Shakespeare Birthplace Trust

'Flowers and Love': https://www.shakespeare.org.uk/explore-shakespeare/blogs/
flowers-and-love/
'Poetry Celebration: Nature and the Environment': https://www.shakespeare.org.
uk/explore-shakespeare/museum-from-home/poetry-celebration/
'Research Conversations': https://www.shakespeare.org.uk/education/research-
scholars/research-conversations/
'Shakespeare Quotes on the Environment': https://www.shakespeare.org.uk/
explore-shakespeare/shakespedia/shakespeare-quotes-theme/shakespeare-quotes-
environment/
'Shakespeare's Favourite Flowers: https://www.shakespeare.org.uk/explore-
shakespeare/blogs/?tag=shakespeares-favourite-flowers
'Sustainable Shakespeare': https://www.shakespeare.org.uk/explore-shakespeare/
blogs/?tag=sustainable-shakespeare
'Tongues in Trees': https://www.shakespeare.org.uk/explore-shakespeare/museum-
from-home/art-and-exhibitions/tongues-in-trees/

Shakespeare's Globe

'Film Students Respond to Climate Change': https://www.shakespearesglobe.com/
discover/blogs-and-features/2021/04/21/shakespeare-and-the-natural-world-
film-students-respond-to-climate-change/
'Research and Collections': https://www.shakespearesglobe.com/learn/research-
and-collections/

'Shakespeare and Climate Change': https://www.shakespearesglobe.com/discover/blogs-and-features/2020/04/22/shakespeare-and-climate-change/

'Shakespeare's Letter to the Earth': https://www.shakespearesglobe.com/discover/blogs-and-features/2019/04/12/shakespeares-letter-to-the-earth/

'Sustainably Improving Shakespeare's Globe Theatre': https://www.lime-green.co.uk/news/globe-theatre-improvements

'Sustainable Shakespeare': https://www.shakespearesglobe.com/discover/blogs-and-features/2023/06/05/sustainable-shakespeare-2023/⊓

REFERENCES

Abram, D. (1996), *The Spell of the Sensuous: Perception and Language in a More-Than-Human World*, New York: Pantheon.

Alaimo, S. (2010), *Body Natures: Science, Environment, and the Material Self*, Bloomington: Indiana University Press.

Apuleius, L. (1566), *The Golden Ass*, trans. W. Adlington. Available online: https://www.gutenberg.org/files/1666/1666-h/1666-h.htm#link2H_4_0001 (accessed 13 November 2023).

Archer, J.E., R.M. Turley and H. Thomas (2012), 'The Autumn King: Remembering the Land in *King Lear*', *Shakespeare Quarterly* 63 (4), 518–543. https://doi.org/10.1353/shq.2012.0059 (accessed 12 December 2023).

Arons, W., and T.J. May, eds (2012), *Readings in Performance and Ecology*, New York: Palgrave Macmillan.

Aronson, A., ed. (2018), *The Routledge Companion to Scenography*, London: Routledge.

Bach, R.A. (2017), *Birds and Other Creatures in Renaissance Literature: Shakespeare, Descartes, and Animal Studies*, Abingdon: Routledge.

Barad, K. (2007), *Meeting the Universe Halfway: Quantum Physics and the Entanglement of Matter and Meaning*, Durham: Duke University Press.

Bartolovich, C. (2022), 'Marxist Ecology and Shakespeare', in C. Lye and C. Nealon (eds), *After Marx: Literature, Theory, and Value in the Twenty-First Century*, 71–86, Cambridge: Cambridge University Press.

Barton, A. (2017), *The Shakespearean Forest*, Cambridge: Cambridge University Press.

Bate, J. (1991), *Romantic Ecology: Wordsworth and the Environmental Tradition*, Abingdon: Routledge.

Bate, J. (2000). *Song of the Earth*. Cambridge, MA: Harvard University Press.

Beer, T. (2016a), *An Introduction to Ecoscenography: The Paradigm and Practice of Ecological Design in the Performing Arts*. Norteas: Aalto University.

Beer, T. (2016b), 'Ecomaterialism in Scenography'. *Theatre and Performance Design* 2 (12): 161–72. https://doi.org/10.1080/23322551.2016.1179437. (Accessed 12 December 2023).

Beer, T. (2021), *Ecoscenography: An Introduction to Ecological Design for Performance*. Singapore: Palgrave Macmillan.

Bendell, J. (2018), 'Deep Adaptation: A Map for Navigating Climate Tragedy', *IFLAS Occasional Paper* 2. Available online: https://www.lifeworth.com/deepadaptation.pdf (accessed 20 September 2019).

Benison, B. (2019), *Jack Lear* in *Five New Plays for the Public Domain*, Tantamount. Kindle Edition.

Bennett, J. (2010), *Vibrant Matter: A Political Ecology of Things*, Durham: Duke University Press.

Berry, R. (2016), *Shakespeare in Performance: Castings and Metamorphoses*, London: Routledge.

Bertram, B. (2018), *Bestial Oblivion: War, Humanism, and Ecology in Early Modern England*, Abingdon, Routledge.

Boehrer, B. (2002), *Shakespeare Among the Animals: Nature and Society in the Drama of Early Modern England*, New York: Palgrave.

Boehrer, B. (2004), 'Economies of Desire in *A Midsummer Night's Dream*', *Shakespeare Studies 32*, 99–117.

Boehrer, B. (2013), *Environmental Degradation in Jacobean Drama*, Cambridge: Cambridge University Press.

Borlik, T.A. (2011), *Ecocriticism and Early Modern English Literature: Green Pastures*, Abingdon: Routledge.

Borlik, T.A. (2013), 'Caliban and the Fen Demons of Lincolnshire: The Englishness of Shakespeare's *Tempest*', *Shakespeare*, 9 (1), 21–51. https://doi.org/10.1080/1 7450918.2012.705882

Borlik, T.A., ed., (2019), *Literature and Nature in the English Renaissance: An Ecocritical Anthology*, Cambridge: Cambridge University Press.

Borlik, T.A. (2022), *Shakespeare Beyond the Green World: Drama and Ecopolitics in Jacobean Britain*, Oxford: Oxford University Press.

Borlik, T.A. (2023), 'Shakespeare and the Snakehandlers: Venom, Vermin and the Circulation of Eco-Social Energy in Renaissance Drama', in B. Angus, L. Hopkins, with K. Davey (eds.), *Poison on the Early Modern English Stage: Plants, Poisons and Potions*, 33–57. Manchester: Manchester University Press.

Bottoms, S. (2007), *Small Acts of Repair: Performance, Ecology and Goat Island*, London and New York: Routledge

Brayton, D. (2011), 'Shakespeare and the Global Ocean', in L. Bruckner and D. Brayton (eds), *Ecocritical Shakespeare*, 173–90, Aldershot: Ashgate.

Brayton, D. (2012), *Shakespeare's Ocean: An Ecocritical Exploration*, Charlottesville: University of Virginia Press.

Brayton, D., and L. Bruckner, eds (2011), *Ecocritical Shakespeare*, Aldershot: Ashgate.

Brokaw, K.S. (2017), 'Shakespeare as Community Practice', *Shakespeare Bulletin 35* (3), 445–61.

Brokaw, K.S. (2024). 'Shakespeare and Environmental Justice: Collaborative Eco-Theater in Yosemite National Park and the San Joaquin Valley', in M. Greenberg and E. Williamson (eds), *Situating Shakespeare Pedagogy in US Higher Education: Social Justice and Institutional Contexts*, 94–110, Edinburgh: Edinburgh University Press.

Brokaw, K.S., and P. Prescott (2022), 'Reduce, Rewrite, Recycle: Adapting *A Midsummer Night's Dream* for Yosemite,' in D. Henderson and S. O'Neill (eds), *The Arden Research Handbook of Shakespeare and Adaptation*, 305–23, London: Bloomsbury.

Brook, P. (1968), *The Empty Space: A Book about the Theatre: Deadly, Holy, Rough, Immediate*, London: MacGibbon and Kee.

Browning, W., C.O. Ryan and J. Clancy (2014), *Fourteen Patterns of Biophilic Design*. New York: Terrapin Bright Green.

Bruckner, L. (2013), 'The Indistinct Human in Renaissance Literature', *Configurations 21* (1), 119–22.

Bruckner, L. (2016), 'Reprocentric Ecologies: Pedagogy, Husbandry and *A Midsummer Night's Dream*', in J. Munroe and E. J. Geisweidt (eds), *Ecological Approaches to Early Modern English Texts: A Field Guide to Reading and Teaching*, 155–68, Abingdon: Routledge.

Bullough, G., ed. (1957), *Narrative and Dramatic Sources of Shakespeare*, vol.1 (including *A Midsummer Night's Dream*), London: Routledge and Kegan Paul.

Bullough, G., ed. (1978), *Narrative and Dramatic Sources of Shakespeare*, vol.7 (including *King Lear*), London: Routledge and Kegan Paul.

Candle Wasters (2023), 'Who are the Candle Wasters?', http://www. thecandlewasters.com/about.html (accessed 24 December 2023).

Centre for Intersectional Justice (CIJ) (2023), 'What is Intersectionality?' https:// www.intersectionaljustice.org/ (accessed 17 November 2023).

Césaire, A. (2000), *A Tempest*, trans. P. Crispin, London: Oberon Modern Plays.

Chaudhuri, S., ed. (2017), *A Midsummer Night's Dream*, London: Bloomsbury.

Chiari, S. (2019), *Shakespeare's Representation of the Weather, Climate and Environment: The Early Modern 'Fated Sky'*, Edinburgh: Edinburgh University Press.

Chiari, S., ed. (2022), *The Experience of Disaster in Early Modern English Literature*, Abingdon: Routledge.

Chiari, S., and S. Clark, eds (2022), *Shakespeare and the Environment: A Dictionary*, London: Arden Shakespeare.

Clark, T. (2015), *Ecocriticism on the Edge: The Anthropocene as a Threshold Concept*, London and New York: Bloomsbury.

Cless, D. (2010), *Ecology and Environment in European Drama*, Abingdon: Routledge.

Cossio, A., and M. Simonson (2020), 'Arboreal Tradition and Subversion: An Ecocritical Reading of Shakespeare's Portrayal of Trees, Woods and Forests', *Multicultural Shakespeare: Translation, Appropriation and Performance*, 21 (36), 85–97. http://hdl.handle.net/10810/60538 (accessed 20 March 2023).

Crane, M. T. (2020), 'Meteorology, Embodiment, and Environment in Shakespeare's *A Midsummer Night's Dream*', in M. Floyd-Wilson and G. A. Sullivan (eds), *Geographies of Embodiment in Early Modern England*. Online edn, Oxford Academic. https://doi.org/10.1093/oso/9780198852742.003.0006,

Crenshaw, K. (1989), 'Demarginalizing the Intersection of Race and Sex: A Black Feminist Critique of Antidiscrimination Doctrine, Feminist Theory, and Antiracist Politics', *University of Chicago Legal Forum*, 1 (8), 139–67.

Daroy, A. (2022), 'Biophilic Shakespeare: Towards an Ecology of Form.' Doctoral Thesis. Monash University and the University of Warwick.

Dawkins, R. (1982), *The Extended Phenotype*, Oxford: Oxford University Press.

Day, T.R. (2018), 'With Parted Eye: *A Midsummer Night's Dream*, Richard Powers' *Orfeo*, and Biosemiotics', *Green Letters*, 22 (3), 247–59.

DCCEEW. (2023), 'State of the Environment Report.' Available online: https://soe. dcceew.gove.au (accessed 11 November 2023).

Deadly Story (2023), 'Life and Lore.' Available online: https://deadlystory.com/ page/culture/Life_Lore (accessed 11 November 2023).

De Quincey, T. (1889–90), 'On the knocking at the gate in *Macbeth*', in D. Masson (ed.), *The Collected Works of Thomas de Quincey*, 14 vols, vol.10, 389–95.

Devall, B., and G. Sessions (1985), *Deep Ecology*, Salt Lake City: Gibbs Smith.

Dionne, C. (2016), *Posthuman Lear: Reading Shakespeare in the Anthropocene*, New York: Punctum.

Dobzhansky, T. (1970), *Genetics of the Evolutionary Process*, New York: Columbia University Press.

Duckert, L. (2019) 'The Climate of Shakespeare: Four (or More) Forecasts', in A. Johns-Putra (ed), *Climate and Literature*, 92–108, Cambridge: Cambridge University Press.

Eckhardt, J., ed. (2013), *Virginia: A Sermon Preached at White-Chappel, Photographic facsimile edition*, ed. Joshua Eckhardt, Richmond, Virginia: VCU Libraries. Available online: https://scholarscompass.vcu.edu/britva/2/ (accessed 24 December 2023).

Egan, G. (2006), *Green Shakespeare: From Ecopolitics to Ecocriticism*, Abingdon: Routledge.

Elam, K. (2022), 'Romancing the Oak: On the Performativity of Trees in Shakespearean Comedy', in J. Drakakis (ed), *Fascinating Rhythms: Shakespeare, Theory, Culture, and the Legacy of Terence Hawkes*, 97–118, London: Routledge.

Estok, S. (2005), 'Shakespeare and Ecocriticism: An Analysis of "Home" and "Power" in *King Lear*,' *AUMLA 103* (5), 15–41.

Estok, S. (2011), *Ecocriticism and Shakespeare: Reading Ecophobia*, New York: Palgrave Macmillan.

Faircloth, N., and V. Thomas (2014), *Shakespeare's Plants and Gardens: A Dictionary*, London: Arden Shakespeare.

Fitzpatrick, J. (2016), '"I Must Eat my Dinner": Shakespeare's Foods from Apples to Walrus' in J. Fitzpatrick (ed.) *Renaissance Food from Rabelais to Shakespeare*, 127–143, Abingdon: Routledge.

Flaherty, J, (2021), '"This Island's Mine": Ecocritical Caribbean Tempests', in *The Shakespearean International Yearbook*, 135–53, Abingdon: Routledge.

Flaherty, J. (2022), 'All is Mended? Activism and Eco-Anxiety in *Bright Summer Night*', *Shakespeare Bulletin* 40 (3): 347–63.

Freestone, E., and J. O'Hare (2021), *100 Plays to Save the World*, London: Nick Hern Books.

Fudge, E. (2002), *Perceiving Animals: Humans and Beasts in Early Modern English Culture*, Champaign: University of Illinois Press.

Fudge, E. (2006). *Brutal Reasoning: Animals, Rationality, and Humanity in Early Modern England*, Ithaca: Cornell University Press.

Galsworthy, J. (1916), 'The Great Tree', in I. Gollancz (ed), *A Book of Homage to Shakespeare*, 37–8, Oxford: Oxford University Press.

Glotfelty, C. (1996), 'Introduction: Literary studies in an age of environmental crisis', in H. Fromm and C. Glotfelty (eds), *The Ecocriticism Reader: Landmarks in Literary Ecology*, xv–xxxv, Athens: University of Georgia Press.

Golding, A. (1567), *The xv. Bookes of P. Ouidius Naso, entytuled Metamorphosis, translated oute of Latin into English meeter*, London.

Gray, D. (2020), 'Command These Elements to Silence', *Literature Compass 17* (3–4).

Groensteen, T., ed. (1998), *La transécriture: Pour une theorie de l'adaptation*, Montreal: Editions Nota Bene.

Gruber, E.D. (2017), *Renaissance Ecopolitics from Shakespeare to Bacon: Rethinking Cosmopolis*, Abingdon: Routledge.

Hamilton, J.M. (2017), *This Contentious Storm: An Ecocritical and Performance History of King Lear,* London: Bloomsbury.

Hamilton, J.M. (2018), 'Constructing Dying and Death as an Eco-Political Concern in Performances of Shakespeare's *King Lear* and Sarah Kane's *Blasted*', *Shakespeare Bulletin,* 36 (3), 485–500.

Hansen, C. (2023a), 'Shakespeare, Climate Change and the Blue Humanities: Imagining an Oceanic Education,' in P. Bickley and J. Stevens (eds), *Shakespeare, Education and Pedagogy: Representations, Interactions, and Adaptations,* 190–9, Abingdon: Routledge.

Hansen, C. (2023b). *Shakespeare and Place-Based Learning,* Cambridge: Cambridge University Press.

Henderson, D. E., and S. O'Neill, eds (2022), *The Arden Handbook of Shakespeare and Adaptation,* London: Bloomsbury.

Höfele, A. (2008), *Stage, Stake and Scaffold: Humans and Animals in Shakespeare's Theatre,* Oxford: Oxford University Press.

Howard, P. (2002), *What is Scenography?,* London: Routledge.

Hickling, A. (2008), 'Jack Lear: Review', *Guardian,* 24 October 2008, https://www.theguardian.com/stage/2008/oct/24/theatre (accessed 24 December 2023).

Hiltner, K. (2011), *What Else Is Pastoral?,* Ithaca: Cornell University Press.

Hogue, J. C. (2021), 'Ariel's Anguish: Doing (Arboreal) Time in *The Tempest*', *ISLE: Interdisciplinary Studies in Literature and Environment,* 28 (4), 1481–1506.

Holling, C. S. (1973), 'Resilience and the Stability of Natural Systems', *Annual Review of Ecology and Systematics,* 4 (1), 1–23.

Hoydis, J. (2022), 'Posthumanism and Drama: From Shakespeare to Climate Change Plays', in S. Herbrechter et al. (eds), *Palgrave Handbook of Critical Posthumanism,* 1–22 New York: Springer Nature.

Jones, G. (2015), *Shakespeare's Storms,* Manchester: Manchester University Press.

Jones, G. (2017), 'Environmental Renaissance Studies,' *Literature Compass,* 14 (10), p.e12407. https://doi.org/10.1111/lic3.12407

Kaiser, S. (2004), 'How Long Do You Think It Will Run?', *Shakespeare Bulletin* 22 (3): 47–8.

Kellert, S. R. (2018), *Nature by Design: The Practice of Biophilic Design,* New Haven: University of Yale Press.

Kerridge, R. (2021), 'All Is Deep: All Is Shallow—Literary Springs, Wells and Depths, from Shakespeare to Ecocriticism', in S. Chiari and S. Cuisinier-Delorme (eds), *Spa Culture and Literature in England 1500–1800,* 263–283, New York: Springer Nature.

Kershaw, B. (2009), *Theatre Ecology: Environments and Performance Events,* Cambridge: Cambridge University Press.

Lanier, D. (2014), 'Shakespearean Rhizomatics: Adaptation, Ethics, Value,' in A. Huang and E. Rivlin's *Shakespeare and the Ethics of Appropriation,* 21–40, New York: Palgrave.

Latulippe, N. and Klenk, N. (2020), 'Making Room and Moving Over: Knowledge Co-production, Indigenous Knowledge Sovereignty and the Politics of Global Environmental Change Decision-Making', *Current Opinion in Environmental Sustainability,* 42, 7–14.

Lavery, C. (2016), 'Introduction: Performance and Ecology—What Can Theatre Do?', *Green Letters,* 20 (3), 229–36.

Lee, S., ed. (1909), *The True Chronicle History of King Leir: The Original of Shakespeare's 'King Lear'*, London: Chatto and Windus.

Lewis, S.L., and M.A. Maslin (2015), 'Defining the Anthropocene', *Nature* 519.7542: 171–80.

Lotker, S., and R. Gough. 'On Scenography', *Performance Research* 18 (3): 3–6. https://doi.org/10.1080/13528165.2013.818306

Lonergan, P. (2021), 'Shakespeare and the Orbis Spike', talk given at the Globe 4 Globe Conference, London. Available online: https://www.youtube.com/watch?v=AhBbsvlVCn8 (accessed 28 December 2023).

Love, G.A. (1999), 'Ecocriticism and Science: Toward Consilience?', *New Literary History*, 30, 561–76.

Love, G.A. (2003), *Practical Ecocriticism: Literature, Biology and the Environment,* Charlottesville: University of Virginia Press.

Love, G.A. (2010), 'Shakespeare's Origin of Species and Darwin's Tempest', *Configurations*, 81 (1), 121–40.

Lovelock, J. (1979), *Gaia: A New Look at Life on Earth*, Oxford: Oxford University Press.

Lupton, J.R. and Gordon, C.J. (2013), 'Shakespeare by Design: A Flight of Concepts', *English Studies*, 94 (3), 259–77.

Machon, J. (2009), *(Syn)aesthetics: Re-defining Visceral Performance*, London: Palgrave Macmillan.

Mack, P. (2010), *Reading and Rhetoric in Montaigne and Shakespeare*, London: Bloomsbury.

Martin, R. (2015), *Shakespeare and Ecology*, Oxford: Oxford University Press.

Martin, R. (2017), 'Shakespeare, Ecology, and Ecocriticism', in J. L. Levenson and R. Ormsby (eds), *The Shakespearean World*, 606–21, Abingdon: Routledge.

Martin, R. (2022), 'The Global Cymbeline Project', https://www.cymbeline-anthropocene.com/article/19311-emancipating-the-anthropocene-%C2%A0the-global-cymbeline-project (accessed 9 January 2024).

Maslin, M. A. (2015), 'Epoch defining study pinpoints when humans came to dominate planet earth'. Available online: https://www.ucl.ac.uk/news/2015/mar/epoch-defining-study-pinpoints-when-humans-came-dominate-planet-earth (accessed 27 December 2023).

May, T. J. (2005), 'Greening the Theater: Taking Ecocriticism from Page to Stage', *Interdisciplinary Literary Studies*, 7 (1), 84–103.

McConachie, B. (2008), *Engaging Audiences: A Cognitive Approach to Spectating in the Theatre*, New York: Palgrave Macmillan.

McDonough, W., and M. Braungart (2002), 'Design for the Triple Top Line: New Tools for Sustainable Commerce', *Corporate Environmental Strategy*, 9 (3), 251–8.

MacFaul, T. (2015), *Shakespeare and the Natural World*, Oxford: Oxford University Press.

McKenna, R. (2017), 'Surviving *The Tempest*: Ecologies of Salvage on the Early Modern Stage', *Shakespeare*, 13 (3), 271–81.

McKernan, L. (2016), 'Shakespeare and Awkward Teenagers', https://lukemckernan.com/2016/07/07/shakespeare-and-awkward-teenagers/ (accessed 23 December 2023).

McKibben, B. (2005), 'What the warming world needs now is art, sweet art', *Grist*, 22 April. Available online: https://grist.org/article/mckibben-imagine/ (accessed 28 October 2020).

Meeker, J. W. (1974), *The Comedy of Survival: Studies in Literary Ecology*, New York: Scribner and Sons.

Mentz, S. (2009), *At the Bottom of Shakespeare's Ocean*, London and New York: Bloomsbury.

Mentz, S. (2010), 'Strange Weather in *King Lear*', *Shakespeare*, 6 (2), 139–52.

Mentz, S. (2011), 'Tongues in the Storm: Shakespeare, Ecological Crisis, and the Resources of Genre', in L. Bruckner and D. Brayton (eds), *Ecocritical Shakespeare*, 155–72, Farnham: Ashgate.

Mentz, S. (2015), 'Phlogiston', in J. J. Cohen and L. Duckert, L (eds), *Elemental Ecocriticism: Thinking with Earth, Air, Water and Fire*, 55–76, Minneapolis: University of Minnesota Press.

Mentz, S. (2018), 'Green Comedy: Shakespeare and Ecology', in H. Hirschfeld (ed), *The Oxford Handbook of Shakespearean Comedy*, 250–62, Oxford: Oxford University Press.

Mentz, S. (2019), 'Shakespeare and the Blue Humanities', *Studies in English Literature 1500–1900 59* (2): 383–392. https://doi.org/10.1353/sel.2019.0018.

Middleton, T., and T. Dekker (1611), *The Roaring Girl, or Moll Cutpurse*, London: Thomas Archer.

Miller, J.A. (2012), 'The Labor of Greening Love's Labour's Lost', in W. Arons and T. J. May (eds), *Readings in Performance and Ecology*, 191–200, New York: Palgrave Macmillan.

Minton, G. (2021), 'Ecological Adaptation in Montana: *Timon of Athens* to Timon of Anaconda', *New Theatre Quarterly*, 37 (1), 20–37.

Monbiot, G. (2014), *Feral: Searching for Enchantment on the Fronteirs of Rewilding*, London: University of Chicago Press.

Monmouth, G. (1904), *Histories of the Kings of Britain*, trans. S. Evans, London: J.M. Dent.

Monowar, T. (2020), 'Indigeneity and Climate Change in Shakespeare's *The Tempest*: A Postcolonial Study', *Café Dissensus*. Available online: https://cafedissensus.com/2020/08/31/indigeneity-and-climate-change-in-shakespeares-the-tempest-a-postcolonial-ecocritical-study/ (accessed 17 October 2023).

Montaigne, M. (1603), 'On Cannibals' in *Essays*, trans. J. Florio, Book 1, 100-107, London.

Montaigne, M. (1991), *The Complete Essays*, ed. and trans. M.A. Screech, London: Penguin.

Montana InSite Theatre (2022), 'Special Projects'. https://www.montanainsitetheatre.org/specialprojects (accessed 10 January 2024).

Morton, T. (2013), *Hyperobjects: Philosophy and Ecology after the End of the World*, Minneapolis: University of Minnesota Press.

Muir, K. (1977), *The Sources of Shakespeare's Plays*, London: Methuen.

Munroe, J., and R. Laroche, (2017), *Shakespeare and Ecofeminist Theory*, London: Bloomsbury.

Munroe, J., E.J. Geisweidt and L. Bruckner, eds (2015), *Ecological Approaches to Early Modern English Texts: A Field Guide to Reading and Teaching*, Abingdon: Routledge.

Nardizzi, V. (2013), *Wooden Os: Shakespeare's theatres and England's trees*, University of Toronto Press.

Nardizzi, V. (2019), 'Shakespeare's Trans*plant* Poetics: Vegetable Blazons and the Seasons of Pyramus's Face', *Journal for Early Modern Cultural Studies*, 19 (4) 156–177.

Nashe, T. (1972), *The Unfortunate Traveller and Other Works*, ed. J.B. Steane, London: Penguin.

Nostbakken, F. (2003), *Understanding A Midsummer Night's Dream*, Westport, CT: Greenwood Press.

O'Dair, S. (2008a), 'Slow Shakespeare: An eco-critique of method in early modern literary studies', in I. Kamps, K. Raber and T. Hallock (eds), *Early Modern Ecostudies: From the Florentine Codex to Shakespeare*, 11–30, New York: Palgrave Macmillan.

O'Dair, S. (2008b), 'The State of the Green: A Review Essay on Shakespearean Ecocriticism' *Shakespeare*, 4 (4), 459–77.

O'Malley, E. (2016), 'You Do (Not) Assist the Storm: A Vibrant and Affective Seascape for *The Tempest* at Minack, Cornwall', *Performance Research*, 21 (2), 81–84.

O'Malley, E. (2020), *Weathering Shakespeare: Audiences and Open-Air Performance*, London: Bloomsbury.

Onions, C. T. (1986), *A Shakespeare Glossary*, 3rd edition, Oxford: Oxford University Press.

Orgel, S., ed. (1987), *The Tempest*, Oxford: Oxford University Press.

Orwell, G. (2022), 'Inside the Whale' (1940) reprinted in *Orwell's Essays 8*, London: Renard Press.

Oxford English Dictionary (2023), 'Literary Criticism'. Online. https://doi. org/10.1093/OED/7576324109 (accessed 14 August 2023).

Parrabola (2020), 'This Distemperature', audio play. Available online: http://www. thisdistemperature.co.uk/ (accessed 12 September 2023).

Poore, J., and T. Nemecek (2018), 'Reducing Food's Environmental Impacts Through Producers and Consumers', *Science*, 360 (6392), 987–92.

Proudfoot, R., A. Thompson, D.S. Kastan and H.R. Woudhuysen, eds (2021), *The Arden Shakespeare Complete Works*, London: Arden Shakespeare.

Raber, Karen. (2013), *Animal Bodies, Renaissance Culture*, Philadelphia: University of Pennsylvania Press.

Raber, K., and H. Dugan, eds (2021), *The Routledge Handbook of Shakespeare and Animals*, Abingdon: Routledge.

Raber, K., and K. Edwards (2023), *Shakespeare and Animals: A Dictionary*, London: Arden Shakespeare.

Raber, K., and M. Mattfeld, eds (2017), *Performing Aanimals: History, Agency, Theater*, University Park, PA: Pennsylvania State University Press.

Reuckert, W. (1978), 'Literature and Ecology: An Experiment in Ecocriticism', *The Iowa Review*, 9 (1), 62–86.

Rowland, S. (2018), *Jungian Literary Criticism: The Essential Guide*, London: Routledge.

Salazar, R. (2018), 'A Rogue and Pleasant Stage: Performing Ecology in Outdoor Shakespeares', *Shakespeare Bulletin*, 36 (3), 449–66.

Salmón, E. (2000), 'Kincentric Ecology: Indigenous Perceptions of the Human–Nature Relationship, *Ecological Applications*, 10(5), 1327–32.

Sanders, J. (2006), *Adaptation and Appropriation*, Abingdon: Routledge.

Sanders, J. (2022), 'What is Shakespeare adaptation? Why *Pericles*? Why Cloud? Why now?', in D. Henderson and S. O'Neill (eds), *The Arden Research Handbook of Shakespeare and Adaptation*, 91-116, London: Bloomsbury.

Schumann, A. (2015), '"But as a Form in Wax"': An Ecofeminist Reading of Shakespeare's *A Midsummer Night's Dream*', *Colloquy*, 30, 42–60.

Scot, R. (1584), *The Discoverie of Witchcraft*, London.

Shannon, L. (2009), 'Poor, Bare, Forked: Animal Sovereignty, Human Negative Exceptionalism and the Natural History of *King Lear*', *Shakespeare Quarterly*, 60 (2), 68–196.

Shannon, L. (2013), *The Accommodated Animal: Cosmopoly in Shakespeare's Locales*, Chicago: University of Chicago Press.

Smith, E. (2022), 'Shakespeare as Adapter' in Henderson and O'Neill (eds), *The Arden Research Handbook of Shakespeare and Adaptation*, 49-67, London: Bloomsbury. Digital Edition.

Steffes, M. (2016), 'Medieval Wildernesses and *King Lear*: Heath, Forest, Desert', *Exemplaria*, 28 (3), 230–47.

Strachey, J. (1906), 'A True Repertory . . .' in *Hakluytus Posthumus, or Purchas his Pilgrimes*, by Samuel Purchas, reprinted, 20 vols, vol 19, 5-25, Glasgow: James MacLehose and Sons.

Suzelis, N. (2021), 'Climate Leviathan and Ecological Accumulation in *The Tempest*', *Shakespeare Studies*, 49, 81–13. Available online: https://www.proquest.com/docview/2582833485/fulltextPDF/ (accessed 20 December 2023).

Symonds, W (1609), 'Virginia: A Sermon Preached at Whitechapel', London.

Taylor, G. (1996), *Cultural Selection: Why Some Achievements Survive the Test of Time – And Others Don't*, New York: Basic Books.

Theis, J. (2009), *Writing the Forest in Early Modern England*, Pittsburgh: Duquesne University Press.

Thunberg, G. (2019), '"Our house is on fire": Greta Thunberg, 16, urges leaders to act on climate', *The Guardian*, 25 January. Available online: https://www.theguardian.com/environment/2019/jan/25/our-house-is-on-fire-greta-thunberg16-urges-leaders-to-act-on-climate (accessed 23 December 2023).

Tiffany, G. (2020), 'Shakespeare's Savage Trees', in T. Willard (ed), *Reading the Natural World in the Middle Ages and the Renaissance: Perceptions of the Environment and Ecology*, 197–208, Turnhout: Brepols Publishers.

Townsend, S. (2019) 'Climate Change Versus Cats . . . Zombies, Cake, Brexit and Gravy', *Forbes*, 15 May. Available online: https://www.forbes.com/sites/solitairetownsend/2019/05/15/cats-versus-climate-change-revealing-issue-coverage-on-our-screens/#66c35b7a479e</ (accessed 28 October 2020).

Turner, C. (2010), 'Writing for the Contemporary Theatre: Towards a Radically Inclusive Dramaturgy', *Studies in Theatre and Performance*, 30 (1), 75–90.

UNWCED (1987), 'Report of the World Commission on Environment and Development: Our Common Future.' Available online: https://sustainabledevelopment.un.org/ (accessed 19 August 2023).

Urban, P., J. Plesnik and P. Sabo (2021), 'How to Define Ecology on the Basis of its Current Understanding?', *Folia Oecologica* 48 (1), 1–8.

Van der Ryn, S., and Cowan, S. (2007), *Ecological Design*, Washington: Island Press.

Vecco, M. (2020), 'Genius Loci as a Meta-Concept, *Journal of Cultural Heritage*, 41, 225–31.

Vitkus, D. (2023), 'Red-Green Intersectionality Beyond the New Materialism: An Eco-Socialist Approach to Shakespeare's *The Tempest*', in R. Arban and L. Ellinghausen (eds), *Intersectionalities of Class in Early Modern English Drama*, 129–47, Cham: Springer Nature Switzerland.

Waage, F.O. (2005), 'Shakespeare Unearth'd', *Interdisciplinary Studies in Literature and Environment*, 12 (2), 139–164.

Watson, R.N. (2006), *Back to Nature: The Green and the Real in the Late Renaissance*, Philadelphia: University of Pennsylvania Press.

Watson, R.N. (2011), 'The Ecology of Self in *A Midsummer Night's Dream*', in D. Brayton and L. Bruckner (eds), *Ecocritical Shakespeare*, 33–56, Aldershot: Ashgate.

Watt, G. (2008), 'The Law of Dramatic Properties in *The Merchant of Venice*', in P. Raffield and G. Watt (eds), *Shakespeare and the Law*, 237–252, Oxford and Portland: Hart.

Weingust, D. (2014), 'Authentic Performances or Performances of Authenticity? Original Practices and the Repertory Schedule', *Shakespeare*, 10 (4), 402–10.

Whitman, W. (1888), *November Boughs*, Philadelphia: David McKay.

Whyte, M. (2016), '"A Midsummer Night's Dream" Web Series "Bright Summer Night" Cast Announced – First Look!', *Hypable*, 10 April 2016, https://www.hypable.com/bright-summer-night-web-series-cast/ (accessed 20 December 2023).

Woods, P. (2012), *Globe Audiences: Spectatorship and Reconstruction at Shakespeare's Globe*, Diss., Queen Mary, University of London.

Yates, J. (2015), 'Wet?', in J. Cohen & L. Duckert (eds), *Elemental Ecocriticism: Thinking with Earth, Air, Water and Fire*, 183–208, Minneapolis: University of Minnesota Press.

Yates, J., and G. Sullivan (2011), 'Forum on Shakespeare and Ecology', *Shakespeare Studies*, 39, 23–116.

Zeunert, J. (2017), *Landscape Architecture and Environmental Sustainability: Creating Positive Change Through Design*, London: Bloomsbury.

Zeunert, J. (2018), 'Challenges in Agricultural Sustainability and Resilience: Towards Regenerative Practice', in J. Zeunert & T. Waterman (eds), *Routledge Handbook of Landscape and Food*, 231–52, London: Routledge.